MAMA RUBY

Also by Mary Monroe

God Ain't Through Yet

God Ain't Blind

The Company We Keep

She Had It Coming

Deliver Me From Evil

God Don't Play

In Sheep's Clothing

Red Light Wives

God Still Don't Like Ugly

Gonna Lay Down My Burdens

God Don't Like Ugly

The Upper Room

"Nightmare in Paradise" in *Borrow Trouble*

Published by Kensington Publishing Corp.

MAMA RUBY

MARY MONROE

Dafina
Books

KENSINGTON BOOKS
http://www.kensingtonbooks.com

DAFINA BOOKS are published by

Kensington Publishing Corp.
119 West 40th Street
New York, NY 10018

ISBN-13: 978-0-7582-3862-7
ISBN-10: 0-7582-3862-2

First Hardcover Printing: June 2011
First Trade Paperback Printing: February 2012

10 9 8 7 6 5 4 3 2 1

Printed in the United States of America

This book is dedicated to Mama Ruby. Yes, Mama Ruby—the real one. The character in this story is a composite of three females in my family, but at least a dozen other "she-devils" in my family claim that I based the character on them. The "real" Mama Ruby crossed over several years ago, but is still a major force in my life and writing career—and always will be.

Acknowledgments

Lots of love and thanks to Bernard Henderson of Alexander Books in San Francisco, California, for making my book signing events so enjoyable, and for encouraging me to write *Mama Ruby*. You are one of a kind.

Thanks and lots of love to Blanche Richardson of Marcus Books in Oakland, California, for being such a beautiful person, for promoting my books, and for making me feel so special before, during, and after my book signing events at Marcus Books. I wish you all the best.

Thanks to the book clubs, the reviewers, the bookstores, the folks in the sales department at Kensington Publishing, the rest of my Kensington family, my agent, Andrew Stuart, and most of all, my wonderful fans.

A very special thank you to the wonderful folks at Open Road Media for filming that incredible video of me, and for promoting my books with so much vigor.

Please continue to share your thoughts, comments, suggestions, and opinions by e-mailing me at Authorauthor5409@aol.com or by visiting my Web site, www.MaryMonroe.org, as often as possible. You can also communicate with me on Facebook and Twitter.

Dear Readers,

For years, a lot of you asked me when I was going to write another story with the characters from *The Upper Room*. I repeatedly told you all that I'd "get to it" someday. Well, I finally got to it and here it is!

First of all, I would like to make it clear that *Mama Ruby* is NOT the sequel to *The Upper Room*; it is the prequel (the sequel is in the works). This is the part of the story that takes place during the immediate years before Mama Ruby enters the upper room. In this book, I will reveal the answer to the big question: why was Mama Ruby so desperate for a daughter of her own that she kidnapped one from her best friend?

I write to entertain, enlighten, and even provoke you wonderful readers. Most of all, I write books because it's what I like to do. And to the small group of readers whom I've offended over the years because one of my characters said or did something crazy (duh, that's what characters do in Mary Monroe books!), my books are based on my own experiences and my characters are composites of people I know, but my books are *fictional*.

If you enjoy this story enough to send me some comments, good or bad, that's enough for me. I've said it before, but I will say it again, your support and interest are sincerely appreciated. As long as you keep reading my books, I will keep writing.

Just wait until you see what I have up my sleeve next. . . .

Peace and blessings,
Mary Monroe
June 2011

CHAPTER 1

Shreveport, Louisiana, 1934

NOBODY EVER HAD TO TELL RUBY JEAN UPSHAW THAT SHE was special, but she heard it from every member of her family, her father's congregation, her classmates, and even the people in her neighborhood almost every day. She was the seventh daughter of a seventh daughter. To some black folks, that was a very high position on the food chain. It meant that she had mystical abilities usually associated with biblical icons. But as a child, Ruby didn't care one way or the other about being "special" like that.

She balked when people insisted that she'd eventually have "healing hands" and the ability to "predict the future" like other seventh daughters of seventh daughters. Ruby didn't care about healing anybody; that was God's job, and those snake oil salesmen who rolled through town from time to time. And she certainly didn't want to be telling anybody what the future held for them. Because if it was something bad, they didn't need to know, and she didn't want to know. The bottom line was—and she told a lot of people this when they brought it up—she didn't want those responsibilities. The last thing she needed cluttering up her life was a bunch of superstitious people taking up her time and drawing unwanted attention to her. Just being the daughter of a preacher was enough of a burden.

And since Ruby was the youngest member of the Upshaw family, her parents watched her like a hawk and tried to monitor and control most of her activities.

"Why do I have to go to church every Sunday?" she asked her mother one Sunday morning when she was just eight. "I want to have some fun!"

"You go to church because you are supposed to, gal. How would it look to the rest of your papa's congregation if his own daughter don't come to church?" Ida Mae replied, giving Ruby a stern look. "Don't you want to be saved?"

"Saved from what, Mama?" Ruby questioned, looking out the living room window at the kids across the street building a tent in their front yard.

"Saved from the world, worldly ways. This planet is full of all kinds of pitfalls out there waitin' on a girl like you. Drinkin'. Men with more lust in their heads than brain matter. Violence. Loud music and sleazy outfits that would shock a harlot," Ida Mae answered.

Ruby already knew all of that. From what she'd been able to determine, it was a lot more fun to be "worldly" than it was to be the way her parents wanted her to be.

"I want to have some fun like the rest of the kids!" she said with a pout, knowing that she faced a no-win situation. Her parents' minds were as nimble as concrete. Once they laid down the rules for Ruby, there were no exceptions.

"You can still have fun and keep yourself virtuous," her father insisted. "Me and Mother ain't makin' you do nothin' we didn't make your sisters do, and look how well they all turned out."

Ruby pressed her lips together to keep from laughing. Before they got married, all six of her older sisters snuck out of the house at night, drank alcohol, slept with men, and wore clothes that would "shock a harlot." That was the life that Ruby thought she wanted, and she had already started on the journey that would lead her to a life of fun and frivolity. And as far as violence, she wondered what her overbearing but naive parents would say if they knew that she was already carrying a switch-blade in her sock.

Ruby made good grades in school and she had a lot of friends, but it was hard for her to maintain both. She didn't like to study, and she didn't like having to attend that run-down school four blocks from her house. Those activities took up too much of her time. She appreciated the fact that her classmates and playmates were at her beck and call, not because they liked her, but because they feared her. They all knew about that switchblade she carried in her sock, and they all knew that she was not afraid to use it. She was the most feared eight-year-old in the state.

Beulah, Ruby's favorite older sister, had started Ruby down the wrong path that same year. Beulah was fifteen and so hot to trot that most of the time she didn't even wear panties. Like her mother, as well as Ruby and the rest of the sisters, Beulah was dark, stout, and had the same plain features. She also had the same short knotty hair that she paid a lot of money to the local beauticians to keep pressed and curled. But her being stout and plain didn't stop the men from paying a lot of attention to her.

Several nights a week, Beulah eased into Ruby's bedroom after their parents had turned in for the night. "Baby sister, get up and come with me," she instructed, beckoning Ruby with her finger. "Lickety-split, sugar."

"Are we goin' back to that bootlegger's house that we went to the other night?" Ruby asked, leaping out of bed, already dressed except for her shoes.

"Yep! And I need for you to watch my back in case we run into a blabbermouth, or somebody that want to start trouble with us," Beulah told her. "If I get in trouble, you can run get help for me."

"Then I better bring my blade, huh?" young Ruby asked eagerly. Even though she had never had to use her weapon, having it made her feel powerful and bold. She hoped that she never *had* to use it. Having her peers *think* that she was "big and bad" was enough for her. Ruby was confused about life. And it was no wonder, with her parents telling her to do one thing, and her sisters influencing her to do another. But one thing she was not confused about was the fact that she didn't want to hurt anybody, physically, or in any other way. However, she had promised herself that no matter what life dealt her, she would do *whatever* it took for her to survive, and be happy.

Ruby had as much fun as Beulah did that night. There had been an abundance of beer and loud music for them to enjoy at a nearby bootlegger's house.

By the time Ruby was twelve, she knew more about sex than her mother. Beulah was engaged to a truck driver, but she was also involved with a married man. When she wanted to spend time with him, she usually dragged Ruby along to act as a look-out while she rolled around with the married man in the bed that he shared with his wife. When the man's wife and three young children were in the home, Beulah and her lover spread a blanket on the backseat of his old car, and did their business there. Ruby sat in the front seat. Her job was to make sure no one walked up on the lovers. But every few minutes, Ruby glanced in the rearview mirror. She was amused and fascinated by what was taking place in the backseat. Beulah and her lover rewarded Ruby with peanut brittle and comic books, which she read in the car with a flashlight.

When Ruby visited her other sisters, who were all married by this time, she liked to peep through their bedroom door keyholes and watch as they made love with their husbands. What she couldn't figure out was what all of the hollering, screaming, and moaning and groaning was about. If she hadn't seen what was going on, she would have thought that some-body was stepping on somebody's toe for them to be making so much noise. That was what piqued her interest the most. Even before she had sex, she knew it had to be good. Married people risked losing everything because of sex. Girls risked getting pregnant, catching some nasty disease, and God knew what else, but that didn't stop them from having sex. Something that powerful *had* to feel damn good.

Ruby couldn't wait to find out. Right after she had watched Beulah and her married lover buck and rear like two horses at a rodeo three nights in a row, she decided that it was time for her to find out for herself what all the fuss was about. She knew enough about boys and men to know that none of them would say no to a piece of tail—her tail especially. Even though she was no raving beauty, she had the kind of body that black southern men worshipped. She was thick from top to bottom—especially her top and her bottom. Her butt was so plump and high and tight that you could bounce a quarter off it. One of the Donaldson boys had proved that during a break from Sunday school studies one Easter morning. But the most impressive part of Ruby's body was her bosom. She had large melonlike breasts that were so firm and perky, she didn't even need the support of a brassiere. She balked when her mother made her wear one anyway.

"Why do I have to wear a brassiere if I don't need one?" she asked her mother the day she steamrolled into Ruby's bedroom with a bag full of those damn things.

"Well, if you don't wear a brassiere because you don't need one, you will sure enough need one eventually. The bigger the titties, the farther they fall, sooner or later." Ruby's mother glanced at her own bosom, which now resembled two deflated footballs. "Don't be stupid like I was." Ruby's mother sniffed. "Had I known what I know now when I was your age, I would have worn two strong brassieres at the same time. Maybe I wouldn't be walkin' around with such a slope of a valley now . . ."

Ruby's face burned. The condition of her mother's bosom was one thing that she did not care to hear about. "Yessum."

"You started your monthly last week. You're a woman now, Ruby Jean," her mother said, obviously embarrassed and even a little uneasy.

When her mother sat her down for that "birds and bees" talk

last week, she didn't tell Ruby anything that she didn't already know. She had learned everything she needed to know, and some things that she didn't need to know, from her sisters and from other worldly kids.

"Dang, Mama. Why you buy up this many brassieres? I only got two titties!" Ruby complained with amusement. She fished one of the plain new white bras out of the bag. She couldn't understand why her mother had purchased so many this time. The bag contained at least ten bras. "I guess this means I can court with boys now?" Ruby asked hopefully.

"Naw it don't! You still a child. You'll have plenty of time for courtin' boys in a few years."

A few years? *Like hell*, Ruby thought.

She was not about to wait a few more years to have some real fun. All she had to do was find the right boy.

CHAPTER 2

*R*UBY HAD NEVER BEEN OUTSIDE THE STATE OF LOUISIANA. Her two oldest sisters, Flodell and Bessie, who had married twin brothers, lived in Texas. The rest of her married sisters lived in various parts of Louisiana.

Shreveport was a fairly large city, but segregation and racial violence were rampant. It seemed like every other week Ruby heard her parents whispering about somebody getting lynched. And it was usually for the stupidest reasons. One seventeen-year-old black boy had been beaten beyond recognition and then lynched for brushing up against a white woman's butt when he tried to pass her on the sidewalk. That had all happened right in his grandfather's front yard in front of thirty to forty black people attending a block party. And none of those thirty to forty people had been able to do a thing to help that boy. What the lynch mob didn't know was that the boy was severely retarded and cross-eyed. He was so clumsy and uncoordinated that he couldn't even ride a bicycle. He used to fall on his face just walking down the street. He brushed against people all of the time, the same way he had brushed against that white woman.

That happened a week after Ruby's mother had given her that bag of brassieres.

"I don't care what nobody say, I ain't goin' to put up with that mess from white folks, or nobody else," Ruby said later that day during dinner.

"Hush up," her father snapped. "You need to learn now that you can't beat them white folks. As long as you stay in your place, you'll be all right. Look what them white folks done to that retarded boy—and ain't nobody been arrested for it!"

"White folks don't scare me," Ruby announced. "Nothin' scares me."

That same night, Ruby snuck out of the house and went with Beulah to visit another married man that she was involved with. "He's right handsome, and he wants me because I'm a virgin," Beulah bragged.

Ruby gasped. She was dumbfounded, and she didn't hesitate to let her sister know. "What? No you ain't! I ain't tryin' to hurt your feelin's, but you must be one of the biggest whores in town, girl." Ruby guffawed and gave her sister a hard look of disbelief.

"He don't know that!" Beulah shot back. "And if you ever tell on me, I am goin' to whup you."

"But you told me yourself that a girl bleeds only the *first* time she's with a man."

A pensive look formed on Beulah's face. A few seconds later, she gave Ruby a serious look. "Listen, a girl can bleed as many times as she wants to, if she knows her business. Them whore women I babysit for sometime, they tell me stuff."

"They told you how to bleed even after you ain't a virgin no more?"

"Men are so stupid! Like that nitwit I'm fixin' to marry next month. He thinks I'm a virgin, and he told me that he wouldn't marry me if I wasn't. Hmmph. I bet there ain't a man alive over twelve that's still a virgin. Them dogs! They got some nerve expectin' so much from us. But do you know what? If virgin pussy is what they want, that's what some of us will give 'em."

"What is this trick them whore ladies told you about?" Ruby

was curious and she had every reason to be. She had already decided that when it involved sex, she wanted to know as many tricks in the book as possible.

"You know them big capsules that Mama gives us when we have cramps? Them red and green things that look like they could choke a mule?"

Ruby nodded. "Yeah. I had to take one last month." Ruby grimaced. "I'm glad to hear that them nasty tastin' things is good for somethin' else."

"You open up the capsule and dump out whatever that stuff is they put in it. You drop some chicken blood into one side of the capsule, and then you press the capsule back together. You have to make sure it's screwed back together right, so the blood won't leak out before it's supposed to. Just before the man, uh, sticks his pecker in you, you slide the capsule up into your coochie. As soon as he hits it, it busts open, and the blood trickles out. But before you do all of that, you have to douche with some vinegar or alum to tighten yourself up the way a virgin is supposed to be," Beulah explained. "I read in a magazine that the women in Europe have been doin' this for years, and gettin' away with it."

"That's nasty!" Ruby hollered. "I hope I never have to fool no man into thinkin' I'm a virgin."

"Let me tell you somethin', girl. When you get involved with men, you will have to do all kinds of shit to keep them in line. Just like a dog. Men have to be fed, petted, and trained right. It's our burden to keep 'em happy if we want to keep 'em. As long as we do what they tell us to do—or let them think we doin' it, I should say—they won't be much trouble."

"I already know that. But that don't mean nothin' to me. When I do get a man, I am goin' to do what I want to do, not what he tells me to do," Ruby vowed.

Beulah gave Ruby an exasperated look, but she really wanted to slap some sense into her head. She couldn't believe that she was related to a girl as naive as Ruby. "Girl, you got so much to learn about men. Don't you know that the man is the head of the house?"

Ruby nodded and gave her sister a mysterious look. "That's what you think, but I know better. When I get involved with a boy, I am goin' to be the one callin' the shots. When I get married, my husband can be the head of the house all he wants. But I am goin' to be the neck, and the neck is what controls every move the head makes. . . ."

Beulah was flabbergasted. She was stunned to hear something so profound coming out of her baby sister's mouth.

"My word, Ruby Jean," Beulah said, speaking in such a sharp tone of voice that it almost sounded like she was whistling under her breath. "You smarter than you look, girl. We ain't got to worry much about you. It sounds like you already got everything under control."

Ruby was enjoying Beulah's reaction to her neck comment. That was why she didn't confess that she had overheard their mother saying almost the same thing to one of her female friends.

True to her word, Ruby controlled every boy she got involved with. When she played stickball, or any other yard game on her block, she and her male playmates played by rules that she made up as she went along.

"Ruby Jean, how come you don't play with girls that much? You gettin' too old to be shootin' marbles and runnin' up and down the street like a savage with them boys," her mother mentioned one Saturday afternoon. Earlier that day, Ruby had shot marbles for several hours with a couple of boys from across the street.

"I don't like girls that much," Ruby admitted. "They ain't no fun. And they way too much trouble."

Beulah had married and moved out, so Ruby had a lot of free time on her hands now.

"Well, you better rethink yourself, honey-child. There is plenty of little girls around here for you to socialize with. It don't look good for my daughter to be spendin' so much time with boys. People will start talkin'," Reverend Upshaw told her.

Girls bored and annoyed Ruby. All of the ones she knew only wanted to talk about school and church, making their own clothes, and baking pies. The only girl in the neighborhood who was even remotely interesting to Ruby was Othella Mae Cartier. But she was *way* off limits. Her mother, Simone, was a part-time prostitute with a seventh-grade education. Other than fucking and sucking, she had very few skills. Everybody who knew her knew that she had sold her body to hundreds of men in several New Orleans brothels. In addition to prostitution, she supported herself and her children by doing a variety of dull jobs for wealthy white women—housekeeping, ironing, and anything else that the women she worked for didn't want to do.

Ruby's parents repeatedly ordered her to stay away from all of the fast girls. She received a sound whupping one day for walking down the street in front of half a dozen witnesses with a pregnant thirteen-year-old. This girl drank alcohol in public and bragged about the dozen or more boys that she'd already slept with. Since Ruby was not allowed to associate with girls like Simone's daughter Othella—who was just as fast as that pregnant thirteen-year-old—she eventually tried to form relationships with other girls. Unfortunately, none of those relationships panned out. Those girls were dull and stupid. They didn't even know half of what Ruby knew!

So by the end of that year, behind her parents' backs, Ruby started paying more attention to Othella.

"I ain't allowed to be seen with you in public, but if you want to, we can hang out together on the sly," Ruby told Othella on the day that Othella invited her to her fourteenth birthday party.

It didn't seem fair to Ruby that Othella had more dolls and other toys than she had. And it didn't seem fair to Ruby that Othella was so pretty. She decided that she could overlook Othella's good looks, because she knew that it took more than good looks to get a boy's attention these days. In spite of her feelings of jealously toward Othella, Ruby liked her and wanted to be her friend anyway.

"That's fine with me, Ruby Jean. I am used to hangin' out with certain kids on the sly. But the real reason I wanted you to come to my party tomorrow night is because my brother Ike likes you," Othella replied.

That juicy piece of information caught Ruby completely off guard. Her eyes got big and her heart skipped a few beats. "Huh? Me?"

Othella nodded. "Yeah. My brother likes you. . . ."

"DAMN!" Of all the boys that Ruby knew, not a single one was as cute as Isaiah "Ike" Cartier. "He's just about the best lookin' boy in town!" Ruby didn't realize she was licking her lips like a hungry dog until Othella snickered. Embarrassed, Ruby blinked and pressed her lips together for a few moments. "Uh . . . he's got all of them cute freckles on his face. And you say he likes me?"

"I know he's cute, he knows he's cute, and so do all of the other girls around here. But he's particular when it comes to girls. He's always goin' on and on about your titties."

Ruby laughed and stuck out her chest.

"What's so funny?" Othella wanted to know.

"Every female has titties," Ruby chuckled.

"Yeah, that's true. But unless she's a big cow, every female ain't got no big healthy rack like you got. One of these days, I am goin' to scrape up enough money and buy me a pair of them fake foam titties that I see all the time in them magazine ads."

There was a smug look on Ruby's face, and that was why what she said next caught Othella by surprise. "Well, if I could give you half of mine, I would."

"And you would end up regrettin' that. Men like big titties. One day you'll be glad for what God gave you."

"I wish I looked more like you," Ruby admitted, gazing at Othella like she was looking at a fancy new bicycle. "You are the kind of girl that colored men really go for. Teeny-weeny body, light skin." Ruby paused and looked Othella up and down. "And all of that long pretty black hair. You look just like one of them white film stars with a tan."

"And lookin' the way I do usually causes me a lot of problems. I swear to God, boys and men sniff after me like dogs in heat," Othella complained, and then she gave Ruby a misty-eyed look and a tight smile. To Ruby, this was an indication that Othella enjoyed all of the male attention she attracted, but she kept that thought to herself. She knew how stuck on themselves pretty girls generally were. "Even my mama's men friends and all of my brothers' friends try to mess with me. If that ain't bad enough, they try to pester all of my girlfriends, too. And a bunch of 'em been askin' me about you, too."

Othella could be as vain and as stuck on herself as she wanted to be as far as Ruby was concerned. It didn't matter. The fact that she was trying to help Ruby jump-start her love life made a huge impression on Ruby. That made up for the few things about Othella that Ruby didn't like.

"Oh? Is that so? Them other boys *and* your brother Ike? They been askin' about me?"

"Uh-huh. *Especially* my brother Ike. I ain't never seen him grin the way he does when your name comes up. Ruby, you need to hurry up and get loose."

"Sure enough!" Ruby agreed, unable to stop grinning. She was ready to "get loose" and she knew that once she did, she'd be loose for a long time to come. "What time did you say your party was startin' tomorrow night?"

CHAPTER 3

*R*UBY WAS AWESTRUCK THE FIRST TIME SHE ENTERED THE
house that Othella lived in with her mother and six siblings.
She had seen the outside on several occasions, but she'd never
been inside until now. It was like walking into a carnival fun
house. The furniture in the congested living room was loud
and mismatched. There was a shabby plaid couch backed
against the wall with one brick on top of another in the place of
a missing leg. A lumpy yellow and black settee faced it. The settee had no legs at all. A bloodred upright piano sat against the
wall by the door.

"Y'all got a piano, too?" Ruby squealed. "Other than my uppity cousin Hattie in Baton Rouge, ain't nobody in my family
got a piano in the house."

"What about the church where your daddy preaches at? I
hear piano music comin' out of there every time I walk by,"
Othella pointed out.

"Yeah, there's a piano in there, but it belongs to the church,
so it ain't the same as havin' one in our livin' room." Ruby
looked around, amazed by all of the pictures on the walls of
dead presidents, and a couple of scowling philosophers that she
didn't recognize.

"Some white lady that Mama did some ironin' for gave this piano to her for payment last December. It was her Christmas present, too. My uncle Ernest hauled it here in his truck," Othella revealed.

"Hey, Simone," Ruby greeted, offering one of her biggest smiles.

Simone lay sprawled on the couch with a catalogue on her lap that was open to a page with an ad for girdles at the top and one for chewing tobacco at the bottom. She was just waking up from a drunken stupor.

"Hey, Ruby Jean. A storm must have blowed you over here. Your daddy don't want his kids hangin' out with mine," Simone said with a sneer.

"Oh, I don't worry about my daddy, bless his soul. What he don't know won't hurt him," Ruby replied with a dismissive wave and a chuckle.

Othella's handsome brother Ike was seated on the other end of the couch with his mother. He winked at Ruby, and that made her heart skip a few beats. She felt the blood rise in her face, heating it like a steamed towel. She had to force herself not to giggle.

"Hi, Ike," Ruby muttered. "Uh, I like y'all's house."

"Yeah," Ike said. "A uptown girl like you must be used to nice things like we got."

"Uh-huh. I'm goin' to have to come over here more often." Now Ruby's whole body felt hot, especially her crotch. She couldn't take her eyes off Ike. Ike was so cute, with his soft, wavy black hair and big brown eyes. His skin tone was what they called high yellow, and he had slightly darker freckles in the center of his face that resembled the footprint of a small cat's paw. He looked like the doll that Ruby's aunt Lucy had given to her a few Christmases ago. Hadn't she heard something about him having a pecker the size of a cucumber? Girls lied and exaggerated, but Ruby had already made up her mind to find out if what she'd heard about Ike was true. Whether it was true or not, she wanted him. And, according to Othella, he wanted her.

"You do that, Ruby Jean," Ike said with a sniff.

"Sure enough. We like company," Simone added with a nod. "We are a real sociable family, if ever there was one."

"I'm glad to hear that, because I really like your house, Simone," Ruby said, putting more emphasis on her words than was necessary. "I ain't never seen no red walls and red curtains, except at that circus that my mama took me to last year." She gasped with glee when she noticed a guitar and a harmonica on the scarred coffee table.

Bright green linoleum covered the floors in half of the six rooms in the house. Wood covered the other three. There was a deep well in Simone's backyard, right next to a chicken coop that she regarded as one of her most prized possessions. The family ate chicken in some form almost every day of the week. Simone and her children shared the well with several neighbors. There was no indoor plumbing, so the whole family bathed in foot tubs or took bird baths in the kitchen sink. And since there was no indoor plumbing, they used portable toilets, better known as "slop jars," when they didn't want to go outside to use the outhouse.

Simone always managed to keep a dependable jalopy in her driveway. As soon as one became inoperable, she acquired another one with a little help from her men friends.

Almost every house in this section of Shreveport, which was an unincorporated district called Thelma City, had a backyard garden that contained everything from collard greens to tomatoes.

As hard as it was to believe, Othella's shabby gray house was on the same street as Ruby's, just three blocks away. But compared to Othella's "neck of the woods," Ruby's house and the other nice houses on her block looked like they were from another planet. Her family home was a large one-story, red-shingled house with a well-kept front lawn, indoor plumbing, four neatly appointed bedrooms, a large dining room, and a living room with impressive imitation leather couches.

Ruby's father always drove a shiny Packard, or a car equally impressive. He bought a new used vehicle every two or three years, not because he was a show-off, but because he had an image to maintain. He was the pastor of the Church of God in Christ, where the members of his large congregation spoke in tongues when the spirit moved them. And if the spirit moved them hard enough, they also twisted, shouted, fainted, and rolled around on the floor. And when it came time to offer a donation, most gave more than they could afford, but they didn't mind. They wanted to make sure that they had a nice-looking church to worship in. And that they lined the preacher's pockets so he wouldn't be tempted to move on to another church like some preachers did. Reverend Upshaw was not hard up for financial aid, but he never refused any. He also worked for a cleanup crew at a turpentine mill on the outskirts of Shreveport. He was the only black employee at the factory. The foreman who had hired him had done so because he had heard that the preacher was an honest, hardworking man who "knew his place" and didn't give white folks any trouble. Reverend Upshaw was a big shot in the black community, but to his employer and coworkers, he was as meek and docile as a saint. He did everything he was told to do, with no resistance whatsoever. One of his responsibilities included a task that no white man in his right mind wanted to do: he maintained the four putrid outhouses behind the mill.

Ruby's mother baked pies for an upscale restaurant that catered to rich white folks. To enforce that, there was a huge sign in the front window that said: WHITES ONLY. Not that any black folks Ruby knew wanted to patronize a segregated establishment anyway. Ruby's parents provided as lavish a lifestyle as black parents could at the time, so she didn't want anything from white folks.

Now that she had Othella as a friend, her life was almost complete. The only thing missing was a cute boyfriend with a nice big pecker between his legs.

"You like ice cream, Ruby?" Ike asked, rising from the couch, hitching up his loose overalls with both hands. He was as glad as Ruby was that she had finally come to the house.

"Uh-huh. You got some?" Ruby tried not to look too eager. But if Ike had placed a stick of butter in her mouth, it would have melted like ice on a bonfire.

"I'll walk you over to Spoons' when you get ready to leave and we'll share a scoop. Vanilla," Ike told her with a gleam in his eye. He was still fiddling with his pants, and Ruby couldn't decide if he patted his crotch for his benefit or hers. She pretended not to notice that bold gesture. She promptly returned her attention to Othella.

After Othella showed Ruby her doll collection in the bedroom that she shared with her younger sisters, Ruby was ready to leave. One reason was because Othella was very touchy about her dolls and she recalled how Ruby used to chase her with sticks, trying to take them from her before they became friends. Now, each time Ruby picked one up, Othella snatched it out of her hand and returned it to its place. There were at least ten dolls, all with rosy cheeks, blue eyes and blond hair, in various sizes. They were all over the bed, on top of the oak dresser, and even in cardboard boxes on the floor. The three largest ones occupied the top of a chifforobe facing the bed.

"How come you so particular about my dolls? Ain't you got none?" Othella asked.

Ruby, with her eyes on the largest doll in the room, turned to Othella and gave her a pensive look. "My mama stopped buyin' me dolls when I turned twelve. She said I was too old."

"Well, don't you still have the ones she did buy you when you was a kid?"

"Huh? Oh, my sisters' crazy kids done either took all the ones I had, or broke off their arms and legs. I just love baby dolls, girl dolls especially. I'm goin' to have all girl babies when I get married. Seven. Just like my mama and her mama."

"Well, when you have you some girl babies, you can do whatever you want with them. But I don't like nobody messin' with my dolls. You can come here all you want, but don't tetch my dolls. I want them to all still be in good shape when I leave home to get married so my little sisters can have them to play with."

Ruby was surprised and disappointed to find out that Othella was so territorial about her things. Now she was having second thoughts about cultivating a relationship with her. But she cancelled that thought as soon as Othella's cute brother Ike ducked into the room and offered Ruby some peanut brittle that he had just made.

Twenty minutes later, Ruby told Ike she was ready to leave and wanted to know if he was still going to treat her to some vanilla ice cream.

CHAPTER 4

ONE OF THE MANY REASONS THAT RUBY'S PARENTS DIDN'T want her to socialize with Simone's kids was because Simone didn't properly supervise them. Ike was only thirteen, but he stayed out all night if he wanted to. So did fourteen-year-old Othella and her twin brother O'Henry. Twelve-year-old Roger often disappeared for days at a time and usually came home drunk. The other kids were younger, and they came and went as they pleased as well.

Othella's two youngest sisters, Yula and Noreen, were only seven and eight. Her other sister, Irene, was eleven. Even though Irene was shy and somewhat slow, she was having sex on a regular basis with a fifteen-year-old boy who had already impregnated one girl. Othella had been sexually active since she was twelve. She and her siblings had access to alcohol and sometimes they got tipsy right in front of Simone. She was usually too intoxicated or too busy doing her own thing to know, or care, what her kids were up to. They had the run of the house, seven days a week, twenty-four hours a day.

When school was in session, the Cartier children attended at their leisure. A thorough education was a dream, therefore not a priority. A lot of black or biracial kids like Simone's, some as young as nine, had already dropped out of school to work in the fields. Sadly, the few who had managed to graduate from high school and attend college found out the hard way that an education didn't really mean much when you were a person of color. They generally took whatever jobs they could get.

One of Ruby's sisters had married an ambitious man who had completed four years of college. He had interviewed for several jobs, and ended up stamping prices on merchandise in a feed store. No one else had offered him any other position. And then there was her father's baby brother, Lewis. He'd completed a two-year course at a culinary school and served in the army. The only job that he'd been offered was a janitor's position at the corner supermarket. To supplement the income that he needed to support himself and a wife and nine children, he baked pies for the same restaurant that Ruby's mother baked pies for. Lewis had been sleeping with Simone for the past ten years, listening to her make fun of him for working for a "pie wagon," which was how she referred to that uppity "whites only" restaurant.

When Othella shared that piece of information with Ruby—the fact that her uncle was paying Simone to sleep with him—Ruby cringed. "If my daddy ever finds out about that, there is no tellin' what he'll do."

As off limits as Othella and her siblings were, Ruby didn't care. As a matter of fact, she enjoyed the excitement and the risks involved in doing something that her parents didn't want her to do. She was having fun, and to Ruby, that was what life was really all about. Especially now that she'd ducked into the bushes with Ike.

The tryst had happened that Saturday afternoon in July on the way to the Spoon family's ice cream parlor, the day before Othella's birthday party. It was over too quick for Ruby. Ike leaped up off her so fast, she thought that maybe a bug or a lizard had bitten him on his butt or something worse.

"What's wrong?" she wanted to know, massaging the insides of her thighs. "Is it over?"

"It is for me," Ike quipped, still huffing and puffing.

Ruby was already puzzled, but she grew even more puzzled when he handed her a large leaf that he'd plucked from a bush. "What's this for?"

"Wipe that blood off your thighs, and get your butt home before somebody catches us."

"But ain't we goin' to finish doin' it?"

Ike snickered. "Girl, we done finished doin' it."

"But it was feelin' so good. I thought," Ruby stopped talking when she saw the mean look on Ike's face.

"Look, Ruby Jean. I like you and all, and I just enjoyed myself. If you want us to stay friends, you won't badger me like you doin' now. We straight on that?"

Ruby nodded. "This mean you my man?"

"I guess," he said, shrugging and zipping up his pants. "As long as you don't tell nobody."

Ruby remained on the ground, lying on her side with her thighs pressed tightly together. She dropped the leaf, watched it flutter to the ground, and then she asked, "I can't tell Othella?"

"Especially not Othella! Her mouth is like a dipper, always open!" Ike hollered, waving his hands in the air.

"Well, what about the next time?" Ruby hadn't noticed it before, but now there was a stinging sensation in her vagina. To her horror, there was so much blood and semen between her thighs, they stuck together when she attempted to rise. Not to look like a damn fool, she rolled over on her back and sat bolt upright. She looked like a damn fool anyway, struggling to get up on her feet.

Ike placed his hands on his hips as he stared at her. He was amused and impatient.

"The next time what?" he asked, finally grabbing her arm to help her up. As soon as he released her, he hawked some spit into the palms of his hands and slicked back his curly black hair. "I ain't got no idea what you talkin' about, girl." He brushed off his overalls and shirt. Despite his dingy cheap clothes, he was sure enough dapper and sexy, Ruby thought. "Why you lookin' me up and down like that?"

Ruby shrugged. "I never thought a girl like me would get a boy like you," she said shyly, her face burning.

"Well, you did. Now I'm goin' to go play ball with the Porter brothers. They are scared to be around you too much on account of your mean daddy. Even I'm scared to death of that man! So don't follow me, you hear?"

Ruby was so taken aback, she almost tumbled back to the ground. She took a deep breath and composed herself. For one thing, she couldn't understand why Ike didn't share his fear of her mean daddy before and while he was making love to her. "What about that ice cream?"

"Ice cream? What ice cream? I ain't got no money for no ice cream. What did you do with that leaf I just gave you?" Ike said, looking around. He didn't wait for Ruby to answer his question. He saw the same leaf on the ground, so he picked it up and handed it back to her. "Wipe yourself off and get on home. I'll see you at the party tomorrow tonight."

Ruby snatched the leaf and began to swipe herself between her thighs. She was greatly disappointed, stunned that her first sexual encounter with a boy had not been more romantic. Ike must have sensed her feelings and thoughts, because he hauled off and kissed her on the lips, harder and longer than he'd ever kissed a girl.

"Next time you won't have to use no leaf to wipe yourself off with. I'll bring a rag or some newspaper, hear?" he said. "By the way, if you do make it to the party tomorrow night, maybe we can do it again then." That made Ruby smile. She didn't care what she had to do, she'd be at Othella's birthday party.

"Bye!" Ike yelled before he took off running.

Ruby stood in the same place like a telephone pole for several minutes after Ike had departed, smiling and looking at the spot on the ground where she had lost her virginity.

The next night around nine, after her parents had gone to bed, Ruby jumped out of her bedroom window and trotted all the way to Simone's house. She wore her tightest, most revealing blouse and a pair of denim pants designed especially for big boned girls, loose in the legs and elastic in the waist. She had applied some lipstick, rouge, and nut brown face powder that she had secretly purchased the last time she went shopping. She kept her makeup and "party" clothes hidden in a box under her bed.

She had not mentioned Othella's party to her parents because as far as they knew, she had nothing to do with Othella. And Ruby wanted them to keep thinking that way, not just so she could maintain a relationship with Othella, but now because of Ike.

As soon as she arrived at the party, which was already in full swing, she spotted at least two-dozen kids from the neighborhood. They all looked surprised to see her, because they knew how strict her parents were. But none of them had any plans to tattle on Ruby. They all knew about that switchblade she carried in her bobby sock. Even though she had never used it, nobody wanted to find out if she would.

Every single one of Othella's guests greeted Ruby with a warm smile. Five minutes after she had walked in the door, Ike pulled her into the room he shared with his two brothers so he could play with her titties. But after that, he practically ignored her.

It was the first time that a lover disappointed her. But something told her to get used to it, because it would not be the last time.

CHAPTER 5

*I*KE PRACTICALLY IGNORED RUBY. HE WAS TOO BUSY DANCING up a storm with that high yellow wench, Willene Starkey.

Ruby was glad that she got sick with a slight toothache and had to leave Othella's party early. She didn't even say good-bye to Ike.

"You want me to go with you so I can help you climb back into your bedroom window?" Othella asked as she walked Ruby to the door, glad that she had agreed to come so everybody could see that she could attract some "decent" friends, too.

"That's all right," Ruby told her, rolling her eyes at Ike. "If I am goin' to be jumpin' in and out of my bedroom window to come see you now, I need to get used to it." Even though Ruby was disappointed in Ike, she managed to smile and tell Othella, "I really had a lot of fun."

"Well, I hope you don't get no toothache the next time. You'll have even more fun, Ruby Jean."

Ruby didn't spend much time thinking about how Ike ignored her. There were plenty of other boys in the neighborhood who were glad to accommodate her. A few weeks after she'd given her virginity to Ike, she had sex with three more boys. Neither one was as cute as Ike, but they had all made her feel just as good as Ike. One boy had made her feel even better.

School started a few days later. Ruby was horrified when she discovered that one of her teachers was the kind of sad-sack old maid who had nothing better to do than give students tons of homework on the first day of school. She rushed home that day, rushed through dinner, and then she rushed to her room to do her homework and Othella's. She was determined to make this friendship work and doing Othella's homework was a small price to pay. Besides, she still wanted an excuse to visit Othella's house in case Ike came to his senses.

Ruby and Othella discussed a lot of things when they were together, but the one subject they talked about the most was sex.

"I can go all night with Steve Wes. He's so cuddly and gentle, and he smells good all the time, like soap. I wouldn't mind mar-ryin' him and havin' his babies," Othella swooned.

She and Ruby occupied the steps to the back porch at Othella's house that September night, a few days after school had started. It was a warm night with the crickets, owls, and other night creatures out in full force. Leaves of various sizes and colors covered the ground like a quilt. Despite the mosqui-toes, which were so aggressive they ignored the fly swatters that Ruby and Othella waved at them, it was a pleasant evening.

"Babies? You want to marry Wes and have his babies? Why?" Ruby asked, stunned, surprised, and disappointed. She didn't even like to think about having to share Othella with a husband and a baby, just when she was getting to really know her and enjoy her company.

"I am goin' to have somebody in my life that I know will love me," Othella said with the sad look of an unwanted puppy on her face. She toyed with a loose thread on the top buttonhole of her flimsy white jumper.

"You got all of them sisters and brothers and your mama, not to mention all of them kinfolks still out in the bayou. They love you," Ruby pointed out, stunned that Othella would make such a ridiculous statement.

"Ruby Jean, you wouldn't understand. You don't know what it's like to live my life."

Ruby was puzzled and it showed on her face. "Othella, please talk with some sense."

"I am talkin' with some sense. My mama ain't the best mama in the world, and everybody knows that. You have to sneak around to be friends with me, and you ain't the only girl that has to do that. Paulette Jarvis said her mama told her if she ever caught her at my house, she was goin' to whup her within a inch of her life. My mama is a whore, and that's what people keep tellin' me I am goin' to be. She's been a whore most of her life, and I suspect she always will be."

Ruby gave Othella a thoughtful look. "Well, you don't have to be no whore if you don't want to be one."

"That's just it, I don't. That's why I want to find me a husband to take care of me. My mama is a pretty woman, and men have always paid a lot of attention to her. But she ain't never been married. Nobody cared enough about my mama to marry her and make her more dignified so people could respect her."

"Well, that ain't the worst thing in the world. Your mama still got a lot of men friends. Ain't she locked up in her bedroom with that man who shines shoes in front of the post office."

"Yeah. She's fuckin' him. She's fuckin' him like she does all the dozens of men that trample in and out of our house every week. She don't care who knows it. And the last thing we need in our house is another baby, because I'll be the one takin' care of it most of the time, not my mama."

"I know I sure don't want no baby right now. I'm havin' too much fun," Ruby said with a sigh and a shudder.

"Uh, I wanted to talk to you about that," Othella said, giving Ruby a serious look. "You gettin' pregnant."

"Huh? What do you mean by that?" Ruby asked dumbly. "I ain't pregnant, that I know of."

"That's just it. If you ain't, that you know of, you need to make sure you don't get pregnant. I hadn't said nothin' before on account of I figured with all them big sisters you got, they done already told you what to do to not get pregnant." Othella didn't like the loud gasp Ruby let out. "Oh, Lord. I guess they didn't."

"Well, if you know, you better tell me what I need to do to keep from gettin' pregnant," Ruby said gruffly.

A coal oil lamp sat on the porch floor between them and there were dozens of fireflies circling their heads. There was more than enough light for Othella to see the confused look on Ruby's face.

"Girl, before you leave this house, I'm goin' to give you a jug of bleach and a bottle of vinegar, and you better use it if you know what's good for you. Mix about half a cup of each together real good, and then you douche with it every time after you've been with a boy—unless you want to be walkin' around here with a baby!"

"How do you know to do stuff like that?"

Othella rolled her eyes and gave Ruby an exasperated look. "I'm a whore's daughter, remember? Knowin' some whore secrets is one advantage I got over girls like you."

"Oh. Well, did your whore mama tell you how to trick a man into thinkin' you're still a virgin?"

Othella's jaw dropped. "No, why would a whore want to do that? Men are stupid, but they are not that stupid."

"My sister Beulah is the first one that told me all about it. She wanted that knucklehead that she married to think she was a virgin on their weddin' night." Ruby laughed.

"Well, even I know that that's a damn lie." Othella clucked like a setting hen. "Beulah was no virgin when she got married.

I used to see her comin' and goin' from the juke joints with that bug-eyed woman's husband that lives on Pike Street. And I know he's a cockhound because he was visitin' my mama back then, and still is."

"And Beulah told me that some of my other sisters tricked their husbands into thinkin' they were virgins, too," Ruby added with a smug look on her face. "They used the same trick she used."

Othella gave Ruby an impatient look. "Well, are you goin' to tell me exactly what this virgin trick is, or do I have to sit here and try and guess it?"

"Oh, it must not be that big of a secret if my sisters all know about it. Beulah said that the women in Europe have been pullin' this trick for a long time. All you have to do is get some chicken blood and open up a capsule, like them big ones I take for my cramps. You drip the blood into the capsule and press it back together." Ruby paused and swatted a few more mosquitoes.

"Is that all? How is that goin' to make some man think you're a virgin?" Othella wanted to know. By now, she was extremely impatient and more curious than ever.

"After you seal the capsule back up, you slide it up into your coochie. When the man puts his pecker in, it'll bust the capsule and you'll bleed." Ruby sniffed. "Just like a virgin."

"Damn!" Othella looked at Ruby in awe. "Damn!" she said again. "That is a good trick—as long as the man don't already know you've been busted by somebody else."

"Well, that goes without sayin'. You can't be fool enough to try and pull a trick like that on a man who already knows your business."

"And you sure couldn't do it if you've had a baby, huh? Jesus's mother was the only woman who was able to pull off a virgin birth." Othella clucked again.

"Well, that's for sure." Ruby sighed. "I love babies, and I will have me a houseful some day. Papa would beat me to death if I got pregnant before I got married, so I'll do that douche thing you told me about. I wouldn't want to end up like your mama. And anyway, how in the world does your mama keep goin' the way she is? Seven kids and she's still kind of young. She can't get a husband, she's fuckin' every man that moves, and she ain't even tryin' to change her ways."

Othella shrugged. "I guess that's her style. She likes to do it with a lot of men, because she wants to. Even with ones that don't pay her. And since she ain't got no pimp makin' her do it, she must like it! I ain't never heard her complain about bein' a whore. Besides, she's gettin' paid most of the time."

Ruby sniffed. "To tell you the truth, I admire a woman who will do what she wants to do, even fuckin' for money. It beats cleanin' toilets for a livin'."

"Would you do it?" Othella asked, giving Ruby a guarded look.

Ruby looked amused. "Who me? I ain't cleanin' nobody's nasty, stinkin' toilet! Shoot!"

"I meant, would you go to bed with men for money?"

Ruby thought about Othella's words. That thought was taking so long because she really wasn't sure how she wanted to answer the question. "I hope I never have to stoop that low. But I have to say that it's better than screwin' them for free like we do now."

"But ain't you supposed to be saved . . . sanctified?"

"So? I'm still saved and sanctified. Me screwin' around with all these boys ain't made me no less a Christian. I'm still the same person that I was before boys got ahold of me, and I still go to church every Sunday. I just have to pray a little harder to cover for all the extra backslidin' I do now."

"I guess that makes good sense," Othella replied with her head tilted to the side like she was trying to balance her thoughts. "Do you ever worry about gettin' hurt?"

"Hurt? Hurt how? It only hurts that first time. We already talked about that."

"I mean hurt some other kind of way. Like a jealous boy might beat you up if he finds out you doin' the big nasty with all of these other boys. Or some jealous girl might jump you for doin' it with her boyfriend."

At this point, Ruby reached inside her bra and removed a switchblade knife with a black and gold handle. It made a loud click when she flicked it open. The four-inch blade was so sharp it could slice a thick piece of sugarcane in two with just one swoop. "I ain't worried about no jealous boyfriend beatin' me for bein' with another boy, or no jealous girl jumpin' on me for pleasurin' her boyfriend."

"So it's true. You do carry a knife, just like my mama told me. Where did you get it?"

"When I was eight, I spent part of my summer vacation with my uncle Mervyn in Slidell. His wife is the one that wanted me there so he wouldn't beat her so much. He was a real mean old pit bull. He used to beat up folks left and right, until his wife scalded him to death with a pan of hot grease. Anyway, his knife fell out of his pocket one day before he died, and he didn't know it. I snatched it off the floor, and it's been mine ever since."

"You ever had to use it?" Othella couldn't take her eyes off the blade. Just the thought of Ruby using it to cut somebody made her flesh crawl.

"Not yet," Ruby answered.

"I hope you never do," Othella whispered, her voice cracking.

"I hope I never do neither," Ruby said, her voice hollow and detached. "But if I ever have to chastise somebody, I wouldn't hesitate to use it."

Othella was concerned and frightened by how casually Ruby talked about "chastising" people. The last thing she wanted was for her to get herself in trouble with that switchblade. "That's what worries me, Ruby Jean. Honest to God. You might get mad at somebody and hurt them real bad."

"Well, as long as nobody messes with me, I ain't goin' to mess with nobody."

But a couple of weeks later somebody did mess with Ruby, and she had to use that switchblade for the first time.

CHAPTER 6

*W*HEN RUBY TOLD SEVENTEEN-YEAR-OLD LONNIE STARKS that she thought she was carrying his baby, he called her a black cow and then he slapped her face so hard, the barrette holding her braids in place flew halfway across his bedroom.

The main reason that Ruby had given herself to Lonnie was because he looked a lot like Ike. He was older and more experienced, but he was not even as good a sex partner as Ike. Ruby didn't let that stop her from being with him several times in the same week.

The only reason Lonnie gave Ruby the time of day was because he had heard it was easy to get between her thighs. He was a red-blooded American boy, and that's what red-blooded American boys did. He had no feelings for a plain Jane like her!

"You ain't blamin' no baby on me! You know I got a girlfriend. If she ever finds out I been fuckin' your stinky black self, she'll drop me like a bad habit! Now you get your husky black ass up off my bed and get the hell up out of here before I slap you again and then beat your brains—" Lonnie didn't even get to finish his sentence. Before he realized what was happening, Ruby sliced him across the front of his neck. Othella was outside in Lonnie's mother's living room acting as the lookout. She and Ruby took turns doing this favor for each other. As soon as Othella heard the commotion, she burst into the room.

Ruby was calmly putting her clothes back on. Lonnie was backed up against the wall holding his neck. "That no good bitch cut me," he said in a weak, raspy voice. He lifted his hand off his neck to show Othella his wound. Her eyes got wide, her jaw dropped. The slash made Lonnie look like he had two mouths.

"Lord have mercy! Ruby, why did you cut Lonnie?" Othella shrieked, her hands up in the air like somebody had pulled a gun on her.

"Oh, that crybaby will be all right. I didn't cut him that deep," Ruby said casually.

"But why did you cut Lonnie, Ruby Jean? What did he do to you for you to cut him up like that? His mama's a school teacher! She's goin' to call the police on you!" At the same time, Othella was running around the room pulling out drawers until she found a towel. She ran to Lonnie and used the towel to sop up the blood oozing from his wound.

"It was his fault. I told him I was fixin' to have a baby, and he got all crazy on me."

Othella froze. "You pregnant? You fixin' to have a baby?"

"Yeah. I guess I am," Ruby muttered with a nervous shrug. "And my daddy is goin' to kill me dead."

Othella had calmed Lonnie down. She had stopped the bleeding and tied the towel around his neck. "You'll be all right now, Lonnie. You shouldn't have messed with Ruby Jean."

"Y'all better not tell nobody about this," Lonnie whimpered, tears rolling down both sides of his face.

"Oh, you ain't got to worry about me tellin' nobody about this," Othella said. "And if you got some turtleneck sweaters, I suggest you wear them until your neck heals up." She turned to Ruby. "And you, girl, you better come up with a real good story about how you got pregnant."

*   *   *

Later that same night a few minutes after eleven, Ruby jumped out of her bedroom window and galloped over to Othella's house. Simone, with a grin on her flushed face, was entertaining company: a fifty-nine-year-old man with eyes like a fish and skin the color of tar. She had just moved the nervous-looking man, who had her red lipstick all over his cheeks and forehead, from her bedroom to the living room. As the man was buttoning his shirt, he froze when he saw Ruby. He had every reason to be nervous; he was the husband of one of Ruby's mother's close friends from church.

"Ruby Jean, you ain't supposed to be here," the busted husband croaked.

"You ain't neither," Ruby said with a smirk.

Without saying anything else to one another, the married man and Ruby knew that they were on the same page. From what he'd just said, apparently he knew that Ruby's parents didn't allow her to be in Simone's house. And the fact that he was married, and a deacon in her father's church . . . well, there was nothing else for them to say on the subject. He knew that she wouldn't tattle on him, and she knew that he wouldn't tattle on her.

"What you doin' out here this late, Ruby Jean? Ain't you got school tomorrow?" Simone snorted, handing her gentleman friend another jar of beer. She wore a short, thin nightgown and it was already hanging off her shoulder like a too-big toga. Even though Simone crossed her legs, Ruby could see that she didn't have on any panties. Nothing Simone did surprised Ruby. But Ruby had done a lot of things herself lately that surprised Simone. Like busting into her house in the middle of the night on a school night.

"I need to talk to Othella," Ruby told her. She was almost out of breath because she had run all the way from her house.

"She's in her room." Simone waved Ruby away and lifted a

broom straw off the coffee table and started to pick her teeth. "Don't you go back there makin' a lot of racket and wake up all my young'uns."

Ruby pranced across the floor and down the narrow hallway to Othella's bedroom at the end of the hall.

Othella occupied a metal folding chair in front of a mirror on her bureau, rolling her hair with pieces of a brown paper bag. The three younger sisters that she shared the room with were already in bed, snoozing like newborn puppies.

"It was a false alarm!" Ruby hollered.

"Shh!" Othella ordered with a finger pressed against her lips. She motioned toward the bed where her sisters lay. "You don't want to wake them little monkeys up so they can broadcast your business all over town."

Ruby tiptoed over to Othella. She cleared her throat and whispered in Othella's ear, "It was a false alarm. My monthly just came on a little while ago while I was sittin' on the commode!"

Othella rose from her seat, instructing Ruby to remain quiet as she led her out to the back porch.

Othella closed the kitchen door and looked around the yard to make sure that she and Ruby were alone. When she spoke again, she used a voice that was just above a whisper. "You was lucky this time. But you might not be so lucky the next time. You use that bleach and vinegar and clean yourself out every time after you been with a boy from now on. And to be on the safe side, use some vanilla extract, too. Stir it up real good until it gets real soupy."

"All of that's supposed to keep me from gettin' pregnant? That's supposed to work?"

"Well, it's been workin' for me all this time. My mama told me to do it."

Ruby gave Othella a curious look. "But it must not work every time if your mama got seven kids."

"My mama got seven kids because she wanted seven kids. She likes puttin' her hands in Uncle Sam's deep pockets. When you get ready to have kids like she was, and you want to milk that welfare cow, you stop douchin' mens' jism out of your pussy. Boom! Them babies start poppin' out like popcorn."

"Oh."

"And I'm goin' to let you in on somethin' else that you probably don't know. If you want to be with your man while you on your monthly, all you have to do is that same douche. It'll stop the blood until you finish your business."

"Is that right?" Ruby said, giddy and impressed.

Othella nodded.

"You got some bleach and vinegar and vanilla extract that I can use right now?"

Othella snickered and shook her head. "Who is it this time, Ruby Jean? I sure hope it ain't that Lonnie again."

Ruby shook her head. "I seen your brother Ike peepin' out his bedroom when I walked by just now. . . ."

Ruby had come to the conclusion that sex was the greatest thing that she'd discovered since peanut brittle and beer. When Ike, or any of her other "boyfriends" were not available to satisfy her, she spent time with whoever was. But even then, she was picky. She didn't believe in screwing ugly boys. She'd done it once on the ground in a cornfield with a long-headed boy who reminded her of an alligator. It had been an unpleasant experience for her. His looks had been too distracting for her to concentrate. The expression on his face had looked so comical when he climaxed, she giggled all the way home from the cornfield behind his daddy's house. She promised herself that she would never stoop that low again.

She liked a certain type that was popular among black females in the region at the time—men of color with exotic features. That included light skin and "good" hair, which meant it had to be wavy, straight, or curly. And with all of the Creoles in Shreveport, she didn't have to worry about running out of partners in that category.

Now that she was sexually active, Ruby had mellowed out. This was a change that pleased her parents as well as the rest of her family.

"Ruby Jean, I guess you really are growin' up," said Lola Mae, Ruby's third oldest sister. Lola, her thin, sad-faced husband, Arlester, and their three owl-eyed sons had come to enjoy another Sunday dinner at the Upshaw home. They had all spent the better part of the day in church, listening to Reverend Upshaw deliver one of his fiery sermons. "You actin' mighty mature these days, girl. You ain't bickered with my rowdy young'uns one bit today."

"She ought to be actin' mature. She's fourteen, goin' on fifteen," Reverend Upshaw pointed out, giving a stern look to Ruby's three impish nieces and nephews for snickering and making faces at Ruby.

"Sure enough. The girl is just glowin' like a coal oil lamp. Y'all better keep her on a short leash . . . all these frisky boys around here lookin' for some juicy-butt girl like Ruby Jean to *dip their tally-wacker* in," Arlester said. Ruby decided that the look on his face and his demeanor was less than brotherly. He was more like a devil's advocate. "Somebody pass the corn bread." This man had no shame or class. He was the only person Ruby knew who used a word like "tally-wacker" to refer to a dick.

Ruby occupied a chair right next to her meddlesome brother-in-law. She was more than happy to pass him the platter that contained a mountain of steaming hot corn bread muffins; anything to divert his attention. For the bag of bones he was, he loved to eat.

In addition to a gallon-size bowl of collard greens with red peppers and smoked turkey neck parts swimming in the pot liquor, a bowl of black-eyed peas and a huge platter of golden fried chicken sat in the center of the table. Surrounding those treats were a platter of fried green tomatoes, a huge bowl of gravy, a meat loaf the size of a full-grown cat, a mountain of potato salad, and a casserole dish overflowing with a peach cobbler. The mixture of so many different aromas was intoxicating. Except for Ruby, everybody was smacking and chomping on something, looking too happy for words.

"If I didn't know no better, I'd swear you was in love, Ruby Jean," Lola added, looking from the reverend to her mother. "Mama, you sure enough better keep both eyes on this girl," she teased, grease and butter sliding down her chin.

Ida Mae was not the least bit amused. "Our girl ain't crazy. She ain't thinkin' about courtin' no boys yet. She's into her school books and the church." Ida Mae paused and turned to Ruby. "Ain't that right?"

"Yessum," Ruby agreed. "Um, Papa, can I be excused. I want to go to my room and do my Bible lesson. . . ."

Reverend Upshaw dismissed Ruby with a casual wave, beaming with pride at how well he and Ida Mae had raised the last of their seven daughters. "That girl is goin' somewhere, someday," he predicted.

Ruby was definitely going "somewhere" and it was today. Earlier that evening when she had run into Ike at the corner store, he had invited her to come to his house after dinner if she wanted to.

She wanted to, so she did.

CHAPTER 7

*A*S SOON AS RUBY ENTERED HER BEDROOM, SHE LOCKED THE door and wiggled out of the high-necked, mammy-made smock she'd worn to church. Within ten minutes, she had on her jeans and a loose, but low-cut blouse. These were items that she had purchased on the sly with her allowance, but most of her new wardrobe items had come from Othella.

That Othella. She had so many talents. One, and it was an important talent, was that she was a cunning thief. That made her relationship with Ruby even more valuable. Once she'd realized what a gold mine Othella was, she wanted to kick her own ass for not becoming friends with her sooner!

Every time Othella went downtown, she came home with all kinds of goodies for her family and for Ruby. And she was no ordinary thief. She didn't always just slide an item or two into the huge, homemade cloth handbag she carried. Othella was ahead of her time. She would mosey into a high-end store, strutting like a white woman with money. She would focus on what she wanted, or needed, and then she would snatch and run—sometimes three or four items at a time. Every black person who shopped in these particular establishments knew that the white clerks took their time helping them—if at all. The clerks would lollygag or chitchat with the white patrons and practically ignore the black patrons, not waiting on them until they got good and ready. Othella visited these stores only when they were too busy to notice her. And by the time they did, she'd be on her way with hundreds of dollars worth of merchandise.

Ruby stood in front of her dresser mirror admiring the cute two-piece ensemble that Othella had given to her the day before. Just as she was about to adjust her blouse to make it look even more low-cut, somebody pounded on her bedroom door.

It was that busybody brother-in-law of hers! "Ruby Jean, your mama and papa and me and Lola was wonderin' if you'd keep a eye on the young'uns while we go visit Sister May. She's on her deathbed, and if me and Lola don't see her before we go back to Bayonne this evenin', we might not get a chance to say a final farewell to her."

"Babysit? Now?"

"No, not right this minute. In about a hour or so. We fixin' to do Bible study right now, and you welcome to join us if you got a mind to."

"I'm doin' my Bible lesson in my room," Ruby reminded, holding her breath, wondering what this sucker was really up to.

"You sure? Somethin' tells me you need a group spiritual shot in the arm."

"Arlester, don't you worry none about me. Now if y'all want me to babysit later on, that's fine," Ruby snapped, surprised at how assertive she had become lately. Her brother-in-law's silence made her nervous. It would be just like him to go running to her daddy to tattle on her for sassing a grown person, even though he was not that much older than she was.

"We'll pay you a nickel tonight, and we'll bring you some peanut brittle next time we come," he finally said.

"In a hour or so? Uh, yeah. I think I can do that," Ruby said, her ear against the door.

"All right, baby sister."

Ruby kept her ear to the door until she heard her brother-in-law's squeaky-shoe footsteps move back toward the living room. After she'd slathered on some of the plum-colored lipstick that she'd gotten from Othella, she crawled out of her bedroom window. Once her feet landed on the ground, she stumbled away from the house like a drunken person.

By the time she got to Othella's house, Ike was home alone. He was in his bedroom, and already naked. Ruby had only an hour to do her business with Ike, so she immediately got naked and flopped into bed with him.

While Ruby's family was studying the Bible and listening to some of their favorite old spirituals on the radio that evening, Ruby and Ike were humping one another like rabbits.

Ike wasn't just good in bed, he was also a good kisser. When Ruby couldn't make love with him, they kissed until they got tired and sometimes that was almost as good as sex to her, and to him. Like Othella, Ike had a lot of talents. He knew a lot of the swing dances, thanks to Ruby. He'd even made up a few on his own. He also played a mean piano. Since Ruby couldn't listen to "worldly" music in her own house, she enjoyed listening to Ike tickle the keys on that old red piano that Simone had acquired. It was scarred with cigar and cigarette burns from top to bottom, even on the keys, but it still made good music.

Ruby stood behind Ike now as he sat at the piano by the living room door. They had put their clothes back on and shared the last beer in the house.

Ike had plopped down on top of an upturned empty fifty-pound lard bucket, playing some tune by somebody named Cab Calloway that he had heard on the radio.

"Ruby Jean, I heard somethin' sure enough bad about you just before you got here," he said out of nowhere. "I heard you been foolin' around with other boys, makin' me look like a fool."

Ruby was curious as to why he had waited until after he'd

made love to her to accuse her of cheating on him. "That's a lie," Ruby lied. "You are my first and only boyfriend." She sniffed. "What busybody told you that?"

Ike didn't stop playing his piano, and he didn't turn around to face her. "It don't matter who told me that," he continued. "And just to let you know, more than one person told me."

"Well, more than one person told you a damn lie," Ruby said calmly. "Now give me some sugar." She puckered her lips and leaned her head closer to Ike's. She was stunned and disappointed when he gave her an annoyed look and moved his head so she couldn't kiss him. It was such a brutal rejection, she almost burst into tears. "What's the matter, baby?"

"Nothin', I guess."

Ruby dropped her head and remained silent for a few moments. She had already wasted a third of the hour that she had to spend with Ike before she returned home. "I got to go babysit my sister's kids, so I can't stay long this time," she informed him.

Ike whirled around to look at her. "Oh? Well, uh, you got time to . . . uh . . . you know again? Mama and the rest of the family won't be home till real late, so we ain't got to worry about them catchin' us." There was a pleading look on his face.

Ruby wondered if she would ever figure out what kind of convoluted brains boys had inside their heads. Here Ike was accusing her of cheating on him, making her think that he was about to dump her. And in the next breath, he was asking her to go to bed with him again.

She also wondered what kind of convoluted brains girls like her had in their heads. Without hesitation, she planted a long sloppy kiss on Ike's puckered lips before they literally ran back to his bedroom.

Ruby didn't see or hear from Ike the rest of that month. But she did spend time with a few other boys.

When her period didn't start on time the following month, even though she had done all that douching with vinegar, bleach, and vanilla extract each time after intercourse, she wasn't that concerned. But when another month went by, and because she threw up bile three mornings in a row, she became a little concerned. But that didn't slow her down. She didn't miss a stride. She continued to see her boyfriends and she got so busy sneaking here and there with Othella, that she put her concerns about her late period out of her mind.

By the end of the fourth month, Ruby finally admitted to herself that she was in serious trouble. "Lord, what have I gotten myself into?" she asked herself one night that February. Even though she was big boned and more than a little plump, her belly had never protruded out from the rest of her body the way it did now. When she turned sideways, it looked like she had swallowed a small watermelon.

She had already temporarily stopped wearing tight, low-cut blouses and any other clothing that didn't hide her expanding body. Since she wore a lot of baggy pieces anyway, nobody noticed that she had been wearing nothing but loose-fitting outfits lately.

Ruby didn't sleep at all that night. She lay awake trying to come up with a believable story that she would eventually have to tell her family and everybody else.

CHAPTER 8

*E*VEN THOUGH RUBY WAS CONVINCED THAT SHE REALLY WAS
pregnant this time, she tried to ignore it as much as she could.
She continued to go to school and church, and she continued to
prance around the house playing with her nieces and nephews
when her sisters visited with their families.

Since she usually wore loose-fitting outfits most of the time
now anyway, she convinced herself that she could conceal her
pregnancy until the end. Hazel Lattimore, one of the neighborhood's fastest teenage girls, had done that last year. Nobody
even knew she was pregnant until she gave birth in the family's
bathroom one night.

Ruby was not worried about any of the busybodies she knew
noticing her expanding stomach. When and if they did . . .
well, she decided that she would worry about that when and if
they did. She was thankful that her bout with morning sickness
had only lasted a few weeks.

Another thing she wasn't really that worried about was the
fact that she was eating even more than usual. Since she had always eaten like a big hog in front of everybody, she saw no reason for anybody to ask why she had suddenly started to eat like
an even bigger hog. But her nosy brother-in-law Arlester asked
her at the very next Sunday dinner!

Of all the comments for that meddlesome fool to make, he had to say the one that almost made her wet her panties.

"Ruby Jean, why do it seem like you eatin' enough for two people these days?" he wanted to know. He gazed at Ruby with both of his bushy eyebrows raised, and one of his crooked knuckled, bony fingers aimed in her direction.

"Who me?" Ruby managed, her mouth stuffed with food.

While everybody else at the table remained silent, looking at Ruby with curious stares, Arlester continued.

"I ain't never seen you eat no five pieces of fried chicken durin' the same meal," he declared. His seat was across the table from Ruby's, so he had a direct view of her horrified face. As he chewed with his slack jaws twitching, his eyes rolled down from her face to her chest. "My Lord, you lookin' mighty thick these days. . . ."

Before Ruby could respond, her sister Lola came to her rescue. "I keep tellin' you the girl is growin' up—and out. By the time she's eighteen, she's goin' to be just as plump as the rest of us Upshaw females." Lola chuckled, patting her stomach, which was almost as big around as her large pear-shaped bottom.

But Lola's husband was not through with Ruby yet. "You ain't courtin' yet, Ruby Jean?" he asked with a suspicious look on his face.

Damn his soul to hell! Ruby thought. She hadn't mentioned boys or anything that had to do with courting in *months* to her parents. She didn't want to do or say anything that might make them keep closer tabs on her activities.

"Ruby Jean ain't thinkin' about no boys yet, praise the Lord," Reverend Upshaw offered. "If she is as smart as she looks, she'll finish school and go on to that colored college in Bayonne, be a school teacher or a nurse, before she ties herself down with a husband and babies." He tickled the side of Ruby's cheek. "Ain't that right, baby girl?"

"Um-hmm. That sure enough is right," Ruby mumbled, nodding as she reached for another piece of chicken.

According to Ruby's calculations, her baby was due to arrive some time in early July, only a month away. She hoped that he or she waited until after the Fourth of July holiday, which was also Othella's birthday. That was the last day in the year that Ruby wanted to be out of commission.

CHAPTER 9

*R*UBY WASN'T ABOUT TO LET THE THREAT OF A TORNADO stop her from sneaking out of the house through her bedroom window tonight. She wanted to help Othella celebrate her birthday and the holiday.

But that wasn't all.

Ruby hadn't had any beer or sex in over two weeks, and it was beginning to get on her nerves. She knew that she could get both at Othella's party.

"Ain't no tornado or nothin' else in the world goin' to keep me from comin' to your house tonight," she had assured Othella earlier in the day. "And I do mean *nothin'*."

"Oh, I ain't worried about you not comin' to my party," Othella told Ruby. "You ain't never missed one of my parties. If your mama and daddy can't stop you from associatin' with me, I know no storm can't neither. Don't forget to wear somethin' that'll keep the boys' attention on you. That low-cut dress I stole for you last week ought to do the trick. You ain't wore it yet, and I want to see how it looks on you. No matter what you wear, them boys will be all over us. I already told 'em how hot and horny we both been feelin' lately. . . ."

But a tornado was not the only thing that was threatening to interfere with Ruby's plans. She was also nine months pregnant with a baby that nobody even knew she was carrying.

Her labor had started at the dinner table this evening. The first contraction had shot through her belly like a red-hot bullet, while she sat eating some of the holiday barbeque and greens that her mother had prepared. The pain reminded her of the time that she'd stepped on a nail with her bare foot at a church event in Baton Rouge. She wanted to scream and roll around on the floor like she had done that time, but she managed not to. She did moan and grit her teeth though.

"Stop screwin' up your face like that, Ruby Jean. Them greens ain't that bitter," her mother scolded, before her teeth chewed a wad of turnip greens to pulp.

Ruby's father stopped gnawing on a rib bone so he could add his two cents. "And she'd better hurry up and eat everything on her plate. If that storm hits, it might be a while before our next meal."

"Can I finish my supper in my room?" Ruby asked, already rising. "I don't feel too good. . . ."

"You don't look too good neither," her mother quickly pointed out. "You must have the cramps again," she added in a whisper, rolling her eyes at her husband, seated directly across the table from her. She could tell from the grimace on his face that this was not a conversation that he wanted to hear. "And I ain't never seen that many pimples on your face."

"Yessum. Cramps again," Ruby responded with a cough and another moan. "And my acne is actin' up."

"It must be that homemade lye soap you been scrubbin' your face with. I'll get you some witch hazel this weekend. Finish your dinner in your room. But don't get too comfortable in case we have to haul ass to the root cellar to dodge that tornado," her mother told her. "And don't forget to say your prayers."

"Yessum. Uh, 'night, y'all," Ruby muttered as she wobbled across the floor, holding her plate with both hands.

Her mother nodded. Her father grunted and kept his eyes on the huge plate of food in front of him. He didn't look up until Ruby had left the room. Then he stopped chewing and shot a hot look at his wife. "Hell's bells, Ida Mae. I wish you and Ruby Jean wouldn't discuss them female issues at the table while we eatin'. That subject is so . . . gruesome," he complained. "Pass the biscuits, please."

Ruby's mother practically threw the bowl with the biscuits at her husband. "Look, old man, you done spent a whole lot of years in this house with eight women—me and them seven daughters we got. What do you expect? You ought to be used to female issues by now."

"Well, I ain't! Even though"—Reverend Upshaw paused and glanced over his shoulder toward the doorway—"even though . . . that's what's torturin' poor Ruby Jean today. Her face ain't never been as bloated as it is now. But there might be somethin' else goin' on with her that she don't want us to know about. After I finish my supper, I'm goin' to go get Dr. Hollis and have him come take a look-see at her."

"That ain't such a bad idea. Maybe I can get him to check my blood pressure," Ruby's mother said as she speared a large chicken wing on her plate with her fork. "Don't forget to take your raincoat and cap with you in case the rain starts back up before you make it over there and back home."

It was a good thing that Ruby had stopped in the hallway to eavesdrop on her parents' conversation. Had she not, she would have had a major mess on her hands. There was no way in the world that she would have been able to hide her pregnancy from Dr. Hollis, even though he was practically blind and hadn't practiced medicine in twenty years.

She held her breath and strolled back into the dining room, still holding her plate with both hands. "I feel so much better," she announced. She returned to her seat and dropped down with a thud.

Both of her parents were surprised to see her back at the table, and even more surprised to hear that she was feeling "so much better."

"You feelin' better already? You just left here a minute ago," Ruby's father said, concerned but relieved. He didn't really want to go out again tonight to get the practically blind doctor anyway. "I was goin' to go fetch Dr. Hollis."

Ruby laughed and waved her hand. "I don't need no doctor and you don't need to bring that old man out in this weather, tornado brewin' and all."

"Well, you still look peaked to me," Ruby's mother insisted.

"And bloated," her father added.

"It's just my monthly, y'all. I can't help myself." Ruby pouted. "I'm bleedin' a little heavier than usual this month, so I hope I don't get no blood on this chair," she muttered, rocking from side to side. She glanced at her spacious lap, thankful that her voluminous duster hid her condition so well. "That was why I asked if I could eat in my room. I know how much it cost to clean these quilted seat cushions. . . ."

"You can take your plate back to your room and finish your supper there," her father said with a heavy sigh. "But don't you leak no pot liquor or no barbeque sauce on your new bedspread."

"Or no blood," her mother said sharply.

Ruby finished her meal in her room. Then she locked her door, not that it was necessary. Her parents rarely disturbed her when she was in her room. She locked up this time because she didn't want them to barge in on her while she was getting dressed and making up her face for the party.

CHAPTER 10

*W*ITH SIX OLDER SISTERS AND SEVERAL OTHER FEMALE RELA-
tives of child-bearing age, Ruby knew enough about childbirth
to know that a woman's first baby usually took his or her time
to enter the world.

She had decided that she had enough time to go to the party,
dance, drink, and fool around with the boys for at least two
hours. She would make it back home in time to have her
baby—which meant she'd be a new mother before midnight.
By that time, both of her parents would be asleep. She'd give
birth in her bedroom.

"You can forget about haulin' water to the root cellar. We
won't need to take cover now. The weatherman on the radio
just said that the tornado threat is over," Ruby's mother yelled
to her from outside Ruby's bedroom door.

"Uh, yessum. Um . . . I think I'll just stay in my room and
turn in early tonight," Ruby yelled back. "My cramps done got
a little worse."

"And it's your own fault! I warned you when you first started
havin' your monthly that you shouldn't be runnin' around outside with your hair or feet wet, but you did. Now you sufferin'.
I'll make you some ginger tea, and I'll get in your bed with you
and rub your stomach till you go to sleep. I wish you had said

somethin' sooner before your daddy took out his teeth and put on his long johns. He's itchin' to get in the bed hisself! But I can still send him to get Dr. Hollis if you want me to."

Ruby's head almost exploded. "Oh no, Mama! You don't have to do all that! I ain't *that* sick!" She paused and glanced around her room, her eyes resting on the makeup and shoes on her bed that she was going to wear to the party. "Uh, you go on to bed now. I'll be just fine." She held her breath and listened. She had eaten in such a hurry, barbeque sauce was on her chin and lips. She licked her lips and wiped her chin with the back of her hand, still holding her breath and listening for her mother's response.

"All right then. 'Night, Ruby Jean," her mother yelled, already padding back down the hall to her room.

Ruby breathed a sigh of relief. " 'Night, Mama," she hollered, listening with her ear against the door. She wore her green terrycloth bathrobe over her loose-fitting blue cotton party dress, not the one that Othella had shoplifted for her and told her to wear tonight. That flimsy green jersey dress was way too tight. It clung to every lump, jellylike roll, and curve on her body. It would make her look pregnant even if she wasn't. She had hidden her condition for nine months, and she was not going to expose herself now, when she was so close to the end.

Ruby cracked open her door to make sure her mother had gone into her room and shut her door. Two seconds later, a super sharp pain shot through the lower part of her belly. It was the most painful contraction so far. It was the only one that made her wish she had never even *seen* a boy in her life, let alone screwed one. She had to close the door fast and cover her mouth with her hand to keep from screaming.

Maybe she wouldn't make it to the party after all. . . .

If Ruby didn't know any better, she'd swear she was carrying a pit bull instead of a baby in her womb, the way he or she was kicking. And to think that some of the women she knew went through this more than a dozen times! Her oldest sister Flodell had given birth to ten children. Ten! The thought of going through labor ten times was enough to make Ruby's heart skip a beat and her chest tighten. More pain was the last thing she needed right now. She pushed the thought of multiple births out of her mind and decided to focus on the only one that mattered to her tonight.

Despite the discomfort that she was experiencing, the fact that she was still a child herself and unmarried, and the fact that she'd gotten pregnant by mistake, Ruby still felt blessed. Like her mother, she believed that every child was a gift from God, even the "mistakes" like the one she was carrying.

Ruby waited another ten minutes. Then she tiptoed down the hall to her parents' room. She immediately peeped through the keyhole. Damn that labor! Bending over to look through the keyhole had caused her another sharp pain, making her legs tremble. She held her breath until that pain had subsided, then she placed her ear against the door and listened. Her parents had turned off their bedroom lamp, and her daddy was already snoring like a moose. She was sure that she was in the clear now, so she tiptoed back to her room. She locked her bedroom door again. Then she removed her bathrobe and placed it on the back of the chair in front of her dresser. After listening for a few more moments, she waddled to the window, opened it, and slid out like a huge snake. She hit the ground running like a track star.

Ruby was not a beautiful girl. Most people thought that she was just a little too stout and a little too dark. Her hair was too coarse and short for her to wear most of the latest styles. She usually wore it pressed, with a few finger waves on the side like now. Her inky black eyes were too small for her large round face. But those "imperfections" didn't stop any of the fifteen boys at Othella's party from wanting to dance with her. For one thing, she was a good dancer for such a husky girl. Nobody could do those swing dances like Ruby. She'd just introduced the jitterbug, a dance that she had picked up in Baton Rouge last month while visiting one of her musician uncles. It was not a new dance, but it was to her friends and they all wanted to learn it.

Another reason why so many boys wanted to dance with Ruby was because other than herself and Othella, there were not that many girls at the party. Othella had invited only three others, and she had handpicked borderline plain Janes. There was a good reason for that; Othella was smart when it came to dealing with Ruby. She read that girl like a book. She knew how important it was for her to get a lot of attention. Since the two of them didn't go for the same type of boy, Ruby had very little competition tonight. She had not stopped dancing since she walked in the door an hour ago. And she'd already drunk so much beer that her contractions didn't seem to hurt nearly as much now.

Six of the boys at the party had had sex with Ruby, each one at least twice. And one was the father of the baby that she was going to give birth to in less than an hour.

While Ruby was in the kitchen smacking on some barbequed ribs, her water broke. It saturated her panties and dripped a small puddle on the floor. Though she knew what was happening, it still startled her. She was glad that nobody else had come into the kitchen with her. She would have dropped dead on the spot if one of her friends had witnessed the gruesome mess she'd just made on the floor. And since nobody did, it was nothing for her to be concerned about. Clumsy partygoers had already spilled beer, soda pop, and other liquids in several other spots on the floor. Ruby didn't think anybody would notice the mess she'd just made.

She was not going to let even this incident interfere with her fun. She ducked into the broom closet facing the stove and removed her wet panties. Then she snatched a dust cloth off the shelf and wiped herself off. She wrung out as much of the water as she could from her panties before she put them back on.

Then she stuffed part of a wadded up brown paper bag from the supermarket between her thighs, lining the crotch of her cotton panties from side to side. When she left the closet, she took a few vigorous steps around the kitchen table to make sure the makeshift diaper was secure. She didn't want it to slide out and end up on the floor, too. Once she was satisfied, she returned to the living room so she could dance some more.

"You sure enough actin' strange all of a sudden," Ike said.

Please, Lord, let Ike be the daddy of my baby, she thought to herself. She blinked at him as he stared at her out of the corner of his eye. "You actin' *real* strange right now," Ike accused. "You was dancin' all right a little while ago. Now all you doin' is stumblin' like you blind, and steppin' on my toes and shit. And don't tell me that it's because of the beer. You drink beer every time you come over here, and it ain't never made you this clumsy. So what's wrong with you, girl?"

"Huh? Um . . . what . . . what do you mean?" Ruby asked slowly and with a pout, hoping that it would gain her some sympathy and end the nosy questions.

"You all jumpy and stuff, too. You got gas or what?" Ike had his arms around Ruby's waist. Before she could stop him, he thumped her stomach with his fingers, like he was inspecting a melon. "And another thing, your belly is as hard as a rock. What do—" He stopped talking and froze, shaking his hand like he'd just burned his fingers. "Girl, your stomach just moved!" With a pinched look on his face, he put his arms back around Ruby's waist.

Ruby let out a loud breath and removed Ike's arms from around her. "Oh, it's been doin' that a lot today. Gas." She gave him a playful pat on his shoulder. "And stop talkin' so loud. I don't want everybody to know about that. A problem with gas at a party is so . . . *unsociable*," she whispered. "Especially when it's a girl with the gas problem."

"You want to sit down before you cut loose and stink up the

place?" Ike asked, rubbing his nose. "I ain't smelled nothin' yet but . . ."

"Oh, I'm fine." Ruby dismissed that thought with a giggle and kept dancing.

"Do you mean to tell me that gas is makin' your stomach move? You must have some bazooka farts tryin' to get out, if gas can make your stomach move like that. It felt like somethin' was kickin' in there, girl," Ike said in a low, guarded tone of voice. He scratched his head and then he attempted to feel Ruby's stomach again. She moved away in time. He cocked his head to the side and gave her a suspicious look. "Gas, huh?"

"Yep! My mama made baked beans to go with them ribs we barbequed, and I ate a mighty big plate," Ruby explained, nervous sweat forming on her face and under her arms. "Go get me another bottle of beer while I run to the toilet and do my business. I don't want to be droppin' no farts in front of all these boys," she said with a laugh, rushing out of the living room before Ike could say another word.

The toilet, which was a large metal bucket with a cover in a closet next to Ike's mother's bedroom, was occupied when Ruby got to it. She didn't want to go outside to use the smelly, spooky, rat-infested backyard outhouse in the dark, so she went back into the kitchen. Another super-sharp pain exploded in her stomach, making her dizzy. All of a sudden everything went black. She fell sideways, her arm hitting the sharp corner of the stove with such force she bled. She came to a couple of minutes later, with a small but nasty wound on the side of her arm. When she attempted to rise, she passed out again on the kitchen floor. That was where Othella and her mother found Ruby five minutes later, with blood oozing from the cut on her arm.

Simone squatted down next to Ruby and quickly lifted the tail of her dress. "Oh shit!" she shrieked, almost falling to the floor herself.

"What's wrong with Ruby Jean, Mama?" Othella hollered, hopping from one foot to the other. She and Simone had come into the kitchen to check on the beer supply. But as soon as they saw Ruby on the floor, they forgot all about the beer. "Look at that blood on her arm." Othella paused and looked at the floor. "And on the floor. You want me to run down the street and get Dr. Hollis?"

Simone didn't answer; she was temporarily speechless. All she could do was stare at Ruby's bloated belly, and the way it was moving.

"She done drunk too much beer, I guess," Othella suggested. "And look at her bloomers. She done peed on herself, too, huh?"

"This gal ain't drunk. And she ain't peed on herself. This gal is fixin' to have a baby," Simone reported, speaking in a low voice out of the side of her mouth. "This sneaky-ass hussy!"

"Nuh-uh!" Othella jumped back and bumped into the front of the stove. "Oh no she ain't! Ruby Jean can't be pregnant, Mama! I would know if she was!"

"Look, girl. I done had enough babies myself to know all the signs. Grab ahold of her arms and help me haul her out of here." Simone lifted Ruby by her legs, and Othella lifted her by her arms.

Ruby regained consciousness again about ten minutes later. She was disoriented, but she was lucid enough to know that she was in Simone's bed, and that her baby was struggling to make it through her birth canal.

CHAPTER 11

SIMONE'S BEDROOM, WITH A WINDOW FACING THE OUT-house in her backyard just a few yards away, was not the ideal place for a baby to be born. But Simone had given birth seven times already in this same gloomy room. And, she decided, if it was good enough for her, it was good enough for Ruby.

Even though it was the largest bedroom in her shabby house, it was a small room with cheap, mismatched furnishings. Simone was a hoarder, so there were at least a dozen medium-size cardboard boxes stacked five high along the walls. Some contained items that should have been discarded years ago: old clothes, old newspapers and magazines, broken toys, cracked plates, and even the steering wheel from a car that Simone had owned ten years ago.

There were large brown paper bags filled with more junk on both sides of Simone's lumpy bed. One contained a dried-out ham bone that she kept forgetting to feed to Hairy James, her nine-year-old sheep dog.

There was a long, deep indentation in the middle of the bed's mattress, evidence that Simone still had a vigorous sex life. There was a wobbly nightstand on the side of the bed by the window. On the stand was a kerosene lamp, an open pint bottle of whiskey, a dog-eared magazine with a lurid cover, an empty jar with plum-colored lipstick on its rim, and crumbs from the chocolate cake that Simone had baked for Othella's party. A large plaid chair, its seat stained with various liquids including menstrual blood and gravy, sat next to the footstool that Othella occupied at the foot of the bed.

"I knew somethin' was fishy by the way this girl's been stumblin' around ever since she got here. I seen her run into a wall a little while ago, but I just figured she was a little drunk," Simone told Othella in a nervous voice. "What's wrong with you, Othella? Why is Ruby here in the shape she's in? What if that fall in the kitchen had killed her? We don't need another peacemaker snoopin' around here askin' a bunch of nosy questions. And I don't want another dead body in my house like that other time." Last December, one of Simone's elderly men friends had suffered a massive heart attack and died in the middle of making love to her. It had been an embarrassment and a major inconvenience for Simone. Dead bodies were too disruptive, especially in her bed. She didn't want to go through that again anytime soon. She glared at Othella. "I ought to whup your behind for lettin' this gal come here tonight in her condition!"

"Mama, I swear I didn't know till now that Ruby was pregnant," Othella defended. "Honest to God, I—"

"Shet up!" Simone interrupted. "Do you mean to tell me that you and Ruby Jean been runnin' around together every day all this time, and you didn't know she was pregnant? You blind, stupid, or both?"

Othella blinked and looked at Ruby sprawled on the bed. Then she looked back to her mother and shook her head. "I didn't know. She was already big. I just thought she was a little bit bigger than she normally was, because she's been drinkin' so much more beer lately than she used to. Look at her, Mama. She don't really look like you did all them times you was pregnant, now does she? Her stomach ain't even pokin' out that far."

Before Simone could respond, somebody pounded on the door. "Mama, can we eat the rest of them ribs in the kitchen?" O'Henry, Othella's twin brother, yelled as he jiggled the door-knob.

"Get away from my door, boy!" Simone screamed, covering Ruby's mouth with her hand to keep her from screaming.

The door creaked open but before the boy could enter, Othella sprang up off the footstool and ran to the door and slammed it shut.

"What y'all doin? Is Ruby Jean in there?" O'Henry asked.

"Get back to that party, knucklehead!" Othella shouted. "Go change the record on the Victrola."

There was a moment of silence before O'Henry spoke again. This time in a nervous voice: "Mama, there's some nasty lookin' bloody stuff on the floor. All the way from the kitchen to . . . uh . . . right here outside your door," he announced. "Y'all know how blood makes my skin crawl."

"Blood? Uh, it's mine. My monthly snuck up on me," Othella offered.

"Again? Already? Wasn't you all crampy and laid up last week? I thought y'all females only went through that nasty mess once a month!"

"It did come last week, but these things don't always follow no time line. Now you get back to that party and change the record on the Victrola like I told you, boy. I'll be back out there directly. I'll mop up that blood before I go to bed," Othella told her brother.

Instead of leaving, O'Henry remained at the door, shuffling his feet and wondering what his sister and their mother were up to. "Is Ruby Jean in there? I want her to teach me that jitterbug dance."

"Yeah, she is in here! Uh—she's helpin' me pick out another frock. I got some blood on the britches I had on when my monthly came," Othella said, becoming more agitated by the second.

"Ruby Jean is helpin' you pick out another frock . . . in Mama's room?" O'Henry asked with a snicker.

Simone beckoned for Othella to move closer to her. As soon as Othella reached her mother's side, Simone grabbed her hand and used it to cover Ruby's mouth. "Make sure she don't holler so somebody can hear her. I don't want nobody to think we beatin' on her or nothin' like that, up in here. We got enough mess on our hands already." Simone wrung her hands and sprinted across the floor. She cracked open the door. She glared at her son with so much hostility that he almost jumped out of his shoes. "Boy, you get your nosy ass away from my door! Now!"

"Yessum," O'Henry muttered, trying to look over his mother's shoulder. "I know what y'all doin' in there," he sneered. "You and Othella and Ruby Jean."

"What?" Simone barked, closing her door a few inches more.

"Y'all in there drinkin' some of the good whiskey," O'Henry accused with a loud belch.

"That's right! If you want some, there's a fresh bottle in the kitchen cabinet over the stove," Simone told him. She quickly closed and locked the door.

"He's gone," Simone said in a low voice, returning to the bed. "We need to hurry this thing up. We got to get Ruby Jean out of here before him and the rest of them kids get too nosy."

For the next five minutes, Ruby writhed in agonizing pain as the baby took its time making a complete entrance into the world.

"Hold your breath and push real hard, Ruby Jean! Push like you sittin' on the commode doin' your business," Simone ordered, hovering over the bed. Ruby still wore the same dress that she had worn to the party. Simone and Othella had pushed it up around her waist and elevated her pelvis with two pillows and a folded up quilt. "That's it . . . that's it. Now give me one more real hard push. . . . The head's out . . . the shoulders is comin'! It's almost here!"

CHAPTER 12

*W*ITH HER HANDS SHAKING AND COVERED IN SWEAT, OTHELLA held Ruby down by her shoulders. There was a sudden, squishy noise as the baby popped out of Ruby's body and slid into Simone's anxious hands.

A few seconds after Simone had slapped the newborn baby's behind, and gently forced open its mouth with her fingers, the baby wailed like a banshee. Othella covered the baby's mouth with her hand to keep the other kids in the living room from hearing. She kept it there until the baby stopped crying.

As soon as Ruby realized she had finally given birth, she sat bolt upright, reaching for her baby. But before she could snatch the baby out of Simone's arms, she passed out again.

Ruby came to less than five minutes later. Simone was standing over her with the baby wrapped up to its neck in a pink towel, all cleaned up and gazing around the room, reaching with one hand. A tiny finger grabbed one of Simone's fingers and held on to it as if it were a lifeline. It was almost as if the baby knew and realized the grim circumstances of its birth. And it was a beautiful child, the most beautiful, most healthy-looking baby that Simone had ever seen before in her life. It had golden brown skin and large brown eyes. A lock of silky black hair spiraled down the baby's forehead, looking like a fishhook.

"This is the most beautiful baby I ever seen in my life," Simone said softly, tears in her eyes. "She looks like a little angel. If God created a prettier baby, He kept it for Hisself."

"Sure enough," Ruby agreed, gazing lovingly at the child as Simone held it close to Ruby's face. Looking at her baby, she had to blink her eyes several times to hold back her tears of joy. She was so pleased, she was beaming with pride, just the way a new mother was supposed to. "This baby is so precious . . . and *perfect*," she managed. Ruby's voice was so hoarse, it sounded like she had a frog in her throat. At that moment, she was convinced that there was nothing on the planet more important to her than this baby—*her* baby. "Hand me my baby," she ordered, grinning so hard her bloated cheeks ached. "I don't care what happens to me now. I am goin' to be proud to show off my baby!"

"Oh no you ain't!" Simone snapped. She moved a few steps away, making sure that the baby was out of Ruby's reach.

Ruby looked at Othella. She was stunned and puzzled by the peculiar look on her face. Othella looked like she was in a hypnotic trance. Ruby returned her attention back to Simone. "What do you mean by that?" she asked. She gazed at Othella again from the corner of her eye, her heart beating like a bongo drum. Her insides, or what was left of them, had formed a tight, painful knot. "What do your mama mean, Othella?" Ruby panicked. It felt like she was losing her breath. She shook her head and sucked in some of the stale air in the musty room. She was light-headed, confused, and frightened by what Simone had just said.

Instead of answering Ruby's question, Othella turned to her mother. "Mama," she said, stopping with a hiccup. "You tell her what me and you talked about while she was passed out."

"Uh, I will in a minute. In the meantime, Ruby, you get a

hold of yourself," Simone advised, moving even farther away from the bed. When she bumped into the wall, she stopped and moved a few feet forward, back closer to the bed. But this time she stood at the foot where it would be harder for Ruby to reach her. "Now, Ruby Jean. Don't you go gettin' attached to this baby. The sooner you forget about this baby, the better."

Ruby's mouth dropped open and she stared at Simone like she had suddenly got naked in front of her. "Woman, what's wrong with you?" she asked. "Forget about my baby? What . . . why . . . I can't believe my ears. What makes you think I am goin' to forget about my own baby?" A strange eerie laugh shot out of Ruby's mouth, a laugh that she couldn't control. She laughed for several moments before a serious look appeared on her face. For a split second, she looked and felt like a very old, very tired woman. She didn't know what to think. She even thought that maybe she was dreaming, because everything seemed so unreal. "Look here," she continued, glancing from Othella to Simone. "I don't know what y'all cookin' up in this room, but I ain't swallowin' none of it."

"Be sensible, Ruby Jean. This baby was a mistake and you know it. You, of all girls, know your folks ain't about to accept you gettin' yourself into a mess like this. But don't worry. I'm goin' to handle everything," Simone insisted with a vigorous nod. The baby began to squirm and whimper, and was about to cry some more. Simone stopped that from happening by gently squeezing and rocking the baby in her arms.

Ruby was glad and grateful that Simone and Othella had come to her aid, but she was not happy about the way they were acting and talking now. It had to be the alcohol they'd drunk, or they had both gone crazy at the same time. There was no other acceptable reason for them to think that she was going to let them tell her what to do with her baby, Ruby told herself.

"What in the world . . . ? This is *my* baby, y'all. I can do whatever I want with it." Ruby attempted to rise again. "Now stop talkin' crazy. Both of y'all," she ordered, her head swiveling from side to side to look from Othella to Simone. Her gaze landed on the top of the baby's head, and she managed to smile. "Now tell me, is it a girl or is it a boy? Let me hold it!"

"It's a girl," Othella announced in a tired, hollow voice. Her face looked like it had turned to stone. It took a lot of effort for her to make her lips move again. "It . . . she looks a lot like me."

Ruby was pleased to hear that. Her next thought was that Othella's brother Ike was the baby's father, like she had hoped.

Simone was thinking the same thing. With hesitation, she placed the infant in Ruby's arms, but she remained close by in case Ruby dropped her. Ruby was, and had always been, as clumsy as an ox. How she managed to be so agile on the dance floor was a mystery to Simone. It would be just like her to drop the baby on her head. "This young'un looks like all of my girl babies," Simone said with a grunt. "But that don't mean nothin'. Even though I *suspect* you and my boy Ike been sneakin' around doin' *somethin'* nasty, this baby looks like that Peterson's boy's sisters, too. He could be the daddy. What I want to know is, how come you didn't tell nobody you had a pig in your poke?"

"I . . . I was . . . I . . . see," Ruby stuttered. "I was goin' to," she said in a very small, very nervous voice. She was unable to take her eyes off the baby's face.

"When? You been walkin' around with this bun in your oven for nine months! Exactly *when* was you goin' to tell somebody?" Simone demanded, tugging the baby girl out of Ruby's arms so hard and fast, *she* almost dropped her.

Ruby stared at Simone with her mouth hanging open again. She wanted to punch this bitch in the nose, but she knew that that was the last thing she needed to do. She still needed Simone's help. "I just found out for sure myself tonight!" Ruby boomed. Her voice suddenly got low and shaky. "I didn't even know I was pregnant till tonight," she lied, her eyes looking at the top of the baby's head again. She was too weak to fight with Simone, and too concerned about her child to risk her being injured in a tussle. For now, she had to remain as calm as she possibly could. For the first time tonight, she wished that she had not come to the party. If she had given birth in her own bedroom like she had thought she would, with her bedroom window facing her mother's impressive flower garden, she wouldn't be in the mess she was in now. However, she realized that if she had given birth at home, she might have been in an even bigger mess.

Ruby had to admit to herself that she was probably better off in Simone's house under the present circumstances. At least Simone and Othella weren't calling her names and threatening to beat her the way she thought her parents would probably be doing by now. She bowed her head submissively and spoke without looking up. "Let me hold and hug my baby again. I should probably be givin' her some of this milk in my titties anyway. I love her already."

"Gal, didn't I just tell you to forget about this baby?" Simone snarled, slapping Ruby's hand. "Shame! Shame! SHAME! You know your daddy would give birth to a baby hisself, if he knowed you just had one. And your poor mama! Oh my Lord in heaven! Sister Upshaw would up and die if she knowed what you—a preacher's daughter—done! You know how hysterical and frantic y'all holy rollers can get. Especially your folks. They are unpredictable, too. You and me both know that your folks could either beat you into the ground or comfort you for a predicament like this. My guess is that they'll beat you into the ground first and comfort you later. That's if you still alive after the beatin'. I know you ain't forgot how that Hardy girl almost died from the whuppin' her daddy laid on her when she fooled around and got herself pregnant last year. Be reasonable, girl."

Simone was right. Ruby knew how hysterical and frantic her parents could get. She also knew how unpredictable they were in some situations. She could imagine her father flying into a rage and tearing down the house with his bare hands if he walked into her bedroom and saw her giving birth. Or her mother fainting and falling to the floor, breaking her hip like the time she'd thought one of her daughters was thinking about divorcing her husband.

Now that she'd had more time to think about it, and the few other things that Simone had pointed out, Ruby wondered how she could have given birth in her bedroom by herself the way she had planned to. *What was I thinking?* she asked herself. Simone's house was bad, but if she'd given birth at home, it might have been a catastrophe.

"Well, my daddy and my mama is goin' to know now. I got to go home tonight, and I got to carry my baby home with me. I already got my story worked out. I just hope they go for it— and let me tell it before they get all crazy on me." Ruby paused and tried to organize her thoughts. But her mind was spinning in so many different directions, she couldn't think straight. "I need to be home in time, so I can straighten everything out before our church revival meetin' tomorrow mornin'. I'm goin' to tell my daddy, and everybody else, that I got raped!" Ruby couldn't hide the desperation in her voice. "I'm goin' to say I got jumped and raped by that hook-hand man that broke loose from the chain gang a while back. The one that they say was so mean that he'd be a danger to anybody he came in contact with—especially females on account of he was in prison for raping a few. Well, I was the unlucky female he snuck up on, as I was on my way to choir practice. He threatened to beat me, and gouge out my eyes with that hook hand of his if I didn't let him have his way with me. He said if I told on him, he'd burn down my daddy's house—with us in it. They never caught that maniac, so it ain't like he'll come out and deny it! Besides, he's a Cajun, and this baby looks like she could be half Cajun!" She was convinced that if her tall tale didn't keep her parents from going crazy on her, nothing would.

"Ruby Jean, that story might not work. Your folks might not even give you time to get it all out before they light into you.

For one thing, that convict with the hook hand broke loose two years ago, way before you got pregnant. He wasn't crazy enough to hang around this state. The newspaper said he was spotted in Arizona around the time you would have got pregnant," Othella pointed out.

"But my story *could* work." There was a pleading look on Ruby's face. "I know it could!" She was frantic. She said the first thing that popped into her head next. "There's plenty of other maniacs on the loose around here, so I could say that it was one of them that raped me!"

Othella shook her head. "Only a fool would buy that foot-long lie. And your folks ain't fools. The bottom line is, you can't go home with no baby tonight. Me and Mama, we got a plan, see. And, I have a feelin' you ain't goin' to like it." Othella paused and turned to Simone. "Tell her, Mama."

CHAPTER 13

SIMONE SNIFFED AND HELD THE BABY TIGHTER, STILL GENTLY rocking her. "I know a preacher that owes me a few favors. I'll get him to bless this young'un tonight. She's a . . . a miracle, and she deserve to be treated as such." Simone paused and hugged the baby even tighter, not because she was afraid she might drop her, but because she didn't want Ruby to jump up off the bed, snatch the baby and run. Simone opened her mouth to speak but paused again. This time it was to tickle the baby's chin. "Oochie coo," she said, smiling.

It was obvious to Ruby that she was not the only one already attached to this unplanned miracle.

Simone suddenly got serious. She pressed her lips together, took a few deep breaths, and then she began to speak slowly and with caution. "Uh . . . them nuns at this asylum I know, they don't turn nobody away. If Satan crawled up to their gate in distress, they would scoop him up and take him in! I'll carry this child to them nuns in my own two hands. It ain't a bad place. . . . I know that on account of it's the same place where my mama dumped me off at for a while, when I was still in diapers. It was the only home I knew for a long time." For a brief moment, Simone looked and felt unbearably sad.

Nobody, not even her children, or the many men in her life, would ever know all the details of her painful past. At the top of the list was a family tree with a drunken Cajun on each and every branch. There had been frequent physical, sexual, and mental abuse in her stormy past so severe, her tortured mind had buried most of the memories.

If all of that wasn't bad enough, Simone's history also included a mother with the mind of a lunatic. She had given birth to eleven children that she never wanted, six of them by her own father. She had left her last child, a severely retarded one-year-old boy, in the back of a wagon on the street while she treated herself to a night out on the town in a rowdy bar a couple of blocks away. When she left the bar several hours later to retrieve her son, it was too late. The boy had rolled around so much, his blanket had accidentally covered his face and suffocated him. When the authorities tracked down Simone's mother a week later, hiding in a barn on her former lover's farm, she was dead from a self-inflicted gunshot wound to the head. Four of her remaining children ended up in other asylums. Simone had not seen or heard from any of her siblings in years. She had a very bleak outlook on life, and often used poor judgment when she made decisions. Like now.

"This child will be safe in that asylum," Simone said, her mind a ball of confusion.

Ruby's breath caught in her throat. The plan that Simone had for the baby was ludicrous! But because Ruby knew Simone as well as she did, nothing the woman said or did surprised Ruby. In spite of that, she still could not believe her ears! Had Simone not only lost her mind, but her memory, too? She must have! Didn't she remember telling Ruby about some of the horrors that she'd experienced in that asylum? She had claimed that most of the mean nuns had used violence to keep things under control. Simone still had scars on the palms of her hands and legs where the nuns had beaten her repeatedly with metal rods and bamboo canes. And what about those male orderlies and how they had sexually abused the most helpless of the females that they had been hired to take care of?

"Y'all want me to turn *my* child over to a hellhole like you was brought up in, Simone? Why would a place like that even want to be bothered with a newborn baby? It don't sound nothin' like them orphanages they put kids in that I read about in school," Ruby said through clenched teeth. She shook her head, trying to release all of the dark, ominous thoughts dancing around in her mind. But she couldn't.

"I know what I'm doin', girl," Simone said firmly.

"Asylums is for crazy people. And the way y'all both actin', if anybody should to go to that asylum, it's y'all!" Ruby hollered.

Simone held up her hand. "Uh-uh! The place I'm talkin' about ain't that bad no more. I heard that they made some real positive adjustments durin' the last few years. They got a new director, and some more sympathetic nuns are workin' there now. They welcome displaced individuals—especially newborn babies. They feel that they are the ones that need the most help. And them hoity-toity orphanages you read about in school, ain't nary one of 'em mentioned takin' in no colored kids, now did they? I know your papa and mama got you on a hog-high pedestal. But in the real world, folks like you and your baby will be considered second class. Compared to most of the other orphanages in Louisiana, the home I'm talkin' about would be more like a walk down primrose lane for a colored baby."

The more Simone babbled, the more she angered, shocked, and confused Ruby. She had to get up and get the hell out of this place before Simone drove *her* crazy.

"And what in the world do you mean by displaced, Simone? My baby ain't nowhere close to bein' no displaced individual. I got a home, she got a home. You want me to let you turn my baby over to some frustrated nuns? I ain't goin' to let you do that. Not after all the trouble I went through to birth her!"

"I'm tryin' to show you that I'm practical," Simone told Ruby.

"The only thing you showin' me is that you done lost your mind!" Ruby shot back.

"Don't you keep sassin' me, girl," Simone warned, shaking a fist at Ruby. "I know I ain't no church-goin', high-level muckety-muck like your mama, but I'm still your elder! So don't you fix your lips to sass me no more tonight. My Lord in heaven. Colored people ain't never talked to me the way you do. It's a cryin' shame."

"I ain't sassin' you. I'm just speakin' my mind, and I ain't goin' to let you stop me from doin' that," Ruby protested. She sucked in some more stale air, and then she adjusted her body on the bed, turning over on her side. As much as she enjoyed visiting Othella's house, this was one visit that she would put out of her mind as soon as possible. She had pressed and curled her hair earlier in the day. It was now nappy, soaked in sweat, and standing up all over her head like tentacles. She thought that the shadow of her head on the wall made her look like Medusa. That almost made her laugh again, but she didn't. She was too angry to laugh now.

"Ruby Jean, be reasonable. Mama is tryin' to help you stay alive!" Othella hollered, her voice so loud it sounded like it was bouncing off the walls. Simone gave Othella a menacing look, and Othella lowered her voice to a whisper. "Don't you want to live, girl?"

"What do you mean by that?" Ruby asked with such a profound gasp, it almost choked her. She had to cough to clear her throat and catch her breath.

Othella rolled her eyes. "Ruby Jean, what good are you goin' to be to a baby if you dead?" she questioned, talking so fast and hard she almost bit her tongue. "How long do you think your daddy would let you live, if he found out you had a baby tonight? I truly believe that Reverend Upshaw would beat your brains out."

"How many times do I have to tell y'all that I can tell my folks that I got raped?" Ruby wailed. "By that hook-hand maniac that got loose from the chain gang—or some other devil!"

"It don't matter. I know your daddy real good, been readin' him like a book since before you was born. He'll feel sorry for you at first, but at the end of the day, you still brought shame on the Upshaw family's good name. I guarantee you, he won't care about no rape. Sooner or later, he might even blame you for puttin' yourself in a position where a rapist could pester you in the first place," Simone hissed, her eyes dark with anger.

"Especially since you parade around town in them skin-tight, low-cut blouses, showin' off your big titties," Othella sneered. "Reverend Upshaw will probably even say you was beggin' for trouble because you tempted that rapist by wearin' one of them low-cut blouses."

"Othella's right," Simone declared. Her voice had softened.

Ruby gave Simone a helpless look, and she gave some serious thought to what she had just heard.

"The bottom line is, *you* got yourself pregnant. If you hadn't been where you was at when it happened, you wouldn't have got pregnant," Simone told Ruby in a voice so soft, shaky, and gentle now, you would have thought that *Simone* was the one in trouble.

"But what if a maniac had knocked me over the head and dragged me into some bushes for real?"

"Ruby Jean, it don't matter—"

"But what if that was what really happened?" Ruby interrupted.

Othella shook her head and sucked on her teeth. "Like

Mama just said, even if that was true, wherever you was at when it happened, *you shouldn't have been there*," Othella said. "That's what your daddy will eventually say. Your daddy is a man, and believe you me, most men think we females are responsible when one of them pesters us against our will. And some women feel the same way."

CHAPTER 14

"*M*Y GIRL'S RIGHT AGAIN. MOST MEN, AND A LOT OF women, believe that if a female didn't put herself in the wrong place at the wrong time, she wouldn't get raped," Simon declared. "Men are naturally lusty and can't control themselves. That's a well-known, scientific fact; so it's our burden to stay out of their way when they need some affection bad enough to take it by force."

Ruby wondered if that was what Simone believed about her own grandfather when he had repeatedly raped her mother and her sisters for so many years.

"Now you listen to me, girl. Let's lay this rapist bullshit to rest. If you smart and do the smart thing, there won't be no need for you to tell that ridiculous story. Enough on that subject." Simone paused to clear her throat. "I know this baby would be better off in that asylum, and you'd be better off if your folks never find out you had a baby. I been around the block a few thousand times, so I know what I'm talkin' about. You let me take care of everything. You are still a young girl. In time, you can forget about this baby. Find yourself a sport, marry him, and let him pester you in the bedroom as often as he wants to. Sooner or later, you'll have more babies than you'll know what to do with."

"But I want *this* one," Ruby wailed. "This is my firstborn—that's somethin' special to a woman! And this ain't your baby, so you ain't got no say-so in the matter, Simone." Ruby leaned toward the side of the bed, looking around the floor. "Othella, where my shoes at?"

Simone hoisted the baby up on her shoulder and leaned forward. Mumbling profanities under her breath, she slapped Ruby's face so hard, Ruby saw stars. "Hush up! I done already decided what's best for this baby! From what Othella done told me, and from the way I seen you and my boy Ike lookin' at one another, this *could* be my grandbaby. And if that's the case, I got a say-so in this matter."

"You . . . can't," Ruby bleated, rubbing the spot on her face where she'd been slapped.

"I said hush up, girl!" Simone stomped her foot so hard, the whiskey bottle on the nightstand shook and rattled. "Now I'm goin' to go get a tub of hot water. We'll clean you up and send you home. Ain't nobody got to know nothin' about this baby. I'm goin' to get Reverend Meacham to bless this baby before I take her to that asylum," Simone announced.

"Reverend Meacham? Didn't you just say that nobody else was goin' to know about this baby? What do you plan on tellin' Reverend Meacham?" Ruby asked with her eyes stretched open wide.

"You let me worry about that. I'll come up with a real good story," Simone said as she reached for the whiskey bottle on the nightstand. She took a long drink and let out a mighty belch. Wiping her mouth with the back of her hand, she continued, "Then I'm goin' to drive this child to that asylum myself tonight in that old jalopy of mine." She paused and turned to Othella, giving her a sharp look. "Go make sure none of my tires is flat. Then go make sure them kids in the livin' room is behavin' like they got some sense. After you do that, trot down to Reverend Meacham's house and bring him here to me. He owes me a few favors, so I know he won't turn me down. I might even get him to drive me to that asylum so I can save my gas." Simone shifted the baby's position in her arms and then she turned back to Ruby. "And that's where this baby will be brought up. Case closed."

"Don't you worry none, Ruby Jean. Your baby will be took care of real good by them nuns," Othella added.

Ruby felt so defeated, she didn't even know what else to say next. All she wanted now was for Othella and Simone to stop ganging up on her, trying to convince her that their decision was the only one to consider.

"Ruby, I know what's best for you. I am your best friend. And I am here to tell you, you ain't got no business tryin' to raise no baby. What can you give a baby?" Othella asked with a weary voice. There was almost as much sweat on her face as there was on Ruby's, and she looked just as tired.

Just when Ruby didn't think she had any more fight left in her, she realized she did. In a strong voice, one that seemed to begin in her toes and work its way up to her lips, she said, "*I can give my child my love.*" The words spilled out of her mouth like lava. "I love kids," she whimpered. She was immediately sorry that she had opened her mouth again to say anything. At the rate things were going, Simone and Othella were going to badger her into the ground with their "We know what's best for you" talk.

"That don't mean nothin'! The witch that tried to eat up Hansel and Gretel loved kids, too. You ain't in no shape to be tryin' to raise no baby and you know it! Now you look, girl. I am your best friend. I am way smarter than you when it comes to things like this here, so I know what I am talkin' about. You ain't got what it takes to raise no baby yet. Your daddy, with all of his preachin' and Bible thumpin', he'll ride your back like he's ridin' a mule, and preach your funeral every time he even *thinks* you tempted and provoked another man. That's the way men's minds work. They can't help it. I'm way more worldly than you, so I know what I'm talkin' about. Now you got that?"

"I . . . I . . . got . . . got that," Ruby stuttered with a heavy nod.

Othella was worldly; she knew things a lot of girls her age didn't know yet. But that didn't bother Ruby much. As far as she was concerned, she was a few steps above Othella. She lived in a nice house with an indoor toilet and two loving and stable parents. She was one of the few black youngsters in the community in such an enviable position. Unfortunately, Ruby's enviable position meant very little to Othella. The only thing Ruby had that Othella envied was an ample bosom. Othella had promised Ruby that one day she'd have enough money to buy herself a pair of those fake foam titties that they advertised in the back of the sleazy magazines that Simone purchased every week. Ruby didn't know why she was wasting time and energy thinking about Othella's flat chest when she had a baby to be thinking about. A beautiful baby girl . . .

Ruby nodded again. She couldn't take her eyes off the bundle in Simone's arms; her first baby. Maybe even her *only* baby.

However, she had to remind herself that if Simone was right, she'd eventually have a house full of children. That was the only thing that she had said all night that kept Ruby from losing her mind.

"All right, y'all. I'll . . . I'll . . . I'll forget about this one baby somehow," she rasped, her voice cracking.

But she wouldn't. Ruby Jean Upshaw would think about her first baby every day for the rest of her life. And, she knew that somehow, some day, somewhere, she would make Othella pay for what she was helping her mother make her do tonight.

Ruby was so distracted by the thoughts swimming around in her mind, she didn't hear Simone's voice again until Simone slapped the side of her head. "You done gone deaf or what? I've asked you three times in the last few seconds, who the daddy of this baby is. Or who you *think* it is? Who you been courtin' the most? Was it really my boy Ike? Was he your boyfriend?"

"I ain't got no boyfriend." Ruby sniffed.

"Yes, you do!" Othella hollered. "You got all kinds of boy-friends, girl. Almost as many as me."

Simone looked from her daughter to Ruby, giving her one of her notorious "you better come clean with me or else" looks. "If you decide to change your mind about lettin' me take care of this baby, I need to know who this baby's daddy is. We need to cover all the bases. Your folks will want to know who done it, too, Ruby."

"I swear to God, I don't know which one done it," Ruby admitted. "But I can't tell my mama and daddy *that*! Y'all know I can't!"

"Well, you got to tell them somethin', girl. Like I said, if you don't let me take care of this child, you can't go home with a newborn baby and expect your folks not to want to know the details," Simone assured her.

"What difference does it matter who got me pregnant now? Ain't you takin' the baby to that asylum place tonight? Ain't we keepin' this a big secret from everybody?"

"In case you change your mind about lettin' me handle this situation, we need to have a backup plan. Now, you tell me, who do you think got you pregnant, Ruby Jean? Give me the name of the boy you *think* done it."

A confused look crossed Ruby's face. "A name? Why?"

"I'll tell you the reason why. If you keep this baby, the daddy should know about it so he can do his part to help raise it. Another reason you need to give up his name is so your daddy can approach the boy for a man-to-man showdown. If my son is the culprit, I want him to know so he can be prepared when your daddy comes after him," Simone snapped.

"Comes after him? What do you mean by that?" Ruby held her breath.

"Everybody in this part of Shreveport knows that your daddy don't take no mess off nobody when it comes to his daughters. He ain't goin' to sit back and let his grandbaby's daddy off the hook without a confrontation. You and Othella is too young to remember, but years ago a musician came through here from Bayonne to blow on his saxophone at the grand openin' of a new juke joint. He already had a wife, but he still tried to pester your big sister Bessie Mae while she was babysittin' his sister's kids. She was sleepin' on a couch that night, mindin' her own business, and that man tore her nightgown clean off her body. If the man's sister hadn't come home when she did, Bessie Mae might have ended up in the same mess you in now. The next mornin', your daddy went after that filthy-minded musician with his shotgun and run him out of town."

Ruby's eyes got big. "Oh Lord! I think your boy Ike is the one," she whispered. "I don't want my daddy to shoot poor Ike!"

CHAPTER 15

"*I* WAS SCARED THAT YOU WAS GOIN' TO DRAG MY BOY INTO this mess." Simone sighed. She looked confused, impatient, and disgusted at the same time. "And what a mess it is!"

"It's my mess, Simone," Ruby said evenly. She wanted to get up off that bed, grab her baby, and run. Years later, when she would recall this night, she would wish that she had done just that. Unfortunately, she was too tired and weak to do something that drastic. She could barely stand up straight, so running was out of the question.

"Your mess? Yeah, it's your mess, girl. But let me tell you somethin'. If my boy is the one that done this to you, it is my mess. Can't you see that?"

"You could send Ike to Uncle Laurent's place out on the bayou where he'll be safe, Mama," Othella suggested in a quiet voice.

"I ain't sendin' my baby no place! I'm his mama and I love him! This is his home and he is goin' to stay here until he gets old enough to take care of hisself," Simone shouted, looking at Othella like she had sprouted horns.

Ruby felt like she'd just been beaten over the head with a sledgehammer. That was how hard her head was pounding now. She couldn't believe what Simone had just said. Here she was ranting and raving about how she wouldn't give up one of her babies, but she wanted Ruby to give up hers. *What a selfish bitch*, Ruby thought, glaring at Simone as she stood there holding the baby that should have been in Ruby's arms. It made no sense at all to her. But despite Simone's attitude, Ruby had to seriously consider the consequences of her actions if she kept her baby. She loved Ike. She did not want Simone to send him to live with the Cajun relatives on the bayou. And she sure as hell did not want him to be beaten or shot by her daddy.

"You think my daddy would do somethin' to my baby's real daddy if I keep the baby and he found out the truth?" Ruby wanted to know. Not only was she extremely worried, she was just as frightened. "He likes Ike, but if he suspects Ike pestered me and got me pregnant, y'all think he really would shoot him or somethin'?"

"I don't know what he'd do if he found out the truth. But you need to think about all of that." Simone paused to let her words sink in, but that was no longer necessary. Ruby had already surrendered completely. Under the circumstances, there was no way she could keep her baby. All she wanted to do now was get up, hold and hug and kiss her baby one last time, and then go home to her own bed. She figured that the sooner she did that, the better off she'd be.

Simone could see that Ruby had almost run out of steam, and that there was hardly any more fight left in her. She was about to roll over like a pig in a mud puddle. But Simone kept talking anyway. "And what if the baby ends up lookin' exactly like the real daddy so much that you can't deny the truth? Folks is smart these days; they'll put two and two together in no time, girl! Why, just look at me and Othella. Except for her bein' a few shades darker than me, me and her could be twins. There is no way I could deny that she is my blood child." It was true. Simone and Othella, two of the most beautiful women Ruby knew, were almost identical. They had the same large brown eyes, high cheekbones, full lips, and long straight black hair.

And when they spoke, their lips curled up at each corner. Even though Simone was in her midthirties and had lived a rough life—and was still living a rough life—she had to practically beat the men off with a stick.

Simone sat down on the bed, at the foot so she wouldn't be close enough for Ruby to snatch the baby away from her. "Listen here, Ruby. By now, me, you, and Othella, we are all in agreement. I done laid out all of the particulars of what could or couldn't happen if you keep this baby." Simone stared at Ruby long and hard. Ruby thought she was trying to stare a hole in her and that weakened her even more. All she could do was nod.

"Ain't nobody never goin' to find out that you had no baby here tonight, right?" Simone said, wagging her finger like a dog's tail in Ruby's burning face.

"All right! I give up!" Ruby hollered, waving her hands high above her head. "Leave me alone—y'all win! I'm too tired to keep goin' at this. Simone, you do what you have to do, and let's hurry up and put this all behind us."

CHAPTER 16

"*R*UBY JEAN, I AM SO GLAD THAT YOU ARE WILLIN' TO LET this child have a chance," Simone said. "This baby don't need to be around people who might not accept her in the long run. Even if you had changed your mind and decided to keep her, and convinced everybody that her daddy is that escaped convict, that plan could have still backfired. Thinkin' she's a convict's child, other kids would tease her comin' and goin'. She'd be self-conscious and lost in a world that's already gone mad. And the good Lord knows that people would be watchin' every move she made, day and night. She'd be miserable."

Simone paused and made a sweeping gesture with her hand. "Look at me. Everybody knows that my granddaddy is also my papa. My very own mama's papa. He raped and had babies with my mama and some of her sisters. He started eye-ballin' me, sizin' me up when I was eleven. I do believe that he would have pestered me, too, if I hadn't got out of that house in time. With a background like that, how could I expect people to accept me and treat me decent? Trust me, you don't want that for your baby girl, Ruby Jean. She'd eventually go crazy, and you would, too."

Ruby couldn't help but feel sorry for Simone. Under different circumstances, she would have offered her a big hug. Simone knew from the frozen look on Ruby's face, that she had made her point. But she kept talking anyway. "I know I'm white Cajun trash, and that's why I do what I do. It's my nature. I'm a bad seed and so is the child you just had here tonight. If this is my grandchild, well, bad seeds can't produce nothin' good. . . ."

After Simone had haphazardly wiped Ruby off, Ruby put her dress back on and sat down on the side of the bed, her eyes on the baby's face as she lay on the bed looking more like a store-bought doll than a real child.

"I hadn't thought about all of that," Ruby admitted. "I wouldn't want my baby to feel that she wasn't as good as every-body else."

"Well, I'm tellin' you, if you tell people she's the child of a fugitive rapist, they won't treat her as good as they treat every-body else. Now hand her here so I can check her out some more. I need to make sure she's breathin' all right, and that she ain't got no other complications that I might have to deal with before I carry her off."

Ruby kissed her daughter on the forehead for the tenth time in the last five minutes. "Since I won't never see my baby again after tonight, can I at least name her?"

"It don't matter to me if you do or not. But you shouldn't waste up a good name on a baby you ain't never goin' to see again," Simone pointed out. "Wait until you get grown and get married and have another daughter. Whatever name you wanted to give to this one, save it for the one you will have without shame. Do you hear me?"

"Yessum," Ruby muttered. "Simone, is Othella's party over with?"

"Naw. I doubt it. Even though I told them young'uns of mine to send their friends home, I got a feelin' there's a few still in the livin' room dancin', eatin', and listenin' to that Davis boy play his guitar. Why?"

"Because I don't want nobody else to get suspicious like O'Henry and Ike done. I need to get back out there and dance

some more and drink a few more beers before I go home."
Ruby handed the baby to Simone, but not before kissing her
again, this time on her cheek. "One more thing. When you
take my baby to that asylum, can I go with you? I'd at least like
to know where I'm sendin' my child to."

"Umpossible! That's *umpossible*! That would be too hard on
you and on me. I ain't goin' to watch you boo-hoo up a storm in
front of them nuns. How would I explain you to them? I done
already decided that I'm goin' to say that this baby's mama died
givin' birth to her. Naw. You can't go with me. I feel bad
enough already!" Simone stopped talking when she felt the
baby wiggle. "Let's keep our voices down so we don't wake up
this child. You go on back out yonder to the livin' room and
dance some more, if that's what you feel like doin'. That'll help
the rest of that birthin' fluid drain out of you. I plugged you up
real good, so you don't have to worry about drippin' nothin'
else on my clean floors. I told Othella to bring Reverend
Meacham in through the kitchen door. He will be in and out,
and none of them kids will even know he's been here. The next
time I see you, you'll be your old self again, right?"

Ruby nodded so hard her neck hurt. She reached back to
massage the back of her neck, eyeing Simone with mild contempt. Simone was a complicated, pitiful woman, and her best
friend's mother.

"All right, Simone. But I need to ask you one more thing. Do
you think I will ever have another child that will be as sweet
and beautiful as this one? Please say yes, because I think that's
the only way I am goin' to be able to get through this. Givin' up
my child and actin' like she was never born is the hardest thing
I ever did. I hope that I never have to go through anything half
as hard as this again."

"Ruby Jean, one day you will have a beautiful daughter that
you can show the world," Simone chirped with a level of confi-
dence that she didn't know she had. "And because of this experience, that child will mean the world to you. She'll be so

special, your life will be almost sacred. Now get on back out there for one or two more dances before I send you home."

Simone stopped talking for a moment and gave Ruby a concerned look. "You been through a lot tonight so you need to take it easy. You don't want no brain damage, or have your body go into no kind of shock. So don't you do no more of them swing dances. Do you think you can hoist yourself up and back into your bedroom window on your own when you go home? If you don't, I can send Othella home with you so she can help you."

"I'm fine, Simone. I can make it back into my bedroom window by myself. I been doin' it for a long time now, and I ain't never had no problem."

Ruby spent the next ten minutes dancing. After drinking two more beers, she had to make a bathroom run. When she returned to Simone's room to use the slop jar, she was saddened to see Simone curled up in her bed rocking the baby to sleep, serenading her with a lullaby that Ruby had never heard.

"I'm fixin' to go back home now," Ruby announced.

Simone nodded. "If you can, sneak over here tomorrow night. I'll make you some peanut brittle," she replied, waving Ruby away.

Ruby didn't use the slop jar, and she didn't return to the living room to dance again. She didn't even tell any of her friends that she was leaving. She eased out of the kitchen door and went home.

CHAPTER 17

*W*HEN RUBY ARRIVED HOME, SHE WAS TOO WEAK AND DIS-
oriented to climb back into the house through her bedroom
window. She stumbled to the backyard. Near the trash cans was
a wooden crate that she thought she could use for a step ladder.
That didn't work because the crate was too flimsy to support
Ruby's one-hundred-seventy-pound frame.

Before tonight, climbing through the window had been no
trouble. It was a large window and very low to the ground. All
she had to do was stand on her toes, grab the windowsill with
both hands, hoist herself up, and crawl in like a burglar.

"I wish I'd let Simone send somebody with me to help me
get back in this damn window," Ruby whispered to herself as
she looked around the area.

There was not much light from the moon or the one street-
light on the block for her to see much. Not that there was much
of anything she wanted to see. There were a lot of trees behind
the houses on the block, and in almost every backyard, there
was some type of vehicle. Most of the folks owned various
models of old trucks and ugly cars. One man even had a wagon
and a couple of mules in the garage that he had turned into a
glorified barn.

Ruby stood under the moonlight for a few moments, breathing through her mouth. Even though she was in the yard on the side of her family's home, she had never felt this lost before in her life. Lost was not the only way she was feeling. She felt profoundly sad. But she had experienced sadness before in her life. Like the afternoon that she had watched in horror as a runaway train hit and kill her aunt Della as she was crossing the railroad tracks out by Miller's Park. Aunt Della had taken Ruby there on a picnic. Had Ruby not skipped and trotted several yards ahead of her aunt, the train would have hit her, too. That tragic event had happened when Ruby was six. But it had been so traumatic, her mind had pushed it so far back into her consciousness that she had only thought about it a few other times before tonight.

And it triggered another grim memory of an incident that had occurred four years ago while she was visiting some of her father's relatives in Baton Rouge. In broad daylight, she watched an angry white mob burn down the house of a blind black man who was also confined to a wheelchair. Ruby never did find out what that doomed man had done to deserve such a fate. Now she would have another incident to bury in her consciousness, and the thought of this particular one was almost unbearable. "I can't . . . I can't let them give my baby away," she said, still whispering as she leaned against the side of the house. Without giving it too much thought, she took a deep breath and started walking back toward Simone's house. But halfway there, she recalled everything that Simone and Othella had said to her. She didn't want to bring shame on her family, and she didn't want people to shun her child. And now she wasn't even sure that her father, or anybody else, would buy her far-fetched story about a rapist.

It was still warm, which Ruby was thankful for. The sleeves on her thin dress were short. She had left her panties back at Simone's house, bloodied and ripped down the side where Simone had snatched them off when Ruby was thrashing around on the bed during the final moments of her labor. Since Simone and Othella were petite, neither one of them had any

panties large enough to accommodate Ruby's hefty bottom.
She was glad of that now, because when a sudden wind blew up
the tail of her dress, she enjoyed the warm breeze on her naked
crotch. It helped to ease the soreness in her vagina. Just before
she had left Simone's house, she had plugged up herself with a
fresh wad of toilet paper, shoving it up into her vagina as far as
it would go so that it wouldn't slide out. But that had been quite
a while ago. She knew that if she didn't change again soon,
she'd drip like a leaky faucet.

Ruby had left her watch at home on her nightstand next to
her bed before she went to the party, so she had no idea what
time it was. She was even more disoriented now, so she didn't
know how much time had passed since she had started for
home. "Lord, let me make it through this night without losin'
my mind. I . . . I done lost enough tonight," she prayed, still
whispering.

She rubbed her eyes to wipe away a few fresh tears that she
had been unable to hold back. Then she looked up at the darkened sky, wondering why the only thing that stars did was
sparkle like diamonds. She forced her mind to dwell on other
subjects that were of little or no importance to her other than
the fact that they were distracting. Like, what purpose did the
moon serve? And, exactly what was God doing these days while
she and almost everybody else in the world were behaving so
badly? Did He think that by NOT preventing the mess that she
was in, she'd benefit from it? The only "benefit" that she could
determine so far, was that the consequences for her behavior
had made her realize what a stupid fool she'd been. She was
sorry that she had screwed around with boys who cared more
about their fishing poles and hunting dogs than they cared
about her. She had had fun getting fucked inside out, but she
had paid a high price for that fun—a price that had no ending.
As far as she was concerned, having a beautiful, healthy baby
and losing it the same night was the ultimate price to pay for
her being such a fool.

Ruby spent more than an hour meandering throughout the backyard vegetable garden that her mother kept such good care of every year. One minute she was feeling sorry for herself. The next minute she was feeling so much anger that she wanted to go back and beat up Othella and Simone.

She got tired and sleepy, not to mention the fact that her entire body was still in shock from giving birth. She thought about going back to Othella's house again, not to claim her baby, but to spend the night—which was what she should have done in the first place, she thought. She was disappointed that Othella and Simone had not insisted that she do so.

The longer she remained outside, the more she regretted not letting Simone have Othella escort her home to help her climb back in her bedroom window. She made a few more attempts to get herself in, but each time she got so dizzy and weak she almost fainted. On her last attempt, she almost made it. But when she tried to lift her heavy leg up to the windowsill, she fell and landed on her back like a turtle.

By now, Ruby realized she had to enter the house through a door. She didn't have her key so she had no choice but to knock. But before she could do that, her father, fully dressed and with his best hat on his head, snatched open the front door and clicked on the living room light at the same time.

Anybody who challenged Ruby's father, Reverend Roebuck Upshaw, was a fool. He was the most respected and feared preacher in the community, and for a variety of reasons. For one thing, he was a large man with a hard, scowling face that rarely displayed a smile. He had a double-barrel shotgun, and he was not afraid to use it. Another reason that he intimidated so many of his peers was because he was very intelligent, especially for a man with just a ninth-grade education. Unfortunately, intelligence generally worked against a person of color in the South at the time.

However, the reverend was smart enough to know when and

to whom to show his intelligence. To a lot of white folks, he was "just another nigger." But to other white folks and almost every black person he knew, he was a very important man. Some of his admirers even thought of him as a visionary. He helped people do their taxes, he doled out financial assistance to those in need, and he had some mysterious, but strong relationships with some of the most powerful white folks in town. Whenever somebody had a problem with the Man, they rushed over to Reverend Upshaw's house. He was always able to "fix" the problem. A lot of people told him that he resembled the genius Albert Einstein, even though his facial features were definitely the full, fleshy characteristics of a middle-aged black man, and his complexion was as brown as the bark of a pecan tree. But Reverend Upshaw had the same penetrating eyes, the same wild, wiry white hair and bushy black mustache that Einstein had.

The only person who was able to pull the wool over Reverend Upshaw's eyes was his youngest daughter, Ruby.

"Gal, where the devil have you been?" he roared. "Go yonder in that front yard and get a switch off that chinaberry tree!"

"But, Papa, I was just out walkin' along Mama's garden. I couldn't sleep," Ruby bleated. Her father blocked the door, but she gently eased around him into the living room. "I wasn't feelin' too good." She winced and added a cough to sound more convincing. "I thought that a walk in the garden in the warm night air would do me some good." She smiled. Her lips were still dry, so dry that the smile she had just forced made her bottom lip crack. "And it did. I feel better already," she said, moistening her lip with her tongue, frowning at the faint taste of blood oozing from the crack.

Reverend Upshaw went from roaring like a lion to purring like a kitten. "Oh. I see. Well, was it that same female issue that had you all balled up with pain at the supper table?"

"That's exactly what it was! That same female issue that ruined my supper!" Ruby said, speaking so fast her words sounded more like gibberish. "Uh-huh. My cramps got worse and worse as the night went on. But I'm feelin' so much better now." She blinked and began to move backward toward the door leading out of the living room to the hallway. "I just need to get in the bed. . . ."

Despite his intelligence, some of the subjects that the reverend avoided discussing were the female-related maladies: pregnancies, menopause (which his wife was currently going through and driving him to distraction), cramps, and that disgusting monthly bloodletting that all women went through. And with a wife and seven daughters, he'd had enough of that to last him a lifetime. However, being a man of God, he didn't let his personal feelings get in the way of his professional duties. He firmly believed that when members of the black community needed help and comfort, if they couldn't count on the black church, they couldn't count on anybody. Despite his feelings about women's female nature issues, he was a man who appreciated women. He worshipped his wife and his daughters. He also worshipped some of the women in his congregation, and within the community, and in more ways than one. . . .

Ruby had never mentioned it to anybody and she didn't even like to think about it, but she noticed how her father's eyes lit up when he saw an attractive woman. She had also never mentioned or thought much about the fact that her father spent the majority of his time making "house calls" to give spiritual comfort to five times more women than men.

Ruby stopped moving toward the door. "I thought you was in the bed, Papa. You had a long day, frettin' over that tornado and standin' over that hot grill cookin' all of them ribs."

Reverend Upshaw walked up to Ruby and gave her a big hug and then rubbed her back so long and hard, she got very suspicious of his behavior.

"And . . . and how come you all dressed up in your black suit, Papa?" Ruby paused and looked off to the side of the room, then to the doorway. She was glad not to see her mother peep-ing around the corner. She didn't want her father to see the suspicion in her eyes. And in case he had some in his eyes, too, she didn't want to see his. "You fixin' to make another one of your house calls to that juke joint dancin' lady they call Martha Lou? The one you been visitin' every week for a month?" she asked, rubbing her belly. She was glad to have something else sordid to focus her attention on, even if it was just for a few moments.

"I was in the bed, but somebody needs my spiritual assistance—and it ain't Sister Martha Lou," Reverend Upshaw responded, giving Ruby a gentle pat on her shoulder. "Othella left here a few minutes ago. Simone got another mess on her hands," he stated.

Ruby gasped. "Oh. What . . . what kind of mess? Othella never comes to our house."

"Well, she came over here tonight!"

"Why? What kind of mess?" Ruby asked again, her voice so low her father could barely hear her. Her heart started thumping in such an aggressive manner that it felt like it was trying to escape. Which is what she was thinking she might have to do! But if Othella had spilled the beans on her, her father would have said something about it immediately. As a matter of fact, had he known that Ruby had given birth to an illegitimate baby a couple of hours ago, she'd probably have black and blue marks on every inch of her body by now from a severe whupping. And that would be just the beginning of her punishment.

"Sugar pie, it ain't nothin' for you to worry your sweet and innocent self about. But I will tell you one thing, I am *so* glad you don't fool around with that Othella and the rest of that clan like some of these kids around here do. Heathens! Every single one of them—especially that Othella. If you had seen the frock she had on when she come to the door—skin-tight britches and a blouse that wouldn't even cover a baby's booty. If she ain't a harlot in the makin', Mary Magdalene wasn't either. I—" The reverend stopped and sniffed in Ruby's direction. "Is that beer I smell on your breath, girl?"

"Beer? No. I don't drink beer, Papa. Remember when Sister Barker next door told me if I rinsed my hair with beer, it would grow faster? I washed my hair last night after you and mama went to bed."

Reverend Upshaw nodded. "And where did you get this beer?"

"From Sister Barker next door." One thing Ruby knew how to do well was to recycle a good lie to be used as many times as possible. She had planted this one in everybody's head several times already. And she didn't have to worry about Sister Barker. She was the town drunk and couldn't remember from one day to the next what she'd said or done.

"I will speak with Sister Barker first thing tomorrow mornin'! But from tonight on, you don't visit that woman's house unless you with me or your mama. Now get to bed." Ruby's father gave her a dismissive wave. "And if I find out from Sister Barker that you drunk some of that beer, you will be sorry."

"Okay, Papa." Ruby was reluctant to leave the room. She *had* to find out *why* Othella had come to the house to get some kind of assistance from her father, tonight of all nights. She was quite sure that Simone had not sent Othella to get her father so that he could come administer her some of his spiritual comfort tonight. "Um . . . Papa, are you goin' to tell me why Simone sent Othella to get you?"

Reverend Upshaw shook his head and gave Ruby a tortured look. "You ain't goin' to believe what went on in that woman's house tonight," he said stiffly, the caterpillarlike brow above his right eye twitching.

"What . . . what went on in that woman's house tonight?" She was so frightened and nervous, she had a hard time controlling her bladder. Not only had she left her panties behind at Simone's house, but the balled up toilet paper that had been used to plug up her vagina had slid out during her walk from the garden to the front door. She could feel fluid sliding slowly down her thighs. All she could hope for was that if her daddy saw blood or urine or whatever else was dripping from under-neath her dress, he'd be too squeamish and too embarrassed to mention it.

Reverend Upshaw did notice streams of bloody urine slowly rolling down his daughter's naked legs, and he was too squea-mish to mention it. At least not directly. What were those damn things females used as a sop during their bloody days each month? He couldn't remember, and it was just as well be-cause he was not about to bring up that subject. "You really need to go back yonder and . . . take care of yourself before your condition gets worse."

"Daddy, I am fine now," Ruby protested, shifting her weight from one foot to the other. "I'll feel even better once you tell me what's wrong at Simone's house, for Othella to come get you out of bed this time of night."

Reverend Upshaw cleared his throat and looked around the room, and behind him toward the door leading down the hall before he spoke again. "There's a baby involved, and it's one ugly mess," he stated, glancing toward the hall again.

Temporarily speechless and so terrified that she could barely remain conscious, Ruby staggered back a few steps. She was still wondering, if Othella had spilled the beans, why her father hadn't slapped her through the wall by now.

"Now don't you be gettin' all upset," Reverend Upshaw said, his hand on Ruby's shoulder, holding her in place. What he said next confused and relieved her. "This ain't got nothin' to do with you."

"It . . . don't?"

"Of course it don't! Why would it? So there ain't no need for you to be lookin' so distressed."

Ruby blinked and folded her arms, more curious than ever now.

"One of Simone's loosey-goosey, feebleminded colored female cousins dumped off a baby at Simone's house tonight." Rev-erend Upshaw was clearly angry. His jaw was twitching, and he had balled both of his hands into fists. "After that heifer dropped off that poor baby, she took her tail right back out in the street, headin' for another juke joint!" he hollered, shaking one fist in the air. "And guess what that peanut-size-brain hussy done before she left?" He didn't wait for Ruby to guess the answer. "She left instructions for Simone to carry the child to some orphan asylum for the time bein'. Simone wanted it to get blessed first. That's why she sent for me. As big a heathen as Simone is, wasn't that a righteous thing for her to do?"

Ruby nodded. "It sure enough was," she agreed.

She was relieved to hear that her role in this mess had not been revealed. But she was still nervous, frightened, and paranoid. And she would be until this nightmare was over.

CHAPTER 18

*A*S IF RUBY WAS NOT ALREADY IN ENOUGH PAIN—PHYSICALLY, emotionally, and spiritually—her head felt like it was going to explode like a hand grenade. Her eyes felt like they were sizzling each time she blinked.

It was a struggle, but somehow she managed to get the words out of her mouth. "I . . . I can't believe Simone's cousin is turnin' her baby over to a . . . asylum."

Reverend Upshaw nodded. "I can't believe it neither. Or I should say that I don't want to believe it. That poor little baby might never know her real kinfolks. I swear to God, Negroes are goin' to hell in a handbasket. Havin' babies and dumpin' 'em off on some stranger is usually a white woman's folly. At least with us colored folks, we always find a relation to drop off a unwanted baby on." Reverend Upshaw paused and shook his head. "This is a sin and a shame. In all the days of my life, I ain't *never* knowed of no colored woman to give up her baby to *strangers in a asylum* . . . until now."

Ruby agreed that it was a sin and a shame for a colored woman to give up her baby to strangers for them to raise. But she couldn't get those words out of her mouth. All she could say next was, "Oh." She felt faint. It felt like her brain was swimming around in her head. For a moment she thought her legs were going to buckle and that she'd end up on the floor in a heap. That was the last thing she wanted to happen. Dr. Hollis would be summoned and she'd be exposed for sure. She felt woozy, but she didn't know if it was from the beer she'd consumed at Othella's party or because she'd given birth, or both. And it didn't matter. The only thing that did matter was that she could not let her father know the truth about what she'd done tonight.

Like a chair with weak legs, Ruby backed up until she touched the wall and that was the only thing that kept her from falling to the floor. She stood against the wall, wanting to disappear into it. But she needed to know more about why Simone had sent for her father instead of Reverend Meacham.

"Ruby Jean, before you go back to bed, go get my Bible off the bureau in the back bedroom," Reverend Upshaw ordered, patting his hair. "And you might as well bring me one of my hymn books, too. And for God's sake, don't wake your mama up. This mess would upset her. You know how she loves babies," he added. "She'll be wantin' to keep it!"

Ruby also needed to know exactly what Othella and Simone had told her daddy about this mysterious colored cousin of Simone's. "Uh . . . what else did they say about this colored cousin? Which one was it?"

"What difference do it make? You don't know them folks. All you need to know is that the whole clan is bad news, and that's why me and Mother don't want you hangin' around with Othella." Reverend Upshaw plucked a large white handkerchief from the breast pocket of his jacket and mopped sweat off his face. "I'm surprised that Othella ain't got herself in the family way yet. But it's just a matter of time before she do. Maybe if I did let you hang out with her, you'd be a good influence on her, huh?" He smiled approvingly at his daughter.

"Maybe so, Papa," Ruby agreed. "Maybe so."

"But you ain't to fool around with that girl! She'd be more of a bad influence on you than you'd be a good influence on her.

Both of y'all might end up lost *and* in the family way at the same time."

"Can I go with you?" Ruby asked in a small voice, holding her breath because the question had slid out of her mouth before she could stop it.

"Say what?" Reverend Upshaw gasped. "Why would you want to go with me, girl? The mess Simone got goin' on might be too traumatic for you to get involved in."

"I want to see Simone's cousin's baby . . . before they take it to that asylum," she pleaded. Now that Ruby knew that Simone and Othella had concocted a story that her father had accepted, she decided that she was in the clear.

"Why in the world do you want to see somebody's baby that you don't even know? I don't even know this female myself, and I thought I knew all of Simone's folks. Them Cajuns and them colored ones on her grandma's side. Hmmm?"

"I just want to see that baby."

Reverend Upshaw gave Ruby a narrow-eyed look. "I still don't know why. With your sisters trottin' in and out of this house with all of them brats they got, how come you so hot to see another baby? Just last weekend you was complainin' about havin' to babysit your sister Lola's three young'uns."

"I know. I just wanted to see the kind of baby that a mother would give up to some asylum."

"I'm kind of curious to see this child for that reason myself. Othella didn't say, but it must be deformed or unspeakably homely. Maybe there's a chance that I can talk Simone into keepin' it and raisin' it as her own. She got so many already, one more won't make a difference."

Ruby's head felt like it was going to roll right off her shoulders. She knew that Simone was a strong-willed woman, but Reverend Upshaw could talk people into doing just about anything. Simone had made it clear that she didn't want to take a chance on having people find out that one of her sons had taken advantage of Ruby and gotten her pregnant. In spite of that, it was not that much of a stretch for Reverend Upshaw to talk Simone into keeping the baby, anyway. Especially once he got in her face with his Bible, beat her down with quotes from this scripture and that psalm, and then crooned a spiritual or two from his hymn book.

If that happened, Ruby was as good as dead. "Oh no, Daddy, don't do that!" she hollered, almost jumping out of her shoes. Reverend Upshaw's jaw dropped, so she immediately toned down her rant, using a much softer voice as she continued. "I hear all the neighbors talkin' about how she complains about havin' so many kids now. Why would you want to talk *her* into raisin' another baby?"

"My role is to try and help people do the right thing. I don't like the fact that there is a single colored child in somebody's asylum, bein' treated like God knows what. If you ask me, I'd say that the child would be better off with Simone. She is a Cajun to the bone, but she done fooled around with colored folks so much, and all of her kids is half colored; she is more like one of us in spirit. Me and the other church elders will do our part on her behalf. Despite her lowly status in the community, Simone knows that she can always get help from the church, and all of the spiritual comfort that she needs from me."

Ruby panicked even more. If her father *did* convince Simone to keep the baby, Ruby was certain that she couldn't go on. The way that Simone and Othella broadcasted their business when they drank, it wouldn't be long before the whole real story came out! And even if one of those two blabbermouths didn't talk, Ruby was afraid that *she'd* be the one to break down.

"Oh, Lord," Ruby moaned.

"Look, you beginnin' to look right sickly again. Almost as bad as you did durin' supper. Ain't there somethin' in the cabinet in the bathroom that you can take for this thing that's ailin'

you? I ain't never seen you look so peaked and lackin' in color."
Reverend Upshaw felt Ruby's forehead. "You want me to go
wake up Mother so she can tend to you?"

"Papa, I keep on tellin' you, I'm all right." Ruby stood back
on her legs. "Maybe some more of that night air might do me
some good. That's another reason why I want to go to Simone's
house with you." She gave her father a desperate look. "And I'd
like to see them red tapestry drapes at her front windows that
I've heard so much about, too."

"Well . . . I guess one visit to that hellhole won't corrupt you.
But just this one time!" Shaking a thick finger in Ruby's face,
the reverend added, "Don't you ever tell Mother, or anybody
else in this family, that I let you accompany me to Simone's
house. But it might do you some good to feel some of that negative energy that that woman and her young'uns generate."

"And to see the kind of baby that a mother could give up,"
Ruby added, following her father out the front door.

CHAPTER 19

"*R*UBY, WHAT IN THE WORLD ARE *YOU* DOING *HERE?*"
Othella, fully dressed in a fresh pair of jeans and one of her
twin brother's shirts, yelled as soon as she spotted Ruby standing on the front porch. It had been about two hours since Ruby
had left Othella's house. When Othella saw that Reverend Upshaw was standing off to the side out of her immediate view, she
covered her mouth. "What I mean is, you ain't never been to
this house before."

Simone ran into the living room. She had also changed into
another outfit, a pair of brown corduroy pants and a loose-
fitting, freshly ironed plaid blouse. She had put on fresh makeup
and pinned her hair up into a bun on her head. She stopped
right next to the lumpy couch. On the couch was a large cardboard box that contained Ruby's baby, wrapped in the same
pink towel as before.

"Reverend Upshaw, I didn't want to bother you," Simone
apologized, waving him and Ruby into the house. "But Othella
tried to get Reverend Meacham to come over here and bless
my crazy cousin's baby. But as he was gettin' dressed, his lum-
bago started actin' up, and then his back went out on him again.
Otherwise, I wouldn't have disturbed you." Simone gave Ruby
a curious look. "Uh, Ruby Jean is your name, right?"

"Yessum," Ruby muttered, nodding. She was glad that Simone was cool enough to act like she didn't know her that well in front of the reverend.

"You and my girl Othella was in some of the same classes last year, huh?"

"Yessum," Ruby muttered again, her eyes on the box on the couch. Only the baby's face was partially visible. She was sleeping, sucking on her knuckles like she had not eaten a thing since her birth, and she hadn't. Ruby, her breasts swollen with milk, wanted to run to her baby and stick one of her nipples in her mouth. "Uh, I begged my papa to let me come see your cousin's baby. I wanted to see the kind of baby that a colored woman would give up to strangers. What's wrong with it?"

Othella and Simone looked at Ruby at the same time, and then they looked at one another and shrugged. "Ain't nothin' wrong with my cousin's baby," Simone answered, a touch of contempt in her voice.

"Oh. I'm glad you ain't goin' to *keep* that baby," Ruby said, putting a lot of emphasis on the word "keep."

"Keep it? Oh no, honey child. I'll tell anybody, it took a whole lot of steam out of me to keep the ones that *I* gave birth to. I'm goin' to tell you the same thing that I told that cousin of mine; seven kids is more than enough for me to raise without a husband," Simone said firmly, giving Ruby a conspiratorial glance and a wink. "I can guarantee you, *I* ain't goin' to keep this baby and raise it. . . ."

"I'm glad to hear you say that, Simone," Ruby said with a sniff. She was relieved, but she didn't want to get too comfortable yet. Simone and her father were both so unpredictable that there was no telling how this situation was going to end. "Raisin' kids must be real hard to do, and like you said, seven is enough for you to be raisin' without a husband." Ruby swallowed hard. She was a little more relieved to know that Simone's mind was made up. She had no intention or desire to keep this baby. But that still didn't mean that the reverend wouldn't try and get her to change her mind.

"If it wasn't a shame, and me and Mother wasn't so old and wore out, I might consider takin' in this unwanted child myself," Reverend Upshaw said, shaking his head. "I love kids, and I wish me and Mother had been blessed with a few more." He bit his bottom lip and looked at Ruby. She froze and held her breath. What he had just said was the last thing that she wanted to hear. The only thing worse than Simone raising the baby girl was Ruby's parents raising her!

"Reverend Upshaw, that's a mighty generous notion for you to have, but I don't think that's a good idea," Simone said, loud and clear. She paused long enough to clear her throat. "See, for one thing, my crazy cousin might try to come back and reclaim this child after you and your wife done got attached to it."

"Babies don't ask to be born," Reverend Upshaw pointed out, mopping sweat off his face with his hand and then fanning his face with his hymn book. "And it's a shame when one comes into this world that ain't wanted."

"True. Babies don't ask to be born, and most young girls like Mama's cousin don't ask to get pregnant," Othella said, giving Ruby the same kind of conspiratorial look and wink that Simone had offered.

"Young girl?" Reverend Upshaw asked, looking from Othella to Simone. There was a harsh tone in his voice now. "Exactly where is this young cousin? I'd like to meet her," he added, one hand on his hip. "She sure sounds like she could use some spiritual comfort."

"That heifer! Right after she dumped off her baby, she left this house runnin' like a dog was chasin' her. She's back roamin' around them juke joints," Simone said quickly. "We tried to get her to stay here long enough to meet you, and to give this child a proper send off, and she said she would. But as soon as she heard about another shindig goin' on at one of them juke joints she can't seem to stay out of, she took off."

"I see. Well, it sure enough sounds like this sister is about as lost as she can be. You said she's a *young* girl? Just how old is this cousin? She can't be no young girl if she already got ten young'uns like Othella told me when she came to my house tonight," Reverend Upshaw said, scratching the side of his neck.

Simone wasted no time responding to Reverend Upshaw's comments. "She's around my age. Crazy as a Bessie bug."

"A sin and a shame. And exactly which one of your cousins is this baby's mama?" Reverend Upshaw asked, shuffling over to the box on the couch. He leaned over and lifted the stiff towel so he could get a better look at the unfortunate baby. "If you want me to try and talk some sense into this child's mama's confused head—" He stopped talking as soon as he saw the baby's whole face and the rest of her tiny body. Simone had wrapped a small pink towel around the baby like a T-shirt. Sadly and ironically, it looked more like a straight jacket—the same kind Simone had once been wrapped in during her residence at the asylum. A face cloth, also pink, had been pinned to the baby like a diaper. Reverend Upshaw stood up straight so fast he almost fell backward. From the frightened look on his face, anybody who didn't know any better would have sworn that he'd just met Satan in person. "Oh, goodness gracious alive! This baby can't be more than a few hours old!" His jaw dropped as he whirled around and looked from Simone to Othella again. "I thought y'all was talkin' about a toddler, or at least a child that's been around for a month or two!"

"Oh, didn't I say it was a newborn?" Othella asked, feeling defensive. "I'm sure I must have, and you just forgot that part."

"You ain't said nothin' about this bein' no fragile newborn baby just a few hours old!" Reverend Upshaw insisted.

"Well, it is. Cousin Anna was so drunk, she didn't even know she was in labor tonight!" Othella blurted, wondering how many more lies she would have to tell before the night was over. She had already told more lies in this one day than she usually did in a whole week. She figured it was good practice, though. From what she already knew, lies were part of the game if a person wanted to enjoy life.

"Where was this child born?" Reverend Upshaw asked, looking alarmed. "What's this loosey-goosey cousin's name again?"

"It's Cousin Anna's baby," Othella said, blinking at Ruby. "She was, uh, at some bootlegger's house when she went into labor. She gave birth just as she was about to sit on the toilet to empty her bowels. She's had ten kids already, so this one just slid out on the floor like a blood clot."

"Thank the Lord that one of them other drunks walked into the outhouse in time," Simone stated. Her hands were shaking because she was so nervous. She hid them by folding her arms. This wasn't going the way she had thought it would. But it was too late now. She had to finish what she had started. "You can see why I sent for you, Reverend Upshaw. I knew we could count on you."

"Bless you for feelin' that confident in me, Simone," Reverend Upshaw croaked. "I'll give thanks to God."

"And you can also thank God that them drunks at the bootlegger's house had enough sense to clean off this baby and make Cousin Anna bring it to us," Othella added. "She walked half a mile in the night air with this child."

Reverend Upshaw strolled over to Ruby and put his hands on her shoulders. "You go on back home, baby girl. This is worse than I thought. I don't want none of this negative energy to rub off on you. You are way too innocent for all of this."

Othella had to force herself not to laugh and it was not easy. But the stern look that she got from Simone was a potent enough warning for her not to laugh at how naive Reverend Upshaw was when it came to his precious Ruby Jean.

"Can I look at the baby first, though?" Ruby asked, anxious to leave. She was glad that her father had advised her to leave the premises. She was sorry now that she had come at all. It had been hard enough to leave her baby the first time. She knew that this would be the last time. She would never see her child again. "Can I hold her?" Ruby was already hovering over the box, looking at the child like she was something good to eat. She had to hold her breath to keep from bursting into tears.

"*Her?* Ruby Jean, how did you know it was a girl baby if you just seein' this baby for the first time tonight? Ain't nobody said nothin' about it bein' a girl," Reverend Upshaw asked with a puzzled expression on his face. He was looking at Ruby like he could see through her. She was glad he couldn't, and doubly glad that he couldn't read her mind.

Othella held her breath. Simone held hers, too, thinking that maybe the preacher wasn't so naive after all. Would he put two and two together and figure out what was really going on?

Ruby couldn't think fast enough. She stood stock still, looking from her father to the box on the couch.

Simone rescued Ruby again. "I guess that pink towel gave it away." She grinned. "Huh, Ruby? Pink is for girls." Simone nodded, prompting Ruby to nod.

"Yeah, it was that pink towel," Ruby muttered, almost biting her tongue.

"Well, it don't matter whether it's a boy or a girl at this point," Reverend Upshaw grunted, shaking his head again. He looked at Ruby as she leaned over the box, reaching for the baby again.

"Ruby Jean, like your daddy said, you go on back home and let us handle this." Simone narrowed her eyes and gave Ruby a threatening look. "You shouldn't have come out this late no how."

Ruby was not about to give up too easily. She straightened up, sucked in some air, and smoothed back her hair with both hands. She had no idea how she looked, but she knew that after what she'd endured tonight, she probably looked a fright. When Simone had bathed her, she had wiped off her makeup and pinned her knotty hair back with several hairpins.

"It's been a while since I seen a little bitty baby up this close, and I won't never see this one again. I feel sorry for her, just like y'all do, so I'd like to hold her just this once." Ruby was determined to hold and embrace her daughter again. And she wasn't going to let her daddy, or anybody else, stop her.

Simone, Othella, and Reverend Upshaw moved aside as Ruby lifted the baby and held her in her arms for the last time.

CHAPTER 20

"*R*UBY JEAN, NOW THAT YOU KNOW WHAT A BABYLON that Simone's house is, I can only hope that you are glad we never let you socialize with that Othella." Ruby's mother paused long enough to take a few sips of her coffee. She resumed her part of the conversation with a tight look on her face. "Your papa just told me that he let you accompany him to Simone's house last night."

"Yessum," Ruby said, struggling to keep the fear out of her voice. "It sure was a pretty little baby, though." She adjusted her position in her seat at the kitchen table.

"All babies is pretty when they that young," Reverend Upshaw said with a nod. "Even when they ugly." He chuckled. His wife shot him an annoyed look, but she didn't look in his direction long. She immediately turned her attention back to Ruby, looking at her like she was trying to read her mind. Even though Ruby knew that her mother didn't know what was on her mind, she was still nervous.

"I'm glad Simone let me hug that baby for a few minutes," Ruby said, trying to keep the conversation light.

"Now, Ruby Jean, you stop that. You don't need to be gettin' attached to no strange baby. You'll have your own babies soon enough. As a matter of fact, me and Mother decided that we're goin' to let you start courtin' as soon as you ready. Them Simpson boys and them Mason boys ask about you every time I see them," Reverend Upshaw said with a wink. "Me, I'd like to see you latch on to one of them Donaldson boys. Not only do they all already have good jobs sharecropping, they are all in the church."

"As long as that courtin' don't interfere with your schoolwork and your household responsibilities," Ida Mae added.

Ruby experienced several different emotions, one right after the other. For one thing, she hated being so deceitful to her parents. And another thing was that she didn't like the fact that they had decided what boys she could see. There wasn't a single boy among the ones that her daddy had just mentioned that she would give the time of day—especially one of the four Donaldson boys. Sharecroppers! What was wrong with her daddy? What in the world made him think that she'd want to spend the rest of her life married to a sharecropper? Ugly sharecroppers at that! They all had big moon-shaped heads, beady eyes, and lips that looked like raw liver. And those were their most *attractive* features. All of those Donaldson gnomes had buck teeth. Leroy, the one who had been flirting with Ruby since she was nine, spoke with a lisp.

"Can I be excused?" Ruby asked, her stomach in knots. "I don't feel too good this mornin'."

She didn't even wait for her parents to respond. She promptly returned to her room and remained there for the rest of the day. She did manage to sleep for a few hours that night. But the next day, as soon as she crawled out of bed, she dressed and snuck back to Othella's house.

Ruby was disappointed to see that Ike was the only one up when she arrived. And that Othella and Simone were not even home. "Uh, where did they go?" she asked, standing on the top porch step.

"Last night, Mama told Othella to get up this mornin' and go over to some white lady's house to help her do some housework that Mama was supposed to do," Ike answered. "Mama said somethin' real serious had come up and she had to drive out of town, so she couldn't go to the lady's house herself."

"Oh? You didn't happen to hear her mention what that 'somethin' real serious' was, did you?"

"Nope. But I heard Mama's car leavin' the yard real late last night. I peeped out the window and I seen her carryin' somethin' in a box. She was still gone when I got up this mornin'. Mama and Othella is up to somethin'. Mama made us all go to bed after the party, but she let Othella stay up. I heard voices comin' from the livin' room all through the night. But I couldn't make out what nobody was sayin'." Ike opened the door wider and motioned with his hand for Ruby to enter.

"O'Henry was a little jealous because it was his birthday, too, but Othella was the one gettin' most of the attention. But he was kind of glad when you and her went to Mama's room and stayed so long so he could be in the spotlight more. And I hope you don't mind me sayin' so, but I thought it was scandalous that nobody brought no birthday presents for Othella or O'Henry."

"Uh, well, I didn't have no money to buy no presents, but I'll get 'em both somethin' when I do get some money. And since Othella planned the party, I didn't think much about it bein' O'Henry's celebration, too. Next time she throws a party, I'll be sure and pay him more attention."

"Why? I thought you was my girl. . . ."

"Huh? Well . . . I . . ."

"Did you come back here last night?" Ike's eyes were on Ruby's bosom. "If you did, you should have come woke me up so we could have had some fun."

"Um, no," she muttered, fingering the top button on her blouse, still standing on the porch step. She was glad that she had worn one of her baggy blouses. Ike could stare at her chest all he wanted to and he would not see her nipples like he usually did. But the real reason Ruby had on such a large blouse was because she had on two bras, one stuffed with toilet paper to prevent the milk from her breasts from leaking through.

Ike glanced around before he spoke again. "Uh, about the party last night . . ."

"What about it?"

"Me and you didn't get to do nothin' nasty last night, so we got to make up for it." He grinned. "I felt so sorry for them other three girls 'cause nobody was payin' them much attention. I tried to make them feel welcome."

"I noticed," Ruby hissed. Her contempt was wasted on Ike because it didn't even faze him. That stupid grin was still on his face.

"Come on in and stay awhile," he insisted, waving her in. As she moved forward, he slapped her so hard on her butt, it felt like a bee sting to Ruby.

She was disappointed that she had not been able to satisfy the urge to have sex that she had experienced before her labor started. That was one of the main reasons she had come to the party. She didn't know how long it would be before she felt like having sex again. When she emptied her bladder this morning, it felt like somebody had stuck a metal rod with spikes on it up into her vagina. But Ike would be the first boy she made herself available to when she felt healed enough, and horny enough, to resume her sexual activities.

"Maybe next week," she told him with a tight little smile. "I'm on my monthly." She looked around the living room. It was such a mess of beer bottles, paper plates with leftover barbeque and cake, and broken glass on the floor, it looked like the tornado had struck after all.

Ike rolled his eyes and gave Ruby a dismissive wave. "Shit. Well, you can still visit for a spell if you want to. The least you can do is help me clean up some of this mess."

"Uh, I think I'll just come back later when Othella gets home," Ruby told Ike, her hand already on the doorknob.

Ike leaned closer to her. His morning breath was so foul and hot on her face, it made her frown. She promptly leaned away from him.

"Ain't nobody up yet so we got the house to ourselves for a little while. We can . . . you know." He licked his bottom lip. "I could use a quick piece of ass. . . ."

Despite the fact that Ike was so cute and the fact that Ruby loved looking at that cat's paw footprint of freckles on his face, he didn't appeal to her right now. She had more urgent matters to deal with.

She gave him an apologetic look and shook her head.

Her response to his suggestion annoyed him to the point of anger. He narrowed his eyes and shook his finger in Ruby's face. "Girl, I been meanin' to ask you; how come you been turnin' me down these last few times I tried to be nice to you and pay you some attention? Who you been foolin' around with—and don't stand here and tell me you ain't been foolin' around with somebody else. I ain't stupid."

"I ain't been foolin' around with no other boys, Ike. How many times do I have to tell you that?"

"Well, you must be! I know how frisky you can get, and I know how much you like the way I lay pipe between your legs. And there's been plenty of times that you didn't let your monthly stop you from bein' good to me. Why you doin' it now? You just want to be stingy with your stuff or what? Now if you got another boyfriend, I want you to tell me so I can go on about my business. I'm a one-woman man, and I want a one-man woman." It was hard to believe that this boy was just one year younger than Ruby. He sounded like a dirty old man.

"Ike, you can go on and be with any other girl you want. Me, I just want to be by myself for a while. I got some thinkin' to do."

"If that's the way you want it, that's fine with me. You want to set down a spell, or what? Or do you want to help me clean up, like I said?"

Ruby immediately shook her head. Next to having sex with

Ike, cleaning up a party mess was the last thing on her mind at the moment. "When Othella gets home, tell her to send for me. I . . . I just want to talk to her about last night."

Ike gave Ruby a suspicious look, his eyes trying to see what she had lurking inside her head. Unlike his other girls, she was a real challenge. Unfortunately for her, a challenge was not what he was looking for in a girl. All he wanted at the moment was just a "quick piece of ass." And that was exactly all she was to him. "What about last night? Did somethin' happen that I need to know about? Did one of my mama's men friends stop by after I went to bed and y'all robbed him?"

Ruby shook her head again, and then she went home.

CHAPTER 21

*L*ESS THAN A WEEK AFTER RUBY HAD GIVEN BIRTH, HER SIS-
ter Lola and her husband dropped by the house to have dinner
again. Ruby got along all right with all of her six sisters' husbands, but Lola's husband was a major thorn in her side. He
was the meddlesome kind, and he kept his meatball of a nose in
Ruby's business. But this time, Lola was the one who got the
ball rolling.

Five minutes after everybody had sat down to eat dinner, the
first thing out of Lola's mouth was, "Ruby Jean, you been sick?
You done lost weight? You was a mite thicker around the middle the last time we was here." The questioning look on her
face made it even worse. Like Ruby, her mother, and the rest of
Ruby's sisters, Lola was dark, stout, and somewhat ordinary
looking. However, she knew enough makeup and hair tricks to
make herself look quite glamorous. Ruby was glad that she
looked more like Lola than any of her other sisters.

The fact that Lola did look quite attractive made her a little
more confident than her sisters. She was bold and often did and
said things that none of the others would. And of all the people
in the family, this sister had no business being suspicious of
Ruby. Not after all of the backsliding she'd done before she got
married. And knowing her, she was probably still doing her

dirty business now for all Ruby knew. Like Ruby's favorite sister Beulah, Lola was also a hypocrite, and an even bigger one than Beulah. Not only had she fooled around with a slew of men while she was engaged to Arlester, but she'd fooled around with women, too! Ruby didn't see anything wrong with women sleeping with women. With men being the only other option, it was no wonder some women turned to other women for romantic attention, she thought. But she knew that her parents considered homosexuality to be one of the most unspeakable acts on the books. One night a few years ago, she had walked in on Lola and Sandra Wooten, rolling around naked on Sandra's parents' living room floor. Lola had paid Ruby a nickel not to snitch.

"How is that *mannish* Sandra woman you used to spend so much time with doin' these days?" Ruby asked, giving Lola a mildly threatening look.

"She's fine as far as I know!" Lola said quickly, clearing her throat and shifting her butt around in her seat. Ruby enjoyed watching Lola squirm. Her question took care of Lola's meddling right away. But Ruby was not out of danger yet. "I'd rather focus on you. . . ."

That's when the husband jumped on the bandwagon, and from the anxious look on his hound dog face, he was itching to stir up some mess that would bring more unwanted attention to Ruby. He took the subject and ran with it. "Hmmph! I ain't tryin' to stir up nothin', but I'm real worried about Ruby Jean," Arlester started, licking his lips and then pressing them together a few times, like he was tuning up his mouth. He wore the same dingy beige suit that he always wore to funerals, weddings, and dinners. Not only was it so thin you could see through it in some places, but it looked so stiff, Ruby was convinced that it could stand up and walk around on its own. Arlester coughed to clear his throat and when he spoke again, it was in a much louder voice. "I sure hope this child ain't expectin' a itty-bitty newcomer," he said with a grunt, his eyes sparkling with mischief. It was obvious to Ruby that this was his way of making sure everybody at the table heard what he had to say about her.

"What do you mean by that?" Ruby asked, offering a silent prayer to God that she wouldn't lose her temper and hurt Arlester's feelings if he didn't back off. As it was, this man was lucky to still be alive. He was lucky that Ruby didn't know some dirt on him like she did with Lola. The way he meddled, not just in Ruby's business but in everybody else's business, too, somebody was eventually going to hurt him real bad, if they didn't kill him first. She didn't know what to say in time to shut him up. It wouldn't have made any difference anyway, because he got on a roll that almost derailed Ruby.

"What do I mean? Well, since you asked, I'll tell you what I mean, Ruby Jean. I know it ain't my business, but you lookin' and actin' the same way my little cousin Mae Ella—y'all remember that crossed-eyed girl that came to the family reunion last year. Anyway, that young sister fooled around and got herself ruined. And I wasn't the least bit surprised, the way she dressed and sashayed around the neighborhood." Arlester paused and sucked in some air, looking around at every face in the room. "She was so loosey goosey, she didn't even know *who* got her pregnant!"

Ruby's parents and her sister looked like they had turned to stone. There was no movement whatsoever on their faces. Not even an eye was blinking. Ruby, horrified beyond belief, stared from the frozen faces to the pug-ugly mug of her brother-in-law, glaring at him like she wanted to bite his head off. And if he didn't straighten up soon, she just might do that.

"I ain't nothin' like that," Ruby insisted, trying to sound as casual as possible. "Y'all know me better than that," she added, looking from her mother to her father. She was glad to see that their faces had softened and come back to life. Her mother smiled.

"Baby girl, we know you would never shame this family by

gettin' yourself into a pickle like that," her father said, smiling. He blinked at his son-in-law. "We trust Ruby Jean as much as we trust all the rest of our girls."

Ruby's mother, her mouth full of corn bread, nodded. "We sure enough do."

"I just hope whatever ailment you got, it ain't nothin' serious," Lola added, giving Ruby a guarded look. "It would break my heart and disappoint me if you brought shame on this family."

Ruby had to grit her teeth to keep her jaw from dropping. She couldn't believe the words that had just rolled out of Lola's mouth.

Lola knew better than to go too far with Ruby. "But I'm sure that ain't the case! Ruby Jean ain't that crazy," she added, all in one breath, talking so fast her last sentence sounded like it was one long word.

"I won't bring no shame on this family," Ruby mumbled, wishing she could melt into the wall behind her. These family meals had become so uncomfortable that Ruby dreaded them now. And this one was especially painful.

"I know you won't, baby sister," Lola said, winking at Ruby. "I want you to follow in my footsteps."

Ruby gave her sister a mild warning look. She knew that Lola was probably thinking that Ruby was thinking about all of the un-Christian-like things she had done before she got married. And she was right. Beulah had told Ruby that Lola had used that chicken-blood-in-a-capsule trick on her fool husband. He thought she was a virgin on their wedding night. "I will follow in your footsteps, big sister," Ruby said with a smirk.

"Uh, I hope so, sugar. But what I meant was, I hope you find yourself a man like Arlester to marry, and live out your life with him the way the Bible tells you to. That's what I meant."

"I know what you meant," Ruby said, the same smirk still on her face.

Ruby loved Lola as much as she loved the rest of her sisters.

But there was a special bond between her and Beulah. She had shared things with Ruby that none of the other sisters would even admit that they knew. Like that fake virginity thing. Ruby had never bothered to ask Beulah, but she wondered how she had been able to get blood from a chicken to put in those capsules. She made a metal note to herself to eventually ask Beulah, or maybe even one of her other sisters. She thought it would be a good idea to know all of the details, in case she and Othella ever needed to fool some man into thinking they were virgins.

"I been havin' a few female issues, that's all. That's how come I lost a few pounds," Ruby volunteered, knowing that this subject would not be explored too much longer with her parents and Lola's goofy husband. "But I'm fine now."

"And it didn't hurt for this girl to lose a few pounds," Ida Mae said. "Ruby Jean, go in the backyard with Lola and y'all bring the clothes off the line. It's gettin' mighty cloudy again, and I don't want my laundry to get wet."

As soon as Ruby and Lola were out of ear-shot, Ruby asked her, "How do you get blood from a chicken to use in them capsules?"

Lola gasped and gave Ruby an amused look. "Why you askin' me somethin' like that?"

"Don't mess with me, Lola Mae," Ruby warned. "Don't you play dumb with me. Beulah told me about that trick that a woman can use when she wants a man to think she's still a virgin."

Lola gave Ruby a dumb look anyway and shrugged her shoulders.

"All I want to know is how do you get the chicken blood from the chicken to put in that capsule?" Ruby asked again.

Lola let out a loud, exasperated sigh and looked around the yard and toward the back door before speaking again. "If you ain't started courtin' yet, that ain't nothin' you need to be worried about. Or is it?" The amused look was still on Lola's face.

"I don't see you or Beulah that often, and I just want to know now in case I don't see y'all for a while," Ruby replied. "I'm goin' to start courtin' soon."

"Well, it ain't no secret. Flodell, Bessie, and almost every other gal I know knows about it. Even Carrie and Vera." Carrie and Vera were Ruby's two middle sisters, born eight months apart.

"I don't," Ruby chortled. "So you need to tell me."

CHAPTER 22

*T*HERE WERE TIMES WHEN LOLA WANTED TO SLAP RUBY. ES-pecially when she displayed a smug look on her face like she was doing now.

"You don't know? I should hope not! Trust me, you don't want to grow up too fast, Ruby Jean."

"But I do want to grow up soon," Ruby wailed.

"What's that got to do with that chicken blood trick?"

"I don't know when I'll meet me a man, uh, like your husband. There might be one or two before him and, you know how it is. . . ."

"You might get weak? You might not be a virgin by the time you meet your husband-to-be?"

Ruby nodded. "I might get weak and do somethin' . . . nasty before my time. I want the man I marry to think he's the first," Ruby whined. "Like you."

"Let me tell you somethin' right now, little girl. Virgins over fifteen around here is as rare as hens' teeth. Other than you, I sure don't know none. And I am stupefied that any man in his right mind is dumb enough to think there is. I mean, there is some somewhere, but virgins is *real* rare. And to tell you the truth, I am surprised that one of these boys ain't already got to you."

"I'm surprised, too," Ruby said with a nervous cough. "But like I just said, I will start courtin' soon and I just—"

Lola held up her hand and gave Ruby an impatient look as they started to remove the clothes, sheets mostly, from the clothesline. "You don't need but a few drops of blood, see. And you get it when you cut up a chicken. You drain the blood into a cup or somethin', then you use a spoon or a eyedropper, and you drip the blood into the capsule. It's so easy, any idiot could do it." Lola paused and narrowed her eyes to look at Ruby. "What you been up to, girl?"

"Nothin' yet. Like I said, I don't see you that often. I want to know this kind of stuff in case me, or one of my friends, need to do it. I think it's a real good trick."

"Honey, we women know all kinds of tricks when it comes to sexin'. Since we're on the subject, I guess I should also tell you how to keep yourself from gettin' pregnant, huh?"

"It wouldn't hurt," Ruby muttered, looking over Lola's shoulder toward Othella's house. She couldn't tell her sister that Othella had already shared that information with her. And she certainly couldn't tell her sister that she had gotten pregnant anyway, knowing that she probably could have prevented it—had she followed Othella's instructions more diligently, or aborted her pregnancy with a triple dose of that harsh Black Draught laxative. But it was too late for any of that now.

"You douche with bleach and or vinegar every time after you do the deed." Lola was curious as to why Ruby was staring at her with a look of disbelief on her face. "You don't believe me?"

"And that's supposed to keep me from gettin' pregnant, huh?"

"It's supposed to, but it don't always work. I hope you know that." Lola paused again and gave her sister a very concerned look. "Baby sister, please don't bring no baby into this world until you know you can take proper care of it. A baby is a gift from God, but sometimes them gifts come before they are supposed to, and the mama ends up sufferin'. . . ."

I know, Ruby thought, blinking hard and fast to hold back her tears.

"You got somethin' in your eyes? Why you blinkin' like that?" Lola wanted to know.

"I got somethin' in my eyes . . . dust, I guess," Ruby told her. "Uh, we better hurry up and get them clothes and sheets off the line. I can smell the rain comin'."

The next couple of days were very difficult for Ruby. She was depressed, she was concerned about her baby, and she was mad with everybody involved. Especially Simone. She was the one who had insisted, no, *forced* Ruby to give up her child. And Othella had not helped Ruby's case at all. After thinking about it, Ruby felt that Othella should have challenged Simone and insisted that Ruby keep the baby, especially if she thought there was a chance that Ike was the father.

Ruby was even mad at her father for being so damn eager to help Simone get rid of that poor little innocent baby.

It was another week before she caught Othella and Simone at home.

"If I didn't know no better, I'd swear y'all been avoidin' me," Ruby accused that Saturday around midnight when she'd tip-toed up on the front porch of Simone's house. Othella had opened the door.

"Other than them bill collectors, we ain't been hidin' from nobody," Othella said in a very defensive manner. "And we sure ain't got no reason to be hidin' from you. You are the one that had a baby that nobody knows about."

"That's what I wanted to talk to y'all about," Ruby said, brushing past Othella. She sat down hard on the couch next to Simone, who was in a short gown and drinking home-brewed whiskey from a coffee cup. "Simone, did you arrange every-thing all right with them asylum folks?"

"If you mean did I get that child situated with them nuns, the answer is yes. Now I suggest we don't talk about this subject no more after tonight," Simone said hotly. She took a long, loud drink from her cup, frowning as the harsh liquid burned its way down her throat. "That was a major ordeal for me to get caught up in. And"—she paused and looked from Othella to Ruby—"I still ain't tellin' neither one of y'all the name or location of that asylum." She blinked and let out a deep sigh, as if gearing up to deliver even more unpleasant news. "I told them nuns that that baby's mama died."

Ruby's breath caught in her throat, along with a huge lump. She held her breath because it was the only way she could keep herself from crying some more. "You didn't have to tell them folks that," she whimpered. "What if . . ."

"What if what?" Simone snapped.

"What if I marry me a real nice understandin' man, and he wants to adopt my child? We might have to deal with all kinds of red tape with them nuns," Ruby said firmly. And she meant every word. In her mind, her fantasy was that she would marry a decent, compassionate man (soon she hoped) and she would tell him about her baby. He would insist on retrieving the baby girl and helping Ruby raise her.

"Girl, have you lost your mind? If and when you ever find a husband, you are goin' to have a hard enough time keepin' him happy and under control with the normal, everyday problems we all have. And say you did do somethin' that crazy, like tellin' your husband you had a baby. What about your mama and daddy? Do you want them to ever find out about this? Well, honey, I am tellin' you right now, if you do, you better not tell them I was involved in this mess!"

"I wouldn't tell them nothin'," Ruby said, her lips trembling. "I don't want to get you in no trouble, Simone. Not after all you done for me. Honest to God."

Simone shook her head and her fist. "Lord, why didn't I send somebody to get your daddy when you first passed out in my house that night?" she muttered, and shot a hot look at Ruby. "Girl, it's too late to be havin' pipe dreams about you and a husband and y'all raisin' that baby and livin' happily ever after. Now like I said, I ain't tellin' you or Othella where that asylum is, or the name of it. So any notions y'all might have down the road about goin' to get that baby—forget it. Them nuns got it on paper that the mama is dead; a colored retarded cousin of mine that died givin' birth to that baby. That's exactly what I told 'em. And y'all both know that when it comes to colored folks, nobody—not even them nuns—is goin' to be too particular about maintainin' the proper paperwork after a while. If anything, Ruby, if you was to ever show up there askin' about a baby, they more than likely will just call the law on you and have you hauled off to jail. They might even wrap you up in a straight jacket and lock you in a room in that same asylum yourself! And I know they would, because I seen 'em do stuff like that all the time. You hear me?"

Ruby stared off into space, but she'd heard every word that had come out of Simone's mouth. She nodded. She sniffed. She wiped a tear from the corner of her eye.

Othella looked toward the back of the house to make sure none of her siblings were lurking about. Then she looked at Ruby and spoke in a low but firm voice. "Mama is right. And to tell you the truth, this subject is gettin' real stale. The sooner we forget about this, the better off we'll all be."

"That's easy for y'all to say." Ruby sniffed, getting more and more depressed by the second. Her eyes were red and slightly swollen. It was obvious to Simone and Othella that Ruby had been doing a whole lot of crying lately. "What if I can't never have no more babies?"

"Oh, I wouldn't worry about that none. You look right fertile to me. And there will always be some boy, or some man, willin' to stick his pecker in you and fill you up with his baby-makin' batter. Like I tell everybody, sex is like gumbo. As long as it's available, even when it's bad, it's good. And that's all that boys and men care about when it comes to that. Othella, go in that kitchen yonder and pour Ruby Jean a glass of beer. She looks like she could use some."

CHAPTER 23

*R*UBY'S DEPRESSION BECAME SO SEVERE THAT HER PARENTS were more than a little concerned. They didn't know what was bothering their daughter, and no matter how much they tried to pry the information out of her, they had no luck.

"Ruby, whatever it is that's got you walkin' around with such a long face, it can't be so bad that you can't talk to us about it," her mother said for what seemed like the hundredth time to Ruby. Her father usually said something similar, or sometimes the exact same things her mother said.

"Ain't nothin' the matter with me," she mumbled each time they asked.

Ruby's sisters and several other relatives also tried to find out from Ruby what was bothering her. But like always, Othella was the only person that she felt comfortable telling some of her troubles to. Lately, Othella didn't even have to ask Ruby why she was so depressed.

"I just miss my baby, that's all," Ruby said. She and Othella occupied Simone's back porch steps around eleven-thirty one Friday night, six weeks after the baby's birth. Ruby was still associating with Othella behind her parents' backs. Ironically, after all these years, Othella was one reason why her life was so dreary now. And it was all because she had not helped her convince Simone to let her keep her baby. . . .

"It's too late to do anything about that now. You need to concentrate on things that you can fix," Othella suggested.

"Like what?"

"Well, your folks still think you too good to hang out with certain peoples," Othella stopped and gave Ruby a hard look.

"They don't want me to get ruined," Ruby explained.

Othella stared at Ruby in slack-jawed amazement. "In *your* case, with them hoity-toity folks of yours, you can't get no more ruined than pregnant!" she shouted.

Ruby gave Othella a disgusted look. "There is worse things that can happen to me than gettin' pregnant," she insisted, her bottom lip trembling.

"Yeah—*dead*. Or locked up for life in some dank prison like my uncle Andre for robbin' a bank."

"Your brother treats me like I'm a stranger these days. Some of them other boys I was with, they treat me the same way." Ruby looked out toward the bushes behind the garden beyond the well. "All them times I went in the bushes with one, and now I can't get them same ones to give me the time of day." Ruby looked at Othella and gave her a warm smile. "I don't know what I'd do if I didn't have you to talk to, Othella. If you ever left here, I'd go crazy or die. Maybe even both."

"Ruby, you need to make some more friends. Forget about my brother, and the rest of them hit and run boys, that hit you and ran."

Ruby shrugged. "As long as I got you, I don't need no other friends. Eventually, I'll get another boyfriend, I guess. One that'll stay my boyfriend for a while."

"Maybe there'll be some new boys in our school. I heard somethin' about some of them sharecropper families havin' kinfolks movin' here from Baton Rouge. I know they must have some boys around our age."

"Oh?" The information that Othella had just revealed obviously pleased Ruby. "That's good to hear. That's somethin' for us to look forward to," she said eagerly. She was even willing to settle for a sharecropper's son for a boyfriend now—as long as he was cute and cool.

"It don't matter to me. I won't be around too much longer, so I don't care," Othella responded, speaking in a flat, detached tone of voice.

Ruby turned her head to the side and gave Othella a confused look, peering at her from the corner of her eye. "What are you talkin' about, girl? Where you goin'?"

"I ain't goin' back to school when it starts back up." Othella sniffed and sucked in some of the night air. "I'm goin' to go to New Orleans and find myself a husband. Last year when I was there visitin' one of Mama's friends, I seen servicemen all over the place. I wanted to marry me one then. A couple of years ago, Uncle Laurent came back from the army with a bullet in his head, so he gets some kind of army money every month now. Even though he dropped his rifle and it went off accidentally and shot hisself, it don't matter. The government got money and they give it to men who serve. With his check from the government, and the money that Uncle Laurent makes drivin' trucks cross country, he treats his wife real good. That's what I want, a man that can offer me some real security and attention."

"You leavin'? Why—I can't believe what I'm hearin'!" Ruby hollered, her eyes opened so wide it looked like they were going to roll out of their sockets. She stood up and faced Othella with her hands on her hips. "You can't do that! You can't just run off like that lookin' for a husband!"

"You just watch me!" Othella retorted, rising. She placed her hands on her hips and got so close to Ruby's face, Ruby could smell the homemade wine on her breath. "I'm sick of livin' the way I been livin' with my mama. She ain't never goin' to change for the better. I'm just fifteen but I feel like I'm fifty, cookin', cleanin', and takin' care of all them brothers and sisters of mine while Mama's havin' a good time with her men friends."

Ruby's lips moved, but no words came out. Suddenly, she started gasping for breath so hard that Othella clapped her on her back. "Ruby, you ain't all the way healed from havin' that baby. You don't need to be makin' yourself upset." Othella wrapped her arm around Ruby's shoulder and guided her back down on the steps. Othella eased onto the steps, patting Ruby's knee.

"What about me?" Ruby rasped, blinking to hold back her tears.

"What about you?"

Ruby gave Othella a desperate look. "What will I do with myself when you leave here?"

"Ruby, me and you are real good friends. You are the best girlfriend I ever had in my life. But we ain't joined at the hip; we had to part company sooner or later. I love you to death, but it's time for me to move on. Now if you want to come with me, that's fine with me. But I am leavin' this place."

"I can come with you?"

"It's all right with me. But you and me both know, Reverend Upshaw and your mama ain't goin' to let you run off with me! They don't even allow you to walk the street here with me! And don't even think about runnin' away without tellin' them. The last thing I want to have to deal with is the law. Knowin' your papa, he'll send the Man after us so fast it'd make your head spin clean off your neck."

"But if he say I can go with you, I will."

Othella gave Ruby a pitiful look and then she shook her head. "What did I just say? Your daddy would never in a million years let you leave town with me."

"When are you leavin'?" Ruby asked in a meek voice. She was so terrified of losing her friend that she didn't know what she was going to do, if and when that happened.

"I don't know yet. I got a few dollars saved up, but I need a few more. I figured if I could boost a few more frocks out of that boutique on Saint James Boulevard, I can sell them to get the rest of the money. If so, I think I'll be leavin' right after Thanksgivin'."

"You ain't goin' to stay around to celebrate Christmas with your family?"

"I don't think I can wait that long. Mama is gettin' lazier and crazier by the day, and I am sick of tendin' to my baby sisters and cleanin' and cookin' and dodgin' Mama's men friends. I need a break from this life."

"I see," Ruby muttered. She rose without another word and headed home. She crawled back through her bedroom window, crying so hard she could barely see her bed through her tears. Othella's news had upset her so profoundly, she forgot to say her prayers. She climbed into bed fully clothed and cried herself to sleep. Now she had something else to be depressed about.

When Ruby's mother got up to fix breakfast the next morning, Ruby was already in the living room staring at the wall.

"What you doin' up so early, Ruby Jean?" Ida Mae asked. "I'm about to fix breakfast. You want grits, rice, or oatmeal? Ham, sausages, or bacon? White bread, rolls, or biscuits?"

"That's all right, Mama. I'll eat somethin' later," Ruby said with a weak smile, shaking her head. "I got a lot of things on my mind, so I ain't got no appetite right now."

Reverend Upshaw sauntered into the room. He was still in his bathrobe, his face was unshaven, and his hair resembled a burning bush. "What things you got on your mind, girl?" he asked, a grim look on his face. "You ready to talk about why you been cryin' so much your eyes is red and swollen, and why you been so down in the dumps lately?"

Ruby remained silent for at least a whole minute with her eyes looking down at the floor. Her parents stood side by side, a few feet in front of her. When Reverend Upshaw cleared his throat, Ruby looked up and began to talk in a slow, mechanical manner. "Most of my good friends done moved away, so I ain't hardly got nobody to hang out with."

"What about us? What about your family? And Lola and Arlester offered to let you come stay with them at their house for a couple of weeks, if you think that would cheer you up," Reverend Upshaw said, trying to sound cheerful. "You can spend your whole Christmas vacation from school with them." He added a smile.

The thought of living in the same house with Lola and Arlester for two weeks made Ruby cringe. She would rather spend her vacation in a dog house! And she didn't care who knew it.

"I wouldn't be found dead in the same house with Arlester," Ruby growled, her lips barely moving. There were times when Ruby actually frightened her parents. She was a good girl, they firmly believed that, but she had inherited some personality traits from a few less than holy members of the family, on both sides. She was moody like her mother's brother Preston in Slidell. She was opinionated like her father's deceased sister Della. She walked, talked, and sometimes laughed in the same high pitched way that her father's oldest brother Moses did. He was in prison for life for killing his wife when she attempted to leave him. Moses was so mean and violent, his own mother had encouraged the district attorney to lock him away for life. Ruby was only four years old when Uncle Moses went to prison, but she had still picked up some of his traits. That was what frightened her parents the most.

"Arlester is a fool," Ruby added, her lips snapping brutally over each word. "If he don't stop runnin' off at the mouth, sayin' all kinds of stupid stuff to people, somebody is goin' to hurt him real bad."

"Well now. That's one thing that me and Mother agree with you on. I just hope that you ain't that person to hurt Arlester, or anybody else, real bad. And don't you worry about all of them outlandish things that Arlester says about you in front of us. Me and Mother don't buy none of it. We know you better. Don't we, Mother?" Reverend Upshaw turned to his wife with a stern look on his face. It was the kind of look that made her agree with him, whether she did or not. She agreed with him this time, and the stern look from him had nothing to do with it.

"We want you to be happy, Ruby Jean. Now I know we been real strict with you and that's because you are our baby. We know when you leave home, we are goin' to have to get used to a completely empty nest, and that ain't goin' to be easy for a couple of old birds like us," Ida Mae said, her voice cracking. "Now we know you want to start courtin', but what else do you want to do that might help bring you out of them doldrums you been in lately?"

Ruby swallowed hard. She had already rehearsed what she wanted to say. "Simone's havin' a backyard cookout next Friday, and I want to go." As soon as she'd released the last word, she held her breath. "Uh, I ran into Othella at the store, and she invited me."

Ruby's parents were still standing side by side, still staring at her. Their bodies looked as stiff as pillars of salt, and their faces looked like they'd turned to wood.

"I know y'all hate Othella, but she's always been nice to me in school and when I run into her at the store and stuff. And I think I'm old enough now to decide who I want to be friends with." Ruby surprised herself at how easy she was able to speak her mind on such an unpopular subject in her parents' house. And even though she was acting and looking bold and confident, inside she was trembling like a leaf. She didn't know what to expect from her parents. "With everybody else married and out of the house now, I feel like a loose wheel."

"What about them Donaldson boys?" Ida Mae asked.

"I wouldn't go to a dog fight with one of them Donaldson boys! They don't even use deodorant!" Ruby hollered. She was surprised to see such a frightened look on both of her parents' faces. "At the rate I'm goin', I'm goin' to be a old maid with not a friend in the world. I'll grow old and die alone. And I wouldn't have had no real fun in my life."

The room got so quiet, Ruby could hear the small clock ticking on the wall above the couch. It was like everything in the house and outside had stopped. She couldn't hear the neighbors laughing and talking back and forth like she did almost every other morning. No cars with loud mufflers, like so many in the neighborhood had, were driving down the street. The chickens in the backyard, which could usually be heard clucking all hours of the day, had suddenly stopped. Reverend Upshaw's lazy old nameless coon dog was usually barking at something or somebody from the back porch, all hours of the day and night. Well, Ruby couldn't hear a peep out of that mangy creature now. It was like the whole world had come to a complete standstill, and everybody and everything in it had become mute. But that was not the case. Ruby's mind had tuned everything out, and it remained that way for at least a full minute. As soon as her mother spoke again, all of the sounds inside and outside the house resumed.

"Will Simone stick around to supervise things at this cookout?" Ida Mae asked, talking loud enough to be heard over the coon dog barking at the chickens clucking. It pleased Ruby to see her mother's hard face soften by degrees, right before her eyes.

"Simone can't supervise herself," Ruby said quickly.

Ida Mae and the reverend both laughed and nodded in agreement.

"The cookout will be in the daytime, and I won't stay more than a hour or two," Ruby added.

Her parents looked from her to one another and shrugged. This was usually a sign of surrender on their part.

"There ain't goin' to be no alcohol served at this shindig, is there?" the reverend asked, his face softening, too.

"If there is, I ain't goin' to drink none. Honest to God," Ruby said, "I swear I won't."

"I'll think on it," Reverend Upshaw told her, turning to leave the room. With a great sigh, his wife followed behind him.

Before Ruby could make it back to her bedroom, Reverend Upshaw yelled from the kitchen, "You can go to that cookout, but you better behave yourself or you will *suffer*. . . ."

Ruby covered her mouth to keep from giggling and it was a good thing she did. Reverend Upshaw appeared in her bedroom doorway within a matter of seconds.

"One more thing," he said, waving a finger in the air.

Ruby gasped and stood trembling by the side of her bed. "What's that, Papa?"

"This ain't no license for you to start runnin' the streets all hours of the day and night with Othella. Me and Mother still don't approve of the way that girl dresses or behaves. If you ain't careful, she could lead you down a real dark path like a Judas goat. However"—he paused and rubbed the side of his sweaty face and neck and then he continued, talking in a loud voice—"I guess you can be *casual* friends with her and still maintain your dignity. When and if she do somethin' unholy in your presence, you remember the way you was brought up, hear?"

"You and Mama ain't got nothin' to worry about. I know right from wrong," Ruby said.

CHAPTER 24

GETTING HER PARENTS' PERMISSION TO VISIT OTHELLA WAS a major move forward in Ruby's life. Her attitude changed immediately. She started to eat right again, she smiled more, and she behaved in a manner that pleased her parents. And, she did not miss climbing in and out of her window to sneak to Othella's house after her parents had gone to bed.

When Ruby went to Othella's house now, she didn't do anything that was hot enough for anybody to report to her parents. And she always returned home when she was supposed to.

She eventually got over Ike, and all of the other boys who now shunned her. She had found a couple of new ones that she liked enough to spend time with, anyway.

However, despite all of these new changes in Ruby's life, there was still one thing from her past that haunted her on a daily basis: the baby girl that she had given up. There were times when she was so broken up about it that she prayed that she'd get pregnant again with another baby girl to replace the one she'd lost. She didn't care who fathered her, what she looked like, or even if she came with two heads and hooves. Ruby had convinced herself that she'd never be whole again until she made up for her loss. She prayed that in some way

Othella would make up for her role in the deception so she could "forgive" her.

It did Ruby no good to try and find out from Simone the name and location of the asylum where she said she had dropped off her baby. She had tried repeatedly, but no matter how much she begged and pleaded, Simone refused to reveal that information.

Othella had not mentioned moving to New Orleans again since that night she had told Ruby. When school started that September, Othella didn't show up. Ruby couldn't catch her at home, and she didn't respond to any of the messages that Ruby had left with her siblings for her to come see her.

Ruby eventually found out from Othella's twin, O'Henry, that she was doing domestic work for rich white women in the suburbs to get enough money to leave home with. Not only did Ruby's depression return, but she panicked. She could not even think rationally.

Without giving it much thought, she told her parents in an "Oh by the way" manner, "I'm goin' to drop out of school and move to New Orleans with Othella so I can find me a husband, y'all."

Ruby had seen some expressions on her parents' faces over the years that would have frightened Satan. But there were no words to describe the looks on their faces this time. Her mother's eyes looked like they had doubled in size. Her lips looked like they had disappeared. She even looked two shades lighter. The reverend's nose flared like a bull's. His mouth dropped open and his lips quivered in a way that made his teeth click.

"What?" Ruby said dumbly. "Why are y'all lookin' at me like I'm crazy?"

Reverend Upshaw's lips were still quivering, his teeth still clicking. He and his wife both remained quiet for a few more moments as they continued to stare at Ruby in stunned disbelief.

Finally, Ida Mae spoke. "Ruby Jean Upshaw, how did you get from wantin' to be friends with Othella and goin' to her cookouts every now and then, to wantin' to run off to New Orleans with her to find a husband? What's got into you now?"

Before Ruby could respond, her father spoke. His voice was so hoarse and deep, it sounded almost like a demonic growl. "Have you lost your mind, girl? YOU AIN'T GOIN' NO PLACE!"

"No, I ain't lost my mind! I—" Ruby began, but she was abruptly cut off by her mother.

"You must have! In the first place, you ain't goin' to quit school! Any colored kid who can go to school these days at all, and not have to drop out to work, is lucky. That's one thing. Quittin' school to run off with a Jezebel like Othella is another thing."

"Go get a switch, Ruby Jean!" Reverend Upshaw ordered, pointing toward the door. "Get your tail out yonder to that chinaberry tree and break off a switch, because I'm fixin' to whup you like you stole somethin'!"

Ruby slunk out of the room, but she did not go to the chinaberry tree in the yard to break off a switch for her whupping like she'd done so many times in the past. Instead, she galloped over to Othella's house to tell her about her parents' reaction to her desire to quit school and leave home. She knew that she had a serious whupping coming when she got back home, but she didn't care.

"I ain't the least bit surprised," Othella told her as she massaged her mother's feet.

Simone occupied a wobbly chair at the kitchen table. As usual, there was a large jar of liquor in her hand. She grunted. "Ruby Jean, if I was you, I'd do what I wanted to do. It's time for you to stand up to your mama and papa. They can't run your life forever."

"They keep goin' on and on about how they want me to make somethin' out of myself," Ruby said. "Be a school teacher or a nurse or somethin', even though that ain't what I want to do with my life."

"The bottom line is, they got to turn you loose, sooner or later. Most of the girls around this place leave home around fifteen or sixteen anyway. Ask your mama how old she was when she left home," Othella said with a smug look. "You ain't no better than the rest of us. School teacher, nurse—my ass. You wouldn't like doin' nothin' that dull, Ruby. You and me is like birds of a feather. We want to have some fun, huh, Mama?"

"Sure enough," Simone agreed. "I didn't let my folks rule my life. Especially after they was the ones that got me on the road to ruin in the first place. I got treated so much better in that asylum than I did at home."

The mention of the asylum made Ruby give Simone a sharp look. But the look that Simone shot back made Ruby reconsider what she wanted to say. As tense as things were about her desire to leave home, Ruby didn't want to deal with the subject of Simone leaving her baby in that asylum again right now, too. If that was what she really did. For all Ruby knew, Simone could have given her precious baby to one of her relatives. Or, she could have even sold it to some desperate childless couple. After all, the baby was fair skinned, healthy looking, and attractive. What childless colored couple wouldn't want such a child? And knowing Simone, she would have sold that baby for the price of a few drinks. Ruby considered the possibility that that was the real reason Simone wouldn't even tell Ruby the name and location of the asylum.

From the angry look on Simone's face, Ruby knew not to bring up the subject. When she looked at Othella's face, the angry look on hers was just as severe as the one on her mother's.

"I'll miss you, Ruby," Othella said. "I'll send you a letter as soon as I get settled in New Orleans. Maybe you can come visit when you graduate from school . . . on your way to that colored college your folks want you to go to."

"I'll probably get a whuppin' when I get home today," Ruby sighed, moving toward the door.

And she did. As soon as she entered the living room front door, Reverend Upshaw lit into her with his belt.

For the next few weeks, Ruby moped around the house like a woman in mourning. She went to school in a daze and came home in a daze. Her homework suffered, she suffered. One day she was so distraught, she had a severe panic attack at the dinner table in front of her parents, her sister Lola, and Lola's busybody husband, Arlester. Not knowing what was really happening, Ruby's mother assumed she'd choked on a fish bone so Ruby went along with that.

"If you goin' to eat fried fish without chokin', you need to eat slower, Ruby Jean," Ida Mae said, clapping Ruby on the back until she stopped hyperventilating. "I thought you was old enough to know that."

"Swallow some corn bread. That'll absorb that fish bone," Reverend Upshaw advised Ruby before he carefully bit a tail in two, his favorite part on a fish.

"I'm all right," Ruby sputtered, still having a hard time trying to catch her breath. Once she'd composed herself, she actually smiled.

"Ruby Jean, the more I see you, the more I think you tryin' to hide somethin' real serious," Arlester said. That signifying monkey sat at the table, spilling his red wine all over Ida Mae's brand new white linen tablecloth. His comments made Ruby so uneasy, her butt started to itch like she'd sat in a bucket of fleas. "You want to talk about it?"

"I don't want to talk about nothin'," Ruby snapped, giving

her brother-in-law a look so sharp he flinched and wiggled in his seat, like his butt was itching, too. "And if you don't mind, please stop tellin' me how bad I look, or how you think I'm tryin' to hide somethin', 'cause I ain't. Pass the gravy, please."

The conversation shifted abruptly to an upcoming church event, but Arlester continued giving Ruby suspicious looks and shaking his triangle-shaped head. The looks that she shot back at him must have been pretty effective because he didn't mess with her again for the rest of the evening. However, as he was preparing to leave, he took her aside and told her, "Baby girl, if you ever want to confide in me, all you need to do is let me know. I ain't no expert, like a psychiatrist or preacher, but I been around enough to know a little bit of somethin' about everything. Maybe I can turn you around."

"Arlester, I don't need to be turned around or nothin' else. Now you have a blessed evenin'," Ruby told him, closing the front door so fast behind him and Lola that she caught the tail of his jacket in it.

The closer it got to Othella's departure date, which Othella had estimated to be the week after Thanksgiving, or at least before Christmas, Ruby was almost as robotic as a zombie.

On Thanksgiving Day, when all of her six sisters and their families and a few members of Reverend Upshaw's congregation showed up for dinner, Ruby remained in her room the whole day. Beulah, knowing how much Ruby liked to eat, and feeling sorry for her, fixed her a huge plate of black-eyed peas, corn bread, rice and gravy, turkey necks so tender the meat was falling off the bones, and yams. She delivered the feast to Ruby on a platter.

When Beulah entered Ruby's bedroom a few hours later, the plate was still on top of Ruby's dresser where she'd left it, and none of the food had been eaten.

The day after Thanksgiving, while Ida Mae was cleaning up

the mess that her guests had made, Ruby finally stumbled out of her room and into the kitchen.

"Ruby Jean, you need to get a grip on yourself. You know we love you and we only want you to be happy," Ida Mae said to Ruby in a gentle voice, rubbing her shoulder.

Ruby had been crying off and on for hours. Her eyes were bloodshot and almost swollen shut. "I ain't never goin' to be happy in this house," she sobbed, blinking hard to hold back her tears. "I am goin' to marry the first man that asks me, so I can get up out of here!" she threatened, pouring herself a large glass of goat's milk, wishing it was beer.

"You do that and you'll be back home in no time. You think you miserable now because you're livin' by our rules? Just wait until you get married and have to live by your husband's rules! You'll come runnin' back here lickety-split—just like all of your sisters keep threatenin' to do. Life ain't easy, girl. Me and your daddy, we are simply tryin' to keep you from experiencin' just how evil and ugly the world really is, for as long as we can." Ida Mae gave Ruby a guarded look as she continued to rub her on the shoulder. "You need to think about somebody other than yourself for a change. Like your daddy, and how hard he works to keep folks around here on the straight and narrow. Do you think he likes spendin' so many evenin's a week visitin' folks so he can minister them, like he's doin' right now as we speak? And the poor soul is another one of them wretched worldly women that done lost her way. Do you think your daddy likes that?" Ida Mae didn't give Ruby time to answer her question. "No. No, he don't like roamin' from the house of one wench to another like he's been doin' so much of lately. Don't make his burden no harder than it already is."

This was not the first time that Ida Mae had complained about Reverend Upshaw making "house calls" and Ruby knew it wouldn't be the last. For one thing, according to Beulah, and a couple of her other sisters, Ida Mae was uncomfortable with her husband spending so much of his time administering spiritual comfort to single women, especially the ones with bad reputations. It seemed like the younger and prettier those women were, the more spiritual comfort they required.

Ida Mae was in bed by the time her husband returned home. He was surprised to see Ruby still up, sitting in the living room enjoying some of what was left of the huge Thanksgiving feast that Ida Mae had prepared.

"Ruby Jean! What—ain't you supposed to be in the bed by now?" Reverend Upshaw exclaimed as he stumbled in the front door. He looked flushed and tired. "Uh, are you all right, sugar?"

Ruby nodded. "Daddy, I told Mama that I can't wait to get married so I can get up out of this house," she muttered.

"Uh, to be honest with you, I can't wait for you to get married, too. The sooner you learn about life, the better off we'll all be," Reverend Upshaw said, as he stood in the middle of the floor moping sweat off his face with the back of his hand.

Ruby noticed that his shirt was buttoned wrong, and the fly on his pants was open. With a stony expression on her face, she looked her father up and down. She wrestled with her thoughts, because she didn't want to believe the obvious: either her daddy was fooling around with other women, or he was one hell of a clumsy ox who had bumped against a woman so hard she left lipstick on his collar.

"You been sippin' on elderberry wine *again*, Papa," Ruby accused. It was hard for her to believe that the average man still had not figured out how easy it was for lipstick to get on his clothes or face if he got close enough to a woman. "You got some red stains on your shirt collar . . . *again*." It was a tone of voice that she rarely used with her father, and she only used it when she knew he would not retaliate.

"Oh?" He rubbed both sides of the collar on his shirt, but all that did was spread the lipstick even more. "I had me a few sips with Sister Blake—medicinal purposes as always," he eagerly offered. He was sweating profusely as he continued to rub the side of his collar, trying with no success to rub off the red stain.

"It's stained on both sides this time," Ruby pointed out. "It is red wine, ain't it?"

"It sure enough is! What else could it be?" Reverend Upshaw folded his arms and gave Ruby a narrow-eyed look, like he was trying to read her mind. "Now you quit bein' so nosy and get yourself to bed. You got Bible study tomorrow."

CHAPTER 25

THE SATURDAY AFTER THANKSGIVING, RUBY PAID OTHELLA another visit around midnight. She had accepted the fact that she was losing the most important friend she'd ever had in her life. She didn't know when, or if, she'd ever see her again after Othella moved to New Orleans. That was why it was so important to Ruby to see Othella as much as she could now.

One thing that Ruby liked about seeing Othella in the middle of the night was that she didn't have to face Ike. He only spoke to Ruby now when he couldn't avoid her, like on the street, or at the corner store. He had not returned to school either, so she didn't have to worry about running into him there. The other boys who had used her had also moved on to other girls. And when she ran into them, they didn't even acknowledge her.

"I got to find me somebody to marry, Othella, and I got to find him real quick, before I go stone crazy," Ruby told her friend as they sat on footstools in Simone's living room, drinking beer and nibbling on cold fried chicken wings.

"You ain't goin' to have much luck findin' one around here. All the good ones have already been snatched up. That's why I'm goin' to New Orleans for a fresh start."

"What if you meet somebody to marry here before you leave? Would you stay then?" Ruby asked with a hopeful look on her tortured face.

A sad look crossed Othella's face and she rubbed Ruby's shoulder. "Ruby, ain't no man in his right mind goin' to marry me knowin' who my mama is. I need to go someplace where nobody knows me."

Ruby had almost given up all hope of changing her life when she found a way out that she never would have expected. That Sunday after her last visit with Othella, Othella came to her bedroom window around two in the morning. She got Ruby's attention by throwing pebbles at her window.

Ruby stumbled out of bed, lit the kerosene lamp on her dresser, and ran to the window. She lifted it with one hand and leaned out. "What's wrong with you, girl?" she hissed, propping open the window with one hand, holding the coal oil lamp in the other. "What you doin' out here this time of night? I just left your house a couple of hours ago. Did I forget and leave somethin' over there?"

"You need to come back to my house with me. You need to come with me right now!" Othella said in a low steady voice, with a mysterious look on her face. She was rarely this serious, so Ruby knew that something big was going on. And whatever it was, it involved Ruby.

Ruby almost peed on herself because she could only think of one thing important enough for Othella to order her out of bed in the middle of the night: somebody had found out about the baby!

"Oh God! Somebody done told on me!" Ruby hollered, almost in tears. "They know I had a baby!"

"This ain't got nothin' to do with your baby!"

"Did—did another man die in the bed on top of your mama?"

"I ain't got time to explain nothin', and we need to hurry up before it's too late! And bring that lamp with you!"

Ruby left the window and grabbed the same off-white shift that she had worn to church earlier in the day. It took her less than two minutes to get dressed. She slid out of the window, hitting the ground so hard she fell, dropping the coal oil lamp at Othella's feet. Othella helped Ruby up with one hand and picked up the lamp with the other.

"What's goin' on?" Ruby asked, brushing off her dress.

"Just follow me!" Othella ordered.

Ruby had a hard time keeping up with Othella as she followed her back to her house. "I want you to know right now that I'm only just findin' this out myself. But I got a feelin' it's been goin' on for a while," Othella said, sounding even more serious.

"What?"

"Hush up! Come on with me!"

They tiptoed up the steps to the back porch. As soon as they got inside the kitchen, Othella blew out the lamp. There was enough light coming from another lamp filled to the brim with kerosene on the counter in the kitchen for them to see their way down the hall. Once they reached Simone's room, Othella stopped and gave Ruby a pitiful look. Then she held her breath and reached for the doorknob. Simone and her lover were so involved in what they were doing, they didn't even hear the loud squeaky door open.

Ruby almost fainted when she saw the bare back of a large, dark-skinned man on top of Simone. He was humping her so hard, the legs on the cheap bed were rising off the hardwood floor, making a click-clacking noise. Ruby turned to Othella with a puzzled look on her face and shrugged. "You dragged me out of bed to come look at your mama fuckin' one of her customers?" Ruby whispered. "Why?"

Instead of answering, Othella cleared her throat as loud as she could. But that still didn't get any attention from the couple in the bed. So Othella stomped her foot so hard and loud, the Bible on the nightstand fell to the floor.

This was the same room where Ruby had given birth a few months ago. This was the *last* place that she expected to see her daddy. Simone, looking over his shoulder, gave Othella and Ruby one of the dirtiest looks she could manage. If looks could kill, Othella and Ruby would have immediately dropped dead on the spot.

"Aw shit," Simone complained, tapping Reverend Upshaw on the shoulder. He stopped humping, but he took his time turning around and rolling off her. Had he seen the Devil himself, he couldn't have looked more frightened or busted.

The funny thing about a married man who gets caught in bed with another woman is that the first thing out of his mouth is usually the universal line: *"This ain't what it looks like—I can explain!"* Those were the exact words that shot out of Reverend Upshaw's mouth like a cannonball. Still huffing and puffing, he scrambled off the bed, his huge bare feet hitting the floor with a loud thud. He pulled the flowered sheet with him, wrapping it around his waist with both hands. "I DECLARE!" he began with his eyes as wide open as they could get. "Ruby Jean, you— you ain't got no—no business bein' up in Simone's bedroom this time of night!" he stammered. "I DECLARE!"

"I declare, you ain't neither," Ruby retorted. She was so stunned, she could barely breathe. For a split second, she thought she was going to have a serious panic attack. She was glad that didn't happen, and that she managed to remain somewhat composed. "At least not like this."

"This ain't what it looks like, Ruby Jean. You know me. This is just business," Simone said, rising. She swung her freshly shaven legs to the side of the bed and didn't even bother to hide her nakedness.

"I can see that!" Ruby screeched, blinking and breathing hard. She could not believe her eyes. Either she was having a bad dream or her eyes were playing tricks on her. But she was not dreaming, and her mind was not playing tricks on her. This was as real as it could get. The room even smelled like hot sex. That was one smell that she'd recognize anywhere. She rubbed her eyes as she moved a few steps closer to the bed. She recognized the Bible on the floor, which had fallen off the nightstand. It was the same one that her father took with him when he made his house calls.

"LORD HAVE MERCY!" Reverend Upshaw roared, his eyes bugged out so far, it looked like they were about to roll down the front of his burning face. This was the last thing that he thought he'd ever have to deal with! It was not the first time he'd been unfaithful, and, it wouldn't be the last. But right now this was the only transgression that required some immediate damage control. "Ruby Jean . . . I . . . Lord Jesus!" he yelled, his voice so hoarse his words almost sounded like a foreign language.

"You better call on the Lord, and I hope you don't have the nerve to tell him 'this ain't what it looks like,' because He knows better, and so do I," Ruby snarled.

"Now look . . . this . . . uh." Reverend Upshaw stood by the bed as stiff as an oak tree. "See, I come over here on spiritual business . . . and . . . but you see, it just happened. Satan has a way of leadin' us so astray. . . ." The reverend stopped talking and ran his trembling fingers through his wild hair.

"I hope my mama thinks it was just *spiritual business*, and I hope she holds Satan responsible," Ruby quipped.

"Now look," he began again, a hand in the air. It was funny how the light from the kerosene lamp on the nightstand seemed to shine more on the gold wedding band on his thick finger than anything else in the room. The sheet slipped, and for the first time in her life, Ruby saw her father's dick. It was long and thick, like the kind *she* liked herself. She could understand why a woman like Simone would want to hop into bed with him. *And how many other women?* she wondered.

"Your mama ain't got to know nothin' about this! She got a weak heart and high blood pressure. This could kill her!"

Ruby had never seen her father look so desperate and frantic before in her life. Seeing him this way now made her want to throw up. She would never look at him the same way again. It was one thing for her to be a hypocrite; she was too young and stupid to know better. But he was a man of God, and he was supposed to be setting an example for her and everybody else. If preachers were this trifling, what did she have to expect from regular men? Those thoughts made her shudder.

Mumbling under his breath, Reverend Upshaw leaned down and picked up the sheet and wrapped it back around his trembling body.

"If you so concerned about Mama's weak heart and high blood pressure, how come you are over here like this?" Ruby asked, making a sweeping gesture with her hand. "If this is the kind of stuff you been tryin' to keep me from doin', why are you here doin' it?"

Reverend Upshaw blinked and then he snatched a damp napkin off the nightstand and honked into it. "I'll say this much," he continued. "Don't you raise your voice to me, girl! I'm still your daddy, and as long as I'm alive and kickin', I'm the one in charge! How many times I got to remind you to do as I say, not as I do?"

His last sentence made Othella and Simone snicker.

"You won't have to worry about me for long, Papa. I am goin' to see to it!" Ruby taunted, clearing her throat. Amazingly, she grinned and batted her eyelashes.

What she'd just said almost made her father, the strongest man she knew, piss his pants. "What do you mean by that, Ruby Jean?" he asked, pressing his legs together to keep his bladder under control.

"You'll find out soon enough, Daddy. Othella, can I get a little bit of beer before I leave? If I ever needed a drink, it's now."

Ruby looked at her daddy, expecting him to comment on her request for beer.

But the disgraced preacher just dropped his head and remained silent. He knew that he had lost the battle with his youngest daughter, and that it was time for him to give in to her demands.

CHAPTER 26

"*W*HAT'S THAT SUPPOSED TO MEAN?" REVEREND UPSHAW asked Ruby, his teeth clattering and his voice trembling like he'd just waded through an ice-cold puddle of water with his bare feet.

Even though Ruby was angry and upset, she had to hold her breath to keep from snickering. She loved her father and didn't like to see him in such a state of panic. But under the circumstances, how could she not find some humor in the mess he'd gotten himself into?

"When Othella leaves for New Orleans, I'm goin' with her?" It was a statement and a question. And it was one that the reverend didn't respond to because he knew that there was nothing he could say or do now to stop his daughter from leaving home.

"With what for money?" Reverend Upshaw asked, reaching for his pants. The sheet fell to the floor again, but this time he acted like he didn't care if his daughter and her friend saw him naked. He took his time sliding his legs into his pants. Brushing off his shirt, which had lipstick stains on the collar, he put it on so fast, it was on inside out. "You can't go nowhere with no money, missy. Now we can talk this, uh, little incident here through. Me and you. You ain't got to let somethin' like this make fools out of us both."

"I'll get some money from somewhere," Ruby vowed, looking at Othella. "I can babysit, clean houses, walk dogs, and I'll dig ditches if I have to. I can even cook pies for that restaurant like Mama."

"Ruby Jean, you ain't got to do all of that. I'm pretty sure I got enough for both of us till we get jobs," Othella said. *Bless her,* Ruby thought. Othella was well on the way to redeeming herself for the mess involving Ruby's secret baby.

Ruby smiled and moved closer to her friend. "Papa, what you do is your business. I realize that now. But I wouldn't want this to get to Mama, whether she has a weak heart or high blood pressure or not. After all she done for you and the rest of us, she don't deserve to be hit with a scandal like this."

Simone sneered. "I got news for you, girl. Your mama ain't no fool. If you think she don't know that the reverend is been suckin' and fuckin' women for years, you dumber than you look."

Ruby looked in her father's burning face and he promptly dropped his head. She knew that what Simone had just said was true. She didn't want him to confirm it, but the look on his face did just that. For such a big man, he suddenly looked very small in Ruby's eyes. And, unfortunately, he also now looked like the Devil. He was a man and like most men, even some of the ones in the Bible, he liked to look at women. She could live with that. But he was the last man on the planet that she expected to cheat on his wife.

And Othella's mother was the last woman on the planet that Ruby expected her father to cheat with.

If he was low-down and funky enough to fuck a prostitute, what else would he do? she wondered. She refused to allow herself to think about that for too long, because there were so many other things worse than adultery that her father could have been involved in. It broke her heart. The man she thought she knew better than she knew herself was actually a stranger to her. As far as she was concerned, she didn't know him after all.

To say that Simone had let the cat out of the bag was an understatement. She'd let a lion out of the bag, but she didn't stop there. "You should have seen him last week! He licked my muff so much, his face looked like a glazed donut by the time he got off me!"

It got worse.

Ruby saw her father do something else for the first time in her life: he slapped Simone's face so hard snot squirted out of her nose. This was the same man who preached on a regular basis that it was a sin and a shame for a man to strike a woman. Here he was doing just that. "Shet up, woman!" Reverend Upshaw hollered at Simone, raising his hand to slap her again. "Ain't you done enough damage already?"

Ruby and Othella yelped at the same time.

Simone had to shake her head to regain her composure before she could speak again. "Preacher Man, if you tetch me again, I will bite your balls clean off and hand 'em to you on a fork!" Simone threatened, glaring at Reverend Upshaw. She massaged her cheek where he had hit her. With a mighty grunt, she spat out some blood. It landed on the floor, missing his foot by a couple of inches.

"Ruby, you ready to leave?" Othella asked, her voice shaking.

Ruby was too horrified and stunned to speak or move. She couldn't believe what she had just witnessed. Her father stood stock still, literally trembling. There was so much sweat on his body, it looked like he had just stepped out of the baptismal pool in his church.

Simone rubbed her face some more and gave Reverend Upshaw another dirty look. "Ruby Jean," she said, "I'll tell you like I been tellin' my girl all of her life. Do whatever you have to do to get what you want. You ain't no Queen of Sheba, but you got the same thing between your legs that me and Othella got," Simone said.

"Simone, that's my daughter you feedin' all of that worldly slop to! I don't want her to end up like you and Othella!" Reverend Upshaw yelled, stumbling around on the floor looking for his shoes. He wanted to slap Simone again, but he knew better. He didn't want to call her bluff and have her bite off his balls. He knew that she was the kind of she-devil who would actually attempt to commit such a vile act of violence.

"That's your problem, Reverend Hot Stuff," Othella said. "You didn't want Ruby to be like me? You didn't want her to get the Devil in her? Well, I got news for you. Satan done paid Ruby a visit and gone. What would you say if you knew—" Othella caught herself.

The room was so quiet, they could hear the crickets and the other night creatures serenading one another outside Simone's open window.

"Hush up, Othella! You done said enough!" Simone warned, giving her daughter a murderous look.

"No, I ain't goin' to hush up. It's high time this man knows—" Othella yelled.

"He knows all he needs to know!" Ruby said quickly, cutting Othella off. Despite the developments that had just unfolded in the last few minutes, she still didn't want her father to know that for years she'd been one of the biggest whores in the neighborhood.

Reverend Upshaw plopped down onto the side of the bed, struggling to put his shoes back on. The whole time that he was doing that, he was shaking his head and mumbling under his breath. When he stood up, he removed his shirt. He put it on right side out, then he raked his fingers through his hair for the fifth or sixth time. He didn't like the fact that the three females remained silent, watching him as if they were waiting to see if he had any more stupid comments to offer. He didn't make them wait long.

"Y'all women don't understand these things!" Reverend Upshaw said, almost losing his breath. He had to pause and cough a few times. "Y'all don't see things the way we men do," he admitted.

"I do. And I know my girl do, too," Simone assured him. "I ain't worried about her makin' her way when she gets to New Orleans."

"Well, I'm worried about my daughter makin' her way in a Babylon like New Orleans," Reverend Upshaw yelled.

"Keep your voice down! You want to wake up the rest of them kids of mine so they can know your monkey business, too?" Simone said sharply, rising off the bed. She moved to the window with her long, deflated breasts flapping against the map of stretch marks on her belly. After she'd closed the window, she grabbed a thin gown hanging from a wire hanger on the wall. Turning to Reverend Upshaw, she said, "I know you didn't finish, but I still expect to get paid. And let me remind you, you ain't paid your bill all month. . . ."

This piece of information was another major blow to Ruby.

Damn his soul! He was *paying* for a piece of ass! This was way worse than Ruby realized. She didn't know how to react to the fact that even though her father was still attractive for a man his age, he still had to pay for sex.

Ruby was so hot with anger, it felt like somebody was holding a flame thrower in front of her face. She was severely disappointed in her father, and it hurt. Her stomach was in knots, her head was spinning. Even her eyes hurt. Just looking at him made them burn. She thought about how he balked when she or her mother, or anybody else in the family, asked him for money. "I ain't got no money to be buyin' you another frock you don't need. Money don't grow on trees, girl," he'd told her last week. She'd asked him to buy her a frilly pink dress that she'd seen in the window of one of the few downtown boutiques that Othella was too afraid to steal from.

It also saddened Ruby to know that one of the reasons her

mother had to pinch pennies was because her daddy had an on-
going sex-on-credit account with Simone to maintain, and
probably other women as well.

"Ruby Jean, go on back home. You done seen enough here
tonight," Reverend Upshaw said, finally speaking in a low
voice, and looking sincerely remorseful.

"I'll wait for you," she told him with a snort.

Reverend Upshaw gasped, and then his jaw dropped. "You
ain't got to wait on me. We done said all we need to say on this
thing here."

"All right, Papa. I'll see you back at the house in a few minutes." She paused and swallowed hard. "Unless you got another
stop to make . . ." Reverend Upshaw didn't respond to her sar-
castic comment.

Ruby turned to Othella and asked, "When are we leavin' for
New Orleans?"

CHAPTER 27

"OLD MAN, IF I DIDN'T KNOW NO BETTER, I'D SWEAR somebody done worked some world-beatin' voodoo on you. How did we get from Ruby Jean barely bein' allowed to even visit Othella's house to Ruby fixin' to drop out of school and run off to New Orleans with her?"

Of all of the outrageous things that Ida Mae had heard in her lifetime, what Reverend Upshaw had just told her was the most outrageous. It made no sense at all. If voodoo wasn't responsible, had the man lost his mind? He must have. *He* was the one who had held on to Ruby Jean with such a short leash. *He* was the one who had decided that she was too good and virtuous to associate with worldly people like Othella. And *he* was the one who wanted her to remain a virgin until he found her a suitable husband like he had done for his other six daughters.

"No, Mother. I ain't lost my mind. It's just that . . . well . . . see . . . I been thinkin'," Reverend Upshaw replied, scratching the side of his thick, mole-covered neck like he usually did when he was nervous or trying to hide something. "Uh, maybe we bein' too hard on Ruby Jean. She's goin' to find out just how wicked life is anyway, sooner or later. We can't protect her forever. Um, we need to let her live her life the way she wants to now."

Ida Mae stared in slack-jawed amazement at her husband, like he'd just sprouted a second nose. She'd known this man for over fifty years, and she thought she knew him as well as she knew her Bible, which she knew from Genesis to Revelations. Apparently she was wrong. She knew her Bible, but she didn't know her husband. "How come you singin' this tune *tonight*? Just last night you was goin' on and on about how proud you was to be the daddy of a girl as chaste as our Ruby Jean."

"I know, I know . . ." He forced a laugh that sounded downright sinister. "Heh heh heh." He stopped laughing when he saw the exasperated look on his wife's face. "But you know me. . . ."

"Do I?"

"Huh?"

"Go on. I'm listenin'."

"Anyway, you know I'm the kind of man who will admit when I'm wrong. After givin' it a lot of thought, I realize we been wrong to be so strict with Ruby Jean."

"Roebuck Upshaw, have you been drinkin' more of that elderberry wine than is acceptable? You drunk?"

"Naw, I ain't drunk."

"You must be. I want to know what done got into you all of a sudden. When you left this house a few hours ago, *after you got back out of bed*, to go minister what you told me was a member of the community in desperate need of spiritual assistance, you seemed like a sane man. Now you seem stone crazy."

It had only been ten minutes since Reverend Upshaw had returned home from his latest "spiritual visit" to someone in need. He had sent Ruby home a few minutes ahead of him, too stunned and embarrassed to walk the short distance with her. He had ordered Ruby to go to her room and go directly to bed as soon as she got home. That was what she had done, part of it at least. She'd gone to her room, but she had not turned in for the night. Instead, she'd stood by her bedroom door with her ear against it until she heard her father come in. As soon as she heard him enter the master bedroom, she crept down the hall to her parents' room and put her ear against the door.

"I been thinkin' on it a lot lately. I . . . uh . . . I think Ruby Jean is grown, smart enough to take care of herself," he stated, his voice cracking over each word.

"Ruby Jean is still a child. She need to finish school so she can get a good job. You done forgot that? By the way, you'll be sleepin' on the couch tonight," Ida Mae said.

Reverend Upshaw ignored the comment about the couch. "Ruby Jean can go to Harvard and get the best education in the world. But it still might not do her nary bit of good," he pointed out, his voice now loud and somewhat angry. "She is still just a colored gal. The white folks is goin' to control almost everything she do once she leaves home and gets out in the real world. You done forgot *that*? She needs to experience real life—and the sooner the better."

Ruby stood up straight. She'd heard all she needed to hear. Her father *always* got his way when it came to family matters. Yes, he consulted with his wife, and she fussed up a storm, but it never did any good. Ruby let out a triumphant sigh, gently rubbed her chest, and then she returned to her room. After she said her prayers, she crawled into bed, slid up under her goose down comforter, and slept like a baby.

She dreamed about a life in New Orleans that only a princess could have imagined. She envisioned herself marrying a handsome, well-to-do, *faithful* man, landing a glamorous job, owning a lavish home, and the most important thing of all: giving birth to a beautiful daughter—and eventually several more—to replace the one she'd lost.

She dreamed throughout the night and almost every other night after that, until she and Othella boarded that segregated train to New Orleans the first week in December.

* * *

It didn't take long for Ruby's dreams to become nightmares. They had only been in New Orleans for one day before Ruby regretted her decision to accompany Othella.

It was raining and cold the day of their arrival. They were not dressed for rain, and they didn't even have umbrellas. They didn't want to spend money on anything they didn't need, but when Ruby suggested they find a department store within walking distance of the train station where they could at least buy rain scarves or a cheap umbrella, Othella protested. "We don't need none of that. It ain't rainin' that hard."

"You ain't got to worry about your hair nappin' up from the rain the way I do," Ruby remarked, looking at Othella's naturally straight hair. "But if a drop of water gets on mine, I got to use the hot comb again, and I just did that before I left the house."

They stood near the train station ticket counter, receiving cold stares from a few white patrons who were not used to seeing black people up close.

"Didn't you bring your hot comb with you?" Othella asked, forcing herself to smile, hoping it would diffuse the situation. "I got plenty of paper bags in my suitcase that we can cover our hair with."

Ruby rolled her eyes and set the large brown suitcase that her father had purchased for her on the ground. "Now what would we look like roamin' around this city with brown paper bags on our heads? These white folks are already lookin' at us like we crazy." Ruby immediately said that after a white man running through the station bumped against her, almost knocking her down. He didn't excuse himself or even bother to look back. "And with all of these uncouth peckerwoods we done run into so far, it would be just like one of them to make a fuss about two colored girls walkin' around with paper bags on their heads."

Before Othella could respond, a grim-faced security guard approached them. He got so close to their faces they could smell his foul, tobacco chewer's breath. "You gals got a problem?" he asked, folding his arms.

"Naw, we ain't got no problem," Ruby responded. "Why, you got one?"

"Y'all can't loiter around here, and that's my problem," the guard informed them.

"We just piled off the train, sir," Othella said quickly, moving between the guard and Ruby. She didn't like the angry look on Ruby's face, or the guard's.

The last thing that they needed on their first day in town was a hostile situation with white folks, Othella told herself. She knew from experience that even the toughest, biggest white man thought that all black people were threatening on some level.

"We ain't loiterin'," Ruby said through clenched teeth, intensifying the angry look on her face. They were near the doorway and Ruby could see that the rain was really coming down hard, like God had turned on a faucet, full force. People with raincoats and umbrellas were running down the street, wading through puddles that looked like small ponds. "We was just waitin' for it to stop rainin'."

"We ain't got no umbrellas or nothin'," Othella said, hoping her smile would make the man feel less threatened.

"Look-a-here, this ain't no way station. Y'all can't stand around here annoyin' people," the guard snapped, making a sweeping gesture with a bony hand. Ruby and Othella looked around the station at the same time. There were at least twelve other people standing around, and half of them had been in the station much longer than Ruby and Othella. The security guard had walked right by all of them and had not told them to move on. Despite the fact that she had lived in the South all of her life and she knew the "rules and regulations" when it came to race relations, Ruby did not fear white people, or the consequences that she might have to face if she got out of line.

"Look, you can stand your white ass here and talk as much

shit as you want to, but we ain't goin' out in that rain until we get ready. Now if you know what's good for you, you'll get the hell away from us," Ruby growled.

It was hard to tell which one gasped louder, Othella or the guard. Othella grabbed Ruby by the hand and attempted to pull her away, but Ruby wouldn't budge. She slapped Othella's hand and assured her, "I ain't goin' out in that rain, Othella."

"That's it! That's it!" the guard hollered, backing away. "You people don't have a clue about the proper decorum around here, but I am goin' to make sure you do!" The guard trotted toward a door near the counter, opened it and rushed in.

"We got to get out of here before he comes back!" Othella said, trembling. Ruby's suitcase was still on the ground. And from the way she was looking, with her arms folded and a scowl on her face, she was not about to go anywhere, anytime soon. Or at least not until it stopped raining. "Ruby, I ain't goin' to jail where them white cops might beat us down or worse. You can wait around here if you want to, but I am out of here!" Othella didn't wait for Ruby to reply. She tightened her grip on the handle of her shabby suitcase and headed toward the exit. She was pleased to see that Ruby was not far behind. It had suddenly stopped raining, and that was the only reason that Ruby had decided to leave.

They walked briskly down the sidewalk, which was cracked in so many places, it looked like somebody had done it on purpose. As soon as they were two blocks from the train station, Othella set her suitcase on the ground and turned to Ruby. "You almost got us killed back there. You can't be talkin' to white folks the way you done that guard, girl."

"Pfff! White folks don't scare me one bit. They bleed, they hurt, and they die just like us colored folks do."

"That ain't what I'm talkin' about. I'm talkin' about the rules. We have to follow them if we don't want no trouble. You know how happy these crackers get when they lynch somebody or burn down some colored person's house. And you and me both know that there is two laws: one for the white folks and one for us. The difference is, the white folks' law is there to take care of the white folks. Them laws is to make sure we don't cause no trouble for the white folks."

"Law shmaw! To hell with it. I don't care who it is, white or colored, ain't *nobody* goin' to make a fool out of me and get away with it. That's *my* rule and I will die makin' sure it don't get broke. Now let's get to steppin' so we can find us a place before it gets dark, or before it starts to rain again," Ruby said, gliding so casually down the street, you would have thought she owned it.

CHAPTER 28

*R*UBY AND OTHELLA WERE UNABLE TO FIND A WHITE-OWNED motel that was willing to rent them a room. One annoyed manager actually chased them out of his motel lobby waving a broom. They had not come across a single motel run by blacks. They couldn't even find a restaurant that would allow them to use their bathroom facilities.

At one point, when Ruby had to empty her bladder, she squatted down between two parked cars. Then Othella did the same thing herself, several times. When Ruby had to relieve herself again, she did it behind a tree, with a stray dog sniffing her behind.

Just before midnight, they ended up in a small, open-all-night colored restaurant where they ate their first meal since their arrival—four slices of buttered toast and some hot tea. The tacky, box-shaped establishment, Boates' Fine Southern Food—a place that Ruby would not have entered under normal circumstances, even if she had been dying of starvation—had no waitresses or waiters. On one of the four tables sat a pile of old newspapers and some empty lard buckets. Thick grease dotted the gummy floor. The stench of burnt grease, and only God knew what else, permeated the entire restaurant dining area.

The place was owned and run by the same man, a long-faced individual in his late fifties who lived in a one-bedroom apartment above the restaurant. He took each order with a tight smile, and prepared the FINE SOUTHERN FOOD that was advertised on the sign outside above the door, and on the smudged, dog-eared menus.

After eating her toast, and anxious to drink the complimentary tea that the man had served in two different size glasses, Ruby gave Othella a curious look and shook her head.

"What was that look for?" Othella asked, finishing her toast. She lifted her glass to drink, but when she saw a gnat floating on top, she set it back down and grabbed Ruby's. When she didn't see any creatures in it, she drank. "Why are you lookin' at me like that?"

"I ain't never been in a place like this before in my life!" Ruby hooted, looking around with her nose up in the air. "Nobody in my family would be found dead in a dump like this."

"Well, excuse me. But all of us ain't as lucky as the royal Upshaw family. Some of us ain't got no choice," Othella reminded. "I don't like places like this no more than you do."

Ruby took a sip of her tea and then she let out a mild burp. "At least the man who runs it is real nice," she said, smiling at the owner as he wiped the counter. He smiled back and nodded.

"Listen, when I went in the bathroom a few minutes ago, I noticed it looked right safe," Othella told Ruby.

"Safe? And it's clean, I hope. Maybe I should use it before we leave," Ruby grunted. "Which way do you want to go from here?"

"Uh." Othella paused and looked at the man behind the counter as she leaned across the table, talking in a low voice. "I don't think nobody else is comin' up in here tonight."

"That's a good guess. We been here for over an hour, and ain't nobody else been in here yet. What's your point?"

"We done tried to get a room and ain't had no luck. We ain't seen not nary a place with rooms run by colored folks."

Ruby's face remained blank as she shrugged her shoulders.

Othella lowered her voice to a whisper. "I don't see why we can't spend tonight in the ladies room here. Like I said, it looks safe enough. And as slow as business is around here, we don't have to worry about nobody walkin' up in there while we sleepin'. Finish your tea, and let's haul our asses out of here. I'm tired."

They paid their check, slapped a nickel tip on the counter, and left.

The ladies room had to be entered from outside, through a door on the side of the building. Ruby was horrified as soon as she stepped inside.

"Othella, we got to do better than this. I wouldn't let a hog I didn't like sleep in here. This place smells like a cow's carcass that's been layin' out in the sun rottin' for a month!" Ruby complained, wiping her face with a damp wad of rough toilet paper. She coughed and rubbed her nose as she stood in front of a cracked mirror above the only sink. Dim yellow light glowed from a naked forty-watt bulb connected to a cord hanging from the ceiling.

Othella had rushed to sit on the commode in one of the three stalls. It was the first time in her life that she'd done her business on anything but an outhouse, a hole in the ground in the woods, or in one of those gruesome metal buckets that her mother kept in the house. She took her time relieving herself.

Her failure to respond right away annoyed Ruby. "You still in there?" Ruby yelled, pounding on the stall door with her fist.

"I heard what you just said. I don't like this no more than you, but I advise you to hush up and find a clean spot on that nasty floor for us to sleep on," Othella snapped.

"A *clean* spot? You seen this damn floor? It looks like somebody spreaded some cow manure on it, and it smells like it, too," Ruby yelled, coughing some more.

"Well, it's either this or we sleep outside on the ground. We tried to get a room at every motel and hotel we saw. We can try another part of town tomorrow." Othella paused and groaned. "Aw shit! My monthly just came on."

"Hurry and plug yourself up and come on out of there. I'm tired and I want to get some sleep," Ruby said in a worried tone of voice.

"Don't you worry about nothin', girl. Everything is goin' to be just fine. Tomorrow is goin' to be a much better day," Othella insisted.

Tomorrow was not a better day.

The restaurant owner entered the bathroom around noon the next day. When he saw Ruby and Othella stretched out on the floor using their suitcases for pillows, he rushed out and returned with a whisk broom.

"Y'all get up and get your tails the hell out of my place! I ain't runnin' no hotel!" the man yelled, poking Ruby's side with the end of the broom, and kicking Othella's side with the toe of his thick black leather shoes. "I should have knowed you two tight-asses was up to somethin' when you sat your tails in my place as long as you did."

Ruby wobbled up first, pulling Othella up by the hand. "We real sorry, sir," she muttered, almost falling back to the floor.

"Sorry is right. Well, you sorry heifers ain't stayin' here!" the angry man shouted, shaking the broom like he wanted to use it on Ruby.

With a pleading look on her face, Ruby continued. "We didn't have no place else to go! We was tired and it was late." She forced a crooked smile and then she fumbled in the quilted purse she carried until she located a crumpled dollar bill. She handed it to the man. He snatched it and promptly slid it into the back pocket of his pants. "It got too dark for us to see too good, so we couldn't find no motel."

"Well, I don't know where you young girls come from, but I'd hightail it right on back there, if I was y'all. Kids like y'all need to be 'round folks that can take care of y'all," the man told them.

"We ain't young. We both fifteen. And we on our own now. We came here to get jobs," Othella said with a wide smile.

The man threw his head back and laughed until tears formed in his eyes. When he stopped laughing, he wiped his eyes with the back of his hand and sniffed. Then he pulled a large red and white checkered handkerchief from the pocket of his dingy white shirt and honked into it so hard he started to choke. Othella didn't hesitate to slap him on his back. Ruby wanted to slap him, too, but she wanted to slap that stupid look off his face. To her, it seemed like he was enjoying the predicament that she and Othella were in, and his role in it. And he was. His life was just that boring and empty. He had just a few friends, and not much of a life outside of his restaurant. "Jobs? Doin' what? What in the world kind of jobs do y'all expect to find around here? If it ain't field work, y'all out of luck."

"And husbands," Ruby added with a nod. "We came here to work and to get married."

The man shook his head and looked at Ruby like she was speaking Italian. Then he laughed long and loud again, clapping his hands together like a trained seal. "Now I know y'all crazy. Findin' a job, any kind of job, is one thing. But a husband *and* a job? Y'all?"

"I don't see nothin' funny about that," Ruby snapped. She realized that this man was old enough to be her grandfather, but she sassed him anyway. "You don't know nothin' about us, so don't be standin' here mean-mouthin' us!"

The man gave Ruby a wide-eyed look and shook his head again, looking her up and down like she had just dropped out of the sky. "Let me tell you somethin', gal. I been strugglin' for the past five years to keep this hole that my daddy left me open. I done laid more eggs than Henny Penny. I am one step from starvin' and endin' up in the streets. Y'all the first business I had in two days—and y'all didn't order nothin' but that toast." The man wiped his hands on the tail of the soiled, bibbed white apron that he wore over his dingy white shirt, and even dingier white pants. He had the nerve to have a white chef's hat on his head, and it was just as dingy as everything else he wore. "And as far as a husband? Pffft! That ain't sayin' much." He stopped talking long enough to hawk brown spit into the sink. "My mama had four husbands and nary one was worth a plug nickel. Let me give y'all some advice: us men is interested in hips, lips, and fingernail tips when it comes to women. Most men—not me, though—they don't bring nothin' to the table but a knife, a fork, and a spoon. Most men—not me, though—is more trouble than they are worth, so a husband ain't goin' to do y'all much good—unless you find yourself a preacher man."

Ruby closed her eyes and exhaled so hard that her nose ached. When she opened her eyes and looked at Othella, she could see that her friend was struggling to keep from laughing. "I don't want to marry no preacher," Ruby announced. "They behave just like all other men."

"Amen to that," Othella offered with a vigorous nod.

"Well, anyway, y'all need to get on back home until things cool off," the man told them.

"Cool off? What do you mean by that?" Othella asked.

The man's eyes got big, and a loud gasp flew out of his mouth. "Y'all ain't heard?" He tilted his head to the side and reported, "Them Japs done blowed up Pearl Harbor this mornin', and there ain't no tellin' what place they goin' to blow up next. Could be us! Them Oriental folks is real mean and sneaky! Now y'all get out of my place. I'm fixin' to temporarily shet down in a few days and go stay in a house with a lady friend of mine, or I may go out to my son's farm in Shreveport where it might be safer."

Othella released a heavy sigh as she lifted her suitcase. Ruby looked the man in the eye and told him, "We'll leave. But we ain't goin' no place until you give me back that dollar I just gave you."

"Pffft!" The man grunted and gave Ruby a dismissive wave. "I ain't givin' you back nothin', girl! I am keepin' that dollar to pay for y'all sleepin' in my place all night. Now y'all git!" He waved the broom in the air but he didn't have to do it for long or too hard. Ruby and Othella scurried out like frightened mice.

CHAPTER 29

"WHERE EXACTLY IS PEARL HARBOR AT ANYWAY?" OTHELLA asked Ruby as they meandered down one street after another. Othella was smart in many ways as far as the street life and high living were concerned. But when it came to the basics of education, there was a lot that she didn't know.

"It's in Hawaii," Ruby told her, wondering why Othella was looking at her with such a blank expression on her face. "That's that place way overseas in them islands where pineapples and hula dancers come from."

"Oh. Yeah, that's right." Othella nodded. "I had forgot."

They roamed the streets for four more hours looking for another place to sleep. Almost every place they came upon was either already temporarily closed, or about to close because of the attack on Pearl Harbor. And that included the black- and the white-owned establishments. The few white-owned places that were still open told them that they had "no vacancies" even though the signs out front indicated that they did. Finally, when they encountered a black maid coming off duty at the run-down Red Moon Motel, she told them that their best bet was to find a black church.

Ruby, from her background, knew that the church was usually a dependable refuge for anybody in need of help. She couldn't count the number of times that people had come to her daddy's church for help, and none of them had ever been turned away. Especially if that person happened to be an attractive woman.

With all of the things that she had on her mind now, the last thing Ruby wanted to spend time thinking about was her father's un-Christian-like behavior and the fact that he had been leading a double life. Despite all of the sex and alcohol that she had enjoyed, she was profoundly disappointed to know that her own father had indulged in his own worldly pleasures.

She didn't feel too bad about her behavior, though. She had a legitimate excuse. She was young and wanted to be like other kids. Besides, it wasn't her fault that she had been born a preacher's daughter. She wondered what other sins her father had committed. But she didn't really want to know. Especially not while she and Othella were currently in such a deep black hole.

Out of exhaustion and desperation, they attempted to get some assistance at a small Baptist church at the end of one of the many streets that they had randomly wandered down. But the preacher's wife had run them off, suggesting that they go home to their families and get in a cellar in case the Japanese had more bombs up their sleeves.

"I'm tired, cold, and hungry," Ruby complained. "And I'm so dizzy I can barely see straight."

"Look, I'm just as tired, cold, hungry, and dizzy as you," Othella snapped.

They set their suitcases on the damp ground on a dead-end street, a few yards from the church that had just turned them away. "I don't know about you, but I can't take too much more of this. I don't care how borin' my life was at home, it wasn't as bad as this," Ruby croaked, as they plopped down on top of their suitcases.

Othella gave Ruby such a disgusted look, it appeared she'd been sucking on lemons. "See, that's because you ain't had it near as hard as me growin' up."

Ruby gasped. "Do you mean to tell me that us roamin' around here with no place to sleep don't bother you? We got money for a room, but don't nobody want to rent to us."

"Ruby, there is a war goin' on right now. As soon as things settle, people will open up their places. Eventually one of them will rent us a room. Trust me."

"Well, it better be soon, because I can't take too much more of this," Ruby snarled. "I knew I should have listened to my folks and kept my butt home!"

"For what? All you did was complain about your home and the way you had to behave. You got away from all of that, and now you thinkin' about goin' back to it? Well, be my guest! You go on back to Shreveport and sit on the porch. I am stayin' in New Orleans, and I'm goin' to make somethin' of myself, even if it kills me."

Othella and Ruby continued roaming around, mostly in silence. Evening had come, and it would be dark soon. Their suitcases seemed to be getting heavier by the minute. Now they were not just tired, but they were also extremely hungry and light-headed. And because Othella was on her period, she was experiencing cramps, too.

"Ruby Jean, we got to do somethin', and we got to do it real fast. These cramps is killin' me. And I can feel blood oozin' out of me so heavy and thick, I am goin' to need to change my plug soon," Othella said, almost in tears.

"I got plenty of them capsules that I take for my cramps. I can give you some as soon as we stop again, and I can root through my purse to find 'em." Ruby said. "And if you got any ideas about what we should do next, I'd sure enough like to hear 'em. I can't believe you came all this way and didn't have no plan!"

Othella stopped walking and set her suitcase down on the ground again. She punched the side of Ruby's arm, forcing her to stop, too.

"I *did* have a plan, and you knew what it was. If you didn't like it, you should have come up with one yourself. And you didn't have to come with me." Othella didn't even try to hide her anger. "Give me one of them cramp capsules." Ruby fished a plastic container out of her purse, removed two capsules and gave them to Othella. She snatched them and swallowed them immediately. "I hope you got a big supply in case I need some next month."

"I got three whole bottles, but I can get more over the counter at any drugstore."

Othella looked relieved.

"Now let's keep walkin' until we do find a place to stay. And if we don't find a place before it gets too dark, you will be sorry because I'm gettin' my tail back on that train and I'm goin' back home!" Ruby hollered.

Othella didn't like to be threatened, and she didn't want Ruby to know that she was scaring her. "Ruby Jean, I know I got us in this mess, and it's up to me to straighten it out. I promise you I will. Please don't go back home and leave me here by myself—"

"You can go back home, too!" Ruby reminded.

"To what?"

Ruby dipped her head and gave Othella a dry look. "You can go back to your mama's house!"

Othella groaned. "Ruby, you ain't got no idea what it was like livin' with a woman like my mama, and I hope you never have to find out. She wasn't fit to raise a cat, let alone seven kids. No matter what I run into out here, in the long run I'll be better off than I was at my mama's house."

Ruby stared at Othella, searching her eyes like she was looking for a deep dark secret that Othella was keeping from her.

"Did she beat you? Is that why you don't want to go back there?"

"I got my share of punishment, and most of the time I deserved it. I sassed my mama a lot. But my mama is a whore. She always been a whore and probably always will be. Every day and every night, her men was after me. And . . . she seen it all and didn't do nothin' to stop it. As a matter of fact, *she* tried to get me to do what she was doin' with all of them men. And she'll groom my little sisters sooner or later, if she ain't started on them already. Her motto was 'more pussy, more money' and that's all she cares about. Now if your mama was that kind of mama, would you want to go back to live with her?"

"I guess not," Ruby responded, giving Othella a sympathetic look. "I didn't know that Simone was *that* triflin'."

"Come on." Othella released a loud breath and picked up her suitcase. "We best keep movin' until we find a place for tonight."

Just when Ruby didn't think she could stand another minute of the madness that she'd let Othella drag her into, they found themselves right back in front of the same restaurant where they had spent the night. Ruby pressed her face against the window. She was glad to see that the same man who owned the place was still on the premises. He was wiping the counter with a white rag. They wasted no time going back in. An elderly couple occupied one of the tables.

"What y'all doin' back up in here?" the man asked, strutting from behind the counter. He stopped in front of Ruby and Othella, hands on his hips.

"Sir, can you give us the name of a roomin' house, or a real cheap colored motel, or somethin'? We didn't have no luck findin' a place to stay," Ruby said. There was a pleading look on her face, and the man felt truly sorry for them.

"We got money, but we'll do anything else we have to do to get a place to sleep," Othella announced. "Anything."

The man's long homely face softened. He caressed his chin as he looked Othella up and down, realizing for the first time how pretty she really was. And that she had the kind of hips and lips that a man like him could appreciate. It had been six months since that lazy bitch he'd married had run off with one of his friends, and he had not enjoyed the pleasure of a female body since. Now here were two young female bodies, practically being served to him on a platter! Christmas was coming early this year, he told himself.

"Anything, huh? Hmm," the man replied, still looking Othella up and down.

"Like housecleanin', washin' dishes, and stuff like that." Ruby tossed that information in as soon as she saw the excited look on the man's face. "We can cook, too."

"Y'all go sit at the table on the end yonder. I'm fixin' to shet down for the night," the man said, now looking friendly for the first time since they'd met him. "Uh, I got some shirts need ironin' upstairs in my place and a sink full of dishes that y'all can wash, I guess."

"We can take care of all that," Othella said with relief. "You goin' to let us sleep in that restroom again tonight?"

"You already took our money," Ruby reminded. "We ain't got that much money, so every penny counts."

"I think I can do better than that restroom for y'all tonight. Even longer than just tonight, if y'all get a notion to stay," he told them.

"What about your lady friend, and your son in Shreveport? When we was here before, you said somethin' about closin' down and goin' to live with one of them until this thing with them Japanese people cool off," Othella reminded.

"I intend to, but that won't be for a few days, or a couple of weeks. And, uh, like I said, I think I can do y'all better than that nasty, funky restroom." The man licked his lips and nodded toward the empty table by the door that led to the restroom. "Now, like I said, y'all go sit down at that table yonder and behave yourselves until I close up. Lemme get y'all nice young girls some hot tea, so you can be more relaxed when we get to my place upstairs."

CHAPTER 30

*T*HE FIRST FEW MINUTES IN THE RESTAURANT OWNER'S cramped one bedroom apartment upstairs was not bad. As a matter of fact, it was almost pleasant. The man was not as crude and rude as he had acted in the restroom. It seemed like he was trying hard to be hospitable.

"Y'all young ladies set down and make yourselves comfortable," he said, waving them to a gray couch with lumpy pillows.

The couch was backed up against the wall in front of a window. Ruby sat down immediately.

"Uh, sir, can I use your bathroom?" Othella asked shyly. She had changed her pad in the restroom downstairs half an hour ago, but she had done it in such a hurry, it didn't feel so secure now. Even though she felt dry down below at the moment, she didn't want to take a chance on her menstrual blood leaking through her clothes and soiling this nice man's furniture.

"Just go in that door by the stove yonder," the man pointed.

As soon as Othella was out of the room, he turned to Ruby and smiled. She smiled back and looked toward a sink next to the stove. The kitchen was just a small area facing the living room. It contained a stove with just two burners, an icebox that was about half the size of the one Ruby's parents owned, and a table with four mismatched chairs. The living room had even less. Other than the couch that Ruby occupied, the only other pieces in the living room were a scarred coffee table with a jar lid on it that was overflowing with cigarette butts and a large easy chair facing the couch.

"You got a nice place," Ruby commented.

"Thank you. I just can't seem to keep it clean though," the man chuckled.

It had started to rain again. It was beating down on the roof and against the window behind the couch. It sounded like a drum to Ruby. She looked out the window, asking herself for the tenth time, *"What have I gotten myself into?"* The sight of an abandoned feed store with every window boarded up and a skinny hound dog chewing on a shabby old shoe made her feel sad for the people who lived in this dreary neighborhood. Old cars rattled down the street. A large puddle had formed on the sidewalk in front of the restaurant. It was a brownish color and looked solid, as if it had turned to ice. Ruby let out her breath and turned back around to face the man.

"New Orleans sure ain't as glamorous as I thought it would be," she remarked, displaying a wide, fake smile. The man stood at the stove with his back to her. He grunted in response to her comment. Ruby noticed water stains and mold on the bottom half of the wall facing her. The dull brown shag carpet on the living room area of the floor was so thin she could see the wooden floor beneath it. And the smell in the apartment was an unholy stench of stale cigarettes, cabbage greens, and grease. What kind of person could live in a snake pit like this and not go crazy? she wondered. She felt so sorry for her "host," she wanted to ease up behind him and give him a hug. But she didn't. A female had to be careful with men. She reminded herself that an innocent gesture like a hug could easily give this old man the wrong idea, and that was one thing that Ruby didn't want to deal with.

Othella returned and dropped down on the couch at the other end where they had placed their suitcases on the floor.

"Y'all hungry?" the man asked, turning around just enough to see their faces.

"Oh, yes!" Ruby said, almost leaping off the couch. Her stomach had been growling for hours.

"I figured so," the man said with a chuckle.

Ruby used the bathroom and returned to the kitchen area, smiling from ear to ear. She was so happy to be off the street.

The man heated some left over collard greens with neck bones, while Ruby and Othella made hot water corn bread and a pitcher of iced tea.

"Sir, how come a nice man like you ain't got no wife?" Othella asked, speaking over her shoulder from where she stood in front of the sink washing dishes for them to eat from.

"I had a wife, but she was triflin'. That heifer! She didn't want to do nothin' that a woman is supposed to do! She didn't know her place. God made woman to take care of man, and I hope y'all already know that!" the man barked. "By the way, I'm Glenn Boates. What do I call y'all? I don't even know who's who." He grinned, looking from Othella to Ruby.

"I'm Ruby and she's Othella," Ruby said with a proud sniff. "We been best friends for a long time." She had just removed the corn bread from the skillet and was standing over the table spooning greens onto three cracked, mismatched plates. She blinked at a plump roach crawling across the top of the table, like the dinner had been prepared for him. She hit at it, knocking it to the floor. The pest scurried off so fast, Ruby didn't have time to squash it. She couldn't remember the last time she'd seen a roach in somebody's house—other than Othella's mama's.

"Where is your wife at now?" Othella asked. She was not prepared for Glenn's hostile response.

"That bitch is long gone! But when she left here, I made sure she had a well-whupped ass! I beat her down before she took off with my so-called friend! If she ever comes back this way, I'm goin' to beat her some more!" Glenn bellowed, practically spitting out the words. "I'll beat her and that black-ass spook she left me for. If I wasn't a church-goin' man, I'd pay a conjure woman to put a serious hex on 'em both!" Glenn snorted. "That bitch!"

Ruby rolled her eyes and eased down in a seat at the table, hoping she wouldn't see another roach, or something worse. "When I get married, the first time my husband beats me, he'd better make sure I'm dead. Or that he can get far away before I can get my hands on him. Because any man that hits me I will seriously hurt . . . real bad," she said.

Othella and Glenn laughed; Ruby didn't.

The dinner conversation was boring because Glenn Boates was a bitter, boring man. He seemed to be mad at the world, because he had nothing good to say about anybody or anything. "Just when this damn country was beginnin' to do right by us colored folks, them damn rice-eatin' Japs had to go and upset things! They got this whole world in a uproar! I hope that four-eyed, punk-ass President Roosevelt sends some troops over there to Japan and blows them all to Kingdom Come!" he snarled. Glenn didn't let the fact that his mouth was full of food stop him from speaking. "Y'all got boyfriends back home?" Pot liquor from the greens trickled down his chin, corn bread crumbs dotted his lips.

Othella nodded, Ruby shook her head.

"I had a few but they turned out to be triflin', too. That's why I left," Ruby said.

"Well, it's a good thing y'all didn't have no babies to worry about. Or did y'all?" Glenn asked, looking from Othella to Ruby.

"I didn't," Othella said without hesitation.

"I . . . I didn't neither," Ruby mumbled, rising. "Uh, we can sleep on a pallet on the livin' room floor." She placed her empty plate in the sink. "It's gettin' late, and we both real tired."

"Go yonder to the bathroom. There's some kivver in there on a shelf, some handmade quilts and some blankets. It's goin' to get mighty cold durin' the night, so y'all take all of the kivver you want. Them handmade quilts—the only decent thing that wench I married done right—is real thick, so that might be enough for young girls like y'all. I know how hot natured some of y'all can be. . . ."

Ruby gave Othella a puzzled look.

It was a quiet, peaceful night. Ruby and Othella slept side by side on the pallet on Glenn's living room floor that night. Even though he had a bed in his bedroom, he slept on the couch facing the girls.

When Othella and Ruby rose the next morning, Glenn was not in the apartment. Ruby was glad to see that their host had already cooked breakfast for them: bacon, grits, and fried eggs. He had run out of sliced white bread, but he had made some biscuits. Everything was on the table, paper napkins included.

"Mr. Glenn sure is a nice man," Ruby commented as she and Othella sat at the table enjoying the breakfast like it was their last meal. "Lettin' us stay here for a dollar, feedin' us and all."

"Yeah, but that don't mean nothin'. I know for a fact that even the worst men can be nice when they want somethin' from you," Othella insisted.

Ruby didn't ask Othella what she meant, but it didn't take long for her to find out.

About an hour later, Glenn pushed open his front door and rushed inside with a mysterious grin on his face. "Uh, it's real slow downstairs, so I decided to lock up for a few hours and come chitchat with y'all for a spell," he said, plopping down on the couch next to Ruby. He removed his run-over shoes and fraying socks, exposing his sour-smelling, lizardlike feet. Ruby wanted to move closer to the window, or anywhere else in the room to get away from the odor of Glenn's feet, but she didn't want to be rude. She decided that it would be better to grin and bear it, which is what she did.

Othella was at the sink, washing the breakfast dishes, but she could smell Glenn's feet, too. She had smelled worse, so she wasn't as offended as Ruby. But, like Ruby, she didn't want to be rude so she pretended not to notice the unholy stench in the room.

"You got somebody to help you run this place, Mr. Glenn? Maybe you can give us a job for a while until we get ourselves situated," Othella said eagerly, rubbing her nose to keep from sneezing. She perched herself on the couch arm on Ruby's side with the dishrag still in her hand.

"Doin' what?" Glenn chuckled. "Y'all ain't blind. There ain't nothin' around here for *me* to do! What I need somebody on the payroll for? There's a war goin' on. And didn't I tell y'all that I was goin' to go to either my lady friend's house or to my son's place to hole up for a spell?"

"I just meant that we could help you out until you leave," Othella said with a heavy sigh. She rose from the couch arm and returned to the sink, dropping the dish-rag onto the counter.

Ruby didn't like the look that was on Glenn's face, but he was looking at Othella, not her. Othella didn't see the disgusted look on Ruby's face.

"Uh, can you give us the address or the names of a few colored churches that we can go to and try to get some help? We went to one a few blocks from here, but there was a real mean lady there. She didn't help us none," Ruby told Glenn, as she crossed her legs and folded her arms. She didn't like the way his eyes roamed up and down her legs and then her bosom.

"Y'all ain't got to rush off," Glenn replied with a series of rapid blinks. "I'm enjoyin' y'all's company, and it's nice to have a couple of sweet *juicy* young girls in my place to gaze at, instead of them old crones I usually get stuck with. Them menopausal bitches!"

"We don't want to put you out too much longer. We'll be out of your hair real soon," Othella said, holding up a hand. The truth of the matter was, she wanted to hang around as long as possible. She'd only mentioned leaving because she thought it was the polite thing to do. "Uh, but if you don't mind us stayin' a little longer . . ." She wanted to hear Glenn mention dinner or at least one more meal, but he didn't. He just looked at her for a few uncomfortable moments, then he looked at Ruby, making them both nervous.

"Is somethin' wrong, Mr. Glenn?" Ruby asked.

Glenn shook his head. Then he ran his fingers through his thin, graying hair and gave them a hard look. "Wrong? Naw, ain't nothin' wrong. As a matter of fact, everything is very, very right. All I want to know now is, which one of y'all sweet young things is goin' to suck my dick first?"

CHAPTER 31

"*M*ISTER, HAVE YOU LOST YOUR MIND? I KNEW YOU WAS too good to be true!" Othella shouted, almost choking on her words. She couldn't believe what she was hearing or seeing. She plopped down on the couch, sitting so close to Ruby their knees touched. Glenn remained at the other end, looking at them like he was inspecting two sides of beef.

Before they realized what was happening, Glenn stood up and unzipped his pants. A second later, his dick was in Othella's face, dangling like a one-eyed snake. He guffawed as he grabbed his dick and shook it from side to side. "I ain't too good to be true, but I'm true to be good. Now like I just asked, which one of y'all want to go first, hmm?" Still shaking his dick, he dipped his head and looked from Ruby to Othella with a silly grin on his face.

"I'll tell you what; if you want to keep that slimy thing in one piece, you better put it back in your pants and zip it up right now," Ruby advised. She and Othella had already seen more dicks than a lot of girls their age. But neither one of them had seen one as long as the one they were looking at now. It had to be at least twelve inches long. But, it was so *thin* it resembled a pencil, and it curved to the side at the bottom tip like a meat hook. Ruby and Othella were thinking the same thing: something that long and thin, and curved at the tip, poking around inside a woman wouldn't have been much fun at all. And sucking it, well, that would have been even less fun. Ruby almost gagged just thinking about sucking on something that "deformed," especially since her mouth had never even been close to a man's private parts before. She wasn't about to start giving blow jobs on this one!

"Let's get one thing straight right now. I don't tolerate no child sassin' me!" Glenn warned, shaking a finger in Ruby's direction as he stood rooted in his spot like a tree. "And another thing is, if y'all think you're gettin' outta here leavin' me all worked up, y'all got another think comin'. I don't let no females sleep in my place and eat up my food for free! Now I'm askin' *again*, who is goin' to suck my dick first? It don't matter to me, 'cause I ain't choosy."

"Look, sir. You took our money so we could sleep here last night, and if you wanted some pussy from us, too, you should have told us from the get-go," Othella said, shaking her fist at Glenn.

"Pussy? *Don't flatter yourself, girl!* Who said anything about me wantin' some pussy? Don't make me laugh!" Glenn let out a laugh that was both hard and long. "I don't want no pussy from no dingy little hoochie coochie gals like y'all. I done had every nasty woman's disease in the book, and I'm gettin' tired of runnin' back and forth to a doctor to get pills and shots in my butt." He looked from Othella to Ruby, shaking his head. "If y'all give me the blow jobs I deserve, I can take y'all with me to my lady friend's place or to my son's place. I can say that y'all is my cousin's kids from Texas or somethin'. Y'all can stay with me and my boy for free, eat three meals a day for free, and all me and him would want is an occasional blow job."

"Well, you ain't gettin' no pussy, no blow job, or nothin' else from us," Ruby said, standing up in front of Glenn, with her breath on his face. She was so close, he moved back a few steps.

"I got news for you, Big Bertha—*somebody* is goin' to suck my dick today," Glenn sneered.

"You are one crazy-ass old man." Othella stood up, next to Ruby. "Ruby, don't waste no time talkin' to this fool. Let's get our shit and get the hell up out of here."

"Uh-uh! Y'all ain't goin' no place!" Glenn barked. Before Ruby or Othella could say another word, he had his hands on Othella's shoulders, pressing down so hard, she thought he'd cut off her circulation. She sucked in her breath and with all of her strength, she pushed him away. He was surprised at how strong she was for such a petite young girl. "Be still, bitch!" he hollered, slapping the side of Othella's face. "You know you want this good dick down your throat. I seen the way you was lookin' at me when I was walkin' around in my long johns last night. You been beggin' for it ever since you set foot into my place. I ain't blind."

Ruby flopped back down on the couch. She was so stunned she couldn't move or speak. All she could do was watch in horror at what was taking place in front of her.

"If you don't turn me aloose, you are goin' to be real sorry later on," Othella advised her attacker as she fell back onto the couch.

"I'm real sorry now!" Glenn yelled. "I didn't know y'all was goin' to be this much trouble! My wife wasn't half this much trouble when I needed to do my business with her!" He snatched Othella off the couch by her hand and pushed her down to the floor onto her knees. Using both of his hands, he guided her head to his crotch. His dick was dripping juice and generating indescribable funk. "Now you get to suckin' and I don't want to feel no teeth! Suck, lick, and swallow, young lady!"

Othella was struggling so much that Glenn fell. But he was back on his feet within seconds, his hands back on Othella's shoulders, his dick still awaiting the blow job he thought he deserved. Somehow Ruby managed to rise again, but she was in a daze. She was still too stunned to speak or do anything else.

"Ruby Jean—do somethin' quick!" Othella yelled.

Ruby finally moved a few steps toward Glenn. As soon as he realized that, he grinned at her and held up his hand. "Hold on, sugar. You next," he told her. His dick, looking like an over-cooked pepperoni and still dripping fluids, slimy and smelly from no soap and water in the past two days, was now in Othella's mouth. The more she struggled, the deeper it went. "Ruby . . . do . . . somethin'!" Othella choked.

Ruby finally got her wits about her. She knew she had to do something drastic, and she had to do it fast. She moved closer to Glenn and slapped his hand so hard he stumbled, but he didn't fall and he didn't pull out of Othella's mouth.

"You stop that! Take that nasty slab of meat out of my friend's mouth!" Ruby ordered. She repeatedly slapped Glenn's face with both hands, like she was playing patty cake.

"Shet up, hussy!" Glenn hollered, ducking his head. Ruby may as well have been slapping the couch because her attack on Glenn was doing no good. He dismissed her with a wave of his hand. Then he placed both hands behind Othella's head and pushed harder into her mouth.

"Mr. Glenn! You behave yourself! Stop that right now!" Ruby shrieked, clapping her hands the way her mother used to do during her Sunday school lesson when she wanted to get Ruby's attention. "I'm warnin' you for the last time! Or I'm goin' to put somethin' on you that voodoo can't take off!"

Glenn still refused to stop. By now he was so worked up, he couldn't wait to get his hands, well, his dick into Ruby's mouth, too. She had such a big juicy mouth and such thick lips, every-thing a woman needed so that she could blow on a man prop-erly, he thought with glee.

From the minute these two heifers agreed to spend the night in his apartment, he knew that he'd struck gold. What did they expect a man to do when a good time got thrown into his face like a ham bone to a dog? Even if they went to the cops and claimed he'd forced himself on them, what judge in his right mind was going to believe them over him? He'd say that they had aggressively propositioned him, but because he was a spiritually strong man, he'd resisted the temptation. Being a deacon in his church, he would swear that he'd never get fresh with two young girls!

Then he'd tell the judge that the stout dark one had attacked him, cussed at him, and held him down by sitting on his legs while the little yellow one went through his wallet. By the grace of God, he had managed to get the bigger one off him, and he slapped them both. That's when they threatened to run to the police with their outrageous lies. Yeah, that was all he needed to say, he told himself. He'd been in a similar situation a few weeks ago. That wench had gone to the cops. By the time he got through telling his version of the story—how she'd drugged him, ate his food, and then robbed him—the cops arrested *her*! Just let these two wenches try to make a fool out of him. They'd be sorry they ever left wherever it was they came from.

"Mr. Glenn, I told you—turn me aloose," Othella begged, her mouth so full of his meat she felt stuffed. All Glenn did was tighten the grip on her shoulders and push even deeper down her throat.

Despite Othella's vigorous protests and Ruby's threats, Glenn Boates was determined to get what he had convinced himself he deserved. That measly dollar that Ruby had given to him was not enough to cover the night they'd slept in his home and the food that they had gobbled up. Who did they think they were to try and take advantage of his kindness? Well, by the time he got through flooding their young mouths with his sweet jism, and them licking his balls, he'd be happy and their young asses would know better the next time.

"Look, fuck face, this is the last warnin' I'm givin' you," Ruby said, beating on Glenn's chest with both of her fists. He pushed her to the side with a mighty shove. She stumbled and fell, hitting her head on the leg of the couch. She was in such a daze again that she could barely move. But her mind became clear within seconds and she had some thoughts that she couldn't get out of her head fast enough.

One thing that Ruby couldn't figure out was what it was about sex that made men, and boys, act like such fools. Why would they want to do it with somebody who didn't want to do it with them? After Ike and the rest of those boys had stopped wanting to give her pleasure, she didn't chase after them the way some girls chased after boys who no longer wanted them. Nobody had to tell Ruby that there were too many more men in the world for her to get all worked up over the ones that didn't want her. What was it about men that made them act like every piece of ass was the last? she wondered. And what made a man so weak that he didn't care where, who, or what he stuck his dick in? Even a strong man like her father. And it was bad enough that he had cheated, but what made it even worse was the fact that he had done it with an ignorant, low-class slouch like Simone.

Ruby blinked and rubbed her eyes as she watched the scene taking place in front of her like it was in slow motion. "Mr. Glenn, please, please, please let us leave your place right now," she begged, rising and rubbing the side of her head that had hit the couch leg. "We won't tell nobody what you done to us!"

Othella was frantic. "Ruby Jean, I told you to do somethin'!" she yelled again, choking on Glenn's dick. "Hit him! Bite him!" She gagged, and almost threw up. "Make this motherfucker un-ass me!" Othella gagged again, and this time she did throw up. The eruption included everything that she had eaten for breakfast and several ounces of green bile. It spattered on Glenn's hand, foot, and the floor.

"You can go on and puke, little bitchy poo! I don't care! I'm goin' to make y'all clean up my whole place before y'all leave anyway," Glenn laughed.

When Othella finally bit him, he slapped her face so hard she almost blacked out.

"Now you bite my dick again, and I'm goin' to bite you back!" Glenn threatened.

"YOU STOP THAT!" Ruby roared, slapping Glenn's forehead and biting his arm.

"Fuck you," Glenn calmly said. Then he pushed her to the side again, and she fell back to the floor. He guffawed some more. He was so worked up by now and enjoying himself so much, that he got distracted. He loosened his grip on Othella's head, blocking Ruby completely out of his mind. He would deal with her in a few minutes when it was her turn.

Ruby wasted no time getting up and running behind Glenn and kicking him in his butt. And she hit him much harder than he'd hit her. As a matter of fact, she kicked him so hard in his butt crack, that he farted and fell again.

But even that didn't stop Glenn. He got up and slid his pants all the way down to his ankles.

"Y'all got me all worked up, so neither one of you is leavin' here until you both suck off this hard-on *twice* apiece! That'll be my dessert for my lunch and my supper! You can't come up into my place and tease me like y'all done! I'm a man! I expect to be treated like a man! But them blow jobs ain't goin' to be enough now!" he hollered, glaring at Ruby. "I'm goin' to go get a switch and whup both of y'all for comin' up in my place—*cussin'* like sailors, pukin' on my clean floor, and actin' like savages! I want what's comin' to me!"

"All right, old man! You asked for it," Ruby warned. "Since you want to be so hardheaded, you goin' to get what's comin' to you!"

Othella closed her eyes. But when she heard a click, she opened them. That was when she saw the switchblade in Ruby's hand.

Glenn saw it, too, and it distracted him. He released Othella's head and moved back a few steps, but it was too late. With one mighty swoop, Ruby sliced off half of Glenn's dick.

CHAPTER 32

*I*T WAS A GOOD THING THAT GLENN HAD CLOSED UP THE restaurant below. Because the screams coming from his apartment were bloodcurdling. Othella's screams were as loud as Glenn's. She was screaming so loud and hard, she thought her tongue was going to pop out of her mouth. Ruby dashed across the floor and covered Othella's mouth with her hand.

Glenn's screams were suddenly reduced to a whimper, as he passed out and fell backward onto the floor with his hands cupping his bloody crotch. His severed penis lay on the floor next to his leg, like a discarded bone.

Othella removed Ruby's hand from her mouth and asked, "Ruby Jean, what have you got yourself into?" She coughed, wiped her lips with her sleeve, and spat Glenn's juices onto his dingy carpet. She had performed a few blow jobs on some of her former boyfriends. Technically speaking, it wasn't such a bad procedure. When she did do it, she always pretended that it was a stick of sugarcane in her mouth. But Glenn had bad hygiene, and he'd forced himself on her so it had not been a pleasant experience this time. Like intercourse, something as intimate as a blow job should only be done for love or money, she thought. Glenn had offered her neither. And a man with a slab of meat between his legs as smelly and crooked as his was would have to pay her a whole lot of money to do it willingly.

Othella was too afraid, and too stunned, to get closer to the injured man. "Is he dead?" she asked, hopping from one foot to the other like a scared rabbit. "That horny demon."

"If he ain't, he ought to be!" Ruby hissed, spit flying out both sides of her mouth.

"I never thought you'd . . . What is the matter with you, Ruby Jean? We could go to reform school. You can't go around cuttin' off men's dicks!" Othella looked up at the ceiling and shook her head. She rotated her neck and then rubbed it before she returned her attention to Ruby. "You cuttin' Lonnie's throat that time was bad enough, but this is the worst thing I ever seen you or anybody else do!"

"Men can't go around makin' young girls suck their dicks or do anything else that we don't want to. Now let's grab our stuff and get the heck out of here."

"I'm with you on that! We can't stay around here no longer!" Othella yelled, wiping her lips some more. She could still taste Glenn in her mouth.

Ruby hopped over Glenn's body and dashed across the floor to the kitchen.

Othella slid into her shoes and put on the thick jacket she'd worn. "Shouldn't we take somethin' out of here for all the trouble he put us through?" she asked, almost losing her breath.

There was a puzzled look on Ruby's face. She was at the sink, washing Glenn's blood off her knife. She dried it with the same cloth that they had used the evening before to dry Glenn's dishes. "Like what?" she asked, looking around the room with a frown. "Out of all of this junk up in here, there ain't nothin' we can use."

"He might have some money in his pockets," Othella said, standing over Glenn. She made sure not to step in the pool of blood that was slowly forming beneath his body.

"And he's goin' to need it to pay a doctor to stitch him up," Ruby said with a sharp nod.

Just then, Glenn came to. He was moaning and groaning, both hands still covering the place where the rest of his dick was, bleeding like a stuck pig.

"What . . . what happened?" he asked, looking up and around. "What did you gals . . ." Glenn was in absolute disbelief when he realized exactly what Ruby had done to him. "You BITCH! You done cut off my dick!" he hollered, rising with both hands still on his crotch. "I'm goin' to kill y'all!" he threatened, stumbling across the floor. But he was too slow and in too much pain. When he saw the top part of his penis on the floor, he stumbled and fell again. "Get a doctor, y'all," he whimpered. "Please . . . y'all . . . got to help me!"

"Ruby, we got to do somethin'," Othella rasped. "We can't leave this old man like this."

"Do you want to go to that reform school you said we'd go to? You want to find out how bad they treat colored girls in them places? This was self-defense."

"Then let's find a peacemaker and tell him that," Othella pleaded. Even though she had avoided stepping in Glenn's blood, the bottoms and sides of both her shoes were now covered in it. She didn't realize that until she felt Glenn wrap his fingers around her ankle, forcing her to look down. He pulled her down on top of him.

"I'm goin' to kill you, bitch!" Glenn said in a weak voice.

Ruby shot across the floor like a cheetah. She leaned over Glenn and began to pry his fingers from Othella's ankle, but his grip was too strong. His fingers remained clamped around Othella's ankle like a vise. When Ruby bit his fingers, he released Othella, but then he grabbed Ruby around her neck and began to choke her.

Just as Ruby was about to pass out, Othella crawled over to Glenn and bit his arm and he released Ruby.

"You no good dog!" Othella yelled. "You almost killed Ruby Jean dead!" Othella turned to Ruby, rubbing her shoulder. "You all right?"

"Let's get out of here right now," Ruby whispered, holding her neck and coughing. "If we stay here too long, he might kill us."

As Glenn lay on the floor cussing, writhing in agony, bleeding profusely, and praying, Ruby and Othella gathered their things and bolted.

The same elderly couple who had been in the restaurant the day before was approaching. Ruby and Othella ran past them like the Devil was in pursuit. They didn't stop running until they'd reached the end of the fourth block from the restaurant. They spent the next twenty minutes sitting on top of their suitcases on the sidewalk, mumbling disjointed prayers and hyperventilating.

"You think that old couple got a good look at us?" Othella asked as soon as she was able to think and speak clearly again.

"I don't think so. Even if they did, can't nobody prove we done nothin' to nobody. Ain't nobody seen us do nothin' to nobody." Ruby sniffed.

"What about Glenn?"

"What about Glenn?" Ruby asked dumbly.

"He's goin' to tell somebody what we . . . um . . . what you done to him. You cut half of that man's dick clean off!"

"He was makin' you suck it! What else could I do?" Ruby wailed.

"I guess you're right."

"You damn right I'm right!" Ruby shrieked.

"And if it hadn't been you or me, it would have been some other girl, I guess," Othella said, already feeling less guilty about what had happened.

"Not no more he won't," Ruby scoffed, removing something from her jacket pocket. She dropped it to the ground. For a moment, Othella did not know what she was looking at. And when she realized what it was, she could not believe her eyes.

It was the top half of Glenn's severed dick.

Glenn Boates didn't die that day. But he would have if Mr. and Mrs. Charles Townes hadn't arrived in time. The way those two strange teenagers with suitcases had run by made the nosy Townes couple suspicious. And since they were personal friends of Glenn's, they had every reason to go to his apartment to check on him.

Mr. Townes, a retired doctor, stopped Glenn from bleeding to death. He and his wife transported him in their truck to another black doctor in the area, and that doctor patched Glenn up and filled him with painkillers. But there was nothing that either of the two doctors could do to restore Glenn's manhood: his sex life was over.

When Ruby and Othella decided to wander around again, Ruby left Glenn's severed body part on the ground. But before she walked away, she covered it with some leaves, pushing the leaves along the ground with her foot the same way she'd helped her mother spread manure in her garden.

"That ain't goin' to do no good." Othella looked at the mound of leaves with a grimace on her face. She hoped that as long as she lived, she'd never see a man's dick—well, *half* of a dick—in a predicament like this again: on the ground with dead leaves and dirty rainwater. "Sooner or later a stray dog or some rogue coon is goin' to sniff it out and . . . eat it," Othella said, wincing.

"It don't matter that much, I guess. Glenn is a real old man. He don't have too many years left to use his pecker, anyway," Ruby offered, trying to justify her actions. "And he ain't got no wife that he needs to pester in the bedroom no more. He said so hisself."

"That's all true, but that was a real bad thing that you done to that man, Ruby." Othella noticed that Ruby's hands were shaking. She didn't know if it was because she was nervous, scared, or what. And she didn't want to know. Just knowing that Ruby was capable of such an extreme level of violence was enough at the moment.

Ruby gasped. "Let me remind you, girl. That was a real bad thing that he was doin' to you, too—and was goin' to do to me!"

"I know, I know. But . . . well, it was still a real bad thing for him the most. I could have got over what he done to me, sooner or later. I been forced to do even worse things by some of Mama's friends, and I got over that. But what you done to Glenn, he won't never get over. Dicks ain't like hair; they don't grow back. He won't be able to have no more kids."

"I . . . I wish he hadn't provoked me. I didn't really want to cut his dick off! I was aiming for his hand but he moved it at the wrong time. . . ."

"It don't matter what you was aimin' at," Othella mouthed. She couldn't imagine the pain that Glenn had experienced, and would probably experience for a while to come, *if he was still alive*. "Can a man die from gettin' his dick cut off?"

"Them dudes in Italy don't die," Ruby pointed out.

"What dudes in Italy?"

"Them dickless dudes that they train to sing like girls. Sopranos," Ruby explained. "Remember we read about them in Miss Spark's class?"

"Oh yeah. Them eunuchs. But they don't go through what Glenn went through." Othella sniffed. "I wonder how he's goin' to pee now."

"What if it had been a little four-year-old girl he tried to mess with?" Ruby asked, getting angry all over again by just thinking about Glenn attacking a little girl. "Men like him, they don't care where or what they put their peckers in. Before my aunt Della died, she caught one of her field hands screwin' one of her sheep."

"A sheep?" That piece of information disgusted Othella. She

shook her head and cringed. "Men are so unnatural," she mouthed. "I wonder what all Glenn would have done if you hadn't cut him."

"After he got his blow jobs, he probably would have killed us. You keep that in mind when you think about what I done to him," Ruby suggested.

"I will," Othella replied with a shudder. "Let's get out of here. This place gives me the heebie jeebies."

They walked for another hour. Then they stopped in front of a large gray house with a sign tacked to the front wall of the wraparound porch that read: ROOMS TO LET. An old wooden icebox with the door slightly ajar lay on its side on the porch. A dusty red truck, at least ten years old, sat on the street in front of the house. There was an old mattress standing on its side in the cargo area.

Ruby and Othella saw a few black folks walking around the area, so they assumed, and prayed, that this was a black-owned rooming house.

They were relieved when a large, friendly-looking black woman in her sixties, who resembled Ruby's mother, opened the front door and greeted them with a big smile.

"Y'all look like you'd be nice tenants. Don't give me no trouble and y'all can stay here as long as you want," the woman told them. She even sounded like Ruby's mother. With her crisp white apron over a floor-length, flowered duster, her thick gray hair in a bun, she seemed harmless enough. For the first time since they'd arrived in this city, Ruby felt comfortable.

"I got two rooms available, but I'm savin' one for a friend who'll be comin' to spend some time with me soon. If y'all don't mind sharin' the other room, y'all welcome," the landlady told them, still smiling.

After their violent encounter with Glenn Boates, this nice old lady was a refreshing relief. This turn of events seemed too good to be true.

And it was.

In addition to the ten dollars a week *each* that Ola Mae
Logan said she wanted, she expected Ruby and Othella to scrub
the floors of all eight of the rooms in the house as needed, and
do all of the housekeeping that she didn't have time to do.

"The first time one of y'all don't pay your rent on time, I add
another dollar for each day it's late. You will be responsible for
spreadin' the roach paste in your room once a week—and you
have to pay for it out of your own pocket. This ain't no charity
house, and I ain't the Red Cross." The landlady paused to catch
her breath. The big smile was no longer on her face. She continued with her arms folded, looking and acting more like a
prison warden now. "No visitors without my approval, no electric hot plates in the room, no pets, no wild parties, no men in
the room after ten, and no alcohol 'less you got enough for me
and my other tenants. And if y'all don't give me a thirty-day notice before you move out, I'll see you in court. Any questions?"

"Is that all?" Ruby asked, her voice dripping with sarcasm.

"Just one more thing," Ola Mae said, waving a finger in Ruby's
face. She and Othella were still on the front porch clutching
their suitcases, Ola Mae still in her doorway.

"That suit y'all, y'all can stay here as long as you want. That
don't suit y'all, I want you out of my house by the end of the
week," she told them.

"But if we are payin' you for our room, why do we have to do
all of that other stuff, too, Ola Mae? We need time to go out
and look for real jobs. That ain't fair, and you know it ain't,"
Othella protested. She was so tired and frightened, she was
ready to agree to just about anything, in spite of what she'd just
said.

"Like I said, if this don't suit y'all, I want both of y'all out of
my house by the end of the week. As a matter of fact, y'all ain't
even got to agree to move in. Go on back out yonder and see if
you can find a better offer than mine. With this ragin' war, and
half of America gone crazy, y'all goin' to need a heap of luck."

"We know that," Othella said with her head hanging so low, her chin was almost on her chest.

"All right, Miss Ola Mae. We'll take that room," Ruby sighed. She knew when to quit, and she was glad that Othella did, too.

Ola Mae nodded and resumed her smile. But that smile was just as empty and false as the rest of her was. "All right then. Come on in and let's get y'all settled. There's three ten-pound buckets of chitlins in the sink that need to be cleaned for tonight's dinner. Y'all need to clean 'em real soon."

CHAPTER 33

WITHIN *MINUTES* AFTER ENTERING OLA MAE'S GLOOMY rooming house, Ruby decided that she didn't like this new arrangement at all.

They hadn't even seen the chitlins in the kitchen that Ola Mae said she wanted them to clean, but Ruby could smell them. As soon as they stepped into the hallway, the stink hit her in the face like a fly swatter. It was a big house, so cleaning it was not going to be an easy chore. But Ruby didn't want to start complaining too soon. She hoped that things would get easier as they went along. After all they'd been through already, she'd bend over backward to make sure they did.

Under the circumstances, Ruby would have been willing to move in to a broom closet, and that was almost what they got. Ola Mae had assigned them to share a roll-away bed in an elevator-size room at the top of the stairs next to the bathroom that everybody used. A roll-away bed! The very thought disgusted Ruby to the bone. The only other time in her life that she'd been reduced to a roll-away bed was during a Memorial Day weekend two years ago when she and her parents had visited her sister Beulah and her husband. She asked herself again, what kind of mess had she gotten herself into? And how long was she going to live like a stowaway? Not long, she told herself. The incident with the horny restaurant owner was reason enough for her to decide that New Orleans was not the place for her after all.

An hour after they'd checked in, Ruby realized that it was going to take a whole lot of effort on her part for her to tolerate living in this place. Before she and Othella could even unpack, Ola Mae had them on their knees scrubbing her kitchen floor.

"Don't y'all forget I need for y'all to clean them chitlins, too," Ola Mae said. She stood stock still, fanning her face with a magazine as she inspected the mottled black and white rug on the kitchen floor that Ruby and Othella had just mopped and waxed.

They cleaned the chitlins, but they skipped the chitlin dinner. Instead, they stumbled out to the front porch to get some fresh air, and so they could converse in private. The porch steps were falling apart, so they had to be careful where they sat to keep from getting splinters in their butts.

"I didn't come to New Orleans to be no slave," Ruby complained, covering a spot with some old newspaper and then sitting down with a thud. Othella had already done the same thing. "I'd rather work in the cane fields than be crawlin' around scrubbin' floors and cleanin' chitlins. This woman is crazy! And did you see the way them two men tenants of hers looked at us when they walked into the kitchen while we was cleanin' that nasty-ass floor? That bug-eyed one, he was tryin' to look up under your dress while you was bent over!"

Othella considered Ruby's concerns and offered her a hearty nod. "You are so right. I think we need to keep lookin' for a place. We don't want the same thing to happen with the men in this house that happened with that Glenn man."

"If you got a better plan, I want to hear it now," Ruby said. "Let's go talk in our room."

The rooming house had electricity, but Ola Mae was so stingy, she made her tenants keep it turned off most of the time. They had to use kerosene lamps, and they had to supply their own kerosene. That meant no electric lights, and no radio to help pass the time. But time was one thing that Othella and Ruby did not have much of anyway.

Right after breakfast the next morning, Ola Mae ordered them to iron three bushel baskets of clothes. One of the other tenants told them that these were clothes that Ola Mae got paid to iron for people in the neighborhood. Then they had to scrub mold off the walls in her pantry, sweep the front yard, and scrub the rest of the floors. What was so frustrating about all of the cleaning was the fact that mostly the house was already spotless. Ruby and Othella spent hours doing unnecessary housework. And if that wasn't bad enough, they didn't see any of the other tenants doing any housework at all!

"How come we the only ones doin' work in this house?" Ruby asked Ola Mae as she stood watching Ruby wash clothes in the kitchen sink using a washboard and homemade lye soap.

"Old lady Royster in the room next to y'all in her eighties. And the rest of my tenants all work. Besides, they are men. Ain't no woman in her right mind goin' to ask no man to do woman's work. You missed a spot," Ola Mae said in a gruff voice, pointing to a dime-size spot of oil on the sleeve of the man's plaid shirt that Ruby had already rinsed.

That night, Ruby was too angry and too tired to sleep. She paced the bedroom floor for twenty minutes, mumbling profanities under her breath one minute and complaining the next. "One of us better come up with a better plan, or I'm goin' to go stone crazy," she whimpered. She was close to tears.

"I'll come up with somethin'," Othella promised. "Now get in your gown and get to bed."

The next couple of days, Othella disappeared from the house

for a few hours before Ruby got out of bed. Each time when she returned, she told Ruby that she'd just been out walkin', but she never said where she'd been "out walkin' " to. She didn't see any reason to tell Ruby that she had been visiting some of the brothels that she knew about from her mother. Her mother had been a very active prostitute in her heyday. When Othella approached some of the same madams who had pimped her mother and told them who her mother was, they wanted her on a limited basis. "Not much work for colored gals, but you might do all right on account of your young age," she'd been told repeatedly. But when Othella told them that she would only work for them if they hired Ruby, they lost some of their interest. And when Othella described Ruby to them, every single madam lost all interest—even in Othella.

"Where you been all this time?" Ruby asked Othella as soon as she returned from one of her mysterious walks. They'd been in town for four days now, and things were still as bleak as the first day.

"Don't worry about it. I'm workin' on a plan," Othella told her.

The next morning when Ruby opened her eyes, Othella was gone again.

"Where is that high yella gal?" Ola Mae asked Ruby, barging into the bedroom without knocking.

"Uh, she's out walkin'," Ruby replied, buttoning her blouse.

"That good friend that I told y'all about is movin' in this evening, and I want this house spotless. When Othella brings her tail back here, you tell her I want her to scrub that commode and spread the roach paste around in every room downstairs. Is that clear?"

"Yessum," Ruby muttered.

When Othella returned around noon, she ducked and dodged her way through the house. She hid behind doors and peeped around corners, hoping not to bump into Ola Mae. She found Ruby in the kitchen, on her knees, scrubbing spots off the floor with a toothbrush.

"Come on with me upstairs," Othella whispered to Ruby.

"Girl, you got to spread the roach paste around in every single room downstairs. And Ola Mae said you have to scrub that nasty commode, too," Ruby said, speaking low. She looked toward the door to make sure Ola Mae was not eavesdropping. "I am so damn tired. . . ."

"Come on with me," Othella ordered again, pulling Ruby up off the floor by the hand.

They stumbled upstairs to their room and locked the door behind them. Ruby still had the toothbrush in her hand.

"I got some good news and some bad news," Othella announced.

"Give me the good news first. After all we've been through already, I can wait a few minutes more before hearin' some bad news," Ruby said, looking at her hands like they'd suddenly developed scales. There were no scales, but her hands still looked rough and ashy from all the scrubbing she'd done lately. And all the harsh lye soap she'd used to do it.

"The good news is, we can get out of here *today*," Othella informed Ruby. "I got jobs and a place for us. And we can stay there as long as we want to."

Ruby's chapped lips curled up at the ends, forming a smile on her face that was so wide it reached from ear to ear. As soon as she had thoroughly digested Othella's words, her smile faded. "And what's the bad news?" She held her breath as she awaited Othella's answer.

"Remember that old white woman that my mama used to work for when she was young?"

Ruby shrugged. "Your mama worked for a lot of old white women when she was young. So?"

"Uh, maybe you don't remember me tellin' you about this one. My mama worked in the District for a old Irish lady named Miss Mo'reen."

Ruby shrugged again.

"I didn't want to tell you unless I had to, but before I left home, my mama told me if I ran into trouble I could probably get help from Miss Mo'reen. She's one of them liberal white women."

"Othella, I know you tryin' to tell me somethin', but I ain't got no idea what it is. Exactly who is this white woman, and what can she do for us?"

"I went to see Miss Mo'reen today. She said we could both work in her sportin' house," Othella said, looking at the floor.

Ruby snickered and clapped her hands together. Then she looked Othella in the eyes and said, "You brought me all the way to New Orleans so some white woman could pimp me?"

"Not exactly. That's the bad news. She don't think you are the type that men would want to pay. But I'm goin' to turn a few tricks for her. . . ."

"Oh." Ruby was pleased that she wasn't going to be asked to sell her body, but she was also disappointed to hear that nobody wanted to buy her body anyway. "So what will I do for this white lady?" She turned her head to the side, looking at Othella from the corner of her eye.

Othella swallowed hard; she had to in order to get rid of the huge lump that had formed in her throat. She was nervous because she didn't know how to tell Ruby what she needed to tell her, but she managed. "She said you could help out around the house. Be a mammy to the prostitutes' kids, cook, and clean . . . stuff like that. Miss Mo'reen runs a real busy house, so I know them cum-stained bedsheets probably need to be changed a lot. She already got a live-in maid, so you won't have to do everything by yourself."

Ruby gave Othella a pensive look as she shook her head. She was still disappointed. "Oh," was all she could manage. Then she let out a loud breath and said, "I'm goin' to be a maid and a mammy? That's what I left home for?"

"At least you won't have to worry about wallowin' around in a strange bed with a bunch of strange white men," Othella said, trying to sound optimistic.

"To tell you the truth, I would have felt better about myself if you had told me that this white woman wanted me to turn tricks for her, too," Ruby whined.

Othella's jaw dropped. "Do you mean to tell me that you'd rather be a whore than a maid and a mammy?"

"No. But it would have been nice of her to ask me to do it. Even though I would have told her no."

"It's the best I could come up with for now. But if you don't want to come with me, you can stay here, or you can go on back home, or you can do whatever you want to do. I can't stop you. But after what you done to that Glenn man, if I was you, I'd lay real low for as long as I could. Cuttin' half of a man's pecker off is probably a real serious crime."

Ruby ignored Othella's last sentence. "If I'm goin' to be cleanin' toilets and floors and shit, I'd rather do it for a colored woman than a white woman. You can go on, and I'll stay here." Ruby returned to the kitchen with the toothbrush to finish scrubbing up the spots on the floor.

Othella immediately began to pack. Her plan was to leave after Ola Mae had gone to bed tonight. That way, she'd get out of paying rent for the week. And as far as Ola Mae taking her to court for not giving a thirty-day notice that she was moving out . . . well, that old bitch had to find her first. And Othella knew Ruby well enough to know that Ruby would not reveal her whereabouts.

Othella was in the bedroom lying across the bed, leafing through a magazine, when Ruby returned. She ignored Ruby, and Ruby ignored her.

A few minutes past six P.M., Ola Mae hollered for everybody to come to the dining room to eat the fried chicken that she had prepared, and to meet her new tenant. Ruby chose to remain in the bedroom, so she could sulk in private. Othella reluctantly went downstairs, but less than a minute later, she came bursting back into the room with a wild-eyed look on her face.

"Girl, you ain't goin' to believe who Ola Mae's new tenant is!" Othella didn't wait for Ruby to respond. She grabbed her by the arm and led her to the stairs. They tiptoed to the landing and peeped around the corner into the dining room.

Seated at the table in a chair across from Ola Mae, flanked by the elderly couple who had rescued him, was Glenn Boates—*the man that Ruby had castrated!* His two shabby gray suitcases sat by the door.

"That's him!" Ruby managed, her hands trembling. "That's that Glenn man that was attackin' us!"

"Sure enough! That's the man whose dick you cut off!" Othella agreed, nodding her head so hard her neck hurt. "And that's them same two old people that seen us runnin' out of the restaurant after you cut Glenn! Do you want to stay here now?"

Glenn's sorry face looked even longer. And it was so gaunt and lifeless, it was hard to believe that he was still alive. The expression on his face was so unbearably sad that Ruby wished, and she had wished this before, that she had not cut him. However, she knew in her heart that if she was ever in the same, or a similar situation again, she would probably do the same thing, if not something worse. This was one of the few times that Ruby felt a real concern about her temper, and what other mayhem she might find herself in the middle of in the future. This was a thought that she didn't like to deal with for too long, if at all. She shook the thought from her head, biting her bottom lip so hard she almost drew blood.

"As soon as everybody goes to bed and them two old people leave, we need to get up out of here," Ruby said, the words fluttering out of her mouth like leaves falling off a tree.

"You better think long and hard about what you want to do, and you better do it fast. Are you goin' to go back to Shreveport, or are you comin' with me to be Miss Mo'reen's maid?"

"I guess I'll be goin' with you, and be that white woman's maid and mammy," Ruby muttered.

CHAPTER 34

*R*UBY AND OTHELLA WAITED IN THEIR ROOM UNTIL ALL OF OLA Mae's other tenants had turned in for the night and the company had left. As soon as the house got quiet and dark, they slipped out the front door with their luggage. By this time, it was almost four in the morning.

It took three hours for them to walk to Maureen's house, and only because they kept getting lost. It was a long and painful walk, with Othella in front, her feet throbbing like she'd stepped on a bed of nails. Ruby marched behind her like a disgruntled soldier, still cussing and fussing. "Lord have mercy! What did I let you talk me into *this* time?" Ruby growled.

Othella whirled around so suddenly, Ruby bumped into her. "I wish to God that you'd stop all that bitchin' and moanin'. I'm doin' the best I can. And if that ain't good enough for you, you can go on back home, Ruby Jean. Or you can go on back to Miss Ola Mae's house. I'm sure she don't know we left yet, and you still got a key to her front door."

"You know I can't go back to that woman's house. Now that we know she knows Glenn, and he's goin' to be stayin' there, too. All I got to say is, this whorehouse-runnin' white woman better come through or I am goin' back home. You can stay here and hunt for a job and a husband till the Rapture for all I care. I just hope that the next time a man tries to make you suck his dick, you can get out of doin' it on your own."

Othella gave Ruby a contrite look. "Ruby Jean, we're goin' to be all right. I know Miss Mo'reen is goin' to take real good care of us. We'll be happy."

"Livin' in a whorehouse?"

"It's better than livin' on the street! It's better than livin' with people like that Ola Mae woman! And besides, we won't stay at Miss Mo'reen's that long. Every chance I get, I am goin' to go out lookin' for a better job and a nicer place for us to live."

"What if you get pregnant by one of Miss Mo'reen's tricks?" Ruby's question caught Othella completely off guard.

"Pregnant?"

Ruby nodded. "We both know that that bleach douche don't work all of the time," she reminded.

"It works for me!" Othella hissed, resuming her walk down the darkened street. "Now come on. Miss Mo'reen is waitin' on us, and we already much later than I told her we'd get there."

As soon as Ruby and Othella entered the notorious red light district, they received a lot of stares. Nobody bothered them, though, because it was assumed that they were maids on their way to work.

"This is it," Othella said, stopping in front of a large light blue house that reminded Ruby of the old plantations that the slave owners used to run. And that was exactly what it used to be. However, it had been renovated, repainted a few times, and brought up to speed as far as the modern world was concerned. Two white gliders sat on either side of the large wraparound front porch. Red and gold brocade curtains covered every window that Othella and Ruby could see. A neat row of fake red roses had been planted in the front yard and on the sides of the house, resembling a necklace.

"This looks like a palace," Ruby said with a loud sigh, gazing around in awe.

"Well, it looks like a palace, but don't expect to get what Cinderella or Sleepin' Beauty got," Othella advised. "Ain't no charmin' prince goin' to come here to rescue us." A sad look crossed her face, one she didn't want Ruby to see. But she turned her head too late. Ruby saw it and it made her sad, too.

"You don't think we'll be happy in this place?" Ruby asked, shifting her suitcase from one hand to the other. She looked around some more, then back at Othella.

"I left home to get away from my prostitute mama, and look at me. I'm fixin' to be one myself," Othella said. There was such a hopeless look on her face, Ruby wanted to grab her hand and run. But she knew she couldn't do that, at least not yet.

"We don't have to do this, Othella. But you need to make up your mind and tell me what you want to do now." Ruby still wanted to grab her friend's hand and run.

"I still say it's better than us livin' on the streets, or in Ola Mae's house. Only until we come up with somethin' better though," Othella answered with a weak smile. "Just one thing; no matter what happens, I hope to God you won't do nothin' crazy. . . ."

"Like what?" Ruby asked, both eyebrows raised. Othella responded with a blink. "Oh, you mean like what I done to that Glenn man? That couldn't be helped, you know that. I won't do nothin' else crazy as long as nobody messes with me."

Fifty-four-year-old Maureen O'Leary was the third of three daughters in a family of Irish-American dirt farmers. She had been living a shady life in New Orleans since the age of seventeen when her family moved to the United States from Dublin, Ireland. She had two ex-husbands and five estranged adult children somewhere in Ireland.

Throughout Maureen O'Leary's youth people—her relatives especially—had told her that she should have been a man. She was almost six feet tall, and as husky as a lumberjack. She kept her thick, but short, jet black hair slicked back like a duck, or hidden beneath a wig. She acted like a man, too. She smoked cigars, gambled, and fought and drank like an Irish sailor.

With work being so scarce for all women, black and white, Maureen had decided that if she was going to work, it had to be a job that was worth her time. Farming and any other type of mundane labor, which her ignorant father and her stupid ex-husbands had settled for, was out of the question. She was too ambitious to even consider such low-life endeavors. She wanted to live the good life and wear fancy frocks, drink good whiskey, eat lavish meals, and live in a beautiful, opulent house. That meant she either had to marry a wealthy man or make her own money by doing something on the shady side. She didn't have the education or desire to do anything practical such as nursing or teaching, like her sisters. Not only were those jobs dull, but they didn't pay enough money to suit her. The only women Maureen knew of who were making good money were the prostitutes, the madams, and women involved in other criminal activity. She had a female friend who smuggled drugs throughout the country for her gangster husband. When things got too slow in that business for the friend, she turned a few tricks on the side.

Unfortunately, Maureen had never enjoyed sex enough to make it her vocation. But she knew that a lot of other women did, and if they had enough alcohol or drugs in them, a good "adviser" could convince them to perform more tricks than a trained monkey.

Maureen knew that she had what it took to be a good madam. She had convinced herself that this line of work was her calling, after several of her lovers had put the idea in her head. That, and the fact that she had skills as good as any man's when it came to manipulating women.

One of Maureen's lovers, after her second divorce, was a man who frequently visited the brothels in New Orleans' notorious red light District. He helped her find the house that she purchased for her new business venture. He also helped her hand pick her first stable of women, finding them everywhere from the bar room floors to the church pews. She was so charismatic and likeable, she became an im-

mediate success. She was now the most beloved, most successful madam in the District.

Despite the war and thousands of people being out of work, business was booming in the brothels. Some men came alone, sneaking in and out like shy burglars. Some came in groups of three or four. One evening, a busload of rowdy sailors showed up, so horny they were willing to fuck each other if they couldn't get to the women in time.

The men didn't all come to have sex. Some came out of boredom, curiosity, and loneliness. The party atmosphere, the alcohol, and the scantily clad women were potent inducements.

An attractive but obese blue-eyed blond woman in her late twenties greeted Ruby and Othella when they knocked on Maureen's front door. Like everybody else who had noticed them, she assumed they were maids. She shook her finger in their faces and scolded them for knocking on the front door when they *knew* that they needed to use the back door. She was stunned when Othella told her the reason they had come. But when Othella got to the part about Ruby's role, the blonde still made Ruby go around the house and enter through the back door. To show her loyalty, Othella accompanied Ruby and entered through the back door, too.

Mazel Hawthorne was Maureen's longtime cook and maid. She was a bitter middle-aged black woman with ordinary features on a face that almost always displayed a menacing scowl. There was a freshly starched red and white checked bandana tied around her head at all times, except when she went to bed or church. She let Ruby and Othella in, looking at them and their suitcases with contempt. She brusquely ordered them to wipe their feet on the doormat before entering.

Mazel was just as fat as the white woman who had refused to let Ruby and Othella enter through the front door. She wore face powder and some rouge, but it did her no good. She was still plain. Ruby was impressed to see that the white uniform that the Mazel woman wore looked expensive and new.

When Othella told Mazel that Maureen was expecting them, she glared at them, wondering what these two black crows were up to. She directed them to Maureen's room by pointing the way with her finger, shaking her head as they marched across the floor like sneaky soldiers.

Mazel Hawthorne was an astute woman, especially when it involved other black folks. She had a keen sense of smell, and she had already sniffed BIG trouble brewing with these two newcomers.

CHAPTER 35

IT WAS EARLY IN THE DAY AND THREE OF THE FOUR FULL-
time prostitutes who lived with Maureen were still in the bedrooms upstairs that they worked and slept in. The fat blonde
was sprawled on a black velvet settee in the garishly decorated
parlor with a cigarette dangling from her lip, sipping wine from
a coffee cup. Brocade draperies with gold, green, and orange
stripes covered every window. Large pictures of scantily clad
women lined one wall. And as hard as it was to believe, on the
opposite wall there was a large picture of Jesus in a lime green
robe leading a flock of sheep.

"Mazel! Uhh, Mazel! Get your lazy tail upstairs and look in
on them young'uns of mine. Then fix me a hot toddy and some
grits!" the blond woman yelled toward the kitchen area.

Before Ruby and Othella could make their way to Maureen's
room, the mean-looking black woman who had let them in the
back door stomped back through the parlor all the way up to
the top of the stairs.

"I hope y'all here to help Mazel with my kids," the blond
woman said with a smile. "I'm Fanny. But call me Fat Fanny
like everybody else calls me. And y'all can see why," she
laughed, slapping herself on her hip. She rose from the settee,
which was a few feet to the side of a large shiny black upright

piano. Crouching on the floor next to it was a life-size ceramic lion with eyes that looked almost real. Fat Fanny strolled over to Ruby and extended her hand and they shook. Othella shook the blonde's hand, noticing how hot, clammy, and sticky it was. Being that they were in a whorehouse and this woman was a whore, she didn't want to know where that hand had been.

"How many kids do you have, Fat Fanny?" Ruby asked, pleased to see that Fat Fanny was even larger than she herself was. Her face was average-looking, but probably would have been pretty without the three chins attached to her thick neck. One thing that Ruby firmly believed about large people was that they were more tolerant of other large people. If that was the case, she and this woman were going to get along just fine.

"Three, but don't let that scare you none. The two oldest is seven and nine, and boys, so they'll stay out of your way. They ain't much trouble. I usually send 'em to my mama when we get real busy. But my baby, Viola, she's just a few months old, so she needs a lot of attention. I like to keep her around me because my mama is too busy for me to leave Viola with her very often."

Just then, Mazel returned to the parlor, holding the most beautiful little blond baby that Ruby had ever seen before in her life. She looked like the rosy-cheeked, blond, blue-eyed angels depicted on most of the religious periodicals and publications that her father shared with his congregation.

Ruby got misty-eyed just looking at little Viola, and Othella immediately noticed that. She tugged on Ruby's jacket sleeve and led her on to Maureen's bedroom.

Still clutching their suitcases, Ruby and Othella slowly entered Maureen's boudoir, a large room that had once been the back part of what was now the parlor. They were dragging their feet like they were on the way to a guillotine. But there was no need for them to be nervous. Maureen lay on her side like a disabled dolphin, glassy-eyed, but eager to talk. First, she made small talk for a few minutes. She complained about how off key Maurice, her piano player, had been all week, but that he'd still raked in some hefty tips. She also laughingly complained about a gassy client who had stunk up the whole parlor so bad she had to have Al, her black maintenance man, spray the whole house with some pine-scented air freshener. This lighthearted conversation made Ruby and Othella feel so much at ease that they became relaxed, and were soon grinning like hyenas.

Maureen's bedroom was just as gaudy as the parlor. On the wall facing the door was a large picture of Moses parting the Red Sea. There was a loud orange bedspread on her bed. The rest of the bedding—pink sheets, large pillows with pink pillowcases, and a red blanket—were half on the bed, half on the floor. A thick red liquid had been spilled on top of the bedspread, where Maureen had accidentally dropped a large glass of cranberry juice and rum the night before. The bed looked like a murder had occurred in it.

After a few more minutes of small talk, Maureen got down to business. "Othella, your mama was one of my best girls, but I had to let her go on account of she got too uppity too often with my gentlemen friends. She was nothin' but an ignorant, backwoods Cajun, so I couldn't have that," Maureen declared.

Othella and Ruby stood by the side of the bed, tired and so groggy, all they wanted to do was get some sleep. Somehow, they managed not to yawn. Their feet were throbbing from the long walk from Ola Mae's house to Maureen's. And, they were hungry. They hadn't eaten since noon the day before, but those discomforts were the least of their worries. Despite what this woman had told Othella earlier, she didn't look too pleased to be talking to them now. As a matter of fact, she looked annoyed.

"Whorin' ain't easy, but it's just a job, and somebody's got to do it. Men are hornier than ever. And let me make one thing perfectly clear: come hell or high water, men will bend over backward to be with a good whore. If you don't think you can please twelve, or even three or four men a night, this ain't the job for you. Men are just like dogs and snakes, thank God. Next to food, water, and sleep, all it takes for them to stay alive is some kind of sexual gratification," Maureen said with what appeared to be a sigh of relief. "I hope you realize that, Othella."

"I do, Miss Mo'reen, honest to God I do. I know how weak men are, and I know what it takes to make 'em happy." Othella gave a vigorous nod.

"Good! And I hope you know the power of the pussy. If your mama had been smarter, she'd be runnin' her own house by now. When she left here and got herself involved with a Negro, and a *foreign* Negro from some heathen place in Africa—or was it one of them islands down yonder below Florida? Hmm. Anyway, that was the kiss of death for her." Maureen waved her hand in disgust. "By the way, how is she doin' these days?"

"She's doin' just fine, ma'am," Othella muttered, almost biting her tongue. "She does all kinds of stuff."

"I bet she does," Maureen snickered. "She always did. . . ."

"And she still got what it takes to get *beaucoup* men to pay her to go to bed with 'em," Ruby added, nudging Othella in her side with her elbow. "She got 'em comin' and goin', day and night."

Maureen considered this information as she looked Ruby up and down. "I'm not surprised. She was the only one in the house who could swallow."

Up to this point, Maureen had ignored Ruby. But when she finally turned to her, she gave her a warm smile and a nod. "And what was your name again, girl?" she asked Ruby. "Ruby, ain't it?"

"Yessum. Othella told me that you told her that I could stay here, too, but that I don't have to turn no tricks," Ruby said with relief.

"Girl, *you* ain't got nothin' to worry about, as far as gettin' pestered. My clients can be real persnickety when it comes to poontang and other female pleasures." Maureen slowly looked Ruby up and down, her gaze landing on her face. "But you are still good for somethin' around here. Hmm." Maureen scratched her chin and gave Ruby a thoughtful look. "I can see that you like to eat. You can help Mazel in the kitchen with all of the meals. And I expect you to keep my chicken coops in the backyard clean as a whistle."

Maureen paused and sat up in her bed. She removed a thimble from a jewelry box on her nightstand and dipped out a thumbnail of cocaine. She sniffed it and swooned like a woman in ecstasy, and she was. Other than money, there was nothing on earth that Maureen loved more than cocaine. For the next two minutes, she ignored her visitors. When she returned her attention to them, she seemed surprised that they were still in her room.

"What y'all standin' here waitin' on?" Maureen asked, rubbing her nose and sniffing so hard her eyes watered.

"Uh, is there anything else you want to talk about?" Othella asked in a nervous voice.

"Like what? Y'all here, ain't you? I told you, you can both stay a spell," Maureen snapped, looking even more annoyed. "What else is there for us to talk about?"

"Like money. Uh, like how much you can pay us," Othella continued.

From the sour, impatient look on Maureen's face, it was obvious that she did not like to discuss money, at least not with these two. "It all depends on what you do and who you do it to. Now you colored gals generally don't bring in much money most of the time," Maureen said.

"That's why we colored gals are generally poor most of the time," Ruby said quickly. Maureen's jaw dropped. She looked at Ruby like she was looking at a creature from another planet. She didn't like her looks, but she did like her spunk.

"Most of these suckers are really easy to please, Othella. Once you learn the ropes, you can get 'em off with a thorough blow job, a hand job, or even less. And if you get 'em drunk enough, you might not even have to go that far. Any questions?" Maureen was still talking to Othella, but looking at Ruby. "Either one of y'all?"

Ruby nodded. "Yessum. Where do we sleep?" she asked, looking around the room.

"Once y'all leave this room, Othella, you go up to Fat Fanny. She'll fix you up. You can share that room at the end of the hall with her. I was goin' to put you in with Cat Fish, but she got a problem with Negroes." Maureen paused and gave Othella an apologetic look. "Cat Fish's use-to-be husband, and most of the men that she fools around with outside the house, are connected to the Klan. As a white woman, I have to respect that," Maureen explained.

She paused again and turned to Ruby, giving her an apologetic look, too. "You, girl, you go to the right when you leave this room. Keep walkin' until you get to a green door right next to the door leadin' into the kitchen—which is a royal mess, so it's a good thing you got here when you did. You can help that Mazel spruce it up. That'll be her room before you reach the kitchen. And don't let her scare you. She's as big and black as a grizzly, but she's as tame as a kitty cat once you get to know her. There's a roll-away bed in her room, and you and her can share it." Maureen shook her head. "You and her are both a little on the heavy side, so that bed will be kind of crowded. But don't worry. As long as you sleep on your side, you won't roll off and end up on the floor with a splinter in your jaw like that last gal I had helpin' Mazel out."

Another damn roll-away bed! Ruby groaned, but she did it under her breath. This Maureen woman was her last hope in this wretched town, so she didn't want to upset her. Ruby had already decided that if things didn't work out with her, she was going to hightail it back to Shreveport, lickety-split.

"A big, young, strappin' girl like you, you might have to help Al do a few other jobs around the house. All of my girls got kids, but Fat Fanny's is the only ones here. You can give Mazel some mammy assistance. Matter of fact, Fat Fanny just birthed a beautiful baby girl a few months ago. You got here just in time, so you can bond with that sweet little thing—that's if you like babies."

Maureen's last two sentences were music to Ruby's ears. "Oh yessum!" she squealed. "I *love* babies, and especially girl babies! I seen Fat Fanny's baby when we was on our way to your room. When can I start takin' care of that sweet baby?" Ruby's response was so loud and quick, Othella shuddered. She knew that Ruby had not gotten over giving up her baby girl and probably never would. At least she would have a substitute for as long as they remained in Maureen's house.

Othella did not like the idea of Ruby nursing and fussing over that woman's baby. However, from the look on Ruby's face, Othella knew that as long as she could do that, she'd be happy.

And part of the plan was to *keep* Ruby happy, Othella reminded herself.

CHAPTER 36

*I*T DIDN'T TAKE LONG FOR RUBY AND OTHELLA TO GET VERY comfortable in Maureen's house, but there were a few things that bothered them both. They didn't like the fact that they couldn't sleep in the same bedroom, and that somebody was always reminding them that they were not white. But the biggest thorn in Ruby's side was Mazel. Working with her in the kitchen was bad enough, but sharing a room with her was torture. That woman complained about everybody and everything.

Ruby didn't waste any time letting Mazel know that she was no pushover. Even though Mazel was three times her age, and about fifty pounds heavier, Ruby sassed her. She stood up for herself every time Mazel tried to boss her around or scold her.

"Look, Ruby Jean, you can't be walkin' around this house grinnin' all the time. These white folks already think we ain't got but half a brain. Make 'em think you sorry you was born, and that workin' for them is the best thing that ever happened to you. That'll make 'em feel sorry for you and even feel less threatened. And believe me, you won't be smilin' when you start emptyin' them slop jars full of piss and shit, and soppin' up puke off the floor like I do. If anything, you'll be rubbin' vinegar under your nose to lighten up the stink," Mazel barked at Ruby, a few days after they had begun to work together.

"Look, lady, I work for Miss Mo'reen. She tells me what to do and how to do it, not you." There was a sinister expression on Ruby's face, complete with narrowed eyes, twitching brows, and flaring nostrils. "If you don't mess with me, I won't mess with you. Now if you'll get out of my way, I got some slop jars to empty."

Ruby continued to do all of her chores with a smile. Even emptying the slop jars and spittoons and cleaning up puke. She knew that at the end of the day, and usually throughout the day, she could fiddle around with Fat Fanny's beautiful blond baby girl.

Othella didn't do as much smiling as Ruby. For one thing, she didn't get to share that nice room upstairs with Fat Fanny after all. Cat Fish, and at least one of the other women, had complained to Maureen about a black woman sleeping in the same room with a white woman. Maureen decided that it would make more sense for Othella to sleep in the room across the hall from Fat Fanny's. It was primarily used for Fat Fanny's three children. There were four roll-away beds in the room, a large chifforobe, and a few chairs. It was the only bedroom in the house that was not used for entertaining clients. But when a part-time, roving prostitute dropped by and wanted to spend the night, Maureen let her sleep in this room in the fourth bed. Now that same over-used bed belonged to Othella

Al Holly was a large, plain looking black man in his forties. He spoke only when he was spoken to, or when he had to. His position was vague, but from what Ruby and Othella could determine, he was a handyman who did a variety of odd jobs around the house. He was also the mechanic who serviced Maureen's Packard and Fat Fanny's LaSalle. He played the piano when the regular piano player, a hatchet-faced Creole man named Maurice Dozier, didn't show up.

Buster Campbell was another large man in his forties, except he was white and just as plain as Al. He didn't talk much either, and his position was also vague. He was the bouncer who ejected unruly clients and dumped them on the front porch of one of the other houses on the block (after Maureen had instructed him to take all of their valuables). He also did some maintenance work around the house, as well as other odd jobs.

None of the male help resided in the house. Al showed up each day before the sun, every day except Sunday. He stayed until the last client left, no matter how late that was. Mazel had said something about him living across town, and that when he didn't walk to and from work like a field hand, he rode up on his son's bicycle. The piano-playing Maurice lived in a little house three blocks away with a wife and six kids. Buster lived in the toolshed behind the house right next to the chicken coops. He'd never been married, didn't have a woman now, so he paid to have sex with the prostitutes. Because of his loyalty, Maureen rewarded him with a freebie every Christmas and on his birthday; he got to choose the woman.

Fat Fanny and Marielle, a cute brunette in her early thirties, liked Ruby and Othella. They immediately regarded them as new friends. Betty Sue, another cute brunette in her thirties, was cordial, but she didn't interact much with any of the other women. The others, especially Cat Fish, who was an attractive brunette in her late twenties, and the part-time workers, ignored Ruby and Othella as much as possible. The only time they acknowledged them was when they had something to complain about, or when they wanted a back rub or a foot massage. There were times when Cat Fish was downright hostile, especially when she thought the others were too friendly with the two newcomers.

Other than that, it was not a bad arrangement at all.

"I've got a woman to suit every man's needs," Maureen often said, especially to new clients. "I'll line 'em up, so you can take your pick. It don't matter which one you choose, I guarantee you she'll do *anything* you ask her to do . . . as long as it don't involve somethin' with a tail and four legs." And that was true. There was nothing of a sexual nature that the women who worked for Maureen O'Leary wouldn't do, as long as it didn't involve something with a tail and four legs.

Most of the men who patronized the brothels in the District were professional white men—doctors, lawyers, politicians, and a few military personnel. And the majority of them were married to women who were either too cold, too dainty, too worn out, too disinterested, too squeamish, or too clumsy when it came to bedroom activities. It didn't matter who or what the men were to Maureen. Even though she considered herself to be a true patriot of her adoptive country, she would accommodate Adolf Hitler as long as he had money and was willing to spend it. To her, a horny man was a horny man. His politics were his business, as long as it didn't interfere with her business.

Maureen played hostess to a lot of men with wives who had "retired" completely from the physical side of their relationship. These men, some of them still young, felt that they had no choice but to visit the brothels—if they still wanted to feel good. And they were willing to pay for the privilege of spending time with women whose business was to make them feel like men, and give them some physical pleasure. However, the majority of the same men typically ignored women of color who expected to be paid for their services.

Maureen didn't have one single client who had not slept with a black woman, even the ones who claimed to be avowed racists. Several of them had fathered children with black women. Some slept with black women on a regular basis, but always in some back room in a shack in a shantytown. Not only did Maureen and her girls glean this type of information from loose-lipped clients, but Al and Mazel, her only other black employees, shared information on a regular basis with her that they picked up from the black blabbermouths that they associated with. Maureen rewarded her sources to deliver information that could be useful to her in some blackmail-related manner, if that client got out of line. That reward was usually an extra dollar, a glass of whiskey, or a few hours off.

Maureen was pleased that there were enough white men willing to pay to sleep with a black woman in her house when they got drunk or curious enough. That justified her decision to hire Othella. For one thing, Othella was not *that* black. Her features were neutral enough that in the dark, a nearsighted man might even mistake her for an Italian or Spanish woman. Ruby didn't fit that mold by a long shot, and that was the reason Maureen couldn't hire her for her body. But things would take a dramatic turn a few weeks later.

In the meantime, Othella made considerably more money than Ruby. Last week, Othella made several hundred dollars, Ruby made twenty; but that was only because Ruby had received some generous tips from clients who'd requested foot massages. Maureen fed and provided uniforms for Ruby, but she only paid her ten dollars a week.

So that Ruby would not feel bad, Othella assured her that the money she made was their money, not just hers. Unfortunately, she didn't make nearly as much as the white women for providing the same services to Maureen's clients. But whether she made fifty dollars in one night or a hundred, it was more than the *zero* dollars that she had received doing all that housework for Ola Mae in the tacky house they'd snuck out of.

"As soon as I sock away enough for us to live on for at least two months, we gettin' up out of here," Othella told Ruby in a low, nervous voice in the kitchen one morning just before noon, three weeks later. She stood by the stove as she watched Ruby drag a broom across the floor.

"That's nice," Ruby mumbled with a shrug.

The night before had been long and busy. Buster had to eject two unruly clients. One highly intoxicated man had kicked over a coffee table in the parlor, spilling several drinks onto the carpet that Ruby and Mazel had just cleaned a few hours before. Ruby had been up since dawn cleaning liquor stains off the carpet, removing stacks of shot glasses, cups, and spittoons from the tables in the parlor to the sink in the kitchen. She had no idea she was going to be this busy. She didn't complain because at the end of the day, and during the day, too, she got to tend to little Viola.

Ruby was glad that Fat Fanny's two boys stayed out of her way. When they weren't in school, or with Fat Fanny's mother, they were usually in the backyard harassing Miss Maureen's chickens or throwing rocks at the shed where Buster lived. Other than that, they usually stayed in the room that they shared with Othella, doing puzzles and whatever else it was that young boys did in a brothel. They also liked to peek through bedroom keyholes at some of the prostitutes when they were doing their business, and they liked to sneak a few sips of whiskey from a shot glass that somebody had set aside. If anybody other than Ruby noticed what Fat Fanny's boys were up to, they didn't mention it. But the boys' behavior bothered Ruby.

"How are you gettin' along with them boys of Fat Fanny's?" Othella asked.

"If them was my boys, I'd whup their behinds, left and right," Ruby complained to Othella. They didn't get to spend much time with each other so whenever they did, they had some interesting discussions. "White folks don't know the first thing about raisin' kids. It's a good thing they got us to help 'em out."

Othella gave Ruby a pensive look. "Colored kids is lucky, I reckon. At least our mamas and papas know how to raise kids right. Look how me and you turned out. . . ."

They both laughed.

Othella had already acquired a regular weekly morning trick—a moon-faced lawyer with an ass so flat it looked like an extension of his back. She had just spent time with him, paddling his flat ass raw for being a "bad boy" and letting him lick whipped cream off her titties. "Lord knows why this buttless fool comes to this house every Wednesday just to get a whuppin' and to lick *my* titties," Othella complained with a dry laugh as she returned a tall can of whipped cream to the icebox. "Him bein' a lawyer, I am sure he deserves a weekly whuppin', but this whipped-cream-lickin' hobby is ridiculous. Now I could see if I had a rack like you, Ruby." Othella chuckled some more.

"And if you did have a pile of meat on your bosom like I got, your trick would just have to lick a little longer," Ruby teased, still sweeping the floor.

"I wouldn't have no problem with that. I swear to God, I am goin' to buy me a pair of them fake foam titties if it's the last thing I do. It'll be real soon, I think. I'm makin' more money in this whorehouse than I ever thought I would make in my life. But I got to work hard because we won't stay in this house long. Hear?"

Before responding, Ruby looked around to make sure nobody was listening or watching. Maureen had made it clear that she didn't tolerate her employees discussing anything that was related to their earnings. There was a lot of competition in her house so naturally some of the girls made more than others. The last thing that Maureen wanted to deal with, was some jealous heifer running out on her because one of the others made more money.

"We ain't got to rush and leave here," Ruby said, blinking. "I don't mind livin' in this nice big house. And that Miss Mo'reen, she is a nice old lady."

Ruby's words caught Othella off guard. She coughed, grabbed her throat, and swayed slightly from side to side. Then she reared back on her legs and held onto the counter. "Excuse me?" she gasped. "I thought you was itchin' to move on as much as I am."

"I am." Ruby stopped sweeping, clutching the broom handle

with both hands. "But this ain't as bad as I thought it was goin' to be."

"It's that baby girl, ain't it? You done got attached to Fat Fanny's baby girl."

Ruby dropped her head and nodded.

"You don't mind livin' in a whorehouse just so you can be with that baby?"

Ruby looked Othella straight in the eye and nodded again. "And you know exactly why I am so attached to that little baby. . . ."

CHAPTER 37

*O*THELLA ROTATED HER NECK AND MASSAGED HER FOREHEAD with her eyes closed. A few seconds later she looked at Ruby and shook her head in exasperation. "Ruby Jean! Do I have to keep remindin' you that you are a preacher's daughter?"

"And do I have to keep remindin' you that that preacher daddy of mine is a low-down-funky black dog that couldn't keep his pecker in his pants where it belongs? You forgettin' I seen him doin' his dirt with your mama with my own eyes?"

"So what? Your papa is just a human bein'!"

"So am I. He ain't perfect, so he don't always do the right thing, and neither do I. There's whores everywhere and men that are goin' to behave the way they been doin' since God put 'em here. No matter where we go, we are goin' to run into them, and every other kind of devil loose in the world. Yeah, I'm attached to Fat Fanny's baby girl. But as long as we stay here, at least we got food, a warm bed, ain't nobody beatin' on us or molestin' us in no other way, and we makin' a few dollars to boot. So I don't mind bein' here in this whorehouse after all."

"That's because you ain't got to be layin' up under all them sweaty men like I do. All you do is cook and clean."

"And take care of that sweet little Viola," Ruby added with a vigorous nod. "And every now and then her two brothers."

Othella let out a heavy sigh and shook her head. "I should have realized this might happen. I should have knowed that you would want to stay around here as long as you could, just because of that little baby girl."

"What's wrong with that? What else is there for me to do?" Ruby asked with a pout, stomping her foot on the hard floor with so much force the empty pots and pans on the counter rattled.

"Look, girl. You need to get over losin' your baby. You can't let that situation rule your life."

"It's a little too late for you to be tellin' me that! That's the one situation I can't get off my mind," Ruby shouted.

"Well, sooner or later you have to! You can't let this one thing keep eatin' at you. You might as well be attached to a ghost, girl!"

A hopeless look crossed Ruby's face and she practically whispered, "My baby didn't die. She ain't no ghost." She sucked in her breath and held it. She looked like she was going to cry, but she didn't want to. She knew that once the tears started, she would have a hard time stopping them. "Sometimes I wish she had died. We could have buried her somewhere. That way I could have had a grave to visit and put flowers on from time to time. At least that way I would have been able to move on, not be left hangin' like I'm hangin' now. That would have been better than me never knowin' how she doin, how she bein' treated."

"Ruby, you don't want to spend too much time workin' in a whorehouse just so you can be close to a young baby. That ain't normal. But I'll pray for you, and I won't stop buggin' God until He do somethin' for you that'll make you feel better."

Ruby was glad that Othella had finally said something that indicated she had more sympathy for her. But she didn't appreciate what Othella said next: "I know how you must be feelin'. . . ."

Ruby was so taken aback by Othella's words, she thought she was going to jump out of her freshly starched white maid's uniform. A headache had formed, one so painful it moved from the back of her head to the front within seconds. It almost brought her to her knees. She moaned under her breath and massaged her forehead. "You didn't have no baby and have to give her up, Othella. How in the world can you fix your lips to say you know how I'm feelin'?"

Othella immediately regretted what she'd just said. "I'm sorry. What I meant was, I hope I never know what it is you feelin'."

"And I hope you don't neither! Especially since you and your mama is the reason I lost my child!"

"How many more times are you goin' to ride me about that? How many more times do I have to tell you that if you had *really* wanted to keep that baby, you could have? Me and Mama didn't hold no gun on you! We didn't twist your arm that night! We didn't beat you to make you do nothin', so stop puttin' all of the blame on me and my mama!" The more Othella talked, the more she stunned and angered Ruby.

"Y'all talked me down to a frazzle that night! I didn't know which way to turn! Y'all rode me down until I couldn't do nothin' but what you and your mama told me to do! And another thing—your mama made it clear that she wasn't about to take a chance on my daddy jumpin' to the conclusion that Ike was my baby's daddy." Ruby didn't care if somebody entered the kitchen and heard her rant. "You owe me, Othella! You are goin' to owe me till death do us apart!"

"Owe you? Owe you what?" Othella cackled like a hen, long and loud. This didn't even faze Ruby because she had already reached her limit of tolerance.

Ruby's lips moved, but nothing came out for a few seconds. She didn't know how to answer Othella's question. "I don't know *what* you owe me, but you ought to care more about what I feel—over losin' my child—than you been showin' so far."

"I do. I do care, Ruby. I swear to God that if I got pregnant today and gave birth to a baby girl in nine months, I'd give that child to you," Othella yelled. She stopped talking long enough to catch her breath. "If I thought it would make you happy. If I thought it would make you stop moanin' and groanin' about that other baby."

If a house had fallen out of the sky and landed on Ruby, she could not have been more stunned by what Othella had just told her. This news made Ruby's whole body tremble.

"You would do that for me? You would be that good to me?" Ruby asked, her voice low and weak. Othella was glad to see that a smile had replaced the hostile expression on Ruby's face. "I could have one of your baby girls?"

"Yeah, if it would make you happy!" Othella barked. She was getting tired of this clumsy conversation, and was willing to say whatever it took to appease Ruby—even if it meant telling Ruby that she could have one of her children if she had some.

Othella wouldn't think about what she'd just said again until many years later when Ruby did *take* one of her children, a baby girl—and not because Othella gave the child to her. . . .

"You been a real good friend to me, Othella. Ain't a woman nowhere, not even in the Bible, that would offer to do for me what you just did," Ruby said, now beaming.

"I'm glad you realize that. Now let's do our business here for Miss Mo'reen and move on. Once we do, we'll find husbands. And with that big juicy body you got, you'll probably have a house full of kids before you reach twenty-one. When this war mess is over, I know a lot of prisoners of war will be comin' home from them foreign countries so desperate and horny that they will marry the first woman they see. And that could be you and me." Othella gave Ruby a harsh look and shook her finger in her face. "In the meantime, you concentrate on somethin' other than babies!"

The smile disappeared from Ruby's face. She gave Othella a look that Othella couldn't interpret. She couldn't decide if Ruby was angry, happy, confused, or what.

"I got to wash these dishes next, so I can go upstairs and tend to that sweet little baby Viola," Ruby said in a calm voice.

Othella returned to the parlor where there was a modest crowd of men waiting to trot upstairs and do their business with the women of their choice. She noticed right away that none of the other prostitutes, including the four rovers who had checked in that morning to work for just a few hours, were present. And there were twice as many men present than there had been when she left the parlor, less than fifteen minutes ago. Maureen occupied the middle spot of the settee, flanked by the Harrison brothers on either side. Four other men stood off to the side of Maureen. She stared at Othella, giving her one of her "where the hell have you been?" looks.

Othella stopped and stood next to Maurice, who had just made it to the house to play his piano. He was playing a lively tune, the kind of swing number that Othella's brother Ike used to play when she threw her wild parties. She wanted to ignore Maureen, but she knew not to. Maureen was still looking at her and her mouth was moving. Othella couldn't imagine what Maureen was saying to the men surrounding her.

". . . that colored gal there, that's Othella. She swallows . . ." Maureen said proudly. The men all started talking at once. "Hold on, gentlemen. She's young and eager and the day is early. Y'all can all spend time with her before you leave." Maureen rose, pulling one of the Harrison brothers up by the hand. "Now you get over yonder and acquaint yourself with Othella." Maureen gently pushed her client with both hands in Othella's direction. She returned to her seat and resumed the conversation that she'd been involved in before Othella entered the room.

"Now where were we?" Maureen asked, accepting a fresh drink from Buster at the same time. Buster gave her a rare smile and quickly returned to his post by the door. He crossed his arms and fixed a menacing look on his face. When he was on bouncer duty, he spent most of his time serving drinks, which he preferred to hauling drunks out on their ears and looting their pockets.

"It was that goddamn war," one of the men drawled.

"They say that damn fool Hitler ain't about to stop until he's ruined all of Europe," somebody else said, his drunken voice full of contempt.

"Who would have thought that we Americans would be fightin' Japs and Krauts at the same time?" another man asked.

After a few minutes of the men's war chatter, Maureen spoke in a voice with extreme exasperation. "Now y'all look! Y'all came here to forget about that damn war. There are much more pleasant things for us to be discussin'," she scolded.

"You're right, darlin'," said a grinning Father Dyer, a priest from a nearby parish. "And I'm lookin' at somethin' right now that's much more interestin' than Adolf Hitler."

Maureen followed the priest's gaze and smiled. Marielle had just returned to the parlor and was moving toward Maureen and her audience. Walking behind her like he had a stick up his behind was Patrick Cone, one of Marielle's regular clients. He tipped his hat and rushed toward the exit.

Maureen lifted her chin to address Marielle. "Sugar, as soon as you slow down, you need to pay a little attention to Father Dyer."

Marielle gasped and tilted her head to the side. Speaking as she raked her fingers through her hair, she said with a snicker, "Slow down? This is the first time I've been able to leave my room since I got up this mornin'. I don't remember the last time I got pestered back to back for several hours straight. By the end of the day, my hole will be so dilated, a train could pass though it!"

Maureen and most of the guests within hearing range guffawed.

"Business sure is boomin' these days," the other Harrison brother agreed, fishing a watch out of his pocket, frowning at the time. "My time is money, and I'm about to run short of it if I don't get some female attention soon."

"Well, be a little more patient!" Maureen said quickly, rising again. She looked toward the staircase and was glad to see that Othella was already on her way back to the parlor. The other Harrison man who had left the room with Othella was a "minute man," literally. That was how much time it took to satisfy him. He appeared a few moments after Othella. There was a huge smile on his flushed face as he smoothed back his thick gray hair with one hand and adjusted his suspenders with the other. He returned to the settee and lit up a thick Cuban cigar. The other men noticed the joy on the Harrison man's face and in his demeanor.

"What's that gal's name?" Father Dyer asked, looking at Othella as she approached an elderly man with a helmet of curly white hair. "She sure is easy on the eyes."

"Her? That's Catherine. She used to be married to one of them fool Fisher boys. We call her Cat Fish," Maureen replied, smiling and nodding toward Cat Fish, who had suddenly appeared behind Othella. "You could put your whole foot down her throat if you had a mind to."

"Pffftt!" the priest snapped, waving his hand like he was shooing away a fly. "Hell's bells, woman! I know Cat Fish! I don't mean her. I'm talkin' about that brown-skinned gal. The one that took a walk with Bob Harrison a hot minute ago. I . . . uh . . . them brown-skinned gals really know their way around the bedroom."

"Her? Oh, that's Othella," Maureen said. "As you can see, she's got another trick already lined up. As a matter of fact, she's booked solid for the next few hours. And let me tell you one thing, she is well worth the wait." Maureen rose. "However, since you have a itchin' for dark meat, I might have another piece that you might like to taste. If you can hold your horses, I'll take you to her after things slow down."

"I can wait," Father Dyer said eagerly. His eyes lit up and he licked his lips.

"Good! Now have another drink," Maureen yelled.

CHAPTER 38

*I*T WAS ALMOST TEN P.M., AND BUSINESS HAD NOT SLOWED down. It had gotten even busier. Not wanting to lose any money, Maureen turned to Father Dyer, who had been sitting patiently on the settee all this time with a major hard-on. "I don't want to hold you up any longer. I can tell from that look on your face, and that bulge in your lap, that you are about to bust out of your pants. Come with me, sugar pie," she told the priest, pulling him up from his seat by the hand.

Father Dyer followed Maureen to the kitchen where Ruby sat at the table, rocking little Viola to sleep.

Ruby wore the blue and white plaid bathrobe that she'd brought with her from home. She was barefoot, and she had just marcelled her hair, something she liked to do even though nobody except her seemed to appreciate it.

Ruby was surprised to see Maureen in the doorway. From her glassy, bloodshot eyes, it was obvious that the madam was highly intoxicated. She was dressed to the nines in a black and gold floor-length dress with a collar that looked like a cabbage leaf. A tapered red wig hugged her head like a skull cap. Her face was more heavily made up than usual. Heavy lines of black eyebrow pencil outlined her eyes, like oil along the edges of a well-paved road. Rouge covered not only her cheekbones, it had been applied all the way down to the bottom of each jaw. Several coats of bloodred lipstick claimed her lips, as well as the top half of her front teeth and part of her chin. She looked more like a piñata tonight than the femme fatale she thought she was.

It was rare for Maureen to be in the kitchen at all during the day, let alone on a busy night like tonight. Ruby was even more surprised to see the tall white man with her—wearing a cleric's collar at that. The first thing she thought was that one of the whores was on her deathbed and required last rites.

"Ruby, this here is Father Dyer," Maureen introduced.

Ruby looked at the priest. She wondered why he was looking like he was so uncomfortable. He kept blinking his eyes and shifting his weight from one foot the other, like somebody with a bladder issue.

"Ma'am?" Ruby said, clutching the baby closer to her bosom. "Is somethin' the matter?"

"I know this ain't part of your job, and you can say no if you want to. But do you think you can help us out tonight? We are busier than ever before," Maureen said, glancing at the priest.

"Wait a minute now!" Father Dyer began, a hand in the air. "I know you don't think—"

"Will she do?" Maureen asked, nodding in Ruby's direction.

Instead of answering, Father Dyer gave Maureen a horrified look, and then he bolted.

"What was that all about, Miss Mo'reen?" Ruby asked, puzzled.

"Uh, nothin', Ruby. You continue with whatever you were doin'," Maureen muttered, giving Ruby a pitiful look. "I thought maybe . . . oh never mind."

Ruby didn't want to admit it to herself and certainly not to Othella, but the truth of the matter was she missed sex! Being in a house that was about nothing but sex, how could she not? It had been so long since she'd enjoyed the pleasure of a man. She was at a point now where she would have jumped into bed with just about anybody, even a white priest. But to get paid for it, too? That would be icing on the cake.

"Miss Mo'reen, I know you didn't hire me to, uh, you know . . . with the men. But I'll do it if one of your men friends want me," Ruby said, speaking in a voice that was just above a whisper. She held the baby closer.

Maureen gave Ruby a dismissive wave, and then she shook her head so hard her wig shifted. "Ruby, I appreciate your willingness, but that probably ain't never goin' to happen. My clients are way particular as it is, and even more particular when it comes to colored women. The truth is, you remind these men too much of the mammies that raised 'em. But if there was somethin' special about you, it'd be a different story. Until that happens, you ain't got nothin' that none of my clients would want, I guess."

Except for the heavy rain, one that flooded some streets and forced several businesses to close for a few days, things went on as usual for the next couple of days. At least they did for Ruby. But Othella was having more racially motivated problems with Cat Fish than usual.

That Friday night, Othella threatened to slap Cat Fish for calling her a coon under her breath as she walked by on her way to a room upstairs with Father Dyer. He had come back and waited three hours for his turn with Othella. But the priest had prevented Othella from getting violent.

"Honey child, I advise you to pray for Cat Fish, and to be a little more tolerant. Because of the way she was raised, she can't help herself. She's from a very conservative family. It's her nature to be a bigot," Father Dyer said gently, his arm around Othella's shoulder as they entered the room that Marielle and another client had just left.

As the priest began to undress, removing his cleric's collar first, kissing it, and then carefully placing it on the nightstand next to the bed, Othella padded across the floor and opened a window. Despite the fresh air, Othella knew that no matter what she did, every business room she entered upstairs would always smell like sex. It was a very distinctive odor, like a combination of sweat, unwashed feet, and raw fish. Spraying the room with air freshener and frequently changing the sheets on the bed didn't eliminate the problem. She could still smell sex no matter what they did. It was like putting perfume on a pig.

Othella promised herself that once she got away from the business of prostitution, she would *never* slide into such a deep dark hole again. Growing up with it had been rough. She wasn't going to grow old with it, too. She didn't want to be like her mother. . . .

"It's goin' to take more than prayin' for me to put up with that Cat Fish wench! She ain't goin' to quit agitatin' me until I slap her silly!" Othella hollered. "That heifer is just itchin' for me to kick her ass, that's all." Othella slowly removed her light blue negligee and eased down on the bed. By this time, Father Dyer was completely naked and in bed with the sheets covering everything but his head. He had even concealed his hands. "What do you need tonight, honey?" Othella purred.

"Whatever you got a good mind to do," Father Dyer said with a grin. He knew what he wanted, but he was too shy to tell Othella. "Um, Maureen tells me that you have a special talent. . . ." he added, hoping that she would know what he was talking about. As a priest who had just recently lost his way, he didn't know how to tell a woman what he wanted the way most men did. In some ways, he was like a young boy, just getting acquainted with the female body.

Othella giggled and rolled her eyes. "You must be talkin' about somethin' in the oral category," she guessed. And from the way the priest's face lit up, she knew that she'd guessed correctly. She immediately snatched the covers off Father Dyer's body and lowered her head into his lap. She was surprised and disappointed to see that the piece of meat between his thighs was about the size of her thumb. She hesitated and then blinked. Then she stared at the man's nub in disbelief. She felt

sorry for this nice man and wondered how a man with so "little" to offer a woman got by in life, especially with prostitutes.
Then she thought about Glenn Boates. Even after Ruby had
cut off half of his dick, he still had more than Father Dyer. That
made her feel even sorrier for this nice man. It was bad enough
that he had backslid from the church to the brothels, but to do
so with such a tiny dick seemed pointless.

"What's wrong, sugar? Why are you takin' so long . . . to . . .
uh . . . you know?" Father Dyer asked with a worried look on
his face. "Would you rather we do somethin' else first?"

"I can do whatever you want me to do," she said, forcing a
smile.

He smiled back and gently pushed her head back toward his
lap.

Othella was glad that he'd taken the time to bathe; he had a
nice clean smell. Some of the men who showed up in expensive
suits smelled like they hadn't bathed in a week. She was trying
to act like she was having a good time; she wanted the priest to
request her again, maybe on a regular basis. But it was taking a
lot of effort on her part, because she couldn't stop thinkin'
about her problem with Cat Fish.

It was a good thing that Maureen had not witnessed the altercation between Othella and Cat Fish that had taken place
earlier. She had warned them that if they didn't get along better, they'd both be working in another house, or on the streets.

"There is more than enough men to go around in this house.
I don't know why that cow won't leave me alone and let me take
care of my business," Othella complained to Father Dyer about
Cat Fish, after she'd made him climax three times in twenty
minutes.

Father Dyer sat up, propping his head with three of the four
pillows on the bed. In the dim light of the lamp on the nightstand, he looked so young and handsome with his green eyes,
big white teeth, and thick brown hair. He had the good looks of
the kind of white man whom Othella wouldn't have minded

marrying. But that was unlikely to happen and she knew it. Despite the fact that her mother was technically white, Othella had black blood on her father's side. That made her, as well as all the rest of Simone's kids, black by law.

"Well, my dear, that young lady is from a family that's even more racist than the general white southern population. You can't expect *her* to be willin' to deal with the same dicks that have been inside *you* on the same night," Father Dyer said with a mild sigh. "Things of that nature just ain't fittin', darlin'. When I was growin' up, the colored woman who was my mammy used to hold me against her ample bosom and rock me to sleep—in my very own bed. She was also as loyal as a puppy to my whole family. But she wasn't even allowed to use the same glasses that my family members drank from. And then there was the bathroom facilities. That was way off limits to my mammy. When she had to go, she had to go in a bucket in my daddy's garage." The priest shook his head. "You people are a strong lot to put up with the way things are in this country and not complain about it."

Othella gasped. "Father, I don't know how well you know colored people, but let me tell you one thing—we do complain. We have been complainin' for almost four hundred years. We can complain our heads off, but if ain't nobody listenin', it ain't doin' no good."

"I know, sugar. But like I said, Cat Fish is from a very conservative family. She can't help how she feels about you people." Father Dyer tapped the top of Othella's head, the same way he petted his dog.

"I don't care how racist her family is. Marielle told me that Cat Fish's daddy got a baby by the woman who cleans for them," Othella said, moving closer to the side of the bed because she didn't like the way the priest was petting her on the head. He didn't get the message, so she grabbed his hand and placed it on his chest. He got the message. "A colored woman black as the ace of spades."

"Honey child, that don't mean nothin'. The fact of the matter is, every dollar you make is a dollar that Cat Fish thinks should be goin' into her pocketbook. I've been one of her regulars for several weeks now—before you came. Heh heh heh." The priest lifted his hand to tap Othella's head again, but stopped. Instead he reached for the package of Viceroy cigarettes that he'd placed on the nightstand.

"But there are women in this house takin' tricks from Cat Fish left and right," Othella wailed, taking a puff from the cigarette that Father Dyer had just lit.

"True. But they are white women. There is a big difference in them takin' business and money away from a gal like Cat Fish. I've been around whores for years. Even before God called on me to serve Him. I know white women who would rather have a snake slide up into them than a pecker with a colored woman's juice on it. That's just the way it is."

Othella liked spending time with the priest. In addition to him being fairly young and fairly handsome, he was a nice man. And not only was he quick, but it didn't take a lot of effort to satisfy him.

"Well, my dear, you can trot on back down to the parlor any time you're ready. I'm done for the night," Father Dyer told Othella, giving her a quick peck on her cheek.

"Uh, if you don't mind, can we lay here like this for a few minutes more? I want to give Cat Fish a little more time to cool off," Othella said.

Not only had Cat Fish not cooled off, she was angrier than ever. Instead of trying to secure another client, she was in her room holding Marielle and Fat Fanny hostage as she ranted.

"Cat Fish, you can stay up here in this room the rest of the night and sulk about what Othella done if you want to. But I got to get back down to the parlor and make my money," Fat Fanny said, checking her makeup and hair in a handheld mirror. "The only reason I'm in this room with you now is because

I had to come upstairs to take another quick douche. I've been itchin' like I got fleas down below." She laid the mirror on the bed and frowned. "I sure enough hope I ain't got the clap again."

"And you need to lighten up on this beef with this colored girl. She's a nice girl, once you get to know her," Marielle said to Cat Fish, adjusting her girdle. "Damn that Mazel! I told her to make sure she bought me the right size girdle, and I see she didn't!"

"My grandpa would roll over in his grave if he knew that I was even in the same house with a nigger whore," Cat Fish complained, as she attempted to help Marielle into her girdle. It was about the twentieth complaint she'd lodged since her confrontation with Othella, and it was one complaint too many. Maureen entered the bedroom just in time to hear Cat Fish's last complaint.

"That's it! That's it!" Maureen hollered, shaking her fist at Cat Fish. Cat Fish jumped back and let go of Marielle's girdle so fast, Marielle stumbled and almost fell to the floor. "I ain't goin' to stand for no more of your foolishness. You got till mornin' to pack your shit and get out of my house!"

All three of the prostitutes gasped. Cat Fish had gasped so hard, she choked on some air. Marielle had to slap her on the back to help her catch her breath before she could speak again.

"But—but, Miss Mo'reen, I'm a *white* woman. You can't fire me on account of a colored woman! It ain't fittin'!" Cat Fish shrieked, turning to the other two women for support. "Fat Fanny, Marielle, y'all say somethin'!"

"See there! I told you this was goin' to happen if you didn't behave yourself," Marielle yelled, shaking a finger in Cat Fish's stunned face.

"Me, I ain't got nothin' to say. I got them three kids to feed, so I can't be put out on the street, and I sure don't want to live with my mama, or go back to my ex. Cat Fish, honey, you started cookin' your own goose from the day them colored girls moved in, and tonight you burned yourself. And don't you forget to return my bustier before you leave!" Fat Fanny hollered.

Just then, Ruby entered the room. There was a huge smile on her face. Viola was in her arms with a smile on her little face that was almost as big as Ruby's.

"Fat Fanny," Ruby began, looking around the room wondering why everybody was so quiet. "Uh, I just wanted to bring the baby in so you can give her some sugar before I put her to bed." She felt the chill in the room, but knew it had nothing to do with her. She held her breath and didn't acknowledge the chill, and she kept her smile in place.

"Miss Mo'reen, there's a man in a white suit at the bottom of the stairs waitin' to speak to you," Ruby continued. "He's right horny and cute, and itchin' for some female attention. He even pinched my butt when I walked by just now." Ruby tried to look serious but it was hard for her not to keep smiling, especially after that cute man had pinched her butt.

Cat Fish's jaw dropped open so wide, you could see the back of her long tongue. "Miss Mo'reen, I will sure enough get up out of your place! Now that I know you got white men comin' here that's got so little shame, they'd tetch a booger bear like *Ruby* on her butt—I wouldn't stay here if you paid me in gold!"

CHAPTER 39

THERE WAS NO END IN SIGHT FOR THE WAR. THOUSANDS OF young, and not so young, men from various parts of the country were dying thousands of miles away from their homes and their loved ones. Some had come home missing a limb or two. But as long as that missing limb wasn't the one between their legs, they made their way to the brothels.

One night, a week after Cat Fish's departure, one of those ex-military men entered the house, grinning like he was ready to fuck the world. There were three fingers missing from his right hand and a black patch covering his missing right eye. He was new in town and had been referred by a friend. He was a small man with a big sexual appetite, and he didn't let his missing fingers, or his missing eye, slow him down. However, he was most interested in one type of female: virgins.

"A virgin? You came here lookin' for a virgin?" Maureen gave the man an incredulous look. She was tempted to feel his forehead to make sure he wasn't sick and didn't know what he was saying. "Sir, this is a WHOREHOUSE, not a convent. You ain't goin' to find no virgin in here," Maureen laughed. "Now if you don't mind some low quality virgin poontang, you might want to take a ride out to the bayou and cut a deal with one of them swamp men. Most of them got at least four or five real young daughters that might suit your needs."

"That ain't what I want to spend my hard earned money on," the man said, looking around the parlor, smiling. His name was Dobie Boyle. His family tree included two judges, a senator, several lawyers, and a beauty queen. He had devoted the last twenty of his forty-five years to a military career. He sniffed when Othella pranced in. "She's a pretty piece for a colored gal."

"And she's been busted more than a drunk driver," Maureen said, shaking her head. "You could probably slide your whole fist up in her."

"Well, you find me a nice clean virgin, and I will pay you four times what you normally charge. As long as she ain't still in diapers and still has her own teeth, I don't care how young or how old she is."

"Oh? Are you that liberal?" Maureen asked, her eyes wide with anticipation. She was so determined to procure this man a virgin, she was already counting her finder's fee.

Dobie wasted no time replying. "I am more liberal than that, my dear. I don't care how fat she is or what color she is. As long as her cherry is still in place, I don't care. I want me some fresh pussy, and that's that. I got plenty of it over there in Germany. As soon as those fräuleins laid eyes on us American soldiers, they practically served us their cherries on a platter. I guess you could say those gals ruined me for life, because I am right spoiled now."

"Oh, I know all about them European gals. Me bein' from Ireland and all, though I no longer speak with a brogue." Maureen paused and let out a coquettish chuckle. She was glad to see that Dobie had such an eager look on his face. "I had a gal from Paris workin' for me last year for a few months. She suddenly got religion and took off. Now I can't help you if you insist on havin' a foreign gal, at least not tonight. But I might be able to locate you somethin' close, say a Creole or a Cajun?"

"No problem. The lady could be from Mars for all I care," Dobie replied, nodding and licking his thin lips. He hadn't even had a drink yet, and his breath was already as foul as cow dung. Every time he spoke, Maureen had to lean her head back and hold her breath to keep from gagging on the fumes floating out of his mouth. But she'd dealt with a lot worse. Bad breath was nothing compared to some of the other things her girls had to put up with. Last night, Marielle had been with a highly intoxicated man who'd lost control of his bowels right after he'd climaxed while he was still on top of her. She'd been so upset that Maureen dismissed her for the night. She had helped her clean herself off, and let her keep all of the money that she'd made for the whole week. But Ruby had been even more upset because she had to clean up the mess in the bedroom. Maureen had given Ruby the rest of the night off, too, and she still wanted to do something nice for Ruby because as far as she was concerned, Ruby had been traumatized by that gruesome episode as much as Marielle.

"You sure you don't care what she looks like?"

"Maureen, I am serious. I do not care about that. I keep my eye closed durin' the whole session anyway. I always did. It adds a bit of mystery to the act," Dobie said with a wink.

"And her size and color don't matter, you say?"

"That's what I said. Nor does her age." Dobie stopped talking for a moment, and scratched the side of his neck. "Hold on. Let me back up. I need to clarify one thing some more, though: no babies and no hags. She's got to be at least thirteen. And no offense, but I don't want some old crone in your age group. Forty-five is as old as I'll accept. As long as she's never been touched."

Maureen wanted to laugh and then show this persnickety fool the way out. Finding a teenage virgin was not that far-fetched, but did he seriously think that he'd find a forty-five-year-old virgin anywhere in New Orleans?

"I get it. Well, I'll see what I can do for you, sir. Now don't

you move until I come back, hear?" Maureen gave Dobie a
thoughtful look before she rose from her settee and shuffled
across the floor to Othella. "Is Ruby still fresh?" she asked,
whispering in Othella's ear with a hopeful look on her face.
While she awaited Othella's response, she glanced at the man
she'd left sitting on the settee, who was dying to bust open a
virgin. She smiled, nodded, and waved at him. He smiled, nodded, and waved back. The way he kept crossing and uncrossing
his legs, Maureen knew that his dick was on fire, and that she
didn't have much time to get this man into bed with a virgin.

"What? What do you mean by that?" Othella asked, her
heart thumping. She had been very cautious since Maureen had
fired Cat Fish. She was still worried that if that racist bitch
came back to make another fuss, Maureen might fire her, too.
"Uh, do you mean is Ruby clean?"

"I know the girl is clean, but that ain't what I meant. She is
fifteen, and I know how frisky you colored gals are when you
get that age. Y'all drop your drawers and spread your legs earlier in life than regular folks. But Ruby bein' a preacher's girl,
and bein' a little on the heavy side and a little plain, I figured
she might not have crossed that bridge yet. Is she still a virgin?
She sure enough looks and acts like one. And I hope you say
she is, because there is a whole bunch of money at stake."

Othella was momentarily speechless. She didn't know where
this conversation was coming from, or where it was going. The
most important thing to her was, she didn't want to disappoint
the madam. She knew that as long as Maureen was happy with
her, she and Ruby would have a place to stay. "Yes, ma'am, she
sure is still a virgin. But let me tell you right now, she can't wait
to get herself busted," Othella lied. The hungry look on Maureen's face puzzled and frightened Othella at the same time.
"But bein' a preacher's daughter, Ruby is right shy when it
comes to things like, uh, you know . . . Before you approach
her about it, let me put a bug in her ear first. She's real mentally

limited. But I got her trained so good, she'll do anything I tell her to do."

"Good! You go hunt her up, and do that right now then," Maureen commanded.

Othella sprinted across the floor toward the kitchen, weaving her way through the crowd squeezed into the parlor. She almost knocked down Fat Fanny and the man that she was buttering up.

As soon as Othella reached the kitchen and swung open the door, she almost gagged on the smell of boiled pig ears and cabbage greens, the same meal they'd had the day before. She didn't have time to complain, but she would later on. "Where is Ruby at?" she asked Mazel.

"I don't know where that lazy heifer at. Them same dishes been sittin' in that sink for two hours," Mazel snarled, chewing on a toothpick. "She probably off somewhere nursin' that white woman's baby like she always do when she supposed to be helpin' me."

"Miss Mo'reen need her in the parlor straightaway," Othella reported.

"For what?" Mazel asked, hand on her hip. "Since when do Miss Mo'reen want the help up in there 'round all them fancy peckerwoods? Especially Ruby with her musty, rusty, dusty self. What done happened in that parlor this time? Another one of them clumsy oxes done wasted a highball on the floor, and Miss Mo'reen want Ruby to sop it up, or what?"

"Never mind all that. If you do see Ruby before I do, send her to me. I'm goin' to wait for her in the parlor by the piano man," Othella said.

Othella left the kitchen, but she didn't return to the parlor. Instead, she galloped upstairs and checked every room that was not occupied, but Ruby was nowhere to be found. Othella returned to the parlor and saw the impatient look on Maureen's face. She skittered back into the kitchen, ignoring Mazel, who was still fussing about the dishes in the sink, and ran out the back door.

Othella found Ruby sitting on a stump in the backyard, serenading Viola with a lullaby that Ruby had made up herself. The baby was cooing like she was in heaven. There was just enough light coming from the moon and the dim coal oil lamp on the back porch steps for Othella to see the ecstatic look on Ruby's face.

"Ruby Jean!" Othella called, almost out of breath. Ruby didn't notice Othella right away. Othella had to call her name again and snap her fingers.

"What?" Ruby said gruffly, clutching the baby like she was afraid Othella was going to snatch her out of her arms.

"Remember that trick with the chicken blood in a capsule?" Othella asked with an anxious look on her face. She had worked up a sweat from running around looking for Ruby. She wiped some of it off her forehead with the back of her hand.

"What? What about that trick?" Ruby asked, wiping a few drops of sweat off Othella's chin with the tip of her finger.

"We might have to use it on one of Miss Mo'reen's new tricks tonight. He's out there in the parlor, ready to mount a goat as long as it's a virgin."

"Well, there is plenty of chicken blood available," Ruby snickered, nodding toward the three chicken coops that Maureen kept at the end of the backyard next to the toolshed. "But you ain't got to kill no chicken tonight to get no blood. There's plenty of blood in a bowl in the icebox, with them three chickens that I helped that lazy-ass Mazel cut up this evenin' in case somebody wants a snack later."

"Ruby, you need to come with me," Othella said, holding her hands out to Ruby. "Now give me that baby. I'll take her to Mazel, or I'll put her to bed myself—which is where she should be now anyway. I swear to God, you spoilin' this child. Come on!"

"You ain't makin' no sense," Ruby commented, handing the baby to Othella.

"You need to get to your room and get them capsules, and we got plenty of alum for a tightenin' up douche. I'll bring that bowl of bloody raw chicken to you so you can drain enough blood to go in one of them capsules."

Ruby chuckled. "That's fine with me. My sister told me that all you got to do is slide it up in you, and when the man sticks his pecker in, it'll bust open right away. Then all you have to do is lay there and moan and hump. After he pulls out, tell him what a Romeo he is. That's all you got to do."

Othella shook her head. "Uh-uh, honey. That's all *you* got to do."

CHAPTER 40

*T*HE ONE-EYED VIRGIN-LOVING MAN WAS SO IMPRESSED AND pleased with Ruby, he kissed her on the lips after he'd busted what he believed to be her cherry. It had been hard for Ruby to pretend she was having sex for the first time. She had hollered and yelped in pain, and then she had moaned like a woman in ecstasy. She had writhed like her butt was on fire, the same way that she had done when Othella's brother took her virginity.

"There, there, darlin'. The soreness won't last but a little while, and the next time will be so much better for you," Dobie told her, massaging her thigh.

"That's . . . that's what Miss Mo'reen told me," Ruby whimpered.

"But the fact of the matter is, it had to happen sooner or later." Dobie sniffed. He felt right proud of himself and more manly than he'd felt in a long time. "I love bein' a gal's first, but it's gettin' harder and harder to be that lucky in this day and age," Dobie told Ruby, kissing her this time on her sweaty forehead. "I know I hurt you." He paused long enough to fish a cigar out of his jacket pocket and light it. After a few hearty puffs he continued. "But a big strappin' gal like you, you'll get over it real quick. Now what did you say your name was again?"

"Ruby, sir." Being polite and demure helped her look more

innocent, and she was having fun playing the part. It just reinforced her belief that a horny man could be played like a fiddle.

"Ruby what?" Dobie sniffed again and brushed a lock of her marcelled hair off her face. He felt so comfortable with her. Even though she was young enough to be his daughter, she reminded him of his mother, a buxom woman with breasts like eiderdown pillows. He gently squeezed one of Ruby's massive breasts, then the other. He was becoming aroused again.

"Excuse me? You want to know my whole name?"

"Whatever it is, it ought to include *Mama* Ruby. For a gal with no experience, you sure enough know how to make a man feel good. And generally speakin', nobody but a man's mama can do that. Not that me and my mama ever did anything unnatural in the bedroom." Dobie chuckled and took another drag from his cigar, then passed it to Ruby. She hated smoke of any kind and couldn't understand how anybody could put anything as vile as a cigar, a cigarette, a pipe, chewing tobacco, or a cud of snuff in their mouth. However, she knew that if she remained in a whorehouse she would eventually put things that were even more vile in her mouth. Othella had told her about a client who had paid her to suck his toes. She held her breath and puffed on the cigar, choking until Dobie slapped her on the back and gave her a mighty hug. He chuckled again. "Sorry, darlin'."

"That's all right. I sucked in too much smoke too fast, I guess."

"As I was sayin', you ought to be called Mama Ruby," Dobie told her again. He was now holding her hand, squeezing and caressing it like a real lover. Ruby just didn't know what to do with herself! Was being a whore this easy? she wondered. It must be. Why else would she be feeling so special lying in this strange white man's arms, and getting paid to be with him? He obviously liked her, and it didn't bother Ruby one bit that it was because she reminded him of his mother. Becoming a mother was her main goal in life anyway!

"Mama Ruby? I like that—and it suits me. See, I always wanted to be somebody's mama," Ruby chirped, surprised at how giddy she was feeling now. She suddenly felt remorseful about deceiving this nice and thoughtful man with the missing fingers. He was probably closer to being a virgin than she was. "Um, you glad you spent some time and money on me?"

"Of course I am, sugar. Now don't you take this the wrong way, but if you wasn't a colored gal you'd be makin' a real killin' in a place like this." Dobie paused and lowered his voice. "Now you ain't no beauty, and I suspect you already know that. But the truth is, most of the women who work here wouldn't win no blue ribbons in a beauty contest. Between you and me and the bed post, that Fat Fanny reminds me of a white elephant. But you . . . you know . . ."

"I know I'm colored, and that's a heavy burden to some folks, but it ain't to me. I wouldn't want to be anything but colored. You white folks got too many problems for me. And, y'all can't cook that good. . . ." She laughed and Dobie laughed and agreed with her assessment. "But I am glad that you didn't let my color stop you from spendin' time and money on me," Ruby said, rising, tickling Dobie under his chin. "I better go now."

Ruby dressed and eased back downstairs to her room where she washed herself up, just enough to remove Dobie's scent and body juices. She also took a vinegar/bleach/vanilla extract douche, and haphazardly prayed that it would prevent her from getting pregnant. But if she ended up pregnant again anyway, oh well. She just hoped that it would be with another baby girl.

Afterward, Ruby returned to the kitchen where Mazel was preparing fried chicken, crawfish, and hush puppies. She frowned as soon as she saw Ruby's face.

"Where you been, gal? I been runnin' around like a fool all night tryin' to keep these stinky white folks happy! They been eatin' like pigs at a hog trough! If you don't get the spirit, I'm goin' to talk to Miss Mo'reen about gettin' me another gal to help out!" Mazel thundered, slathering the crawfish with home-made butter and then sprinkling them with cayenne pepper. "When I was your age, I was way more responsible!" She accidentally dropped a crawfish on the floor, stooped down to retrieve it, blew on it, and returned it to the tray. She looked at Ruby again. "You done put that baby and them other two young'uns of Fat Fanny's to bed, girl?"

"Yessum," Ruby said, grabbing her apron from a hook on the back of the door and joining Mazel at the counter. She ignored the suspicious look on Mazel's mean face.

"You smell like smoke," Mazel noticed. "And why you got on that blue dress instead of your work uniform? You goin' to church or a juke joint later tonight, or what?"

Ruby rolled her eyes and reared back on her legs, hand on a hip. "So what? What damn business is it of yours?"

Mazel gasped and shuddered. Then she blinked hard a couple of times, clearly frightened by Ruby's outburst. "I . . . I just thought I'd mention it."

Ruby let out a disgusted sigh and shook her head, not taking her eyes off Mazel's face. "What do you want me to do now?"

"You can haul this tray into the parlor and see who needs a drink refill. I swear to God, these white folks get on my nerves so bad with they lazy selves! Ain't no reason in the world why Miss Mo'reen can't get them whore heifers to take turns carryin' these trays and refillin' glasses. I been on my feet, workin' my fingers to the bone since eight this mornin'." Mazel was about to say something else but she held her tongue when she noticed the smug look on Ruby's face. "You look like you just swallowed a carp. One of them horny crackers lose his billfold and you found it or what?"

"Oh no. It ain't nothin' like that," Ruby said. Just then Fat Fanny rushed into the kitchen holding Viola, who was wide awake. As soon as the baby spotted Ruby, she started to sniffle and reach for her.

"What's wrong with the baby, Fat Fanny?" Ruby asked, alarmed. "She was sleepin' like a log when I checked on her a little while ago." Before Fat Fanny or Mazel could say anything, Ruby was already on the other side of the room, pulling Viola out of Fat Fanny's arms.

"I declare, this child has become so fussy. Must be the croup." Fat Fanny was exasperated and slightly drunk. She was slurring her words and swaying from side to side. "Ruby, you are the only one that knows how to calm her down. She was makin' such a fuss, them boys of mine couldn't get to sleep if you knocked 'em out with a baseball bat. I had to leave Mr. Stanton in the middle of his session. Poor thing. This is the second time I've done that to him this week. With his sensitive male equipment, I sure hope he don't end up with the blue balls again."

As soon as Ruby wrapped her in her arms, the baby stopped fidgeting. And even as young as she was, she was obviously pleased to be back in Ruby's arms. She immediately stopped crying and started smiling, cooing, and beaming like a lighthouse.

"Ain't it a wonder to see a baby that young smilin'?" Fat Fanny noticed, fanning her face with a dustpan that she had snatched up off the floor.

"That's just gas," Mazel suggested. "A child that young don't know nothin' about nothin'."

"This one does. She always behaves like a lamb when she is with Ruby. I swear to God, Ruby, if you still around when she start talkin', I wouldn't be surprised if she called you mama."

"That's *Mama* Ruby," Ruby indicated.

"Huh?" Fat Fanny responded, puzzled. She fanned herself faster.

Mazel snickered and shook her head.

"Mama Ruby. That's my name now," Ruby said, putting a lot of emphasis on her words. She lifted her chin so that her nose was way up in the air, where she thought it should be. "I'd ap-

preciate it if y'all would remember that." Ruby turned to Mazel
and added, "All of y'all."

Mazel glared at Ruby and was tempted to maul the side of
her head. If there was one thing she couldn't stand, it was an
uppity colored woman, especially a young one. And as far as she
was concerned, that's just what *Mama* Ruby was. Her attitude
was going to get her in a whole lot of trouble, maybe even mur-
dered. But what was even worse was the fact that she seemed
like the kind of wench who thought she could get away with
murder. A cold chill crawled up Mazel's wide back like a lizard.
She didn't know if the cold chill meant she was having a bad
premonition or if she'd drunk too much of Miss Maureen's
elderberry wine. But there was suddenly something very ominous about Mama Ruby, and that scared Mazel.

"Mama . . . Ruby is your new name, you say?" Fat Fanny
mouthed. She looked like a snowman dressed in a snug white
floor-length negligee, her hair pinned back on her head. She
raised an eyebrow and gave Ruby a curious look.

Mazel rolled her eyes and gave Ruby an impatient look. She
still had on the white uniform and white apron that she wore
every day. As big as she was, her bosom was flat. Her breasts,
even longer than Fat Fanny's, had dropped from her chest and
settled on her stomach like bibs.

"Yep! I'm Mama Ruby from now on," Ruby said with a mysterious smile on her face. She gently rocked the baby, thumping her cheek at the same time.

"Hmmph! Why would a girl your age want to be called
Mama anything?" Mazel asked. Even though Ruby was scaring
her, Mazel's tone of voice was as abrasive as ever.

"Because that's who I am now," Ruby said firmly, shooting
Mazel a hot look. Mazel felt another cold chill on her back.
And the ominous feeling that had come over her a few mo-
ments ago seemed even more ominous.

"Well, I must say, it is a cute nickname. How did you come
up with it, sugar?" Fat Fanny smiled.

Ruby shrugged. "Oh, it just came to me out of the blue, I guess," she said with a tight smile.

From that day on, Mama Ruby was the name that everybody called Ruby Jean Upshaw. And that was the name that she would be called until the day she died.

CHAPTER 41

MAZEL WAS IN THE PARLOR SERVING MAUREEN'S GUESTS. IT had been two hours since Ruby's tryst with the nice one-eyed gentleman. She was glad that she was alone in the kitchen, until Maureen's sudden appearance.

"I thought you had put that child to bed for the night," Maureen said, entering the room where Ruby sat at the table rocking baby Viola and chomping on some pork rinds.

Ruby stopped chewing and swallowed hard. With a giggle she said, "I did. But I just love holdin' her. I can't wait to have my own baby."

"Well, I hope you will. But in the meantime, I just wanted you to know that you really came through for me tonight."

Ruby wiped crumbs from her lips and chin with the palm of her hand. "Thanks, Miss Mo'reen," she fumbled, rising. The baby was sound asleep and had been for over an hour. But Ruby had become so attached to Viola that whenever she got a hold of her, it was hard to let her go.

"Miss Mo'reen . . . uh . . . do you mind callin' me Mama Ruby from now on?"

Maureen gave Ruby a puzzled look. "Mama what?"

"Mama Ruby. That's what I want to be called now." Ruby blinked and rolled her eyes.

"Why?" Maureen folded her arms, but at least she didn't look mad or annoyed. "Where is this comin' from?"

"It's a real long story, Miss Mo'reen," Ruby said with another giggle. "I'll tell you all about it when you got some free time."

"All right. I'll call you whatever you want me to call you, if it'll make you happy. Who is this *Mama Ruby*? A elder relation of yours?"

"No, ma'am. It's me."

Maureen gave Ruby a blank look. "Ruby, I mean, Mama Ruby, have you been in my liquor?"

"No, ma'am, I ain't been in your liquor or nobody else's liquor. I am stone cold sober."

Maureen moved closer to Ruby. She leaned forward and sniffed, wiggling her nose like a rabbit. "Naw, I can't smell no alcohol on your breath, so I guess you are sober." Maureen shook her head and looked Ruby in the eyes. "You don't like your regular name? You got to dress it up? And if you don't mind me sayin' so, 'Mama' is not such an attractive nickname on anybody, unless they happen to be a mama, which you ain't yet."

Ruby pressed her lips together for a brief moment. She gently rocked Viola, even though she was still snoozing like a puppy. "Miss Mo'reen, if it'll make you feel any better, I like your name. When I have my first girl, I'm goin' to name her after you."

This information pleased Maureen. She smiled. "Hmm. That's a right nice thing of you to say, Ru, uh, I mean Mama Ruby. I hope I'm around when you do. It'd make me right proud." There were tears in the old woman's eyes. She started to dry her eyes with the tail of her flowing black dress, but Ruby snatched a towel off the table and handed it to her.

"Did you want me for somethin' else, Miss Mo'reen?" Ruby asked, lowering her voice. "Is there another gentleman you want me to socialize with?"

"Come here," Maureen said, beckoning with her finger for

Ruby to follow her out to the hallway. As soon as they reached the parlor room entrance, Maureen leaned close to Ruby's face, smiling like she had won a prize. "Dobie was so pleased with your, uh, *talent*, he gave *us* a huge tip." Maureen handed Ruby a wad of cash, all in one-dollar bills. "Now what else did he give you?"

Ruby looked at the money in her hand. Then she looked up at Maureen. "Nothin', ma'am. He told me that you told him to pay you, and that you would give me my share."

"That's right. And I just did." Maureen cleared her throat and gazed at Ruby with mild contempt. "Any questions?"

Ruby exhaled as she counted the money. Her mouth dropped open and both of her eyebrows rose. Then she looked at Maureen and asked, "Ten dollars? Is this all I get for all I done for that missin' fingers, one-eyed, white man?"

Maureen's eyes got big and she placed her hands on her hips. Even though she was one of the most liberal madams in the District, she still maintained a certain level of decorum when it came to dealing with low-level people, meaning people of color. "Now I like you, Mama Ruby, and I hope that you will be with me for a long time to come. But you know better than to cross the line with *me*, girl."

"But Miss Mo'reen, I done that deed for you on account of, I thought I'd get some big money. I can't do a whole lot with the ten dollars a week you pay me to cook, clean, and babysit." Ruby paused and shifted the baby around in her arms. "And I take care of them chickens you got in the backyard, I wash clothes, I maintain your flower garden, and I—"

Maureen's eyes got even bigger. She gave Ruby the most incredulous look she could manage. "Hush up! I know everything you do around here! And I have to admit, you do it damn well—which is why I make you do things that Al or Mazel ought to be doin'. Them lazy boogers! But this is the thing, darlin'." At this point Maureen steered Ruby back toward the kitchen. "You are livin' here in my house, free. You are gobblin' up my food—that I pay good money for—like a 'gator, free. I even give you them maid frocks you wear, free! What more do you want, girl—diamonds and gold? I bet you can't go no place else and make out this good! Now you count your blessin' and behave yourself, you hear?"

"Yessum," Ruby mumbled, surprised at how well she could hold her tongue when necessary. "I guess I'll take little Viola upstairs and put her back to bed." With a contrite look on her face, she turned to walk away.

"And another thing," Maureen hollered, tapping Ruby on the shoulder.

Ruby stopped, but she didn't turn to face Maureen. "What is that?"

"If you stay in your place as long as you're in my house, me and you will be real good friends. Don't start no mess, won't be no mess. Is that clear?"

Ruby turned her head around just enough so that Maureen could see the contempt on her face. "That's clear. It's so clear I could see it even with my eyes closed," she said dryly, her lips barely moving.

"That's better. Now you put that young'un back to bed, and take the rest of the evenin' off and do whatever it is you want to do. You deserve it. I've been meanin' to show my appreciation for all you've done lately. Go do somethin' that'll make you feel good. Go to that night revival at that colored church tent thing across town that I heard about from Mazel and Al. They went to it last Sunday, and it done them both a world of good. They've both been real humble most of the week, like they should have been already. I didn't even have to remind Al to spray the mattresses this mornin'. And Mazel hasn't been burnin' the grits like she used to every mornin'."

"Mazel said I had to help her serve your guests later when it gets even more crowded and busier tonight," Ruby said. "Do I?"

"Mazel don't pay your wages. She ain't got no more say

about nothin' around here than this itty-bitty baby in your arms." Maureen removed the child from Ruby's arms and started to walk away. "You tell Mazel that if she's got a problem with anything you do, she can talk to me about it. And take my word for it, I'll straighten her out real quick. Now you git! Go put on some glad rags, and go out and enjoy yourself some-where. I'll put this child to bed myself."

An hour and a half later, Ruby entered the Smart Set. It was a run-down bar on a dark narrow street that catered to black folks, and also white folks who didn't have enough money or class for anything better. Other than a few servicemen at the bar, there were only about five other patrons present.

Ruby didn't want to spend her money on a drink. And she certainly didn't want to take a chance on the bartender embar-rassing her by asking her to show some ID to prove she was of legal drinking age. She ordered a large root beer and took it to one of the six booths in the dimly lit place.

It had been a long, busy day, but Ruby had enjoyed it. She couldn't stop thinking about her intimate encounter with the man who had suggested her new nickname. Mama Ruby . . . oh, she liked that.

When a tall black man in his midtwenties approached her and asked her name, she promptly answered, "Mama Ruby." He was in a soldier's uniform and that impressed her. To her, a military uniform was an indication that a man had some dig-nity. He was cute, too, and that almost made her giggle. Her oldest sister, Flodell, had told her one time that calling a grown man "cute" was an insult. Dancing bears and trained seals were cute; good-looking men were handsome, her sister had in-sisted. And this one certainly was handsome. He was almost as dark as Ruby. He had dimples and nice thick juicy lips. His slanted brown eyes gave him a slightly Asiatic appearance, which Ruby found very exotic. She cleared her throat and shook her head to put her thoughts on hold.

The soldier didn't even ask if he could join her. He removed his cap and slid it securely under his belt—a belt that seemed like it had been glued to his trim waist. Then he slid into the booth, sitting so close to Ruby their knees touched. She liked his smell. It was a deep husky smell that she wouldn't have been able to describe if somebody asked her to. But at least it was a clean smell. She glanced at his big hands, glad to see that each one still had four fingers and a thumb.

"Mama Ruby, you ain't got no business out here by yourself this time of night. A pretty young thing like you," the bold soldier said, grinning. It was the first time in her life that a man had called her pretty. All of the males she knew had only referred to her as looking "healthy" or "juicy" when they paid her a compliment. A few had told her that she was "ripe," which she assumed was another vague compliment. "Where is your man at tonight?"

"I ain't got no—uh, my man is overseas fightin' in this crazy war," she lied, blinking and pressing her lips together so she could keep her face straight. "We got married last month. . . ."

"Your man is lucky," the soldier mouthed.

"You mean because he ain't been killed or shot or nothin' over there where they fightin' the war?"

"Well, that too. But what I meant was, he's a lucky man to have a woman like you."

CHAPTER 42

*R*UBY WAS GLAD THAT SHE HAD DECIDED TO WEAR ONE OF her low-cut blouses. Even though people told her on a regular basis that she was not pretty, *until tonight,* she knew that she had at least one thing on her body that most men appreciated: titties to die for. The soldier's eyes spent more time inspecting her bosom than her face.

"Them Japs and Germans is blowin' up the world, and this is a time for Americans to be together," the soldier added. "Especially us colored folks."

"You got that right. So how come you out here by yourself then?" Ruby asked, sitting up straighter in her seat to make her titties look even bigger. She felt sorry for Othella from time to time. In spite of her beauty, it must have been hell having a chest like a boy. Maybe if she could afford to, she'd buy Othella some of those fake foam titties herself when Othella's next birthday rolled around.

"That's why I came over here to talk to you," the soldier answered with a grin. "Uh, that's a nice blouse you got on there. A real good choice for a spectator like me." He laughed. Ruby laughed with him as she gently touched his hand on the table and squeezed it. It was so refreshing to hold a hand that had all of its fingers. A sad thought crossed her mind as she thought about that nice Mr. Dobie, who had paid so dearly for her virginity. She wondered if he had ever tried to fondle a woman with so many pieces of his right hand missing. Well, she thought, part of a hand was better than part of a dick. She had no idea why she couldn't stop thinking about Glenn Boates and how she had castrated him for trying to take advantage of her and Othella.

"You seem distracted. Your eyes keep wanderin' off," the soldier noticed. "You must have a whole lot of other things on your mind."

Ruby let out a mournful sigh and placed a hand over her heart. "Oh, I was just thinkin' about my husband, hopin' he's safe, and that he makes it home like you." She squeezed her admirer's hand again.

She was enjoying the soldier's attention, and she didn't hesitate to accept the beer that he offered to share with her.

The handsome soldier told her that he had just come home from Italy with an honorable discharge. And that despite several surgeries, he still had a bullet lodged in the back of his right thigh, and a "few other injuries" that he didn't want to discuss. "I will be gettin' a nice check from Uncle Sam till the day I die, and I got a good job drivin' for a dizzy old peckerwood that's so forgetful he pays me twice for doin' the same job. Now I'm sittin' here with my pocket full of money, and I sure would like to spend a few dollars on you."

"If you give me twenty dollars, I'll do anything you want me to do," Ruby said, surprised at how bold she was behaving. And she was thinking, *If I'm goin' to be a whore, I want to be a good one.*

"I was thinkin' more like *two* dollars. I ain't no Mr. J. P. Getty, and to tell you the truth, *you* ain't no twenty-dollar piece. Shit. Them white gals over there in Italy, they did it with me for even less than that! Some did it for free!"

The soldier didn't wait for a response from Ruby. He grabbed what was left of his beer and returned to the bar.

Ruby finished her root beer and exited, unaware that the horny soldier was right behind her.

"All right. I'll give you twenty dollars for a piece of tail, and yours better be worth it!" he yelled as soon as he caught up with her.

The soldier resided in a flophouse two blocks down the street from the bar, and that's where he took Ruby. He was good to her. He gave her a twenty-dollar bill before she even got naked. Then he made her climax within one minute after he'd eased her down onto the hard roll-away bed in the middle of his one-room residence. As soon as he finished his business, he played with her titties for a few minutes. Then he turned over on his side with his back to Ruby. When he began to snore about ten minutes later, she assumed he was asleep. She got up and quietly dressed in such a hurry that she put her panties back on inside out. She left the room running, carrying her moccasins in her hand. As soon as she got out of the building, she slid her feet into her shoes and smoothed down the sides of her corduroy skirt. She looked up at the window in the soldier's room. He had already turned off the light and for some reason that made her feel cheap and sad. It seemed like the end of another chapter in her convoluted life in New Orleans.

During the long walk back to Maureen's, Ruby realized how much she had missed having sex. The white man who had paid for her bogus virginity earlier that night had not been that good of a lover, but he had aroused her. The soldier who never even told her his name had intensified things and finished what that white man had started. And the way he had humped and pumped into her in that squeaky roll-away bed of his, it was hard for her to believe his story about the bullet in the back of his leg.

Ruby didn't know how much longer she and Othella would be living in Miss Maureen's house. But one thing she did know was that she had to have a man, or some men, who could give her some pleasure on a regular basis. If not, she was going to go crazy.

The next morning, Ruby knocked on Maureen's bedroom door and entered before she answered. "Miss Mo'reen, I need to talk to you about somethin'. Uh, a business deal."

Maureen was surprised, annoyed, as well as curious. She waved Ruby into her room and motioned for her to lock the door. Ruby did as she was told, then shuffled over to the side of Maureen's bed and stood in front of her as stiff as a stuffed bird.

"What's the matter? What business deal do you need to discuss with me? Them chickens got loose durin' the night again?" Maureen asked, rising with the white cut-off stocking cap that she slept in every night still covering her head. She removed the cap and swung her bony, varicose-vein-covered legs to the side of the bed, giving Ruby a harsh look.

"Your chickens is fine, Miss Mo'reen. I just come from takin' a look-see at 'em."

"Why ain't you in that kitchen yonder helpin' Mazel out then? You done tended to them kids of Fat Fanny's?"

"Yessum. I did everything I am supposed to do every mornin'," Ruby said proudly. "I done even emptied all of the spittoons, ashtrays, and every single slop jar from last night. I got the first batch of sheets soakin' as we speak. And I didn't forget to use that Epsom salt solution on them jism stains that some of the men leave behind."

"Then why do you have that hang-dog look on your face?"

Ruby swallowed hard and looked Maureen in the face, staring at her in a way that made the madam uncomfortable. "Miss Mo'reen, you know any other men that want to pay to be with a virgin?" Ruby asked, speaking in a slow manner, shifting her weight from one foot to the other.

Maureen was pleased to see that Ruby had put on her apron, something she had to be reminded to do from time to time. She was going to suggest to her that she might also consider wearing a checked scarf on her head like Mazel. Maybe that would help her remember her place.

Maureen dipped her head and narrowed her eyes as she gazed up at Ruby, wondering what kind of business deal this oafish youngster needed to discuss with her. "Uh . . . why?"

"Because I know now how bad some men want to be with virgins." Ruby paused, pleased to see a smile forming on the madam's face.

Maureen sat up ramrod straight and gave Ruby a critical look. She didn't know Ruby that well, but just from interacting with her on a limited basis, she knew that Ruby was not retarded. Now she was not so sure. "Well, I got news for you, darlin'. You ain't a virgin but one time in your life. Unless you know somethin' the rest of us don't know."

Ruby pressed her lips together to keep from looking too smug. "That's just it, Miss Mo'reen." She blinked. "I do. . . ."

"I get the feelin' that you are tryin' to tell me somethin'. Whatever it is, you better spit it out soon. I don't have all day."

"Miss Mo'reen, I know I can trust you, so I will tell you. See, my sisters told me about a trick with some capsules, the ones I take for my cramps every month, and some chicken blood. A woman can put the capsule, with some of the blood in it, up in her, uh, female area. When the man, uh, pesters her, she bleeds like a virgin." Ruby paused and rolled her eyes. "One more thing—the woman should probably douche with some alum, too, just so she'll be tight like a virgin."

Maureen looked at Ruby with great interest. She cleared her throat and attempted to look more authoritative. But Ruby could tell from the amused look on the madam's face that she was definitely intrigued. "My dear, men are as *stupid* as hell in the bedroom, but not *that* stupid. Do you think you can fool a man like that?"

"I fooled Mr. Dobie," Ruby reported. "My sisters' husbands thought they were virgins when they married them."

"Do you mean to tell me . . . you"—Maureen stopped talking and stared at Ruby, looking her up and down like she was inspecting a hog—"you wasn't no virgin when you got in that bed with Dobie Boyle?"

"I ain't been a virgin in a while, Miss Mo'reen. I've probably been pestered as many times as one of your girls, and I ain't even a prostitute. Well, I wasn't until I done it with that nice, one-eyed Mr. Dobie for money last night."

"Where did this chicken blood thing come from? One of them jungle tribal things that the slaves passed on? Like they done with that voodoo?"

"No, ma'am. It ain't got nothin' to do with no jungle people that I know of. My sister told me that the women in Europe started it, and have been doin' it for years. I am surprised that a sophisticated white woman like you don't know about it. . . ."

Maureen gave Ruby a thoughtful look. "This European woman ain't never heard of such a thing until just now." Maureen laughed. "And you think that we can milk this cow?"

"I don't see why not. As long as we watch our step, this is one cow that we can milk dry. A lot of men passin' through town come here once and never come back. We have to do it only with them. Othella knows about it, but I don't think this is somethin' the other girls need to know."

"That's for sure. But the thing is, not all of my clients want to spend time with a gal like you, you know."

"Miss Mo'reen, you don't have to keep remindin' me that I ain't no beauty queen. I hear that enough from everybody else. But it didn't bother Mr. Dobie, and I know there must be other men that will overlook the issue, too. And if anybody can steer them men in my direction, it's you. We can work real good together, me and you. I know my stuff, and if you can round up a few more men that want what Mr. Dobie wanted, we can make a few more dollars."

Maureen bit her bottom lip and gave Ruby a guarded look.

For about half a minute, the two women just stared at one another. Ruby broke the silence.

"Now you think on it and let me know, hear?"

"I'll think on it, Mama Ruby." Maureen winked, something she rarely did to anybody other than a client she was sizing up. This was a good sign, a real good sign, Ruby decided.

"I'll get your mornin' coffee for you, Miss Mo'reen," Ruby said, already opening the door.

"Good. And bring a cup for yourself so you can keep me company. Things just might get real busy around this house for you, and I want to make sure that you and I are always companionable," Maureen said, already counting the money in her mind that men would pay to be with a virgin.

CHAPTER 43

"*Y*OUR FOLKS WANT TO KNOW HOW COME YOU DON'T never write," Othella informed Ruby. "Every time I get a letter from my mama, she tells me that your daddy always asks her that."

"I will write to my folks when I get a chance," Ruby answered, annoyed. "I been real busy since we left Shreveport."

"That was a few months ago, and you ain't been no busier than me. I find time to write letters to my mama a couple of times a month."

"When you write her the next letter, tell her I said to tell my mama and my daddy that I'm a real big success. Tell 'em that I'm doin' real good and that I miss them."

"How come you can't do that yourself?"

"I ain't got no stamps," Ruby said with a pout. "Uh, you got some garters I can borrow? They make me feel real sexy."

"What happened to them garters I gave you last week when you was entertainin' that doctor man?"

"He liked 'em so much, he wanted to take them for a souvenir," Ruby explained. "Bless his horny heart."

She and Othella were in the dreary little room that Ruby shared with Mazel, sitting on the side of the bed. Ruby still didn't like sharing a room, or a bed, with that beastly, musty, snoring-ass Mazel. She woke up almost every morning with a cramp in her neck from sleeping on her side in that roll-away bed. And she didn't like the fact that Mazel was still trying to find out her business.

"What's wrong with you, woman? I don't get involved in none of the things that go on in this place that don't concern me," Al told Mazel the last time she asked him if he knew anything about Ruby. "Why do you care?"

"I just like to know what's goin' on around here when it involves us."

"Us who? If you mean Mama Ruby and Othella, I can tell you now to your face, they done become Miss Mo'reen's pet monkeys. You don't want to make neither one of them mad enough so that they complain to that white woman. By the way, Mama Ruby just told me to tell you to run out in the backyard and wring a chicken's neck. Then bring the carcass in the kitchen and drip the blood into a cup."

"Again?" Mazel rolled her eyes.

Al's lips curled up at the ends. He scratched his chin. "You ain't goin' to ask me why? Not that I know what she always needin' chicken blood for anyway."

"If it's what I think it is, you don't want to know why." Mazel knew about the chicken blood in a capsule trick. She'd done it to make her first and third husbands, both long dead now, think that she was a virgin on her wedding night. And, if the people she associated with outside of Maureen's place didn't know that she had given birth to four kids, all grown now, she wouldn't hesitate to kill a few more chickens for her own use again.

"Ruby, how many more times do you think you can pull off this virgin trick? You've done it eight times now. And is it safe to be puttin' chicken blood up in your coochie? Chickens is pretty nasty out there cluckin' around, eatin' bugs off the ground and stuff."

Ruby gave Othella a dismissive wave. "Don't worry about it.

I ain't never heard of no chicken causin' nobody to get a cancer or no other disease. Besides, they can't be too dangerous if we all eat 'em four to five times a week."

"Well, if you ain't worried about the chicken causin' you no difficulties, what about them silly horny men?"

Ruby threw her head back and laughed. "Look, Othella. Them poor devils. They ain't as dumb as we think, but they are less to worry about than them chickens. Anyway, Miss Mo'reen got it all figured out. We only do it with a first-time, one-time only client." Ruby gave Othella a curious look. "What I don't understand is, why would a man want a virgin so bad, when she supposed to be so naive that all she can do is lay there and holler? That don't sound like much fun to me."

"Just lay there and holler? Is that all you have to do?"

"That's all so far. Oh, there was that one man from Baton Rouge that wanted me to pee on him, too," Ruby snickered.

Othella gasped. "That nasty dog! What's pee got to do with sex?"

Ruby shook her head. "Beats me! That just goes to show you how confused men are, generally speaking. That same man asked me to suck on *his* titties. But you know what the best part of bein' with him was? His pecker was so stubby, he couldn't even reach my, you know, what was supposed to be my cherry."

"If that's the case, what's the point of him wantin' a virgin? If he can't even do the deed properly."

"That poor thing. He was so embarrassed about that little nub between his legs, he thought a virgin would be the only female that wouldn't poke fun at him. But do you know what? I told him he was lucky. I told him that havin' a big dick is not all it's cracked up to be."

"If he thought you was a virgin, didn't he ask you how you knew all of that?"

"I told him that I'd heard so much about how rough men with big dicks could be, and how the girls hated havin' to be with them, that that was the reason I was still a virgin. Boy did he get bug-eyed and frisky, thinkin' that I'd been savin' myself for a man like him." Ruby gave Othella a wan look. "I am so glad I wasn't born a boy. They are so dumb and gullible. That's why I want me a girl baby so bad. . . ."

It had been a while since Othella had had to suffer through another one of Ruby's "I want me a baby girl" conversations. She decided right away not to go there with her end of the conversation.

"What if that man decides to come back to the house and gets wind of you tryin' to fool another man into thinkin' you still got your cherry? This is a small town, you know. Look how fast we ran into that man whose dick you chopped half in two."

"Like I said, Miss Mo'reen got this thing worked out, sewed up like a goose-down pillow. She don't let the same man that's been here for a virgin come back no more. She ain't stupid, and she done told you that you better not blab, or you will be right out there where Cat Fish is—wherever that is."

"I don't like this trick that you and Miss Mo'reen keep runnin' on them men. It don't feel right. Especially since the ones who come here lookin' for virgins seem so nice and easy."

"You let me and Miss Mo'reen worry about it, hear? We ain't goin' to do it too much longer. It is gettin' kind of risky, I guess."

Two days after that conversation, Ruby found herself inserting one of her cramp capsules filled with chicken blood into her vagina for the ninth time.

"I got a real nice strappin' brunette," Maureen told Dr. Charles Ligget, handing him a large hot toddy. He'd been to the house only a few times before, five years ago. As far as Maureen was concerned, he was like a new client. It was safe to use the virgin trick on him. If he came back after that, Maureen would keep Ruby out of sight. Now that his wife had died of breast cancer, after suffering for two long years under his care, Dr. Ligget had a lot of catching up to do. He was not a good-looking man. In fact, he was fiercely ugly with his mulish face, crooked teeth, and droopy eyes. The only saving grace on him was his thick head of silver hair, but he was smart enough to know that it took more than that these days for him to attract a woman. The only reason his wife had married him in the first place twenty years ago was because she had also looked very much like a mule herself. They'd been a good match and he'd been faithful, most of the time. Well, he was lonely now and since his wife had not been able to perform her wifely duties in the bedroom throughout her illness, he was severely horny also. And after closing an important business deal earlier that day, he wanted to reward himself by spending some time with a virgin.

"As long as she's patient with me, I'll be patient with her," Charles Ligget grinned. "I suspect that girl of Marielle's ought to be about the right age now? Sookie is her name, right?"

"Sookie's thirteen now," Maureen told Dr. Ligget. "But she's already been used up. She got her cherry busted last year. But she ain't workin' here no more, no how. Believe it or not, the same joker that busted her married her a month later. I don't know what this world is comin' to."

One of the things that Ruby and Maureen had agreed upon was to keep Ruby's virgin ruse a secret from the other girls. Othella knew about it, but she knew to keep her mouth shut. Maureen couldn't risk the other girls running out to buy themselves some capsules, killing her chickens for their blood, and then passing themselves off as virgins. It wouldn't take long for that information to leak to the wrong person.

"I see. Well, I know none of your regular girls fit the bill. But if you do know of somebody, say a nearby relation or a gal at one of the other houses in the District that's free tonight, I'd be much obliged."

"Now Dr. Ligget. I know you've been out of circulation for a while, but this is America. You know how we do things here when it comes to sportin'. I don't do business with that damn bitch Jeanette Ledbetter across the street, or most of the other District madams. That ain't never goin' to change. You ought to know better."

"Suit yourself, darlin'. I was willin' to pay you a right generous finder's fee. . . ."

Maureen shook her head and looked around. Then she leaned over and whispered into Dr. Ligget's ear, "You still into dark meat, darlin'? I hope you say you are. If so, you ain't got to wait till Thanksgivin' to get a piece."

"Lady, my dearly departed wife and I spent the better part of a year, a few years ago, in a place where there was nothin' but dark meat. And I do mean DARK meat. Senegal. The girls down there run around half naked, with their big asses jigglin' like hog-head cheese! Mercy me. I had no choice but to mount a few from time to time," Dr. Ligget answered with a gleam in his eye. "But it was acceptable down there. Why do you ask me that?"

Maureen looked like she had swallowed three canaries. She was as close to heaven as she would ever get. "It's acceptable in my place, too. Come let me find my girl Mama Ruby. Now I have to warn you up front, she ain't no Nefertiti—and what the hell kind of name is that?—or whatever that jungle queen was named. But my Mama Ruby's got everything else you need."

"*Mama* Ruby?" Dr. Ligget gave Maureen a suspicious look. "How old is this Mama Ruby? From her name, I suspect she may be a bit long in the tooth."

"She ain't but fifteen, and she's so ripe she's about to bust open on her own," Maureen quipped. "And she's got such a sweet, docile disposition, you'd think she was brain dead."

"Oh? Well, for goodness sakes, woman—bring her to me!" Dr. Ligget said, rubbing his hands together like he was about to devour a meal fit for a king.

CHAPTER 44

*R*UBY COULDN'T BELIEVE HOW POPULAR SHE HAD BECOME IN such a short period of time. Had she finally struck gold? It seemed that way to her. Here she was having sex on a regular basis—three virgin hunters in the last week—and she was getting paid! And, unlike the first time when Maureen had given her only ten dollars, Ruby's cut had multiplied considerably by now. Earning half of the *four hundred dollars* for each hit was enough of a bonus. And as long as she drank enough beer to dull her senses and make her less inhibited, she was enjoying it. However, the men who patronized Maureen's brothel were typically not as good in bed as some of the other men, or boys, whom Ruby had been with back home in Shreveport. Othella's mama Simone had told her last year, "Sex is like gumbo: even when it's bad, it's still good." Ruby had decided that that was a damn lie. Maybe that was the case with men, but it was not the case with women. Bad sex was bad sex, period. It didn't take long for her to get to the point where she hated sleeping with strange men for money.

As time went on, she began to hate tricking the men into thinking she was a virgin. It became just another household chore to her, like mopping the kitchen and emptying the spittoons and slop jars. But Ruby continued to do it because she and Othella needed enough money to pack up and move on. She also continued to do it because Maureen kept telling her how "lucky" she was to be so popular.

Ruby prayed that her luck wouldn't run out.

But it did, and in more ways than one.

She didn't really know what "bad luck" was until she got involved with a pit bull of a lawyer in a suit and a Stetson hat named Wally Yoakum.

Even the smartest madams made stupid mistakes. Maureen O'Leary was no exception. She didn't know when to stop using Ruby for her virgin scam. Even after Ruby had suggested that maybe they were "milking that cow" too much and should consider using another girl for the same purpose, Maureen rejected Ruby's request.

"Hog wash! My girls are too well known, and they blab too much. Besides, most men are too stupid for their own good. Anybody who would pay four hundred dollars for some fresh poontang *has* to be as crazy as a Bessie bug. As long as we are careful, we don't have a thing to worry about," Maureen squealed. "Now run out to the backyard yonder. Pick us out a chicken, a real nice plump one with enough blood for at least two dates. With them military men comin' in left and right, I'm goin' to line us up some pigeons for the weekend. In the meantime, I got a true gentleman in the parlor right now. He's here to celebrate his fiftieth birthday in style. Wally Yoakum seems like a decent man, so I expect you to show him a nice time. And don't you forget what I told you; no matter how good it feels inside you, act real surprised, boo-hoo for just a few minutes. Then when he gets all apologetic and gentle, you start humpin' like hell. Make him think that he's a straight-up Romeo and that he's doin' such a good job, you can't control yourself. That way, he will think you are havin' the time of your life, and all because of him. The damn fool." Maureen snickered. "The better you make him feel, the bigger the tip he'll leave."

"What do this Wally Yoakum look like?" Ruby wanted to know.

Maureen let out a cackle first. Then she sucked in some air, like she was about to reveal a deep dark secret. "Moon-faced, potbellied, a mustache that looks like a longhorn steer's horns, but his looks don't matter! As long as a man is payin', he can look like an aardvark and we, I mean you, should still be happy. Now go make that money, honey!"

As soon as Ruby entered the bedroom in the middle of the hallway upstairs, she got a bad feeling. But she closed and locked the door behind her anyway. Then she slowly opened the pink negligee that she had borrowed from Fat Fanny and forced herself to smile.

The man sitting on the side of the bed didn't smile back. He was naked except for his baggy white shorts and his knee-high socks, which were held in place by black garters. He looked at Ruby and frowned.

"What the hell is goin' on here?" the man demanded, rising off the bed with his hands already on his hips. "Who the hell are *you*, gal? What the hell are *you* doin' in this room?"

"Miss Mo'reen didn't tell you that I was colored?" Ruby asked dumbly, trying to look and sound demure. The forced smile was still on her face.

By now Wally was on his feet, and there was a severe scowl on his face. "Are you the same wench that was here last month?"

"Huh? Oh, I . . . I don't know what you mean, sir."

"Uh-huh. Last month I came here with a friend. I couldn't hang around long on account of I had a previous engagement. But later on that same night, my buddy told me all that went on with him after I left. He described *you* to a capital T!"

"But, sir—"

Wally darted across the floor and lunged at Ruby, grabbing her by her wrist and holding on to her so tight, she couldn't move.

"Now look, gal. Don't you stand yourself here and tell me

that Maureen got *two* colored gals like you in this place. As a matter of fact, there can't be that many sluts that look like you in this whole area. YOU ARE NO VIRGIN!"

"Huh? Uh—yes I am! You can stick your finger up in me and tetch my stuff!" Ruby reared back on her legs. She snatched open the negligee all the way, exposing her naked body. "That's what all of them other men did so they could make sure they was gettin' a virgin before they stuck their peckers in." Ruby was nervous and frightened. That was why she didn't realize her last statement was the wrong one, until it was too late. She had just cooked her own goose. "Oh shit!" she hollered, stomping a bare foot so hard on the floor, the perfume bottles on the dresser by the bed rattled.

"Nobody makes a fool out of me!" Wally hollered.

He slapped Ruby's cheek so hard she hit the floor like a rock, holding the side of her face. But that wasn't enough for him. He sprinted back to the bed where he'd left his clothes draped across the headboard. Without a word, he removed his wide, thick leather belt from his pants. Before Ruby could get off the floor and compose herself, Wally attacked her with his belt. He beat her on her back, her arms, her head, and her face. He was cussing loud, and Ruby was screaming even louder. Within minutes, Maureen was banging on the door with both fists.

Wally didn't stop beating Ruby until he got tired. While she lay in a heap on the floor crying hysterically, he quickly got dressed, still cussing and spewing threats of more violence.

Maureen was still outside banging and kicking on the door, screaming for Wally to unlock it. But he ignored her. When he did finally open the door, Othella, Fat Fanny, and Marielle, all three half dressed, rushed in with Maureen.

"What in the hell is goin' on in here?" Maureen demanded, eyeing Wally with a horrified look on her heavily made-up face. She let out a yelp when she saw Ruby on the floor, still struggling to rise.

"Ask your virgin!" Wally roared, shaking his fist at Maureen.

"Woman, by the time I get through with you, you won't be able to pimp a nanny goat to a horny billy goat in this town!" Wally spat on the floor. Then he ran out of the room, still cussing and fussing at the top of his lungs.

Maureen waved her arms high above her head in exasperation as she ran over to Ruby. She attempted to help Ruby up off the floor, but Ruby was so dazed she could barely move, let alone stand up straight. The other prostitutes had to help Maureen lift Ruby and hold her in place to keep her from falling. She had numerous welts on her body, even her neck and ears.

"That man beat me," Ruby whimpered, tears sliding down her bruised face. Most of her injuries were on her arms because she had used them to try and defend herself and to shield her face.

"Othella, run get a wet cloth and some salve," Maureen ordered. "Fat Fanny, trot downstairs and make sure he's gone. Tell Buster I said to guard that door like this is the White House, and don't let Wally back in here until I sort this mess out."

When Fat Fanny returned ten minutes later, Wally was with her.

"I couldn't stop him from comin' back up here, Miss Mo'-reen!" Fat Fanny hollered. "And Buster wasn't nowhere to be found so he could help stop him!"

Without a word, Wally shoved Fat Fanny to the side, and then he rushed over to a terrified Maureen. She stood in the middle of the floor with her eyes stretched open wide, her jaw twitching, and a scream trapped in her throat.

"YOU BITCH!" Wally roared. He knocked her to the floor with his fist. Then he kicked her repeatedly, like he was kicking a mad dog. He left no stone unturned. He kicked Maureen in the head, the stomach, on her legs, her butt, and on both sides of her torso. Even with all of the other women in the room beating him on his back, and trying to pull him away from Maureen, he managed to beat her so severely she passed out.

Ruby was still too dazed to be of much help. She sat on the bed the whole time that Wally was stomping Maureen to a pulp. By the time he'd satisfied his need for revenge, Ruby had wiped the blood from her own face and composed herself. But by then, Wally was gone.

Fat Fanny took charge. She ordered Marielle to escort Maureen to her room downstairs where she could take care of her injuries with wet ammoniated pads and Epsom salt. After that, as the madam's "representative," Fat Fanny closed the house down for the night. She explained to the seven disgruntled clients and the piano-playing Maurice that there had been a "freak accident" upstairs involving the madam.

Othella had discretely escorted Ruby to her room downstairs. As soon as she had Ruby calmed down, she sat down next to her on the bed. Mazel was still in the kitchen cleaning up, but she came into the bedroom unexpectedly, horrified to see Ruby's face covered in welts and bleeding from several spots.

"What in the world happened? Mama Ruby, I guess you done finally crossed the line and sassed the wrong one of them white folks. I hope to God Miss Mo'reen get rid of you after this! This house ain't been the same since you and Othella came here!" Mazel hissed, glaring from Ruby to Othella. "You two pickaninnies give the rest of us colored folks a bad name! Shame, shame, shame!"

Ruby cleared her throat and sat up straight on the bed. Then she rose, as ramrod straight as a lamp post. She looked at Mazel like she was seeing her for the first time. "Mazel, if you don't get your black ass out of this room right now, you will get the same thing that that peckerwood Wally Yoakum is goin' to get. . . ."

CHAPTER 45

Mazel's jaw dropped, but she didn't speak again. She muttered something unintelligible under her breath and then she stumbled backward out of the room. Ruby and Othella heard her frantic footsteps running toward the kitchen.

Othella looked at Ruby. "Mama Ruby, you can't be thinkin' about doin' nothin' to that white man. Let this thing go. Let Miss Mo'reen handle it," she pleaded, shaking as she dabbed at the bloody wounds on Ruby's face and neck.

"Other than my daddy, or one of my uncles, ain't a man alive goin' to beat me and get away with it," Ruby stated, her voice sounding more like the bray of a mule.

"Now, Mama Ruby, you listen to me. Don't do nothin' stupid. Like I just said, Wally Yoakum is a white man. You don't want to mess with him!" Othella insisted, her hand on Ruby's shoulder.

"Jesus was a white man, and look what they done to him," Ruby reminded, pacing the floor.

Just then, the door opened again and Fat Fanny walked in, looking disheveled and nervous. There was a large glass of whiskey in her hand. With a desperate look on her face, she mumbled some gibberish, and then she lifted the glass to her lips and took a long drink. Her bloodred lipstick was all over her mouth, chin, and even on her teeth. Her mascara had melted and slid down both sides of her face. She looked like a clown. As soon as she finished swallowing her long drink, she slurred, "Listen up, y'all. Uh, this is the thing: Miss Mo'reen put me in charge, and I just shet the house down for the night. Y'all can go to bed and get some rest. Miss Mo'reen said she might have to stay closed tomorrow, too. If that happens, we'll all be sure enough busy when she reopens for business."

"Fat Fanny, I need for you to crank up that jalopy of yours so you can carry me out to Wally's house," Ruby said calmly.

"What? Why—I don't know where that man lives! Forget it!" Fat Fanny protested. "He's a newcomer to the house."

"You know where Miss Mo'reen's phone book is?" Ruby asked through clenched teeth.

"Yeah, but—"

"Look up his address!" Ruby ordered.

Othella whirled around so fast to look at Ruby, the bones in her neck cracked. She was speechless.

"I ain't no fool, and I don't want you to be one neither," Fat Fanny told Ruby. "I don't know what you done to make that man so mad, but I'm sure he'll get over it. I suggest you let this thing go. Let Miss Mo'reen deal with Wally. I did hear tonight from another client that Wally Yoakum is an important client in the District, and that he's acted a fool with other madams in the past. We all have to eat a nut pie like him with a real long-handled fork. I heard from another client downstairs before I closed the house down that Wally pulled out his gun and shot a hole in the ceilin' at Susie Jameson's house earlier tonight. All because he couldn't get an all-night session with a redheaded gal he wanted. It don't take much to set him off real bad."

Fat Fanny paused and looked at the floor. When she lifted her head, Othella and Ruby could see that she was more angry than she was embarrassed. "That same source told me that last month, Wally got drunk and almost bit that redheaded gal's titties clean off. She was out of commission for a whole week. A week later, he went back to Susie's house. He paid double for the next two times that that same girl spent the night with him. And if that wasn't enough, he took her shoppin' and let her pick out two expensive frocks from Paris. Y'all seen me in my purple and white calico? That was one of the same pieces that Wally bought that girl that day."

"I don't think Wally will be takin' Ruby on no shoppin' spree. And I sure enough don't think he's goin' to come back over here and apologize to her," Othella said. "And what about him beatin' up on Miss Mo'reen? I don't think she's goin' to let somethin' like that slide. Not even for ten frocks from Paris."

"The bottom line is, this is Miss Mo'reen's call. Y'all need to stay out of it before you end up out of a job, in jail, or the guests of honor in that colored cemetery out by the river," Fat Fanny said, shaking a finger. "Now like I said, the house is closed down for the night, so y'all need to get to bed."

After Fat Fanny had left the room, Othella turned to Ruby and shook her head. "She's right, Mama Ruby." Othella left Ruby and headed upstairs to her room. She climbed into bed fully dressed.

An hour later, Mazel entered the bedroom that she shared with Ruby, looking and acting as meek as a lamb. Ruby stood in front of the small window that faced the bed, with her back to Mazel. Neither woman spoke as Mazel wiggled out of her uniform and slithered into a flannel nightgown.

Right after Mazel crawled into bed, Ruby eased out of the room. She padded up the stairs to Fat Fanny's room and entered without knocking.

Fat Fanny was not surprised to see Ruby. She greeted her with a tight smile and a sharp nod. She sat on the side of her bed, sipping a large hot toddy. "Mama Ruby, I didn't want to say too much in front of Othella; she don't look trustworthy to me. But I hope you do go out to Wally's house and straighten him out. Give him a thorough tongue lashin' so he won't never misbehave again the way he done tonight. I heard he overreacts for the least itty-bitty thing. But what he done tonight wasn't fittin'. We can't tolerate no mess like that. He has to be chastised. If not, other fools will think it's open season on Miss Mo'reen's house."

"You didn't mean none of that stuff you said downstairs?"

Fat Fanny hesitated and sucked on her teeth. "Yes and no. I am still mad as hell about what he done to that other girl; she happens to be my first cousin on my daddy's side. I wouldn't be the least bit surprised if her injuries eventually grow into a cancer, or somethin' worse. I am appalled by what he done here tonight!" Fat Fanny paused and shook her head. She rubbed the back of her neck and blinked back a tear. "But the thing is, I need my job, so that's why I think we should be real careful with Wally. I suspect that whuppin' him would cause more harm. He just needs a good talkin' to, so he won't do nothin' else crazy."

"Can you take me to his house tonight to . . . uh . . . *talk* to him? Now. I need to take care of business while things is quiet and Miss Mo'reen ain't in the way tryin' to stop me. You can sit in your car and wait while I go straighten him out. Ain't nobody got to know you helped me."

Fat Fanny looked at Ruby for a long time, like she was trying to read her mind. She could not have guessed in a thousand years what was on Ruby's mind.

"I'll get the phone book and look up Wally's address. Then I'll carry you over to his house. But I don't want to get too involved. Like you said, I can wait in my car. I'll keep the motor runnin' in case he gets crazy again and we have to make a fast getaway."

"I hope he lives alone," Ruby said thoughtfully.

Fat Fanny finished her drink and set the glass on the floor. "I hadn't thought about that," she grunted, releasing a mighty belch. "You want to wait until we can find that out? We don't need no spectators."

"I can't wait. I want to see him *tonight*," Ruby growled. "And I want him to see me."

"Now tell me, just what do you plan on doin'? Just cussin' him out and callin' him a few choice names, I hope. That ought to do it. I hear that Wally is a Christian, so I think a real subtle approach might work."

"Fat Fanny, you let me worry about that," Ruby replied, removing her switchblade from her bra and caressing it. The only time the weapon wasn't in her bra was when she was with a client. If she had had it during Wally's attack on her, he'd be stretched out on a slab in the morgue by now. *Or at the very least, missing half of his dick*, Ruby thought.

"Sweet Jesus! Mama Ruby, I didn't know you carried a knife," Fat Fanny gasped, her eyes on the weapon. She looked into Ruby's eyes. "My daddy always told me not to possess a weapon unless I had enough guts to use it. You'd cut Wally for what he done to you tonight?"

"I had to chastise two other men with my knife a little bit, for doin' less than what Wally done. Now, are you goin' to get his address and crank up that old jalopy of yours, or what?"

Fat Fanny didn't answer right away. First, she checked to make sure that all three of her children were asleep. Then she changed into a pair of pants, a man's shirt, and a pair of clodhoppers, the best shoes in the country for running.

"The knife is just to scare him, right?" Fat Fanny asked, her voice cracking and shrinking to a whisper by the time she uttered the last word.

"Uh-huh," Ruby mumbled. "That's all."

"Mama Ruby, if Wally even acts like he's goin' to get violent, will you promise me you won't cut him? Promise me you'll run like hell out of that house; promise me you won't stop runnin' until you get back to my car. Promise me that."

"I promise," Ruby muttered.

A few minutes later, Fat Fanny and Ruby eased quietly out of the house and climbed into Fat Fanny's LaSalle. They headed to the street that the phone book listed as Wally's address.

CHAPTER 46

*I*T TOOK FAT FANNY ALMOST HALF AN HOUR TO DRIVE TO THE
neighborhood where Wally Yoakum lived. Even in the dark,
Ruby could see that this was a location that catered to a very
high level of white society. It contained large expensive-looking
houses, most appearing very similar to one another, and each
one very well tended. Impressive decorations dominated the
large front lawns. Expensive cars and even a few buggies occupied most of the driveways.

"Damn," Fat Fanny mouthed, looking up and down the
street where Wally's house was located. She was glad to see that
there were no lights on in his house. "It must take a real pretty
penny to live in this neck of the woods."

"And the right color of skin," Ruby added, not trying to hide
the anger in her voice. "I bet every last one of these crackers
got up this high by takin' advantage of people like me." Ruby
rolled down the window on her side and breathed in some of
the night air. "It even smells white over here."

They parked across the street from the large, two-story beige
house that Wally shared with an aging tabby cat and a lot of sad
memories of the wife and six children who had deserted him. A
shy black man, who worked as Wally's cook and butler, occu-

pied the studio apartment above the two-car garage attached to the house.

Fat Fanny had cooled off considerably during the drive. She was already regretting that she had agreed to assist Ruby. She liked Ruby and didn't want her to get in trouble. She knew that it was one thing for a white woman like her to exact revenge against a white man. But the law would treat her differently, and way more humanely than they would Ruby.

"Uh, maybe we should go on back home and forget about this man," Fat Fanny suggested, silently praying that Ruby would agree with her. "I am sure he'll be all right once he cools off. By the way, what made him so mad at you?"

"Uh, it was just a little misunderstandin'. Kind of delicate and embarrassin', so I really don't want to go into it right now. You know how it is."

"I guess," Fat Fanny said with a shrug. "I had a problem with a trick last year. After he'd rode me like a cowboy, he had the nerve to tell me that I had such a loathsome pussy, he wanted his money back. He slapped me when I didn't give it back to him. Thank God Buster got up to the room in time. A week later, that same client came back and apologized, and he wanted to ride me again. That's a man for you." Fat Fanny chuckled. "Well, like I said, I'm sure Wally'll be all right, once he cools off," she added with a hopeful smile.

"What if he don't cool off? Then what?" Ruby asked through clenched teeth. "I don't let nobody get away with hurtin' me." She rubbed the side of her arm, which was sore and bruised from Wally's attack. "What if he comes back to the house with a gun or somethin', and finishes me and Miss Mo'reen off?"

Fat Fanny released a loud sigh. "Well, that could happen, but it's highly unlikely. Um, the other two men you mentioned that you chastised? Were they colored?"

Ruby looked at the side of Fat Fanny's face. "Why? What difference does the color make?" She had changed into one of her low-cut blouses, but this one had long sleeves. Sleeves that were long enough to cover the bruises on her arms, and the top half of the handle of the switchblade she had in her hand.

"Color will make a big difference if you get caught, Mama Ruby."

Ruby looked straight ahead. "Them other two low-down, funky devils was colored."

"What did you do to 'em?"

"Huh?"

"Did you hurt 'em real bad?"

Ruby recalled the incident with Glenn Boates, something she thought about almost every day. She was sorry about what she'd done to him, but she rationalized her actions by reminding herself that he'd gotten what he deserved.

"Uh, yeah you could say that," she admitted. "The last one especially."

"Oh. Well, do I want to know exactly what you did to them two colored men? The last one especially?"

Ruby looked down for a few seconds, and then she faced Fat Fanny and shook her head. "Naw. You don't want, or need, to know none of that. But I can tell you this much. That last man won't be attackin' no other woman, no time soon. He threatened to kill me and Othella. It was him or us. . . ."

"I see." Fat Fanny was moved by the look of sorrow on Ruby's face. She gave her a gentle pat on her shoulder and a quick hug. "You poor thing, you. In that case, the law don't care too much about whatever you done to that man. Him bein' colored and all. But this is different. See, not only is Wally white, he ain't no redneck from the bayous. He's one of them high-falutin lawyers that's never lost a case, so you know he's a man with a bunch of money! You can see that from the way this neighborhood looks. I'm sure he's got a whole lot of powerful friends. He might be plottin' somethin' else to get back at you and Miss Mo'reen by now hisself. You thought about that?"

"I ain't thought about nothin' but that. That's why I wanted to get to him—in case he's plannin' to get back to me and Miss Mo'reen first."

"Mama Ruby, I'm a whole lot older than you, so I know a whole lot more than you. I know you are still upset, and I am, too. But don't mess with this man. You'll only make things worse. I realize that now. Let me carry you on back to the house so we can check on Miss Mo'reen. I noticed a knot risin' on her forehead when I put her to bed. I'll fix you a highball myself. Or better yet, one of my real strong hot toddies. If that don't calm you down, nothin' will."

"I don't need no highball or no real strong hot toddy," Ruby snarled. "I need to settle my business with Wally."

"It don't look like he's home no how, sugar. Ain't a single light on in his house," Fat Fanny said, breathing a sigh of relief. "And I ain't surprised. This is his birthday, so he's probably at another whorehouse or some joint gettin' drunker."

"Do you know where that might be?" Ruby mumbled, caressing the tip of her switchblade some more.

"No, I don't know the man like that. I just met him in person tonight," Fat Fanny said, starting up the motor again. Before Ruby could object, Fat Fanny made a U-turn and headed back to Maureen's house.

On the way, just one block from Wally's house, Fat Fanny almost hit a squirrel that was trying to cross the street. Two blocks down the street, she almost ran into a tree.

"How come you so nervous?" Ruby wanted to know. "Wally didn't try to beat your brains out like he done me and Miss Mo'reen."

"It don't matter. Anything that happens in Miss Mo'reen's house affects all of us," Fat Fanny replied. "I hope you keep that in mind until this thing blows over."

Maureen's house was completely dark by the time Ruby and Fat Fanny returned.

"Listen up. I advise you not to tell nobody where we went tonight," Ruby whispered. "Not even Othella or Miss Mo'reen. Do you hear me?"

Fat Fanny was not stupid. She had this crazy young black woman's number. She could tell a veiled threat when she heard one. "I didn't plan on doin' that no how."

Fat Fanny made herself a hot toddy and then she rushed upstairs and checked on her children. She pulled Viola from her bed and took her to her room across the hall. After saying her prayers on bended knees, she climbed into bed with her drink in one hand, her daughter in the other.

Ruby gulped down a few beers standing over the sink in the kitchen. Then she retreated to her room where Mazel was snoring like a bull. She stayed up all night, sitting on her side of the roll-away bed, staring at the wall, looking out the window, and pacing the floor. As soon as it got daylight, she crept upstairs to Fat Fanny's room and entered without knocking again.

Fat Fanny was still asleep, but Viola was sitting up in bed, cooing, grinning, her fingers playing with her mother's matted hair. As soon as the baby saw Ruby, she started to whimper and reach for her. It was the sight of that precious little baby that softened Ruby's vengeful heart. She let out a mighty sigh and padded across the floor and pulled Viola into her arms.

"If I still had my own child, I wouldn't be in this mess," she said to herself. She gently placed the baby back into the bed and quietly left the room.

Othella rose early enough to have a serious conversation with Ruby in the kitchen before Maureen or any of the prostitutes got out of bed. Mazel was hunched over the sink marinating an enormous rump roast. As usual, she looked like she was angry enough to cuss out the world.

"Mama Ruby, can I talk to you about somethin'?" Othella asked, rolling her eyes at Mazel. "It's private so we need to go out on the back porch, if you don't mind."

"Y'all ain't got to be hidin' nothin' from me. I know all about that ruckus that went on upstairs last night," Mazel said with a smirk, directing her attention toward Ruby. "I declare, all these years I been workin' for Miss Mo'reen, I ain't never knowed nobody, man or woman, to hit her." Mazel sniffed. She gave Ruby and Othella a scornful look. "Things was fine till y'all got here. . . ."

"So you keep tellin' us," Othella snarled.

With a snort, Mazel turned her attention back to the rump roast in the sink as Othella and Ruby walked briskly out to the back porch.

"With all of this sneakin' around that me and you do, I feel like a criminal," Othella complained as soon as she and Ruby got outside. They stood at the top of the porch steps, facing one another. It was windy, but it was still warm. So warm that the maid who worked in the brothel next-door was outside hanging just washed sheets on the clothesline. There was a sudden burst of cold air between Ruby and Othella that they both felt on their faces; neither could understand what it meant. Ruby assumed that it was just because she was nervous and uncomfortable. Other than the fact that it was so odd and unexpected, Othella didn't know what to think about the cold air on such a warm day. Neither one shared her thoughts about it, but they both experienced an ominous feeling because of it.

"I know what you mean. I feel the same way," Ruby admitted with a mild groan. Looking at the three chicken coops in Maureen's backyard made her nostalgic. It seemed like it had been years since she'd stood on her mama's back porch steps and looked at her chicken coop. But it had only been a few months.

Othella touched Ruby's arm and leaned closer, her stale breath on Ruby's cheek. "I think Miss Mo'reen's goin' to be all right. One of her doctor man clients is with her now," she reported. "White as her skin is, she'll be black and blue for a few days, though."

"Don't forget I got a few bumps and lumps on various parts of my body from where he hit me, too," Ruby whined.

"I know you do, but you are way younger and tougher than Miss Mo'reen. White women, especially old white women, they got real delicate skin and thin, brittle bones. A big, strong strappin' girl like you can take a beatin' better than any white woman ever could," Othella decided.

"I can take a beatin', but I ain't goin' to," Ruby vowed. "And you know I mean it."

Ruby's tone of voice and her choice of words made Othella's chest tighten. She was glad that her best friend was so fearless, and she felt sorry for anybody who crossed her. The most important thing was, fortunately, that she and Ruby were on the same side. Other than the situation with Ruby's baby, Othella had never done anything to make her mad enough to "chastise" her. And Othella knew that if she wanted to keep her name from moving up any higher on Ruby's shit-list in the future, she'd go out of her way to keep their friendship intact. But she knew now that she had to feed Ruby with a very long-handled spoon.

"Ruby, I love you like you are my own blood kin, and I don't want to see nothin' bad happen to you," Othella declared.

Ruby gasped. "Somethin' bad done already happened to me," she reminded. "Wally Yoakum beat me like a dog."

"I know, I know, and I don't want it to get no worse. But the thing is, I think we need to be gettin' ready to haul ass," Othella insisted, her voice trembling. "We need to get away from this place before we do somethin' crazy."

"I don't know about you, but I ain't goin' to do nothin' crazy. Fat Fanny talked me out of it," Ruby said.

Othella shook her head. "I ain't talkin' about Wally and that mess that he caused last night."

Ruby's eyes searched Othella's. "Is there somethin' else goin' on that I don't know about?" she asked, her eyes narrowed into snakelike slits. Othella hated when Ruby did that with her eyes. It made her look even more menacing, and that was one thing that she didn't want to deal with right now.

"Ain't nothin' else goin' on, other than what's been botherin' me for the past couple of weeks." Othella stopped talking and looked off to the side. When she looked at Ruby again, she was disappointed to see that her eyes still looked like the slits of a snake's.

"I just don't want to keep doin' what we been doin' in this whorehouse no more. I can't." Othella stopped again. She was crying. "If we do stay on here, all I will be willin' to do is help you and Mazel cook and clean," she sobbed. She wiped a string of snot from her top lip with the back of her hand and sniffed hard. "I wasn't meant to be no hoochie coochie woman!"

"But what about all of them boyfriends you had back home? You didn't complain about bein' no hoochie coochie woman then."

"That was different. I was in love with every single one of them boys, and I was just havin' fun. The stuff we do here ain't half as much fun. I wasn't meant to spend my life lettin' white men use my body like it was a toilet . . . and you wasn't neither, Mama Ruby."

CHAPTER 47

"*T*OILET? NOW WHAT THE HECK IS THAT SUPPOSED TO mean?"

"Mama Ruby, think about it. Whores ain't nothin' but receptacles! Somethin' for men to leave their body drippin's in. Same as they do . . . with slop jars. No wonder decent people call us trash."

Ruby searched Othella's face. "It ain't that bad, sugar. I don't like it neither, but it's better than where we was when we first got into this town."

"You ain't listenin' to me. What I am tryin' to get you to see is that me and you, we ain't cut out to be whores. We left home to find husbands and jobs, not this." Othella nodded toward the back door and then shook her head, like she was trying to shake off a bug. "I am so sorry I got you mixed up in this mess."

Ruby was glad to hear that Othella was taking most of the blame for the mess they were in, but she wouldn't let her best friend suffer alone. "Honey, you didn't make me do nothin' I didn't want to do. But if it'll make you feel any better, I can't stand these men touchin' me, either, and I will be glad when we do get up out of here. But we need to come up with another plan before we make another move. Now tell me this, have you worked us out a backup plan?"

Othella shook her head again. "All I know is, when I get up out of here, I am goin' to walk the straight and narrow. I won't never get involved in another whorehouse as long as I live. I don't like the person I was before I got here, and I don't like the person I am now."

"Othella, what are you tryin' to tell me?"

"I'm goin' to be the kind of woman I wish my mama had been. You noticed I don't steal clothes from stores no more?"

"Yeah, I noticed that. I'm glad. And I'm glad that you want to be the kind of woman you wish your mama had been."

"I know we got a good thing goin' here, and we might have a hard time tryin' to find us another place when we do leave. . . ."

"Then what's the rush?"

"I'm fixin' to have a baby," Othella whispered, wiping tears from her face. "I don't want my child to be born in no whorehouse and turn out like . . . like my mama and them other whores that work here. I want my child to have a chance at enjoyin' a *decent* lifestyle." Othella shuddered. She didn't notice how Ruby was looking at her with her mouth hanging open. "I am so ashamed of myself, and how easy I let this happen. I want to leave here and forget all about it as soon as possible. Just like I've forgotten about stealin' clothes and stuff. I want to be a good example for my baby."

Ruby finally closed her mouth but it didn't stay that way for long. First, she smiled and then a full-blown grin slid across her face like a tidal wave. There was such an ecstatic look on her face that you would have thought that she was the one expecting a baby. "A baby?" she croaked. Her eyes got big, her chest tightened, a knot formed in her stomach. That was how happy she was. She stumbled, almost falling flat on her face. "You? You fixin' to have a baby?"

Othella rotated her neck and folded her arms. "Is that all you got to say?"

Ruby stared off to the side, and then an indescribable look

appeared on her face. She shook her head until that look disappeared and then she turned back to Othella. Now there were tears in Ruby's eyes, and her nose was threatening to run. "I wish it was me," she admitted.

"Mama Ruby, don't neither one of us need no baby right now," Othella insisted.

Ruby gave Othella a brief hug. "What you want to do then? You want to go back home?"

Othella shook her head so quick and hard her bangs resembled a beaver's tail flapping across her forehead. "That's the last place I want to be right now." Othella paused and looked toward the door. Ruby followed her gaze. They watched as the curtains at the window moved. "One of my clients told me about a carnival that's in town right now that he took his kids to. He said he went to school with one of the big shots who run the show, and he thought it might be somethin' for us to look into. We won't have no trouble gettin' jobs there. He said that outfit would hire a goat."

"Yeah, I bet they would—as long as that goat is white!" Ruby snapped. "I don't know what makes white folks think *anything* is easy for us."

"The other thing my client told me was that the same white man, the one who does the hirin', he likes colored girls."

"What white man don't? I know that now. But I don't want to leave here and go to no carnival and end up pleasurin' them low-class carnival workin' peckerwoods. We might as well stay here. At least we do our business in warm clean beds in a warm clean house."

"The man who does the hirin' is seriously involved with a hoochie coochie colored woman already, so I doubt if he'll be wantin' us, too. At least not as long as the hoochie coochie woman is handlin' her business proper," Othella said.

Ruby clucked long and loud, like a wet hen. "First, you woo

me away from my happy home to work in a whorehouse. Now you want me to move on from here to go work in a carnival. What outrageous foolishness will you come up with next, girl?"

"Suit yourself, Mama Ruby. If you want to stay here, you go right ahead. Me, I am gettin' out while the gettin' is good. I got a baby on the way that I need to be thinkin' about now."

They remained silent for a few moments. Othella looked toward the kitchen door again and let out a weak sigh. "We best get back in the house and see what's goin' to happen next. I hope Miss Mo'reen keeps the house closed up for the day. I could sure use the rest."

Despite her injuries, Maureen decided to open for business. She received a visit from Dr. White, one of her horniest and most frequent clients. The good doctor bandaged several different places on Maureen's battered body. He also gave her some strong pain pills. Shortly after his arrival, she was up and about, barking orders like a drill sergeant.

"Othella, get up those stairs yonder and put on some face powder and rouge. You look like a haint. Fat Fanny, Dr. White is upstairs in the end room waitin' on you to give him a eye-opener to get him off to a good start today—and don't bite him like you done last week!" Maureen paused to catch her breath. She glanced around the room with a sorry look on her face.

"Damn that Buster! Some bouncer he is! He picked a fine time to go visit his daddy in that old folks' home this mornin'. I suspect that he would be real sorry if Wally had done more damage than he done! I sure enough hope we don't have no more violent commotions around here before Buster gets back!" Maureen stopped talking again and looked around some more. "Betty Sue, when you see that Al, tell him I said I want him to stick close by us till Buster gets back. Him bein' colored, I don't expect him to put his hands on none of my clients to keep them in line, but just his presence might make them behave. I wonder if I can round up somebody white to fill in for Buster till he gets his tail back here tonight."

Maureen groaned and rolled her eyes when she looked at Ruby, staring long and hard at her. "Mama Ruby, I guess you'll be workin' in the kitchen only from now on."

Maureen paused when someone started to bang on the front door. She dismissed everyone before she answered the door, but less than a minute later, her screams brought them all back into the parlor. Even Dr. White. He came stumbling down the stairs with his silk shirt unbuttoned and his alligator shoes in his hands.

Standing over Maureen as she lay on her back on the floor in the middle of her parlor was Wally Yoakum. He still wore the same outfit that he'd worn the night before. He was cussing and beating Maureen with his fists and feet again.

Marielle, Fat Fanny, Betty Sue, and Othella grabbed Wally by his arms and legs, pulling him off Maureen. Dr. White, who was too horrified and stunned to do much of anything, stood in the middle of the floor adjusting his disheveled clothes, with his mouth hanging open. Maureen rose from the floor, stumbling around like a freshly decapitated chicken. She plopped down on the settee, breathing through her mouth. A curly black wig that she had recently purchased had flown off her head and landed in a heap in a corner, looking like a dead animal. Wally had ripped her nightgown down the front, revealing her long, floppy breasts and stretch-marked belly.

Ruby and Mazel stood in the doorway, looking at Wally like he was the Devil himself.

"Ain't you done enough harm in this house?" Fat Fanny screamed at Wally. "You done made your point a hundred times over! Now if I was you, I'd get out of here and I wouldn't come back here no more! You might not be lucky enough to leave here unscathed the next time. Al! Uhhh, Al! You in the house? Get in here and help us out!" But Al was not in the house. The women were all alone with a madman who was determined to make them all suffer for the indignity he had endured the night before. "Have you lost your mind, Wally?"

Wally was about to respond to Fat Fanny, but he stopped when he noticed Ruby standing in the doorway. "And I ain't through with you yet neither," he hollered, shaking his fist at Ruby. "I ain't had the chance yet, but I am goin' to broadcast to every man and boy I know that bogus virgin scheme y'all been pullin'! I don't know exactly what y'all done to fool folks, and I don't care. But whatever it was, the jig is up!" Wally calmly lifted his hat off the floor and ran out the door, still cussing.

Everyone in the room looked from Maureen to Ruby with puzzled expressions on their faces.

"What was he babblin' about? Somethin' about y'all pullin' a bogus virgin scheme?" Marielle asked.

"He was delirious, talkin' gibberish," Maureen insisted, waving her hand. "Don't worry about it!"

"But what did happen between him and you and Mama Ruby last night?" Fat Fanny asked. "I think the rest of us need to know so we won't do the same thing."

"Like Miss Mo'reen just said, the man was delirious, talkin' gibberish. I'm goin' to settle this business with Wally once and for all. Fat Fanny, go crank up the car," Ruby ordered, snapping her fingers.

"Why don't I fix us all some breakfast? I can make us a big pot of grits," Mazel volunteered. "And let's sort this thing out before company starts trackin' in here." Mazel forced herself to appear indifferent. But she was as curious as the other people in the room. She wanted to know what Ruby and Maureen had done to make Wally go on such a violent rampage.

"Me, I best be hightailin' it on out of here," Dr. White said, talking over his shoulder as he headed for the door. He snatched it open and fled like a thief, his shoes still in his hand.

"Fat Fanny, did you hear what I just said? Go crank up your

car," Ruby barked. "Miss Mo'reen, after today you won't never have to worry about Wally Yoakum again."

Maureen was still on the settee, bleeding and moaning like a dying animal. "I can't believe this is happening," she said before she fainted.

CHAPTER 48

A FEW DAYS BEFORE HIS BIRTHDAY, WALLY HAD BOUGHT HIM-self a brand new Packard. He had parked it on the street in front of Maureen's house when he'd gone in to teach her and that black bitch whore of hers a lesson.

Wally stumbled and fell down Maureen's front porch steps as he made his way back to his car. He bruised the palm of his hand and ripped the knee on one leg of his expensive pants. That made him angry, too. It was something else for him to blame on those damn whores, he thought as he snatched open his car door and climbed in. Before he pulled away, he spotted Dr. White rushing out of Maureen's front door. The doctor stumbled off the porch and trotted down the street to a dusty Plymouth parked at the end of the block. Wally wondered if that quack scalawag was in on that virgin scam. Well, whether he was or not, if he was present when Wally returned, he'd teach him a lesson, too.

As soon as Wally's Packard shot off down the street like a tor-pedo, he began to spew cuss words and slap his steering wheel. Even though he had been up all night and was still fairly drunk, he was able to make it home without hitting a pedestrian or a squirrel.

"Damn bitches! I'll destroy every last one of 'em!" he yelled, talking to himself as he staggered around in his house, undressing. He fixed himself a drink, knocked a cheap birthday card to the floor that one of his sons had sent to him, along with a note asking for a five-thousand-dollar loan. "Damn everybody to hell!" he boomed. "I'll show 'em! I'll show everybody that they can't mess with Wally E. Yoakum and get away with it." He grunted. "No siree—nobody makes a fool out of Mr. Yoakum!"

Mr. Yoakum was about to have visitors. This time it wasn't just Ruby and Fat Fanny. Marielle, Betty Sue, and Othella had squeezed into the backseat of Fat Fanny's car, with Fat Fanny behind the wheel and Ruby in the front seat with her. Mazel had wanted to come. By now she was so curious, she wanted a ringside seat at the next round of events. But since Al and Buster were still away from the house, and Maureen had more injuries to be dealt with, Fat Fanny had ordered Mazel to stay in the house to look after her.

When Maureen came to, she was surprised to find herself in her bed dressed in a different gown, with more bandages on new wounds. She was also surprised, but pleased, to see that Dr. White had returned. He and Mazel were leaning over Maureen's bed with concerned looks on their faces.

"Don't move, sugar. You've got a nasty bump on the back of your head this time," the doctor said, gently patting Maureen's shoulder.

"A bump that's as big as a goose egg," Mazel decided, shaking her head. "I ain't never in my life seen no man beat down a woman the way that Wally done you."

"A woman your age can't take too many knocks like this, you know," Dr. White said, shaking his head. "It's a good thing I left my billfold on the stand upstairs and had to come back after I'd run out of here." The doctor paused and cleared his throat. "By the way, I didn't get to finish my session. . . ."

"Don't worry about that. I'm a businesswoman, so I know how important it is to keep you men pleased and pleasured," Maureen croaked, coughing and rubbing her forehead. "I'll make sure you get a double dose of whatever it is you want when my girls get back. You can even get a blow job on the house. I don't know when those gals will be back here, but if one of my drop-in girls drops in, you are more than welcome to pester one of them."

"I appreciate your generosity, ma'am." Dr. White grinned, relieved that he was not going to miss out on his weekly escapade. "I could sure use a good female workout after witnessin' that fracas in the parlor." He sniffed. "Now I don't know what y'all did to make Wally mad enough to jump you twice, but whatever it was, I suggest you settle the score and settle it soon, before somebody gets hurt real bad."

Somebody was getting hurt "real bad" just like the doctor predicted. While Dr. White was trying to make Maureen more comfortable, Ruby and her posse were inside Wally's house where Ruby was beating him with her fists and feet. The only reason she was not using her switchblade was because she had dropped it on the floor in the parlor before they'd left Maureen's house.

Wally had already passed out, but Ruby continued to pummel him as Fat Fanny, Othella, and the other two prostitutes watched in horror. They had already given him a few slaps and kicks themselves before Ruby took over. When Wally swung at Ruby and hit Marielle instead, she slapped him.

By the time it was over, Wally was barely recognizable, but he was still alive.

"I'm goin' to have to kill him, y'all," Ruby said, out of breath. Wally's blood had spattered all over her, leaving red polka dots of various sizes on her face, arms, legs, and dress. Had there been any more blood on her face, she would have resembled one of the clowns in that carnival that Othella had mentioned to her.

"No! Sugar, you can't do that! You can't kill this man!" Othella shouted, as she and the other women began to pull Ruby toward the door. "Let's get while the gettin' is still good."

"But he'll tell!" Ruby protested, pulling away.

"Listen to me! You beatin' up a white man half to death is one thing; you killin' him would be suicide, Mama Ruby!" Othella cried.

"It was self-defense," Fat Fanny hollered. "We are all in this together. Mama Ruby wasn't the only one involved. He started it and we just finished it, that's all. Ain't a judge in this state goin' to send nobody to jail for protectin' themselves."

There was so much confusion, nobody was thinking straight. Fat Fanny, Marielle, and Betty Sue couldn't believe that they'd allowed themselves to get dragged into such a big mess. By them coming with Ruby and Othella, and Wally seeing their faces, they had some additional concerns. Adding to everything else that had transpired, now they had to worry about Wally coming back to Maureen's house to attack *them*.

"Self-defense? That's easy for you to say, and you're probably right. But it would be a whole different ballgame for me and Ruby and y'all know that," Othella yelled, looking from one white face to another. "If we let Mama Ruby kill this white man, they'll deep fry her quicker than they would a jumbo prawn. And probably me along with her. I say we get the hell up out of here now before he comes to."

"As soon as that happens, he'll be blabbin' all over town tellin' everybody who beat him up," Betty Sue said, tears streaming down her face. "I didn't know y'all was goin' to beat the man half to death. I wouldn't have come if I did know. I thought we was just goin' to *talk* to him!"

"If you thought that, you should have kept your dumb white ass at the house with Miss Mo'reen!" Ruby boomed. "And don't forget, you gave him a few licks yourself!"

"I was upset and confused! I was drunk! I didn't know what I was doin'!" Betty Sue said in her defense.

"I ain't never seen such persnickety peckerwoods as the three of y'all. No wonder y'all couldn't keep your husbands," Ruby said, blowing out the words like she was blowing out smoke.

Despite their roles in the melee, all three of the white women gasped at the same time. Marielle stumbled, and if Fat Fanny hadn't grabbed her around the waist, she would have landed on the floor with Wally. Neither one of the white women had ever heard a black person, especially a woman, address another white person the way Ruby had just done. And not a one of the white women had ever seen a black person attack a white man the way that Ruby had just done. She was way too bodacious for her own good, they all decided. They all predicted that her disregard for the proper protocol and her bad behavior toward white folks was going to be her downfall. Didn't she know better? Didn't she read the newspapers and listen to the news on the radio? Just last week another black person, and this time a woman, had been found hanging by the neck from some tree in a farmer's field. Ruby had dug her own grave. By beating Wally down like a mad dog in his own house, she already had a foot and a big toe in the grave that she'd dug.

"We shouldn't have come here," Marielle said, talking out the side of her mouth. She dabbed at her eyes, then blew her nose into a white handkerchief. "I don't need to be involved in no scandal."

"None of us need to be. I should have run out the door in the opposite direction when Mama Ruby told me to go crank up my car," Fat Fanny said, looking from Marielle to Betty Sue. "We ain't got no business gettin' caught up in this mess. If a race riot comes out of this, a lot of folks will suffer—colored and white."

"You should have thought about that before we left the house. You didn't have to bring Mama Ruby out here. Y'all know how she is," Othella shrieked.

"I had to do it," Ruby insisted with a pout. "I had to come over here and teach Wally a lesson, y'all."

Wally stirred and moaned like a dying man. It was the sorriest, most frightening sound that Othella had ever heard before in her life. She shuddered and whimpered as she moved toward the door. "Let's get out of here, y'all," she insisted. Nobody moved. All eyes were still on Wally. "I'm gone!" Othella snatched open the door and took off running toward Fat Fanny's car. Before she could get into the backseat and close the door, the rest of the women ran out of the house and piled into the car.

By the time they made it back to Maureen's house, Maureen had everything that Othella and Ruby owned packed and ready to go. As soon as Ruby got close enough, Maureen handed her the switchblade she had dropped.

"Miss Mo'reen, what's all this?" Ruby asked, looking at the luggage on the parlor room floor.

Just then, Mazel entered the room with a wet towel that she immediately placed on the wounds on Maureen's forehead. Maureen had a black eye, a busted lip, and numerous other injuries on her body, from her head all the way down to her toes.

"Y'all stupid as hell, but you ain't blind," Mazel sneered. "What do it look like? Miss Mo'reen done fired y'all!"

Maureen sniffed and nodded. "Mama Ruby, I want you and Othella to get out of my house—lickety-split," she told them in a weak voice.

"Please don't do this to us, Miss Mo'reen," Ruby begged.

"At least give us a chance to come up with a plan. All we need is a few days. We might even be out of here by the end of the week." Getting fired and evicted was a blessing in disguise as far as Othella was concerned. It would save her the trouble of having to tell Miss Maureen that they wanted to leave. However, she didn't want to leave before she could come up with a plan.

"Y'all got to be two of the craziest niggers I ever seen in my life!" Mazel roared, shaking a finger in Ruby's direction. She glared from Ruby to Othella, so angry with them you would have thought that they'd beaten her down, too. "I been prayin' to God that Miss Mo'reen would come to her senses and run y'all off her property! It's colored buffoons like y'all that gives us decent colored folks a bad name!"

"Shet up, Mazel, or you're goin' to be prayin' to God again! This is between us and Miss Mo'reen," Ruby advised, hands on her hips.

"Shet up my ass! Look at all that blood on you, girl! Lord knows what you been up to now! Y'all can't hang around here and get us all killed," Mazel hollered, stomping her heavy, flat foot. "I been here longer than anybody, and I ain't goin' to stand by and let two uppity heifers like y'all ruin my life."

"It don't take no genius to know where y'all went, and I got a pretty good idea what went on," Maureen said, dabbing tears and snot from her eyes and nose. "Mama Ruby, you and Othella are too dangerous to remain in this house. Like Mazel said, y'all might get us all killed, and I can't allow nothin' like that to happen. The Klan'll come burn down my house in no time—with me in it! Now tell me this, is Mr. Yoakum still alive?"

"Yessum. We just wanted to teach him a lesson," Ruby volunteered.

"All I did was kick him, and bite him, and pinch him a few times," Marielle said quickly. "Didn't I?" she said, turning to Betty Sue for support.

"Sure enough. And I didn't even do that much. I spit on him, and I just slapped him about the head a few times," Betty Sue admitted. "Mama Ruby done the most harm. The way his jaw was juttin' out like a iceberg, I suspect she broke it."

"Fat Fanny, you know that old colored sportin' house out on Granger Road?" Maureen asked through her busted lips, immediately turning to Ruby and Othella. "A colored woman that used to clean for me runs it. I sent a note to her by Dr. White a little while ago, that y'all was comin' to see her." Maureen paused and looked at Fat Fanny again. "You drive these two colored young'uns out to that house. Don't say nothin' to nobody about it, or about anything else that went on here between us and Wally."

"I don't want to go to another whorehouse," Othella wailed,

looking at her suitcase on the floor next to Ruby's. "I'm tired of suckin' and fuckin' strange men! I want to do somethin' else!"

"You ain't goin' to be doin' nothin' if you're dead! Now if you want my help, you better take it now on account of I ain't goin' to let y'all stay in this house another night!" Maureen yelled, wincing from all of the pain that she was in. Part of her pain was severing ties with Othella and Ruby, two young girls whom she had come to care deeply about. She felt sorry for them. They were way ahead of their time, too bold. Colored women like them didn't live long. "Maybe some time in the distant future, when things cool way down, y'all might be able to come back here. But for now, y'all can't stay here. Now git!"

It was a quick but tearful farewell. Maureen, Marielle, Betty Sue, and Fat Fanny hugged Ruby and Othella and wished them well. Mazel remained in the doorway leading to the kitchen with her arms folded and a look of scorn on her face. Ruby couldn't imagine what she was thinking now, and she didn't care.

"What about the children?" Ruby sobbed, looking toward the stairs. "I can't just run off and not give little Viola a good-bye kiss."

"Forget about them young'uns! Y'all git the hell out of my house while y'all still can!" Maureen boomed, marching on her injured legs toward the door with Ruby and Othella close behind. Maureen wanted them to leave before the tears that she had been holding back rolled out of her swollen, bloodshot eyes.

It had only been a few minutes since Ruby and Othella had returned. Now they were on their way back out, and to an uncertain future.

CHAPTER 49

*T*HE COLORED SPORTING HOUSE THAT MAUREEN HAD OR-
dered Fat Fanny to drive Othella and Ruby to was just what
they expected. Like so many other things in the South associated with black folks, it was about as low-level as it could be.
Even though it was a fairly large house, and had a huge front
yard with a gate, it was so old and shabby it looked like the next
strong storm would be its last. The shutters on the windows
were rattling like snakes, and there wasn't even a breeze. There
was no glider, settee, or high-backed chairs with pillows on the
seats on the front porch for the residents and guests to lounge
on like at the brothels in the District. There was only a cheap-
looking rocking chair with a flat pillow in the seat. Next to it
were two empty barrels turned upside down. A Bible, with its
cover missing, sat on top of one of the barrels next to a spittoon
running over with thick brown slime and huge clumps of dried
snuff.

Fat Fanny parked in front of the house behind a caravan of
other dusty old jalopies. She left the motor running as she tumbled out. She beckoned with her gnarled hand for Ruby and
Othella to follow as she strutted up the walkway, kicking empty
cans out of her way. A plump rooster strutted by as Fat Fanny
stomped up on the porch and knocked on the front door. The

door eased open and a big eye peered out. "It's me, Emma. Fat Fanny from the District. Miss Mo'reen sent me 'cause she want to collect on one of them favors you owe her."

The door eased open with a loud creak. Whoever was on the other side opened it just wide enough for Fat Fanny to squeeze through.

Othella looked at Ruby as they remained outside at the bottom of the front porch steps, their feet surrounded by chicken and dog droppings.

"I don't know about you, but I ain't about to stay in this place," Ruby told Othella. "I'd rather let them put me *under* a jailhouse and melt the key."

Before Othella could respond, the door swung open. Fat Fanny and a tall, brown-skinned woman with dark brown freckles all over her face, neck, and hands piled out. The brown-skinned woman was breathing hard and wiping sweat off her face with the tail of her yellow apron.

"Y'all clean?" the woman asked, looking down her nose at Othella. When she looked at Ruby, she stared for a moment, then she pulled out a pair of glasses from her apron pocket and held them up to her eyes. "What happened to you, girl? You look like you been run over by a tractor."

"A dog attacked me," Ruby said without hesitation.

"Well, I hope that dog didn't have no rabies."

"He didn't," Ruby muttered.

The woman didn't seem satisfied with Ruby's explanation about the injuries on her face, but she decided to overlook that for the time being. "I *guess* I could use y'all for a few years," she said, not sounding too sure of herself.

"This is Emma Metcalfe," Fat Fanny introduced. "She's goin' to look after y'all for a while. Be nice," she added, forcing herself to chuckle.

"Before I even let you two young she-monkeys in my house, we need to get somethin' straight right now. Just because y'all been doin' your business for the white folks, don't think y'all no better than the girls that's been workin' for me for years. Y'all ain't got nothin' they ain't got, so don't think your coochie is worth more than theirs. Four dollars a trick to start, and if you work out good, and I don't get too many complaints about y'all from my tricks, and if y'all still here by the end of the year, you'll get six dollars a trick."

Ruby and Othella looked dumbfounded. Fat Fanny spoke for them because they both looked too stunned to do it themselves. "They made a lot more than that at Miss Mo'reen' house."

"This ain't Mo'reen's house!" Emma hollered. "What's wrong with you, Fat Fanny?"

"There ain't nothin' wrong with me, Emma. But be reasonable. These two girls are way younger than all of them old hags you got workin' for you now. For that reason alone, you ought to cut 'em some slack. Besides, they are kind of new in town and just want to turn a few tricks to get enough money to get 'em a place and stuff, see."

"Can we talk to you in private?" Ruby said to Fat Fanny, tugging on her sleeve.

"Anything you got to say, you can say in front of me. You ain't goin' to start out by keepin' no secrets from me," Emma snarled, her teeth looking sharper to Ruby each time she opened her mouth.

"That's fine with me, sister woman," Ruby said in a casual voice, her brow furrowed. "Fat Fanny, can you drive me and Othella back across town?" She paused, and when she spoke again, it sounded like she had carefully rehearsed her words. "I wouldn't allow a dog I didn't like to stay in this butt hole of a place."

Emma clicked her teeth and gave Ruby and Othella the meanest look she could manage, and then she went back into her house and slammed the door shut. Othella noticed the curtains moving in every single one of the windows upstairs.

"Ruby's right," Othella said, shaking her head when she saw the Emma woman's angry face appear in the window on the side of the door. A man who looked like a baboon lumbered up the walkway, grinning and looking at Othella's legs first, then Ruby's breasts.

"Yeehow! Look like Christmas is comin' early this year," the man swooned, stopping in front of Othella, licking his lips. "Y'all new around here?" he asked, looking from Othella to Fat Fanny and then Ruby, still licking his lips.

Without a word, Fat Fanny stumbled off the porch back to her car, with Ruby and Othella close behind. They remained silent as they drove off, and didn't speak again until ten minutes later.

"Mama Ruby, what did you and Miss Mo'reen do to Wally to make him so mad?" Fat Fanny couldn't stop herself from asking. "It don't matter now, so you can tell me. I think I deserve to know."

"Me and Miss Mo'reen tricked him into thinkin' I was a virgin," Ruby answered without hesitation. "Him and a bunch of other men. They paid big money to bust my cherry. Or what they thought was my cherry."

Othella gasped. Fat Fanny almost ran up on the sidewalk.

"And how in the world did y'all manage to do that? I been in this business for years, and I thought I knew every trick in the book. I guess I don't," Fat Fanny said. "Do I want to know this one?

"Take my word for it, Fat Fanny. You don't want to know," Othella told her.

"I'll take your word for it," Fat Fanny said with a grimace on her face. They remained silent for another five minutes before Fat Fanny spoke again. "Y'all better make up your minds where you want me to drop y'all off at soon. I've been drivin' around for the longest time, and I've spent a whole day's pay up on gas already," Fat Fanny complained.

"We'll pay you for the gas," Ruby said, looking anxiously out the window from the front seat of Fat Fanny's car.

"And if I don't get on back to the house soon, Miss Mo'reen

might have my shit all packed up and ready to go like she done y'all. Now if the train station ain't really where y'all want to go, or the bus station, where is it we off to now? The only other place that I can think of, is a house on Creely Street run by another colored lady named Isabel Cooper. She's a real nasty piece of work if ever there was one. She's way meaner than Mazel."

"Don't take us to no more whorehouses!" Othella erupted.

Fat Fanny shook her head. "It ain't no whorehouse. She's kin to Mazel some kind of way, and she's been takin' in strays for years."

"We got money," Ruby said. "We can pay for our room and board."

"That's somethin' you need to discuss with her," Fat Fanny suggested. "I only met her a few times, and I just know about her by what Mazel claims. This woman even takes in dangerous colored felons just gettin' out of prison until they can find their way. Rapists mostly. That's why Mazel don't have nothin' to do with the woman no more. She's scared one of them lusty ex-cons might lose control and grab her. In case y'all don't know it, Mazel had to have a piece of her female equipment removed after her last child. She's as good as dead down below."

The last thing in the world that Ruby wanted to discuss was Mazel's sex life. "Keep drivin'," she ordered. "The first open-all-night place you see, drop us off there. We can sit there for a while, all night if we have to."

"Just make sure it's a place that they allow colored folks in," Othella added. "I ain't in the mood to deal with no segregation rigmarole right now."

Fat Fanny finally reached her breaking point. It was dark by now and her car was almost out of gas. "This is it! Y'all get out of my car!" she hollered, stopping in the middle of what looked like a deserted neighborhood. "Go behind this warehouse and keep walkin' till you get to a field. There's a long-runnin' carnival there that's open all night."

It was the same carnival that one of Othella's clients had told her about. They would soon find out that the man had told the truth about the owner, a white man named Mr. Peterson, being the kind of person who would "hire anybody," because that's just what happened.

With their suitcases in hand and despair on their faces, they approached the carnival owner literally begging Peterson for work and a place to sleep. He hired them on the spot, no questions asked about age, experience, work history, or criminal background. Several workers had suddenly quit the day before, so Mr. Peterson was so desperate he would have hired a goat.

That night, Ruby and Othella moved into a small, but clean and neatly organized trailer that they had to share with a middle-aged black woman named Lilly Parker. Lilly did some cooking and cleaning for Mr. Peterson and a few of the other carnival employees. She resembled the mean-spirited Mazel, but she was a lot friendlier. The first night, she offered to scratch and grease Ruby's and Othella's scalps and braid their hair, telling them how much they reminded her of her own children.

"I think this place might be just what we need for the time bein'," Ruby told Othella after Lilly had finished their hair and turned in for the night.

"I hope it is, Mama Ruby. I hope it is," Othella said.

That night they slept better than they'd slept all week.

The next morning they began their new jobs, which included scooping up elephant and monkey manure, hauling water to and from the animal cages, and selling balloons.

"I didn't even know they had animal acts in carnivals. I thought animal acts was only in a circus," Ruby commented, scratching her head.

"Well, this carnival's got animal acts," Othella sighed tiredly.

At the end of the next day, when Othella balked about cleaning up the animals' manure, Ruby told her, "We could have done a lot worse."

"And we probably will. Mr. Peterson told me that the carnival is only goin' to be here for another couple of weeks. Then they are goin' on to Florida where they come from, and will stay there for the whole season." Othella gave Ruby time to process this information. "But . . ." she began again, pausing as a weak smile appeared on her face.

"But what, Othella?"

"He said he never has much luck keepin' people on his pay-roll for long. Miss Lilly done already told him that she's goin' to Chicago in a few days so he said that if me and you want to go with the carnival and take over some of her chores, too, we could," Othella revealed. "He said he'd even overlook the fact that we still underage and colored."

"Florida? Hmmm. Now that don't sound like such a bad idea to me. I been thinkin' that we should leave this state anyway before we run into somebody we know and they find out what we been up to. The last thing I want is for folks to find out I sold myself in a whorehouse."

"And don't forget about what you done to Glenn. And to Wally Yoakum in his own house, in front of me and all of them white witnesses," Othella reminded.

"Well, that too, I guess."

"I'll tell Mr. Peterson we want to travel to Florida with the carnival."

"I don't know about that, Othella. I have to think about it."

"What's there to think about? Either you come with me or you don't."

"I told my folks that I was goin' to be livin' in New Orleans. They didn't like it, but at least they knew I wouldn't be that far away from home. Now you talkin' about draggin' me even farther away from them."

"This is what bein' a grown woman is about, Ruby Jean," Othella hissed. Ruby hated when she was called by her given name, especially by Othella. She'd made it clear to her and everybody else that she wanted to be referred to as Mama Ruby. Othella read Ruby like a Bible, so she knew why there was such a tight-lipped, hard look on her face. "I meant to call you 'Mama Ruby' like you told me. . . ."

The hardness immediately disappeared from Ruby's face, but the tightened lips remained a few seconds longer.

Finally, Ruby chuckled and shook her head. "Othella, I know you are real upset and stuff about gettin' me involved in a whorehouse and all. But to tell you the truth, I don't want to spend my best years cleanin' up elephant shit neither." She looked at her hands, palms first. Then she turned them over, frowning like she'd just sucked on a rotten lemon. "My hands ought to be burpin' a baby or givin' my husband nightly foot massages by now, not spreadin' manure. I sure as hell don't like this situation," she whined.

"So you keep tellin' me! Look, girl, I am doin' the best I can, but you ain't makin' it easy. Maybe you should go off on your own. That way, if things don't go the way you want them to, you ain't got nobody to blame but yourself. You and all of your complainin' done got on my nerves."

"I ain't complainin'! I'm just lettin' you know how I feel!" Ruby wailed. "I thought we'd at least have husbands by now. . . ."

CHAPTER 50

*O*THELLA EXHALED LONG AND LOUD. AND THEN SHE RUBBED the back of her neck, her eyes, and her swollen belly. "I don't know about you, but once we leave here, I'm goin' to marry the first man that asks me to. I don't care if that man has two heads and a tail," she told Ruby, rubbing her belly some more, which was still as flat as her chest. "I want my baby to have a real home." Othella chuckled.

"What's so funny, Othella?" Ruby asked.

"I hope some of my milk stays in my titties once the baby gets here. That might be cheaper than me tryin' to buy me a set of them fake foam titties that I been cravin' all my life." Othella chuckled again.

"My sister Beulah said that if a man played with your titties enough, that would make 'em grow," Ruby said.

"And that's another reason why I want to get married. It would be nice to sleep with and cuddle up to the *same* man every night. Especially after all we been through."

"Well, in case you ain't been payin' attention, the men folks ain't linin' up to marry you, or me. That's one notion that you need to get out of your head right now and leave it out for good, or at least for a while. We ain't nothin' but whores, me and you. Just like them girls that work for Miss Mo'reen. Just like your mama. Even if we married saints, that wouldn't change the fact that we are whores. A monkey in a ball gown is still a monkey. And you, you are the most pitiful kind of whore. You pregnant with some unknown white man's baby. What decent colored man would want to marry girls like us now? And there ain't a chance in hell that a decent white man, or even some snaggletooth red neck, would marry us."

"You finished?" Othella smirked. "Can I say somethin' now?"

"You can say whatever you want to say. We ain't got nothin' to hide from one another."

"Well, since you mentioned white men, I don't think I'd want a white man who would marry girls like us," Othella admitted. Her voice was even more plaintive now, and so detached it sounded like it was coming from another person. There was a look of total defeat on her face. She sounded like a woman who had practically given up on life. For a moment, Ruby thought she was going to burst into tears.

What Othella had just said disturbed Ruby, and made her sad. She had no idea that her best friend, a girl she thought she knew better than she knew herself, had such low self-esteem. "You don't think much of yourself, do you?" Ruby asked, her lips so stiff she could barely move them.

"I care a whole lot about myself," Othella defended. "But that don't change the fact that I been whorin' around and done fooled around and got myself pregnant by one of them white men I jumped into bed with."

"Nobody needs to know how you got pregnant," Ruby insisted. "You can say . . . you can say you got raped like I was goin' to. . . ."

Othella shook her head. "I don't want to touch that with a bean pole." A great sadness suddenly consumed Othella and she knew why. It was because she knew what was on Ruby's mind: her baby in that asylum. She decided not to remove the scab off that old wound. "We'll be all right. We'll find some nice men. Other than us and the folks back at Miss Mo'reen's house, ain't nobody else ever got to know what we been up to. Once we get to Florida, we'll start out fresh."

"I'll think about it. But to tell you the truth, I just might stay on here," Ruby said. "I'll get me a room somewhere, somehow. As long as I stay away from certain parts of town, I don't think I have to worry about runnin' into nobody that we already done screwed up with."

Ruby was wrong again. The next day, she and Othella walked to an outdoor market two miles from their carnival trailer to purchase some vegetables and fruit, and a carp to fry for dinner. Right after they had paid for their purchases and were about to leave, Ruby heard somebody call out her name. "Ruby! Uhhh, Ruby! Yoo hoo!" She and Othella turned around at the same time.

"Cat Fish! What the hell—" Ruby stopped. She was surprised and thoroughly annoyed to see the white woman who had been such a thorn in her side at Miss Mo'reen's house. Othella was even more annoyed. She still wanted to slap Cat Fish for the way she had verbally attacked her in front of Maureen's clients.

"Don't say nothin' else to that heifer," Othella ordered, grabbing Ruby by the arm. But it was too late.

"Cat Fish, what are *you* doin' in this part of town?" Ruby asked, a hand on her hip. She and Othella were stunned and dumbfounded at the way Cat Fish was smiling at them. They were even more stunned when she hugged them both.

"It's so good to see y'all! I ain't seen nobody from the old neighborhood since I left!" Cat Fish squealed.

Ruby and Othella looked at one another, then back to Cat Fish.

"What house are you workin' in these days?" Ruby asked, looking at Cat Fish with guarded caution. The way she had warmly "greeted" them didn't impress Ruby. She was surprised to see that their old nemesis had lost a considerable amount of weight, and that she looked at least ten years older. There were

even several thick swatches of gray hair on her head. The drab
brown dress she wore, with a large safety pin dangling from
one sleeve, looked like it belonged to a woman three times her
age. She had on a pair of backless men's house shoes, both with
holes. And even though she had on lipstick and a dab of rouge,
she looked like a woman who had seen the last of her best days.

Cat Fish seemed genuinely happy to see some faces from her
sordid past. She had never displayed such a wide grin in front of
Ruby and Othella. And despite her tired look, a smile improved
her appearance. "Me? I ain't workin' in nobody's whorehouse
these days. Somebody bad-mouthed me in a big way to all the
District madams."

"I wonder why?" Othella clucked, giving Cat Fish a narrowed-
eyed, suspicious, sideways glance.

"Most people don't know I'm a Jew unless I tell 'em. Miss
Mo'reen didn't even know, and neither did any of her girls,"
Cat Fish confessed in an almost apologetic tone. Her smile
faded, and her face suddenly looked like the mask of a hag.
"This is a real bad time for us. Especially Jews that don't have
much money or a real good education. We can't reach a single
one of our kinfolks who still live over there in Germany."

"Oh? Why is that?" Othella asked with a curious look on her
face.

Ruby, who had always paid more attention to what was going
on in the world than Othella, knew a little about Hitler's pro-
posed plan for the Jews. "This is a real bad time to be a Jew
anywhere in the world, I guess," Ruby said, actually feeling
sympathetic.

"We are hopin' for the best, but expectin' to hear the worst.
I . . . I'm pretty sure some of them are in serious trouble.
Maybe . . . maybe even dead. I've been goin' to synagogue a lot,
and sittin' shivah." Othella and Ruby looked at one another,
then back to Cat Fish and shrugged. "Shivah is a seven-day
mournin' period that my people go through when there is a
tragedy." Othella and Ruby shrugged again. "Anyway, I couldn't

hide all of that from too many people. I couldn't stop myself from talkin' about it to the folks I thought were my friends. Well, apparently, one of the people I thought was a friend I could trust, wasn't. That's how word got around to the houses about me bein' a Jew."

"But you still white," Ruby reminded.

"I'm still a Jew, too," Cat Fish pointed out, tears in her eyes. "You might not believe it, but some folks feel the same way about Jews that they feel about you people. I realize all of that now."

"Uh-huh," Ruby said, nodding and looking profoundly smug. It gave her great pleasure to say what she said next. "Now you know how we feel."

Cat Fish shook her head. "I can't say whether I do or don't. I just know that things got real hard for me once the wrong people found out I was, you know, different. My last boyfriend is in the Klan. When he found out I was a Jew, he almost slapped my face clean off." Cat Fish blinked, but she couldn't hide the sadness that had already consumed most of her spirit. "I work at that restaurant on Willow Street across from that fish market these days. I wait tables, do a little cleanin' when the regular colored woman don't show up. . . ."

Othella could tell that Ruby was as uncomfortable as she was by the way Ruby kept shifting her weight from one foot to the other. They both got even more uncomfortable after what Cat Fish said next.

"A few of the District whorehouse clients pop in from time to time. Y'all remember a lawyer named Wally Yoakum? He told me he'd been to Miss Mo'reen's house after I left. He had one of them handlebar mustaches, so he'd be easy to remember."

"I remember him," Ruby said stiffly, rearing back on her legs, preparing to defend herself. "What about him?"

"He pretends like he don't know me in front of his friends and business associates, but he's met me after work a few times for a little fun. He ain't too particular, so if y'all need to make a few dollars on the sly that you ain't got to split with Miss Mo'reen, I can let him know. Ruby, he's so liberal, he'd even go for a girl like you."

"We don't work for Miss Mo'reen no more," Othella said quickly.

"Oh? Whose whorehouse are y'all workin' in now? Y'all live around here?"

"No," Ruby said. "We live across town, but we are in the process of movin' from there. And we don't work in nobody's whorehouse no more."

Now Cat Fish was the one with a guarded look on her face, looking from Ruby to Othella. "Uh-huh . . . I see. Well, let me give y'all my address in case y'all change your mind and stay here and ever need a few dollars." Cat Fish dug down into her purse until she fished out a pen. "That Wally. He's a real character, if I don't say so myself. And, by the way, he's a 'minute man.' Except when he's drunk! I declare, when he's wasted, he couldn't 'cum' if I called him." She tilted her head to the side and chuckled as she continued to root around in her purse. "I know I got a piece of scratch paper in here somewhere. Would y'all believe Wally's got the nerve to crave virgin pussy? That's a damn shame!" Cat Fish let out such a shrill laugh she sounded like a hyena, but even that couldn't hide her despair. "But he told me he ain't havin' much luck findin' too much virgin pussy in this town. Can y'all just imagine that? Shoot! I got everything in my purse but what I need!" Unable to find anything to write on, Cat Fish scribbled her address on the palm of Othella's hand. Then, she surprised Othella and Ruby with another hug and told them she hoped to see them again.

As soon as Cat Fish departed, Ruby told Othella, "I'm goin' to Florida with you and that carnival. This town ain't big enough for us and some of the folks that we don't want to deal with no more."

"She'll probably tell that Wally that she seen us as soon as she sees him again," Othella said, glancing at the information that Cat Fish had written on her hand. "And as soon as we get back to our trailer, I'm goin' to scrub my hand, and we are goin' to get the hell out of this town."

CHAPTER 51

SILO, FLORIDA, WAS A SMALL FARMING COMMUNITY THIRTY miles west of Miami. It was not the paradise that Ruby and Othella had expected. The very first day got off to a bad start.

They'd arrived with the rest of the other carnival employees in a battered old bus that June morning, a few minutes before noon. The blazing hot sun had already rolled up into the sky with rays that felt more like weapons. Within an hour, the humidity was almost unbearable. Handkerchiefs, fans, and large paper cups of iced water seemed to be useless. And the bugs, flies, grasshoppers, gnats, and even a few creatures that no one could identify, were much bigger, bolder, and hungrier than the ones that inhabited Louisiana.

"Well, I told y'all that Florida wasn't what them travelogue people make it out to be," Mr. Peterson told Ruby and Othella the first time they complained. "And if y'all want to leave and go back to where you came from, that's fine with me. I do wish you gals would stay, though." Mr. Peterson was in his forties but he had the cute pudgy face of a little boy. It was a shame to see such a nice man pouting like a two-year-old. "I was hopin' you two gals would stay on, especially since I bent the rules and hired y'all. . . ."

Mr. Peterson made Ruby and Othella feel so guilty, they decided to remain with the carnival. One of the main reasons that they decided to stay was because Mr. Peterson was probably the nicest man, white or black, that they'd ever encountered.

When the Fourth of July rolled around, two weeks after they'd arrived in Florida, Ruby got depressed. Othella didn't have to ask her why: it was Ruby's baby's first birthday. It was also Othella's sixteenth birthday and she wanted to celebrate it.

"Mama Ruby, you know how you and me always celebrate my birthday in style because it's on a holiday, and I hope that we will continue to do so. But after what else happened on the same day last year, you don't have to keep helpin' me celebrate it," Othella told Ruby that morning.

Ruby shook her head. "It's the blackest day in the year for me," she admitted. "And it will be every year for as long as I live."

This was the first year that Ruby and Othella didn't celebrate that day, at least not as a birthday. However, since it was a national holiday, they attended the carnival's holiday barbeque that included a fireworks display. During that celebration, another carnival worker announced that it was his birthday. Somebody ran out and purchased a cake and more beverages. Othella and Ruby left when a small group started to sing "Happy Birthday" to their coworker.

"I'm glad you didn't tell these folks that your birthday is today, too," Ruby told Othella as soon as they made it back to their trailer. "I wonder if them asylum nuns did anything for my little girl. . . ."

"I'm sure they did," Othella said, trying to sound hopeful. "You know how nuns like to make a fuss."

Less than a week after Othella's birthday, things really fell apart. Mr. Peterson received a wire from his estranged wife in Brooklyn. She informed him that their only son had died in the war. Mr. Peterson rushed to be by her side and to make funeral arrangements. Three days after he'd arrived in Brooklyn, he sent a wire to the carnival headquarters in Miami informing them that he had reconciled with his wife and had decided to remain in Brooklyn.

Two days after Ruby and Othella had been told that Mr. Peterson was not going to return, they met their new supervisor. Unfortunately, he was the exact opposite of his predecessor. Not only was Roland Miller more like a disgruntled pit bull than a man, he was also a bonafide bigot, who vigorously supported segregation. He didn't even allow the black employees to use the carnival toilets or eat in the same makeshift tent cafeteria with the white employees. When nature called, the black employees had to do their business in metal slop jars or in the nearby woods, using leaves, old rags, or old newspaper for toilet paper. But that wasn't enough for the mean new supervisor. He also cut Ruby's and Othella's pay twice in the same week.

"Business is slow . . . ain't much money comin' in since we cut one of them elephant acts," he explained, rolling a wad of chewing tobacco with his tongue around in his jaw. Brown spit oozed from one corner of his mouth. He didn't know that Ruby and Othella had been told by some of the white workers that he had not cut their pay. Then he grinned, revealing two broken rows of dingy yellow teeth. "Y'all some smart gals, so y'all will make do somehow with less money. You people always do manage."

Ruby wanted to slap the white off his face. "You right about that, Mr. Miller. We people always manage somehow," she agreed, grinding her teeth.

As soon as Mr. Miller walked away, Othella said, "You need to stop talkin' to Mr. Miller in such a uppity way, Mama Ruby. Now that he done run off all of the other colored workers, he is just itchin' to get rid of us, too."

"Fuck that hateful bastard and the woman who gave birth to his ass. He don't scare me! If he's smart, he'll stay out of my way!" Ruby hurled the words at Othella like rocks.

Othella shifted a bucket of water from one hand to the other and took a deep breath. "That's the problem. Don't nothin' scare you and I'm scared that one of these days, that's goin' to get you in some knee-deep trouble."

Ruby was also hauling a bucket of water to the dancing elephant in the main tent. She stopped walking abruptly and turned to face Othella. "Trouble don't scare me no more. You ought to know that by now," she announced. "I will always do what I have to do, and anybody that makes me mad . . . well, they'll be real sorry."

Othella knew how sorry Glenn Boates was that he had made Ruby mad. She wondered how a violent sexual predator like him was getting by with only half of a dick. She also wondered how Wally Yoakum was doing, and if he was still angry about the beating he had suffered.

"Lord knows I feel sorry for the next person that makes you mad," Othella muttered.

Ruby gave her a serious look. "I do, too." When Ruby laughed, Othella joined in.

Ruby and Othella did not have a lot of expenses, and they still had a fairly substantial amount of the money left that they'd earned at Maureen's house. Othella didn't know how much Ruby still had, and vice versa. Even though they were in the same mess together, they had both decided to keep certain pieces of information to themselves—in case something drastic happened and they split up on a bad note.

One thing they did share with one another was the desire to get separate places as soon as possible. They had begun to get on one another's nerves lately, so two separate residences was not such a bad idea. And that's why it was important for them to continue working as much as they could.

Ruby and Othella started to work on some of the nearby farms when business got slow at the carnival. Another reason they signed on with the farms was to have something to fall back on in case Mr. Miller abruptly fired them. And the way he had been complaining about their work performances lately, getting fired was a strong possibility. According to Mr. Miller, they didn't clean up after the animals fast or well enough, they used too much water by taking baths every day, and they acted too "uppity" with the white carnival patrons.

Working in the fields was not that much more pleasant than the carnival.

"I never thought I'd see the day that I'd be slavin' away under a blazin' sun pickin' strawberries," Ruby complained for what was probably the fifth time in the last hour.

It was hard to believe that only three months had passed since they'd fled from Maureen's brothel.

"I'd rather be doin' this than pickin' beans. At least we can eat while we work," Othella said. She bit into a large strawberry that she had sliced with a blade that was as sharp as the switch-blade that Ruby had used to downsize Glenn Boates's dick. Othella didn't know that Ruby had replaced her first switch-blade with one that was even sharper. "I can't wait for that man to let us work in the sugarcane field and pick oranges. I can eat as many oranges as I want and reap the benefits from all of that vitamin C in 'em. I don't want to birth no sick baby. That's the last thing I want on my hands. Takin' care of a baby all by my-self is goin' to be hard enough."

"I told you, I'm goin' to help you with the baby when it comes. That is, *if you keep it.*"

"Of course I'm goin' to keep my baby! What's wrong with you?"

"Nothin'," Ruby muttered.

"Now look. I know what you thinkin', and I am tellin' you right now, don't bring up that subject. That's the last thing I want to talk about right now. We got enough mess on our hands already, so don't make it no worse by remindin' me about the baby you gave away."

"It's gettin' late. Let's finish up and get up out of here," Ruby said. "All this hot sun and this hard work can't be doin' you much good. You really beginnin' to look like a sick woman."

Othella was a sick woman. Within the last hour, she had begun to ache all over. Then without warning, she threw up. By the time they made it back to their carnival trailer in a field on a dirt road across from a lake, Othella was so weak and in so much pain she had to lie down on that lopsided roll-away bed that she and Ruby shared.

Ruby went to get some pain pills for her from the bearded lady in the trailer next door. She was gone only a few minutes and when she returned, Othella had sat up on the bed and was looking much better. This puzzled Ruby, but she handed Othella the pills anyway. Othella swallowed the pills without water, and then she started humming gibberish under her breath, like a woman who had lost her mind.

"Othella, you beginnin' to worry me for real. You . . . you just take it easy," Ruby said, silently praying that they didn't need a doctor, or a psychiatrist. She knew that they were in one of the most segregated areas of Florida. The hospitals didn't admit black folks, and she didn't know of any black doctors or anybody else they could turn to.

"I hope you and the baby are goin' to be all right," Ruby told her, worried and frightened. One thing she had not considered was one, or both, of them getting seriously ill or . . . killed. After all they'd been through Ruby decided that they were lucky to still be alive. "All of this hard work and that blazin' hot sun ain't good for you. You really have to take it easy and slow down some." Ruby stood by the side of the bed looking at Othella. She wondered why Othella was taking so long to respond. "You hear me? We don't want you to have no defective baby, now do we?"

Othella stopped humming and gave Ruby a strange look. She didn't look or seem sick at all now. Maybe she'd only just lost her mind. . . .

"It don't matter now. There won't be no baby," Othella sputtered. "And I'm real relieved."

Ruby's jaw dropped. She was clearly alarmed. "What? Did you do somethin' to it? Did you swallow some of that Black Draught laxative to get rid of it?" she asked, giving Othella an accusatory look. "I thought you told me you'd never get rid of no baby!"

"Calm down, girl. I didn't get rid of no baby. I wouldn't never ever do nothin' as unspeakable as killin' my own baby." Othella paused and let out a loud breath. Then her voice came out in a deep croak, "There wasn't no baby to begin with."

Ruby felt the blood drain from her face. She thought she was going to pass out. "What? All this time—"

"It was a false alarm. My monthly just came on while you was next door gettin' them pain pills. I guess all of that activity in Miss Mo'reen's house and my bad nerves threw my cycle off. And all of that backbreakin' work in them fields didn't help much."

A tear rolled down the side of Ruby's face like a marble. She had been looking forward to cuddling a new baby. . . . She sniffed and blinked hard to hold back any additional tears. "Oh. Well, maybe this is a good thing. Now that you ain't pregnant, we can both start workin' longer hours and more days in the fields until we get enough money to move on with. It don't seem like we goin' to be gettin' married no time soon." Ruby stopped talking when she realized there was a look on Othella's face that she could not interpret. "What else is the matter with you? Why you starin' at me with that strange look on your face? You can't be smilin' about not bein' pregnant, when you thought all this time you was."

"You know I wouldn't smile about nothin' like that!" Othella erupted. It was hard for her to control the tone and speed of her voice. She was giddy and excited, and it showed on her face now. This puzzled and disturbed Ruby even more. It took Othella a few moments to summon enough nerve to say what she had to say next, because she knew it was something that Ruby was not going to like. "I got somethin' I need to tell you, and I already got a feelin' you ain't goin' to like it. . . ."

"Just from the way you actin' and soundin', I already got that same feelin' myself," Ruby wheezed, folding her arms.

"See, I didn't want to say nothin' too soon, Mama Ruby. But the thing is . . . uh, I done met me a man and now he wants to take care of me . . . *permanently*."

Ruby's heart was beating with fear. Her stomach muscles tightened, and her head felt like it had just been mauled. Now she wished that she had gotten a few pain pills from that bearded lady for herself. She could not have been more upset if Othella had told her she had terminal cancer or some other deadly disease. She tried, but was unable to hide the way she felt.

"You ain't got to look like the world's comin' to a end! You know that a husband is what I always wanted," Othella told her.

"You . . . found . . . you . . . a . . . man?" Ruby barely managed, asking the question like it was more of an accusation, and in a way it was. "Do you mean to tell me that you went behind my back and hooked up with a man?"

Othella nodded. "I ain't done nothin' behind your back. From the get-go, I been lookin' for Mr. Right. You *always* knew that!"

Ruby swallowed hard. "I know, I know. And . . . I'm happy for you, I guess. But how? Where and when did you meet a man?" Ruby gasped and her eyes widened. "Is he . . . *white*? We ain't had much contact with no eligible colored men since we joined this carnival."

"I have . . ."

"I guess so! The least you could have done was to let me know sooner. I think I had a right to know, so I could have been expectin' this!"

"What? What do you mean by all of that? You ain't my

mama. I don't have to tell you nothin' that I don't want to tell you."

Ruby dropped her head and stared at the gummy trailer floor for a few seconds. When she looked up, she was not surprised to see Othella with her arms folded and a stiff, hostile look on her face. She didn't want to lose her completely, so she decided to soften her attitude.

"What I mean is, where did you meet him? And, who is he?"

"He's a travelin' salesman. He works for some outfit based in Miami. He drives his station wagon from town to town, followin' the carnivals and circuses to sell them stuff. I ran into him the day he was here sellin' balloons, stuffed animals, and that cotton candy stuff to the man who buys all the rest of the carnival prizes. I didn't want to say nothin' to you, because I didn't want to count my chickens too soon. Anyway, he came up to me in that dart throwin' tent yesterday and he invited me to his church this comin' Sunday. I told him that I would love to go. I could sure use some spiritual nourishment. Next thing I know, he's talkin' about how lonely he is and how he's been lookin' for a spouse all of his life. You should have seen the look on his face when I told him that I'd been lookin' for a spouse all of my life, too."

Ruby gave Othella a strange look.

"What . . . I mean . . . uh—what about *me*?" Ruby rasped, suddenly feeling even more fearful.

"What about you?"

"Did you tell him about me? Did you tell him I been lookin' for a spouse, too? He got any men friends?"

"I don't know. But I will find out as soon as I see him again. I'll tell you now, though; I'll do whatever he asks me to do if it'll get me out of this damn carnival and them fields."

Ruby had to force herself to remain composed, and it was not easy. She couldn't stand the thought of a man replacing her in Othella's life yet. And the last thing she had expected Othella to do was abandon her. She had hoped and prayed that they would find suitable mates at the same time.

"I hope . . . you will be real happy," Ruby managed, choking back a sob.

"I know I will be, Mama Ruby. And I hope you will be, too, some day."

CHAPTER 52

*T*HE VERY NEXT DAY, WHICH WAS A SATURDAY AND THE busiest day at the carnival and in the fields, Othella disappeared before Ruby got up.

Ruby didn't know where Othella had gone to, nor did anybody she asked. However, the bearded woman next door told her the last thing she wanted to hear. "I seen Othella leavin' with a man in a red suit early this mornin'. That balloon sellin' man . . ."

Later that evening after Ruby had dropped down on the bed and made herself as comfortable as she could under the circumstances, Othella moseyed into the trailer accompanied by a black man in a red suit. They were holding hands and grinning like fools.

"This here is Eugene Leroy Johnson, my *husband*," Othella introduced, her face practically glowing. "Eugene, this here is Mama Ruby."

HUSBAND!

Ruby was horrified. She had a hard time processing what she was seeing right before her burning eyes: Othella's husband! She stared at this grinning intruder who Othella had slid into their lives like a slippery eel. She was temporarily unable to speak or move. The pain in her heart was excruciating. After all that they'd been through together, she could not believe what was happening now. It was bad enough that Othella had kicked her out of her position and replaced her with a man. But for her to sneak off like a spy to *marry* him and not give her the opportunity to be with her during the ceremony was unspeakable! And if all of that wasn't bad enough, she'd dumped Ruby for so little, *literally.* Eugene was barely over five feet tall, a whole head shorter than Othella. His short, chubby, block-shaped body had short chubby legs and arms like a baby bear. Had he been any shorter, he would have been a midget. And that was not all. He looked more like a bulldog than a man. He had a round jowly face, just like a bulldog! On top of all of that, the man was at least thirty years old. Had Othella lost what was left of her mind? Ruby wondered. Or did her no-neck groom have a magic wand between his legs?

"Mama Ruby, I done heard all about you, and I want to let you know right off that I ain't goin' to come between you and Othella," Eugene sputtered. At least he had nice white teeth and fresh-smelling breath. Ruby came out of her self-induced trance when Eugene hugged her and rubbed his hand up and down her back, making her cringe. "Gimme some sugar!" Before she could stop him, he hauled off and kissed her cheek, making her cringe even more. She couldn't understand why she hadn't fainted by now.

"It's . . . uh . . . nice to meet you, too," Ruby told him in a shaky voice, her eyes rolling to the side to look at Othella. She was disappointed to see that Othella looked like she was in a dream world. Ruby couldn't remember the last time she saw such a glassy-eyed, ecstatic look on Othella's face. And since she wanted the same thing for herself, she felt a twinge of guilt for not immediately embracing Othella's actions.

"Mama Ruby, Eugene is the man I been waitin' on all of my life." Othella swooned, winking at Ruby.

"Well, you ain't got to wait no more," Ruby responded, finally forcing a weak smile. "I hope . . . I hope you both will be

happy." She had to stop talking because she didn't want to say
the wrong thing. She really did wish them well. Now all she
wanted to know was: what was in this sudden turn of events for
her?

"And Eugene's got plenty of single men friends," Othella
added with another wink. "Single men with money and nice
enough houses, lookin' to settle down."

Othella's statements got Ruby's undivided attention. Her
thoughts immediately shot off in another direction. Maybe
there *was* something in this sudden turn of events for her, too!

"Oh? Is that a fact?" she asked, scratching the side of her
face, wondering if she was desperate enough to settle for a man
as homely as Eugene, or even worse.

"That's a fact, sugar. And I want you to know right off the bat
that one of my best single buddies done already put in a bid for
you," Eugene told her, looking at Othella before he spoke
again. Then he looked at Ruby and gave her an ear to ear grin.
"My boy, his name is Roy, he went to town with us and witnessed our blessed event. Me and my sugar pie told him all
about you, so he's itchin' to meet you. He would have come
with us today to meet you, but he had to visit a sick cousin. I
hope you still available."

"And interested," Othella said quickly.

"Oh yes! I'm available and interested. Real available and real
interested," Ruby blurted, talking so fast she almost choked on
her words.

"Roy is self-employed and he rents a real nice house right
down the street from a colored man that use to be a lawyer. And
it's real close to the house where Eugene lives. Roy done made
it clear that he's ready to get married real soon," Othella added.

That made Ruby smile like she had not smiled in months. A
home, security, and a companion meant a lot to her. If there
was anything to justify marrying an ugly man, that was it. She
didn't care if this Roy was a naked ape. If he was willing to take

care of her and give her the family she needed, that was enough for her.

"I can't wait to meet Roy," Ruby squealed. She licked her lips not because they were dry, but because what she had just heard about this Roy made her salivate.

Othella stopped working in the fields, and she quit her job at the carnival and moved in with Eugene that same night. It was difficult for her to leave Ruby behind to have to deal with that elephant shit by herself, and that racist-ass Mr. Miller, but she did. However, from the next day on, Ruby spent so much time at the house Othella shared with Eugene that his neighbors thought that she had moved in with him, too.

Roy Montgomery couldn't find time to meet Ruby right away because, as Eugene explained, "He's visitin' some sick relatives in Key West." She was disappointed, but the fact that she had to wait a while made her that much more anxious to get her hands on him. She was already head over heels in love with the man, and she hadn't even seen a photograph of him. When she asked Eugene what his friend looked like, the description he offered was so vague it did her no good at all. "He ain't the best lookin' man I know, and he ain't the ugliest," he said. That could have meant just about anything, so as soon as Ruby got Othella alone, she asked her.

"Well, for one thing, he's light skinned like you prefer your men," Othella told her.

"Pffft!" Ruby rotated her neck and snapped her fingers. "I was color struck when I was young, but I ain't that shallow no more. I just want me a decent man now, and I don't care if he's purple. Other than light skin, what else can you can tell me about Roy's looks?"

"Looks ain't everything, Mama Ruby," Othella said defensively. "At least not to me . . ."

"I figured that out."

"If you are concerned about givin' birth to baboons, I wouldn't worry about that if I was you. All babies is beautiful. Didn't you tell me that yourself?"

"I did, and it's true. Any gift from God is beautiful. Othella, I wouldn't care if I did give birth to babies that looked like baboons. And to be honest with you, all I'm really interested in now is a man who treats me good and takes care of me. Even if he looks worse than Eugene—" Ruby stopped and covered her mouth with her hand.

"I know the man I married is ugly, but I don't care. He's beautiful on the inside."

"I didn't say Eugene was ugly!"

"You didn't have to."

"Anyway, if Roy looks like a cross-eyed, sway-back mule, I don't care at this point. In the dark, men all feel the same to me anyway."

"Well, like I said, Roy is light skinned. He's a bootlegger, but that don't matter because he goes to church every Sunday."

"And he just bought a house full of fancy new furniture," Eugene added, leaving the bathroom and coming back into the kitchen of the small shabby house he rented. "Roy's one of the few colored folks I know that's doin' real good these days. He don't have to put up with none of the Man's bullshit, like punchin' a time clock or payin' taxes."

Othella and Eugene didn't have to say much more to get Ruby more interested in Roy. She was ready to follow him to another planet, sight unseen.

What Eugene didn't mention, and what Othella didn't know, was that Roy Montgomery was a notorious womanizer—and was with another woman as they sat telling Ruby more about him. Roy had already been married to five different women, he currently had three lady friends, and a few exes that he still spent time with.

There was one more very important thing about Roy that

Eugene didn't bother to mention: he had a violent streak and had spent time in jail for beating his wives.

Unfortunately, Ruby would find out all of that on her own.

Roy Ernest Montgomery was the kind of man who loved women more than he loved life. He didn't care what type of woman she was, what age group she was in, or even what race she was. The day that Eugene told him about Ruby and how anxious she was to meet him, Roy thought that he had hit a jackpot.

"I love all women, but I especially love *big* women because there is so much of them to love. I love *young* women because they got so many years ahead of them to be women," he told Eugene. Even though he was laughing, he was serious and meant every word he said. He *loved* women, and the only problem with that was, he loved too many at the same time. "I can't wait to find enough time so I can fit Mama Ruby on my schedule!"

"Well, you better hurry up and find the time to fit this one on your schedule. She ain't the kind to wait around. Even though Mama Ruby wouldn't win no beauty contests, she's a nice young girl so somebody would love to marry her." Eugene held his breath as he awaited his friend's response.

"Brother, you wouldn't win no beauty contests neither, and that didn't stop Othella from marryin' you," Roy teased.

Othella was as anxious as Ruby was for her to get herself a husband. Though Othella loved her friend, she didn't like the fact that she spent so much time with her and Eugene at their house. Ruby slept on the roll-away bed in their spare bedroom several days out of the week and showed up for dinner almost every day. Ruby's presence put a serious block on Othella and Eugene's lovemaking activities.

Eugene had made several attempts to get Roy to his house to meet Ruby, but each time Roy had to cancel. Even when Eu-

gene offered to bring Ruby to his house, Roy still came up with excuses, usually with names like Martha Ann, Lucy Jean, and Bobby Mae.

Othella finally ran out of patience with Ruby breathing down her neck in her house, hours at a time, every single day now. She went to Roy's house and told him that if he didn't find time to meet Ruby, she was going to introduce her to one of his rivals. That got his attention right away. He instructed Othella to arrange a "blind date" for him and Ruby at the backyard cookout that she had been planning for that upcoming Saturday afternoon.

"Now if you don't like him, make out like you do until he leaves. I don't want my first cookout to be a disaster," Othella told Ruby as they prepared the potato salad and baked beans that would be served with the barbequed ribs and chicken.

"What makes you think I won't like him?" Ruby asked, dipping a finger into the bowl with the potatoes, licking it with a loud smack. "I already like him."

"Well, you might not like him when you meet him. He might be a real jackass to you, and you might not like the way he dresses or acts, not to mention the way he looks. After all, he is in his thirties."

"Look, he can't look no worse than none of the other men I been with, and I survived them. Bring him on!" Ruby giggled. She and Othella had been in Florida for five months. Ruby was glad that things had finally begun to fall into place for her, too.

Before Othella could continue voicing her concerns, Eugene arrived with Roy. As soon as he laid eyes on Ruby he was in love with her, just as much as she was in love with him. He wore a gray seersucker suit with a white shirt and a red tie. A white Panama hat covered most of his head, but Ruby could see that he had thick, curly black hair with a few strands of gray. She was happy to see that he was not the gargoyle that she was afraid he might turn out to be. He was no Adonis either, but he had fairly nice features. He had small, wide-set brown eyes, well-cared for teeth, and the kind of squared-jawed face that Ruby found very attractive on a man. And unlike the gnome that Othella had married, Roy not only had a neck, but he was taller than Ruby by several inches. Had she resorted to voodoo, she couldn't have conjured up a better specimen of a man, she thought to herself.

Despite the fact that he had taken his time to meet Ruby, Roy said, "I been dyin' to meet you." His eyes rested on her ample bosom.

Ruby was beside herself with glee. She giggled like a love-struck schoolgirl. "I been dyin' to meet you, too, Roy."

From that day on, Roy and Ruby were inseparable.

CHAPTER 53

*I*T DIDN'T TAKE LONG FOR ROY TO DECIDE THAT RUBY WAS just the kind of woman that he needed at the time. In addition to her being so young, she was also stout, so she could do most, if not all, of the housecleaning, and even some of the heavy maintenance work around the house. She obviously liked to eat and he was glad to hear that she was a good cook, too. She could do everything he wanted her to do—wash his clothes out by hand and even scrub the hard wooden floors in his neat little house on Board Street.

Ruby Jean Upshaw was perfect. He loved everything there was about her, even her unlikely nickname. "Mama Ruby sounds like a name for a much older female," he mentioned to her, not that he was complaining. "We called my grandma Mama Daisy."

"I love kids and they love me. I been wantin' to be a mama all my life. And not too long ago, a real good friend told me that I reminded him of his mama. That's why he gave me that nickname," Ruby explained.

Ruby was like a totally different person when she was with Roy. There were times when she was so docile and demure, Othella wanted to laugh. And when she and Ruby were alone, she did laugh at the way Ruby was portraying herself around

Roy. "I wonder what he would say if he knew about us workin' for Miss Mo'reen," Othella snickered.

"You'll never know what he would say if he ever found out about us workin' for Miss Mo'reen, because he never will find out!" Ruby thundered, looking and acting like the Ruby that Othella was more familiar with. "I'm goin' to be everything he thinks I am."

"Hmph! I declare, sister. That brother must be layin' some serious pipe in you," Othella teased.

"What do you mean by that?"

"You know what I mean! I know how you like to get nasty," Othella reminded.

"Well, Roy ain't laid no pipe in me . . . yet."

"Girl, you got to be kiddin' me! You been with him goin' on two months now and you ain't rode on his train yet?"

"Naw! He thinks he's goin' to be my first. . . ."

"Your first what?"

"My first man."

Othella's jaw dropped. "He thinks you still a virgin?"

"Yes, he thinks I'm still a virgin, and you know that I know how to make him believe that!"

"Hmmm. Well, if I hadn't thought I was pregnant, I could have used that trick on Eugene. I think he might have appreciated me even more."

"Roy said he was glad to finally meet him a woman as virtuous as me," Ruby said with a dreamy look in her eyes. "I want him to keep on thinkin' that."

Othella stared at the side of Ruby's face, shaking her head. "You better make sure you stick that chicken blood capsule up in your coochie real good, so it will do the trick. And you better hope he never finds out what you done."

"He won't find out from me. And you'd better not blow the whistle on me," Ruby warned. "If Roy is fool enough to believe that I'm a virgin, the least I can do is be fool enough to pretend I am." Ruby snorted. "If he's already treatin' me like a queen, can you imagine how good he's goin' to be to me once we get married?"

Roy did believe that Ruby was still a virgin. That was one of the reasons he loved very young women. Even though he'd been with females younger than Ruby, she was the first virgin that he'd lucked upon. The fact that he had never experienced a virgin had bothered him for years. He had six brothers, dozens of other male relatives, and a lot of male friends. He got sick of listening to them brag about how they'd broken in a virgin, and what a fantastic experience it was for a man's dick. Some claimed to have done the deed with several virgins. His own brother Mason claimed he'd been with three virgins in the same family!

Yes, Roy loved the idea of getting involved with a virgin. Finally! It had taken him long enough. He was a lot of things, but he was no fool. He was not marrying Ruby just because she was a virgin, he was marrying her for a variety of reasons. She had everything he wanted in his next wife. Besides, she had told him from day one that, being a preacher's daughter and all, she couldn't go to bed with a man unless he married her.

Roy loved sex, but he didn't pressure Ruby to sleep with him. He didn't have to. What he couldn't get from her, he got from other women. *That* was the main reason he didn't pressure her to sleep with him.

Three months after they'd met, Roy married Ruby in the courthouse with Othella and Eugene in attendance. And he made her quit her job at the carnival the next day. He even told her that she didn't have to work in the fields anymore if she didn't want to. She thought she'd died and gone to heaven.

Ruby's "honeymoon" didn't last long. Things started to slide downhill at the wedding reception in Othella and Eugene's house, just hours after she had become Roy's wife.

In front of some of Roy's drunken male friends and their significant others, Roy laid down the law, so to speak.

With a bottle of beer in each hand, he stood in the middle of the living room floor in his black suit and one of his four white Panama hats and proclaimed, "Mama Ruby is goin' to do everything I tell her to do! She don't make a move without my permission! And I ain't goin' to tolerate no complaints, no messy house, no burnt or late meals, and no bothersome in-laws! I pay the cost to be the boss! That's that. Case closed!" He laughed after he finished his long-winded declaration, so no-body took him seriously. Ruby even laughed herself, but Othella didn't see the humor in the remarks that her best friend's new husband had just made. The first chance she got, she grabbed Ruby by the hand and took her aside.

"It sounds like he's goin' to be one big-ass head of the house-hold. I hope you can deal with that," Othella told Ruby as they stood in Othella's backyard under a moss-draped tree. "Him makin' up all the rules . . ."

"A real wise old sister, who also happens to be my mama, told me when I was a little girl that it don't matter if the man is the head of a household. He can be as big a 'head of household' as he wants to be, and that's usually the case most of the time any-way. If the woman is smart and strong, she's the *neck*, and with-out a neck, the head can't even move," Ruby told Othella. "I'm smart and I'm strong."

"Sure enough," Othella agreed. "But Roy's older than you, and set in his ways. And he sounds like he means business. I don't want to see this man control you to the point where you'll end up miserable—and me mad at myself for bringin' him into your life."

"Girl, I'm blessed! I love this man from the bottom of my heart, and he loves me! I know he ain't goin' to do nothin' to upset me. You don't need to worry about gettin' mad at yourself today, Othella."

And Othella didn't. She had never seen Ruby as happy as she was now, so there was no reason for her to get mad at herself for bringing Ruby and Roy together. At least not yet . . .

Even though Roy was a bootlegger, selling alcohol without a license from a back bedroom in the two-bedroom house that he shared with Ruby, she didn't complain. For one thing, she now had access to all of the beer she wanted. And that was a good thing because beer had become like a drug to Ruby. She drank it all day, every day of the week.

People came to the house all hours of the day and night, the same way they did with the man who sold heroin in the red house across the street. Other than taking care of the house, and helping Roy host his guests, Ruby spent most of her time lounging on the living room couch eating rich food and drinking beer.

But the thing about the dope dealer across the street was, his customers would purchase their drugs and leave right away. They didn't hang around making a mess for his woman to clean up. When Roy's customers came, they came to stay awhile, partying until all hours of the night, and sometimes until past noon the next day.

It didn't take long for Ruby to get tired of cleaning up the mess the drunks made. And she spent more time in the kitchen than she did in the bedroom. She fried fish of all kinds, boiled greens of all kinds, and baked more pies and cakes from scratch than she could count. She didn't complain to Roy, but she complained to Othella every time she saw her.

"Othella, last night I was up until four in the mornin' fryin' bass and makin' hush puppies. I didn't work this hard at Miss Mo'reen's place."

"Well, at least you won't have to do much cookin' next weekend. I hope you and Roy still plan on comin' to my cookout to help us celebrate the Fourth of July and my birthday. . . ." As soon as Othella had released her last sentence, she wished that she could take it back.

"I know what you thinkin,' and I didn't mean to remind you of *that day* again. I can't tell you how much I wish I had kept my tongue still just now," Othella apologized.

"Othella, that day rolls around once every year. You don't need to remind me about what all happened on that day. I ain't never goin' to forget that that's the day my child was born . . . and took away." Ruby blinked back a few tears. "I already told you, the Fourth of July will be the hardest day in the year for me to get through for the rest of my life. And we can't change that, or the fact that it's still your birthday, too." Ruby released a wistful sigh and then she smiled. That unexpected smile made Othella relax.

"And another thing," Ruby continued. "I guess you know that Roy's got a few kids here and there by some of his exes. He ain't that old, but I hope his sap is still strong enough to stir up a few kids for me. . . ."

CHAPTER 54

*R*OY MADE A LOT OF TAX-FREE MONEY AS A BOOTLEGGER. IN fact he made more than any of the other bootleggers in the neighborhood. For one thing, he paid off the right people in city hall, so he didn't have to worry about getting raided and put out of business like so many of his competitors. He was also very shrewd when it came to making money. He watered down his drinks so he didn't lose any money with his "buy one drink, get one free" scam. And some people got so drunk that they couldn't remember whether they paid their tab or not. In most cases, they ended up paying the same tab in full, several times over.

But Roy's best rip-off scheme involved Ruby, who found it original, funny, and profitable. More money for him meant more money for her. She would complain to his customers about him being too stingy to let her have free drinks, so she would ask a male customer to buy her a few. When he did, Roy served her a glass of colored water and a real drink to the customer. Ruby was a heavy drinker by now so it was not unusual for a dozen men a night to "buy" her a drink from her own man's supply. When Roy closed down for the night, he rewarded Ruby with as much real beer as she wanted and money to spend on whatever she wanted.

"Mama Ruby, me and you are goin' to live like kings," Roy assured the new woman in his life, and he was being truthful with her. He was very generous with his money where Ruby was concerned. He gave her more than enough to purchase the things she liked. Peanut brittle, pickled pig's feet, rouge, and beer were her favorite guilty pleasures. He liked to take her to the beauty parlor to get her hair pressed and curled, her face made up, and her nails manicured and polished. He liked to take her on shopping sprees so she could pick out the kinds of clothes she liked.

Roy didn't just give Ruby the things that she wanted, he gave her things he thought she needed. One was a pearl-handled pistol that he'd won in a poker game a year ago.

"What do I need a gun for? I been carryin' a switchblade in my brassiere for years. And it's sharper than a serpent's tooth," Ruby said to Roy when he handed her the gun that evening during a lavish dinner of smothered pork chops and black-eyed peas.

"I don't care how sharp a blade is, a blade ain't goin' to do you no good if somebody get up on you too quick. Besides, you got to be a magician to handle a knife right if somebody get up on you too quick," he told her, lifting his shirt. There was a small, but ugly scar just above his left nipple. "The last time I tried to defend myself with a knife, the devil that had jumped me took it from me and cut me before I knew what was happenin'. I been carryin' a six-shooter ever since. Now you put this here gun in your pocketbook. It's real easy to use," he said, cupping her hand in his and holding the gun up to her face, pointing the barrel toward the door. "All you need to do is aim and press the trigger. POW! Do you think you can do that?"

Ruby nodded. She stared at the gun in her hand like it was a rattlesnake. "I guess I could, if I ever have to." Ruby paused and shook her head as she gently laid the gun on the table right next to a pan of buttered corn bread. "Everybody I done met in this town been real nice to me." She frowned at the gun some more, it's barrel pointed directly at Roy. "If I was goin' to chastise somebody, a gun is just too mean for my tastes."

Roy gave her an incredulous look and shook his head in bewilderment. "You think a switchblade ain't as mean as a gun?" He guffawed. "Girl, you are so damn young. Now you take this gun and when you get up from this table, you put it in your pocketbook like I told you. It's already loaded. Before we go to bed, I'll take you out to that pasture off Buchanan Road and you can practice shootin' a few squirrels, or empty cans, or a few tree trunks or somethin'. I want to make sure that when you do shoot it, you don't miss your target."

That evening, Ruby shot the gun several times at a spot that Roy had marked on a tree. Each time she hit her target, and that made Roy feel good. He loved his young bride, and he wanted to make sure she knew how to defend herself when he was not around.

Ruby ended up being glad that Roy had made her take that gun. Just five days after he'd given it to her, she had to use it.

The house to the left of Roy's was supposed to be a rooming house where black folks traveling through the South could rent rooms when the white establishments turned them away. The woman who owned the house was Maggie Lou Baxter, a once attractive but now plain woman with a Cherokee mother and a black father. Times were so hard for black women that Maggie never had to worry about keeping her rooms filled. There were a lot of women who had been either displaced due to circumstances beyond their control or deserted by their men. They had no choice but to resort to prostitution for money on an "as needed" basis. The men in the neighborhood knew about these desperate women, and sometimes men from outside the neighborhood showed up at Maggie's door looking for some female company.

Quite frequently, a horny man got confused and knocked on Roy's door by mistake. Over the years, Roy had gotten used to it. He even thought that it was funny. Ruby did, too, until a big grizzly bear of a man knocked on the door one day when she was home alone.

"I'm sorry, but you at the wrong house," she politely told the man. "You want Maggie's place next door," she whispered, nodding toward the rooming house to the left.

"You'll do," the man said. He was obviously intoxicated and determined. He looked Ruby up and down with his fishlike eyes, nodding his approval. "Uh-huh, you'll do," he said again.

"No, I won't do. Like I just told you, you at the wrong house." Ruby had escaped the grip of prostitution. And that was one ugly episode in her life that she did not like to be reminded of. "I'm a Christian woman, so what you got on your mind is offendin' me to death. I advise you to get your nasty self off my porch right now!" she growled, stomping her foot and shaking a finger in the man's face.

This just happened to be one of the days that Ruby had decided to wear one of her most provocative blouses. It was an eye-catching red, sleeveless, and it amply displayed her impressive cleavage. This was her favorite blouse because every time she wore it, Roy stopped whatever he was doing, grabbed her, and made passionate love to her. Another reason she liked this particular blouse was because Othella admired it on her so much. Othella was still talking about how she was going to purchase herself a set of those fake foam titties so she could look good in sexy blouses, too. She was coming to visit Ruby later today, and that was one of the reasons Ruby wore her sexy red blouse.

But Ruby didn't expect or want attention from a strange man like the one on her front porch now.

"What's the matter? You think you too good to sell me some pussy?" the man asked, fumbling around in his pants pocket. He pulled out some bills and shook them in Ruby's face. "Now here's my three dollars!" The horny man sniffed. "If your twat is good, I'll tip you fifty more cent."

"Sir, I done told you, this ain't the sportin' house! It's the house next door! Now if you don't leave, I'm goin' to have to make you leave!"

The man cussed under his breath, and then he lunged at Ruby, grabbing her by the throat. For the next few minutes they wrestled in the doorway of the front porch. Ruby was a big girl, but this man was bigger and she was no match for him. He pushed her into the house and was on her before she knew it. She kicked his leg and bit his hands and that only made him angry. But when he slapped her face, she snapped.

With one hand, she pushed the man halfway across the living room where he fell to the floor like a sack of rocks. He was so stunned at the nerve and strength of this young woman, that it took him a few moments to compose himself. By the time he was back on his feet, Ruby had grabbed her pocketbook off the coffee table and whipped out the gun that Roy had given her.

"If you want to live to see tomorrow you better get your tail up out of my house right now, or I will blow you to smithereens," she told her assailant, aiming the gun at his head.

"What's wrong with you, girl? Don't you know who I am? You can't be pullin' no gun on me and gettin' away with it! I know where you live—"

Ruby was glad that the window behind the man was open, and that the only thing directly outside it was an old tree. When she pulled the trigger, the bullet whizzed past the man's head, went out the window, and lodged in the tree.

"You crazy bitch! You shot at me!"

Ruby shook her head. "No, I didn't! I shot at that tree on the side of my house. But the next time, I will shoot you and where I shoot you at, well, let's just say that it won't matter what I hit on you—you won't like it. Now you get yourself out of here. And if you come back, I'll shoot first and ask questions later."

The man stumbled out of the house and shot down the street like a cannonball. Ruby went out to the sidewalk with the gun still in her hand. She watched the intruder until he was out of sight.

When Othella arrived a few minutes later, she immediately started to rave about how sexy Ruby looked in her blouse. As soon as she stopped doling out compliments, Ruby thanked her and then she told her about the incident that she'd just been involved in.

"My Lord, Mama Ruby. Would you really shoot to kill?" Othella asked, sipping from a large jar of mint julep.

"I sure enough would," Ruby told her. She showed Othella the gun, and then she wiped it and returned it to her pocketbook, glad now that Roy had made her take it.

After what had happened to Ruby today, she knew that there was a strong possibility that she'd have to use that gun again. Therefore, she had to make sure that it was always loaded and close by.

CHAPTER 55

"*F*OLKS IS GETTIN' CRAZIER AND CRAZIER. I BETTER MAKE sure you got plenty of bullets to keep in the house," Roy told Ruby after she told him about the horny intruder that she'd scared off.

"I'd rather have a new pair of red high heels," she whined. "To go with that new red dress you bought me last week."

"You can get a new pair of red high heels, too. And anything else you want. You are just the kind of woman a man like me needs," Roy assured her.

Ruby's face got hot, her crotch tingled, and her stomach fluttered. She grinned like a Cheshire cat. "Why thank you, sweetie pie," she purred.

Roy had realized right away that flattery went a very long way with Ruby. It was like mental nourishment. The more he fed her, the more she became like putty in his hands. He was molding her well—the same thing he had done with all of his other women. Being able to control a woman was one of a man's most important responsibilities. If a man could keep his woman happy, she'd keep him happy.

"Don't thank me; thank the good Lord. He outdid Hisself when he made a luscious woman like you. I could understand why that sucker tried to get his hands on you."

"Luscious? Me?" Ruby's voice was so thin, she barely recognized it. She was not used to this much flattery, and it felt damn good.

"Damn straight! And I'm keepin' your luscious self all to myself. I ain't never leavin' you!"

What Roy didn't tell Ruby was that he'd told his other wives the same things he'd just told her. He also didn't tell her, or the exes, that he only kept a particular woman all to himself, and would never leave her, *until* he found another woman that he liked better.

"Well, I'll be bound," Ruby said with a dreamy sigh. "Listen, sugar, all I want to do is keep you happy. You are a double blessin', and you deserve only the best treatment. If I ever do somethin' to disappoint you, just let me know and I'll straighten out whatever it is that I done wrong. I love you to death."

"I love you to death, too, Mama Ruby. You done made me a real happy man," Roy swooned.

Ruby couldn't have been happier. Each new day was better than the last. She couldn't wait to take Roy home to Shreveport to meet her family, which she hoped to do soon. She couldn't wait to see the looks on her six sisters' faces and their uppity husbands when she paraded her husband around in front of them. Ruby was almost afraid that if she got any happier, her heart would explode.

Roy couldn't have been happier himself. Each day his new young wife seemed more and more like a dream come true. She didn't nag him when he stayed out all night. She didn't make a fuss when too many people came to the house and got so drunk and loud in the back room that she couldn't get to sleep. And she didn't complain when the married people who came to the house to drink brought single, unattached female friends with them. Even though most of these friends were man-eating hoochie coochie women who brazenly flirted with Roy, Ruby didn't complain. She didn't complain about anything. At least not to Roy.

Despite the fact that Ruby used Othella as her sounding board, Othella thought that Ruby had a damn good thing going with Roy. He gave her a lot of attention, even in public. He held her hand, kissed up and down her neck, and he even pinched her titties right in front of Othella.

Othella was mildly jealous, and it was no wonder. Roy treated Ruby like royalty. She had married a Prince Charming, Othella had married a scalawag. Not long after her marriage to Eugene, he began to travel around the South even more in that loud old station wagon of his. He was now driving around selling knickknacks to carnivals, circuses, and amusement parks in a couple of additional states. Whenever Othella complained about his frequent absences, he reminded her that she was lucky to have a man who had a good job.

"Ain't too many colored men can get hired to travel around the way sellin' stuff like me," he reminded her. "I'm one of the best salesmen there is."

"If you think you such a good salesman, why don't you get a job that you don't have to travel so much for? You can sell the same things that them Raleigh men drive around town sellin': hair products, kitchen doodads, and sheets and blankets."

Eugene gave Othella an impatient look, something he did almost every time she spoke to him now. His job wasn't the reason he spent so much time on the road, *she* was! That was how irritating she had become. She whined like a puppy, day and night. She was like a fish stick in bed, a frozen one at that. Every time he asked her to cook him a neck bone casserole, she burned it to a crisp. It seemed that no matter what she did, it got on his nerves and annoyed him to the point of no return. She had become a nuisance, an albatross around his neck. She was smothering him and sucking his spirit out of him. The sight, the sound, the touch, the thought, and the smell of her offended him.

"Woman, what's the matter with you? What company is goin' to send a colored man out to sell women's whatnots?" Eugene growled, holding his breath to keep from gnashing her neck.

"Women buy them things! They buyin' them from them other Raleigh men!"

"For one thing, them products is expensive. Ain't enough colored women got that kind of money to make it worthwhile. Another thing is, if only white women can afford to do regular business with a Raleigh man, do you think my company is goin' to allow me to call on white women in their own homes durin' the day while their husbands and kids and whoever is out and they all alone? The first time I run into a white woman with a bad attitude, all she got to say is that I looked at her the wrong way. And the next thing you know, I'll be swingin' from a tree by my neck!"

"I know all of that," Othella said. "I just wish we had more time together. I married you so I wouldn't be so alone."

"Alone? You?" Eugene guffawed long and loud. "As long as you got Mama Ruby, you ain't never got to be worried about bein' alone. Now didn't you tell me somethin' about her havin' a birthday comin' up in a few days?"

Othella nodded. "And I bet that Roy's got all kinds of nice things planned for her."

For Ruby's seventeenth birthday, that following Saturday, Roy gave her a fistful of money and told her to go shopping on her own, because he had to visit a sick friend.

What Ruby didn't know was that the sick friend was Roy's latest girlfriend, the same woman that he had spent the night with the day before he married Ruby.

What Roy didn't know was that Ruby thought she was pregnant. She wanted to buy some baby items that she would display at a special dinner, when she would announce her good news to him. She bought the baby blankets, booties, undershirts, and other baby items. Unfortunately, by the time she got home that day she discovered that she'd bought them too soon. Her delayed period had started. She was devastated. When Roy got home an hour later, he found her in a fetal position on the couch, crying like a baby. As a matter of fact, she was so distraught she didn't even bother to ask him about his sick friend.

"Now don't you worry none, baby. You still young and healthy, so you'll get pregnant soon," Roy told her, bouncing her on his lap, lucky that she didn't smell the other woman's perfume on his shirt or see her lipstick on his collar.

A week later, when Roy came home again with the smell of another woman on his person and her lipstick on his collar, Ruby noticed. "I smell perfume," she said as soon as he strolled into the house. She sniffed some more, moving closer to him. "And I see lipstick on your shirt."

Roy was a careless man, even more so now. Ruby was so in love with him that she had lost her common sense, and sometimes it seemed like she had lost her vision. He decided that with Ruby being so lovesick, young, and stupid, he could convince her that black was white if he had to. He had Ruby so deep down inside his hip pocket that he could, and did, tell her the first thing that came to his mind when she questioned him. This time was no different.

He sucked in some air, rolled his eyes, shook his head in protest, and stuck out his chest. But this display of displeasure didn't stop him from acting like he was being accused of something un-Christian-like. "Didn't I tell you? It was Sister Barkley's birthday today. I dropped her off some of that new smell-good that the women wearin' these days, and she had to try it out right away. I didn't realize when she was huggin' me, to thank me, that she got perfume and some lipstick on me. And right in front of her husband."

Ruby leaned back on her legs, arms folded. "Who is this Sister Barkley, and how come you ain't never mentioned her to me before, sugar pie?"

Roy rolled his eyes again and brushed past Ruby. "Now, baby, you know what kind of business I do. I know *beaucoup* folks, half of 'em women. This ain't the first time a woman hugged me and got lipstick and perfume on me."

"Oh, it sure enough ain't," Ruby commented, giving Roy a stern look. "And this ain't the first time I seen lipstick on your shirt, or smelled another woman's smell-goods on you. . . ."

Roy shrugged. "I'm a bootlegger, baby. You knew that when you got with me." Roy decided that if he was going to save his face and ass, he had to defend himself more vigorously. "I know you ain't decided this late in the game to get jealous!"

"I didn't say nothin' about bein' jealous," Ruby said, pouting. She followed Roy as he moved toward the kitchen, strutting like he was a barnyard cock. And as far as he was concerned, that was exactly what he was.

To keep his role intact, he had to divert his wife's attention. "Do I smell some turnip greens cookin'?" he asked, sniffing so hard his nose twitched like a rabbit's.

Another thing that Ruby liked about Roy was his dry sense of humor. He didn't display it that often but when he did, she appreciated it. "Now you stop that, darlin'! You know you don't smell no turnip greens cookin'." She giggled in spite of herself.

"Well, can I smell some turnip greens cookin'?"

"I . . . I don't see why not. Let me go get out the Crock-Pot," Ruby said, moving toward the cabinet where she stored her cookware. "I just washed a mess of turnip greens a little while ago—"

"Hold it! Hold it right there! Come here, baby," Roy interrupted. He grabbed Ruby and pushed her up against the counter. Then he hauled off and kissed her long and passionately. And even though it was a struggle for a man his size, he managed to lift Ruby's hefty frame into his arms and take her to the bedroom.

By the time Roy finished making love to Ruby, she was so dazed and pliant, she almost slid off the bed.

CHAPTER 56

WHEN RUBY'S PERIOD WAS LATE AGAIN THE FOLLOWING month, she went out and purchased more baby clothes. She also purchased a crib and several pieces of baby furniture. By the end of that month, Ruby had everything in her house that indicated she was a mother, except a baby.

A year later, when she finally did get pregnant, she didn't believe it until two doctors confirmed it. And a week later when Othella discovered that she was also pregnant, Ruby was the first person she shared her good news with.

"And it's a damn shame that your husband ain't here to hear this blessed news before I did," Ruby told Othella, giving her a much needed and a much appreciated hug. "I guess we both know by now that when we can't count on our men to be there for us when we need 'em, we can always count on each other."

"I wish we women could marry women. That would solve most of our problems," Othella quipped, her voice cracking.

Ruby shook her head and patted her crotch. "Not all of our problems, honey." She laughed, and was glad that Othella did, too. But she knew Othella well enough to determine that she was not happy about the way her marriage was going.

"I hope my next husband is more like Roy," Othella said, her voice dripping with sarcasm.

Eugene was away on another alleged sales trip for a "few days." He had been gone for a week, but was supposed to be home by now. He had disappointed Othella in every way possible. She didn't know how to get in touch when him when he was working, she didn't know how much money he made at his mysterious job, and she never knew when he was going to give her any money to spend. Not just on herself, but for the household incidentals. When she wasn't babysitting some of the neighborhood children or cleaning somebody's house to make money, she borrowed from Ruby. The money issue and Eugene's frequent absences were bad enough as far as Othella was concerned. But the man was also flawed in other ways that irritated her. He did not pay much attention to her, even when they were together. And he didn't seem to care about her feelings at all. Last month when he was home for a two-week period, she talked him into accompanying her on the bus to visit her family in Shreveport. The visit was supposed to last for a week. When they returned, four days after they had departed, Othella was too upset to tell Ruby why the trip had been cut short until three days later. And by then, Eugene was gone again.

"He claimed he had to rush off to go check on a sick sister in Memphis that I didn't even know he had," Othella complained to Ruby. "Now don't you take this the wrong way, but I wish I had been the one to get Roy. He's perfect, ain't he?"

A thoughtful look spread across Ruby's face like butter. But just a split second later, she looked confused and uneasy. "What's wrong with you, girl? You know the Bible almost as good as I do. Even Moses wasn't perfect!"

"Oh, you know what I mean. I mean that for a regular man, Roy is about as close to perfect as one can get, right?"

"Well, he tries to be," Ruby answered slowly, and with a mysterious gleam in her eyes.

"Well, at least he is tryin' to be perfect!" Othella said. "And that's way more than I can say about that *thing* I married."

Roy continued to give Ruby large sums of money to go shopping, and he was just as happy as she was about the fact that she was finally pregnant. But it was not because he wanted to be father of the year, or because he loved kids. He knew that a baby would keep Ruby even busier. Once she had the baby, she wouldn't have time to badger him as much about the things that he did when he wasn't with her, and the things he didn't do when he was with her.

Ruby was so excited that she couldn't buy enough baby clothes, and she couldn't buy them fast enough. And Roy couldn't make the money fast enough for her. He didn't discourage her when she answered a newspaper ad and started babysitting for the niece of Silo's mayor.

"You just make sure you take real good care of that white woman's kids. It don't matter how young they is, don't sass 'em. And you sure better not whup 'em, no matter what they do or say to you. You don't want to upset the mayor," Roy warned Ruby.

"I know how to handle white kids. I took real good care of a white woman's baby in New Orleans. That baby wanted to be with me more than the mama," Ruby replied. Just the thought of little Viola back at Maureen's house made her feel sad. She couldn't wait to have her own baby so she could know exactly what it meant to be a mother.

One month before Ruby's due date, she stretched out on a red leather couch in the living room of the woman who had hired her to look after her two young sons. She had consumed a five-pound box of peanut brittle, three sugar tits, a large moon pie, and nine bottles of beer since Roy had dropped her off, two hours ago. Not only was her belly stuffed, she was enjoying a very nice buzz.

"Now look, Bobby, Jimmy is your baby brother so stop teasin' him," Ruby scolded, thumping the five-year-old on his blond head, making him howl like a baby wolf. She rose and glanced out the window, clutching one-year-old Jimmy in her arms. She gasped and set the boy down on the couch as she rushed out to the spacious front porch. "I don't believe what I'm seein'," she said, talking to herself as she stared at the car moving slowly down the street.

Ruby trotted down the porch steps. She didn't stop trotting until she reached the end of the block. The car that she'd seen had stopped at a red light, and before she could catch up to it, it shot off as if the driver knew she was in pursuit.

And she was in pursuit. She knew who was driving that dusty black Chevy, and she had a good idea where it was going. It took her twenty more minutes to reach Smoky Moe's bar.

Roy was surprised and annoyed when Ruby stormed into the bar and stomped over to a booth in the back that he occupied. A thin, attractive woman in her early thirties with thick brown hair and a silver plated front tooth was on his lap, kissing his cheek.

"Mama Ruby, what the—what the hell you doin' in here?" Roy yelled, rearranging the woman on his lap. "You supposed to be watchin' that white woman's kids!"

"Baby, who is this beast?" the woman sneered, looking Ruby up and down.

"Woman, if you want to live to see tomorrow, you better get your skinny tail off my husband's lap!" Ruby erupted. A small crowd quickly formed in front of the booth.

The owner, a gray-haired white man in his sixties, held his breath as he stood behind the counter. He owned the only establishment in the area that served blacks. They had to enter through a back door and were only allowed to occupy the back booths. Ruby had done the unthinkable, or at least something that no other black person had ever done; she'd entered through the front door, just like the white couple that she had come in behind.

"Don't you be gettin' crazy in this white man's place now, woman," Roy warned Ruby, shoving his girlfriend off his lap.

"We need to take this mess home," he said, rising. "And you better make this the last time you clown me in public!" Roy didn't wait for Ruby to respond. He grabbed her by the arm and attempted to steer her out of the bar. He managed to smile as he waved to the nervous owner, who had already picked up a telephone on the counter.

"Roy, is this that teenage battle-ax I heard you got married to?" the woman asked, scooting out of the booth. The woman stood next to Roy as she laughed and shook her finger in Ruby's face. "You must be stupider than I heard you was! Roy is *my* man and he's been my man for a long time. As soon as I get rid of that old dog I married and Roy gets rid of you, with your husky self, me and him will get married." Ruby's eyes followed the woman's hand as she grabbed Roy's hand and held onto him like he was made of gold.

Had Roy pushed the woman aside and denied what she'd just said, it might have made all of the difference in the world. But he didn't. He stood there looking at Ruby with contempt. All he could think about was how he was going to get a switch and whup her ass as soon as he got her home. Didn't she know that he was only doing what men had been doing since the beginning of time? There wasn't a man on earth who could be happy with just one woman in his life! Didn't women know that by now?

He finally spoke again. "Mama Ruby, tonight me and you are goin' to sit down and have a long talk. I told you to your face, on the same day I married you, how it was goin' to be with me and you. I PAY THE COST TO BE THE BOSS, BITCH! You will not be spyin' on me like this no more! Do you hear me?"

Ruby calmly looked from her husband's face to the woman's as they stood smack dab in front of her, holding hands like they were Romeo and Juliet.

When Ruby lunged at the woman, Roy grabbed Ruby's arm. He attempted to punch her in the face, but he was no match for

her. She swiveled her head out of the way just in time so he
missed. Just as he was about to swing at her again, she slapped
his face so hard, his false teeth—that she didn't even know he
wore—flew out of his mouth. He yelped and kicked her leg,
bringing her to her knees. A split second later, she sprang up
like a jack-in-the-box. There was a look on her face that words
could not describe. It was a look that frightened everybody in
the bar, even the owner, and he was an ex-cop. Her nostrils
flared, her eyes darkened, her jaw twitched, and her lips quivered. If there was such a thing as a she-devil, Ruby was it.

"I . . . I ain't goin' to put up with this mess. I'm goin' to beat
you like you stole somethin'," Roy told Ruby, looking angry
and embarrassed at the same time. "Don't you worry none, Mr.
Brown, I got this situation under control!" he told the bar
owner. He ignored his false teeth on the floor and proceeded to
punch Ruby in her stomach, her chest, and on her arms. He
and everybody else present were stunned: none of his punches
fazed his enraged wife. She stood there glaring at him with one
hand calmly rooting through her purse. Roy delivered a blow
to her face that was so severe, he broke the knuckles on two of
his fingers.

But even that didn't faze Ruby.

The woman who had accompanied Roy to the bar dropped
to her knees and crawled under the table in the booth, shaking
like a leaf.

Roy was sweating bullets. That was why he didn't feel the
one that Ruby fired into his heart. He was dead before he hit
the floor.

Ruby had not contacted her parents or anybody else in her
family since she'd left home. But they were not worried about
her, thanks to Othella. Othella still wrote to her siblings and
her mother on a regular basis. In each letter, she gave her family a sanitized version of what she and Ruby were up to. Most of
the information that she fed to them was ninety percent false,

such as part of her most recent letter: . . . *Me and Ruby Jean clean houses for rich white women, and we are out here in Florida living like kings in a rich white woman's guest house. And we are both married to real handsome businessmen.* . . .

"I wonder why they left New Orleans and went to Florida," Simone asked Ike after he'd read Othella's letter to her.

"You know Othella and Ruby, Mama. They like to get around," Ike surmised. "And ain't it a pip them gettin' married, too?"

"Sure enough. And to *businessmen*! I always knew that them two had real high expectations," Simone said with a profound sigh. "I'm so glad my girl didn't end up like me."

Ruby's father was still giving "spiritual comfort" to Othella's mother, and he was still paying her to let him do so. She was the one who relayed information about Ruby to him.

"I'm so glad I can tell Mother that Ruby Jean done settled down and got herself married," he said, grinning after Simone read Othella's letter to him. "I always knew my girl was goin' to make somethin' of herself. I just hope this man of hers can control her enough to keep her out of trouble."

At the same time that Ruby's father was speaking those words, Roy was being loaded into a hearse.

And Ruby, handcuffed and dazed after she'd been subdued by the butt of a deputy's revolver on the back of her head, was being transported to jail.

CHAPTER 57

RUBY HAD NOT HAD THE TIME NOR INTEREST IN JOINING A new church since she left home. Not only did she not have a church home to fall back on in times of need, she didn't know of one single preacher that she could call on for spiritual comfort.

"Othella, I been in this jailhouse for two days, and they ain't told me nothin'. I don't know what they goin' to do with me," Ruby sobbed. "I wish my daddy was here to pray with me!"

"I can find a preacher if you want me to," Othella offered. "Roy's brother stopped by the house last night, and he told me that he was handlin' the funeral arrangements, and that the service will be at the little Pentecostal church on Jersey Street if I wanted to come. If you don't mind, I can ask that preacher's name and have him come see you."

"I don't think that's such a good idea. I don't think anybody that knows Roy would want to have anything to do with me after . . . after what I done to Roy."

"You want me to send a wire to your daddy? I know he'd be here lickety-split if you want him to. Your mama and probably all six of your sisters would come, too."

"Oh good gracious no! I don't want my family to know what

a mess I done made of my life. I am . . . I am so ashamed of the way I turned out. Look at me!"

"Mama Ruby, you got a baby in your belly to consider. Florida ain't no state to mess with when it comes to crime. What if they put you in the 'lectric chair, or whatever it is they do down here to killers."

"Killer? Is that what you think I am?"

"That's what people usually call people who kill other people. And you bein' a colored woman, them white folks wouldn't think twice about killin' you before that baby gets here. Lord have mercy, what a mess this is," Othella moaned, rubbing her own belly. "And Eugene ain't nowhere to be found. I tried to wire him at that motel that he told me he'd be at while he was in Pensacola. They told me that he checked out two days ago."

"And?"

"And where has that jackass been for two days? I ain't seen him. None of his friends or family will tell me nothin' about his whereabouts. Now with this mess you done got yourself into, I got a feelin' I'll be all alone when my baby comes."

Ruby rubbed her belly. "You think they'll let me out to have my baby? I don't want my child to be born in no jail cell."

"Mama Ruby, think about what you done. You done killed a man. They might not care enough to execute you because Roy was a colored man, but the white folks will sure enough send you to prison, maybe even a chain gang. They don't care about you bein' pregnant. At the very least, they might lock you up for life."

"You got the key to my house. Go into my bedroom and raise up the linoleum by the window with the lamp next to it. There's a bunch of money hidden there. Roy didn't trust banks and he didn't want Uncle Sam nosin' around, askin' how he made his money."

"You got a lawyer? You want me to give him that money?"

"Yeah, unless you know a good voodoo woman."

"I don't know no lawyer, and I sure don't know no voodoo

woman." Othella paused and a wistful look appeared on her face. "But I can assure you that I will hunt up a good voodoo woman that'll turn things around for me and you. Maybe I'll even have her teach that husband of mine a lesson or two, so he won't be strayin' like a dog every month. I can't think of no other way to make Eugene straighten up and stop leavin' me on my own so much."

"You can kill him. If that don't stop him, nothin' will," Ruby said.

"Mama Ruby, I know you ain't tryin' to make light of what done happened. You goin' to prison and there is just no tellin' how long you'll be there. Now shet your eyes and let's pray for mercy."

Ruby and Othella prayed for ten minutes. Right after Othella left, Ruby sat down on the hard cot in the cold, ominous cell and cried like a baby. When she finished, she prayed some more. She promised God that if He kept her from going to prison for killing Roy, she would never shoot another man as long as she lived.

Her prayers were answered in a roundabout way. The judge had reduced the charge of murder against Ruby to self-defense, which is what she had claimed in the first place. And with the people in the bar who had witnessed the altercation, the self-defense claim worked in her favor.

However, the same judge told Ruby that she had committed more than one crime that day: she had jeopardized the safety of those two white children who had been left in her care by leaving them in the house alone when she went to the bar to shoot Roy. Didn't she remember that the older boy liked to play with matches? the judge had asked. As soon as Ruby had left that firebug alone with his baby brother, he'd searched around until he'd located a box of matches. His mother arrived home just in time from the beauty parlor to put out the fire that he'd started in the kitchen with some old newspapers. And these were not just two random white kids. The mother was the mayor's niece—

his favorite niece at that! The judge told Ruby that she had cooked up a "mighty big mess." And for that, she most certainly had to be appropriately "chastised."

The judge sentenced Ruby to one month and a day in the county jail for leaving the two white children in the house alone.

Othella was there to escort Ruby home from jail by bus on the day that she was released. They spent the first couple of hours drinking as much of the liquor that they could that Roy had left behind. Then they packed up everything else in the house. Roy's brothers were coming to get his car, his furniture, and his other belongings. He had paid three months rent in advance the week before his death, but Ruby had vowed that she'd never spend another night in that house. And, since Roy was not going to return, unless he returned as a ghost, the landlord promised Ruby that he would reimburse the extra rent money to her.

"I'm right back where I started," Ruby complained to Othella, minutes after they'd collected some of Ruby's possessions and begun hauling them down the street in two large wheelbarrows to Othella's house. Ruby had purchased so many new things for herself and her baby that they had to make several trips with those wheelbarrows. But Ruby didn't mind doing that. She had other things to worry about. One was being alone again. "I ain't got no husband no more." She sniffed to keep herself from crying. She had done enough of that since she'd killed Roy.

"I guess I could say the same thing myself. Eugene was home for one day last week and now he is on the road again. He could have at least come home to attend Roy's funeral," Othella lamented, sounding even more morose than Ruby. She saw the pitiful look on Ruby's face so she decided to lighten up the conversation. "I know you will feel so much better after your baby gets here. The midwife that lives across the street from me, she's goin' to deliver for me and you both for twenty-five dollars apiece. They don't admit colored folks in the hospital here."

"That ain't nothin' new to me. Me and all of my sisters was born right in my mama's bed with a midwife. And don't forget about my . . ." Ruby gripped the handles of her wheelbarrow tighter and looked straight ahead. Othella was surprised to see a smile suddenly appear on Ruby's face. "My baby's due any day now, and I know your due date ain't too much farther away. But even after all that's happened, we'll still have each other and our babies. I guess I'll have to work in the fields again, and take on as many babysittin' jobs as I can get until my baby comes. And I'll have to get back to work right away after that." Ruby sniffed. "Boy, what I wouldn't do to have my mama with me."

"Mama Ruby, your mama would be glad to have you back at home. And she'd be happy as pie to be with you when your baby comes."

Ruby shook her head. "I'll send her a letter. You got a stamp?"

Othella rolled her eyes. "I got plenty of stamps. You ask me about stamps all the time, but you never take them. But don't worry. Every time I write a letter to my folks, I tell my mama to send word through somebody to your folks that you're doin' just fine."

"And I am doin' just fine, Othella. I'm about to be a mother, and that's what I need to focus on now," Ruby said with a heavy sigh. Less than thirty minutes after they reached Othella's house, Ruby went into labor.

Othella watched Ruby give birth, just like the first time. Virgil Lee Montgomery entered the world with a chip on his shoulder. Even with his eyes closed and his mouth stretched open as he screamed like a banshee, he challenged his mother. When the midwife placed him in Ruby's anxious arms, he kicked his long, plump legs and waved his arms, hitting Ruby in the face several times, leaving a bruise on her bottom lip.

"He's a feisty little booger," Othella noticed, hovering over the midwife's shoulder as Ruby lay on the bed, still writhing in pain. "You ain't goin' to have to worry about nobody messin' with him, Mama Ruby."

Once again, Ruby was happy. Or at least she appeared to be. She was proud of her son and started parading him around the neighborhood two days after his birth.

"He's such a pretty little yellow thing! And with all of that wavy hair, he should have been a girl!" one woman commented.

"My next one will be a girl, God willin'," Ruby predicted, wondering how long it would be before she got pregnant again.

The first couple of weeks went well. And things got even better when Othella gave birth to her son Clyde a week later. Even though money was tight and their future more uncertain than ever before, Ruby and Othella spent their days and nights fussing over their babies.

When the money got even tighter, they were forced to go back to work sooner than they had planned. Once again, they were performing the backbreaking farm labor that they had both come to despise. Neither of the new mothers wanted to leave her baby in the care of a babysitter, even though there were several competent babysitters in the neighborhood. Ruby carried her son in a pillowcase pouch around her waist when she picked oranges at the Gembing Brothers' orange grove. Othella was too frail to work ten hours a day with her baby strapped to her body. She placed her son in a basket on top of a flattened out pillow and set the basket on the ground under a palm tree while she worked.

But the babies didn't fulfill all of their needs. At least not for Othella. Being a mother wasn't enough for her. She was lonely. She hadn't seen Eugene in two months and when he showed up a week later, it was just to take a quick peek at his new son and to get more of his clothes.

"I think my husband is involved with another woman,"

Othella told Ruby. "And if he don't come to his senses soon, I just might not be here when he gets back the next time."

Eugene was a few steps ahead of Othella. He had already moved in with another woman in Sarasota. And when he did come home again, two weeks later, it was only to get the rest of his belongings. That was the last time Othella saw or heard from him. He never bothered to check on his son or send a dime to help support him.

"Let that fool go on about his business," Ruby told her. "So far, all men have done for us was get us in trouble."

"What about the babies?"

"And that, too," Ruby said with a gasp and a cackle. "That was all Roy was good for. May he rest in peace until I get there. . . ."

CHAPTER 58

OTHELLA LOVED HER SON, BUT THERE WERE TIMES WHEN she resented being tied down with a baby. It took a lot of money to support Clyde, which meant more hours of backbreaking work in those damn fields. She had begun to hate oranges, beans, sugarcane, potatoes, cabbage greens, and cucumbers from the bottom of her heart.

With the sun beating down on her for up to ten hours a day, five to six days a week, Othella had begun to lose her looks. Another reason that Othella was not too thrilled to be a mother was that she could no longer come and go as she pleased. And even though she had started seeing other men, she couldn't entertain them as freely as she wanted to. She was disappointed that Ruby didn't feel the same way.

Ruby *loved* being a mother. Despite the fact that she didn't give birth to a baby girl, she didn't let that stop her from treating her son like a daughter. She dressed him in frilly bonnets and ruffled gowns. She even adorned his thick hair with pastel-colored barrettes and ribbons, or braided it, despite his tearful protests.

At first, Othella didn't give too much thought or concern to the way Ruby was dressing that poor baby. For one thing, Ruby had already purchased most of her baby's wardrobe way before his birth, or before she even got pregnant for that matter. And since she'd been convinced that she'd give birth to a girl, she had purchased only feminine items. But as the boy grew, Ruby continued to purchase girly clothes for him. She bought a doll for him to play with, but that didn't last long. The very first time that Virgil's little friends saw him carrying a doll, they taunted him and called him a sissy. He ran into the house and cried and then he ripped off the doll's arms and legs and bit its nose down to a nub. Ruby laughed it off, but she never bought him another doll.

Othella became concerned when she went to visit Ruby in the little three-room house she rented a couple of blocks away, finding Ruby ironing a girl's bonnet that she had purchased for Vigil. Raising him like a girl had not been so bad when Virgil was an infant. But by this time, he was a year and a half old.

"Mama Ruby, I ain't tryin' to tell you how to raise your boy, but you don't want no sissy on your hands. Remember that sissy man what lived on Powell Street back home?" Othella said.

"You mean the one that everybody called Punk Willie?"

"That's him. Remember how people used to mess with him all on account of him bein' a sissy?"

"He was a sissy and if he ain't dead, he probably still is a sissy," Ruby replied. "He didn't try to hide it. He wore makeup, fixed his hair like a woman, and wore dresses from time to time. He looked better as a woman than he did as a man!"

"My mama told me that when he was a little boy, his mama used to dress him like a girl. She'd even marcel his hair to make him look like that Shirley Temple."

"What are you tryin' to say?"

"Don't make your son's life no harder than it's already goin' to be. He's goin' to have to deal with a lot of things because of his color. That's enough of a burden; me and you both know that. Don't add to his burden by makin' him be somethin' that so many folks don't accept."

"At least I don't put dresses on my boy, and I don't marcel his hair. He likes the way I dress him in all them pretty blouses and sandals."

"But you do everything else that you'd do for a little girl."

"Virgil is too young for it to bother him. And he looks so cute in his bonnet! Besides, by the time he's old enough to know better, I'll have me a new husband and a girl baby or two. Matter of fact, I got me a date lined up for tomorrow with that new overseer at the grove where we picked oranges at last week. He just might be *the one*."

The man who took Ruby and her son on a picnic the next day was not "the one." After he slept with Ruby that night, he never spoke to her again.

As the months crawled by, Ruby predicted that each new man whom she allowed into her life and bed could be "the one." But the one that she spent the next few years preparing for never came.

Five more years passed, and the only male who remained in Ruby's life for more than a night or a few weeks was her son Virgil. Ruby had become hopelessly addicted to beer. She drank up to twelve cans a day when she could afford it. She had also gained eighty more pounds. But since that didn't stop men from approaching her, her weight didn't faze her one bit.

Othella's luck with men was not much better than Ruby's. She had lovers come and go. And the only indication that she'd had lovers at all was the fact that she'd had five more children, four of them girls!

Each time Othella gave birth to a girl, Ruby slid into a deep, painful state of depression. But she didn't want Othella to know that. As difficult as it was, she kept a smile on her face when she was around Othella with her babies. She wanted her friend to believe that she was happy enough with just her son, and she was—somewhat. Even though she still dressed him like a girl most of the time. But Virgil was not a weak or docile little boy. He eventually started to rip off and dispose of those frilly flowered blouses and lace panties. And as fast as Ruby dolled up his hair, he snatched those pastel-colored barrettes, ribbons, and bows off and either stomped them to pieces or threw them at her.

"I ain't no girl, Mama Ruby! I ain't wearin' no girl stuff no more!" Virgil yelled on the day that Ruby attempted to make him wear a ponytail with a black ribbon dangling down the back of his head like a python. He was six years old now, and she had never had his hair cut. By this time, it was past his shoulders.

"But, honey baby, everybody talks about you bein' way too pretty to be a boy. And the way they fuss and fawn over you, they wouldn't do it if you was a *regular* boy!" Ruby reasoned. "Enjoy it as long as you can, sugar!"

"If you want a baby girl so bad, go take one from Othella! She got way too many—you said so yourself!"

That much was true. Not only did Othella have too many baby girls, but Ruby often told her so. "Othella, if it wasn't a shame I'd sneak in your house one night, snatch one of them girl babies you got, and I'd run like hell. I'd raise her as my own." Ruby laughed.

"And I wouldn't try to stop you," Othella told her. She laughed, too. "Maybe then poor little Virgil can lead a normal life."

"Don't worry about my boy. He ain't goin' to grow up to be no sissy. The boy is way too mean for that."

Virgil was just mean enough to cut his own hair that night with the scissors that Ruby kept in her sewing basket next to her bed. He wanted his mother to give birth to a baby girl just as much, if not more, than she did.

When Ruby walked into the tiny room that was supposed to be a pantry and saw her son sitting on his roll-away bed scooping his shorn hair up off the pillow, she screamed and swayed from side to side. And then she fainted.

After that day, she never treated her son like a girl again.

* * *

When Ruby and Othella were not working in the fields, they spent hours at a time on Othella's front porch kicking back, chitchatting about one thing or another, and drinking beer. Their lives had become predictable and routine. And in some ways, empty.

"Mama Ruby, you ain't got to be over here all the time. With this house full of kids I got, they can help me all I need with these younger ones," Othella told Ruby. It was a Saturday afternoon in March.

"You know I don't mind comin' over here," Ruby mumbled. "After slavin' away in them fields so much, this is real relaxin' and I love watchin' you with all of them kids."

"Listen, I don't want you to take this the wrong way, but I really do feel bad for you and the fact that you can't seem to get the family you really want."

"What's that supposed to mean?"

"I love my babies, and you know I do. And no matter how many times I douche myself out after I been with a man, I keep gettin' pregnant. It ain't fair for women like me to keep havin' babies. It ain't fair that there's women like you with just one child that really wants a house full and can't seem to have 'em."

"Well, I guess it wasn't meant to be. But the good Lord did bless me with one child, when there is women all over the world that can't even have one. So I still feel blessed."

"But you still want a baby girl to . . . you know . . . to replace that other one."

"We ain't talked about that in a long time," Ruby mumbled, tears forming in her eyes.

"I know we ain't, but I know you like I know the back of my hand. Ain't a day goes by that you don't think about that baby you gave up."

"The baby you and your mama *made* me give up," Ruby reminded.

"We won't go into all that. But the thing is, you ain't never goin' to get over that until you have another baby girl. Maybe not even then. You been harpin' on this for so long that by now you probably think you deserve a few baby girls, not just one."

Ruby had stopped believing that she'd ever find another husband. But she still believed that she would eventually have a daughter.

"You know you can always go get you a baby girl from one of them orphanages. Even if it's just a foster child. Them orphanage folks don't care who they place colored kids with." As soon as those words left Othella's mouth, she wanted to bite off her own tongue. What she had just said was the last thing that Ruby needed to hear. Othella sucked in her breath and awaited Ruby's wrath.

"What in the world makes you think I'd do somethin' like that?"

"Well, I . . . I thought . . ." Othella couldn't even finish her sentence.

"The *only* baby girl that I would want from a orphanage is the one you and your mama made me give up!"

"I'm just tryin' to help!" Othella whined. She was holding her daughter, Mae Alice, so tight, you would have thought that she was afraid Ruby was going to snatch that baby and bolt. "I don't know what else to say to you when you get like this."

"Then maybe you should stop sayin' anything about it at all!" Ruby hollered.

"Don't you put all the blame on me, girl! You always the one that brings the subject up, most of the time!"

Ruby bowed her head and shook it. Then she looked up and gave Othella a tight little smile. "I know," she said with a heavy sigh and a dismissive wave. "Give me that baby so I can burp her. You look awful. You need to get some rest." Ruby paused and widened her smile. "Me and you both hope you don't get pregnant so quick with the next one."

"I hope there ain't no next one. I done had enough babies."

"Well, as long as you keep spreadin' your legs, these babies will continue to come."

"I know, I know, Mama Ruby. And I know none of them daddies will stay around to help me raise them kids neither."

"Men! Low-down, funky black dogs. Just like Satan." Ruby laughed. She hugged Othella's new baby against her chest and patted the baby's back. "I just hope I get me one of them dogs with some sap potent enough for me to have the baby girl I deserve."

"Well, I hope I don't hook up with another one with no potent baby-makin' batter no more." This time Othella laughed.

CHAPTER 59

*T*IME MOVED ON FOR RUBY AND OTHELLA. OTHELLA'S NEXT lover arrived less than two months after she'd given birth to her eighth child. When she didn't get pregnant by him during the three months that he courted her, she decided that her baby-making equipment had finally shut down and not a minute, or a baby, too soon.

Ruby purposely got involved with a man who had fathered twenty children with three different women. "If *his* sap ain't strong enough to make me a girl baby, I'm goin' to throw in the towel and get me a girl puppy," Ruby said to herself two days after her son's eleventh birthday. She was joking, of course. Because by now Ruby was convinced that she would never have another child.

Ruby, Othella, all of their children, and Bo, the man Ruby was involved with at the time, celebrated Ruby's birthday that May in Ruby's backyard. Bo and the two oldest boys, Virgil and Clyde, had built a picnic table where they all sat munching on spicy ribs that Bo, who was from Jamaica, had cooked using his mama's special recipe. It was May 21.

"This is de best cookout I've attended since I left de island," Bo said, giving Ruby a loving look. Ruby thought that he was too good looking for his own good, with his naturally curly red hair and dimples. Which meant he wouldn't be with her too much longer. Men who looked like him, who approached women who looked like her, were usually after the same basic things: convenient sex, a few home-cooked meals, a "few dollars till I get on my feet" that they never paid back, and a place to sleep until they found one better.

"You should have seen what all we had last year at Mama's birthday cookout," said Othella's son Clyde. He was lucky that he had inherited her good looks and build, and not his beastly, short-legged father's—who hadn't been seen or heard from in years now.

"Oh? When was that?" Bo asked, smacking on a roll, looking around the table at each face. He didn't like kids, and that was the only reason he'd approached Ruby instead of Othella at the juke joint the night they'd met. He could deal with the one that Ruby had, but not the mob that Othella had produced. "I hope I'm able to attend it this year. When is your birthday?" he said, looking at Othella.

She didn't have a chance to answer. Ruby did it for her. "Fourth of July," she said in a strong voice.

"Ow wow wow! On de holiday! We'll have a double celebration! And oh, what a happy day it will be!" Bo sang.

Like so many others before him, his lip service was just that—lip service. Bo had gone on his merry way by the time July rolled around, and it was just as well. Even though it was Othella's milestone birthday, and she wanted to mark the occasion, Ruby came down with a devastating summer cold and had to remain in bed for a week and a half. The very next day after she recovered, Othella took to her bed with the same symptoms. Then the kids took turns getting sick with one childhood malady after another.

By September, they had all forgotten about celebrating Othella's thirtieth birthday. For once, Ruby was glad. Each year she dreaded that day in July. And even though the tragedy that had made it such an undesirable date in her life had occurred fifteen years ago, it still caused her a tremendous amount of pain. By now, she knew that it would be painful until the day she died, or until the day she got her baby girl back. . . .

A few weeks later, Othella got sick again at Ruby's house. This time it was nausea, a migraine headache, and dizziness. She reluctantly broke the news to Ruby that she suspected she was pregnant again. That information didn't even faze Ruby. As a matter of fact, she even made a joke about it.

"If this one is a girl, I just might run off with it." She laughed, rubbing Othella's belly.

Ruby said the same thing a few months later when Othella went into labor as they sat drinking beer in Ruby's kitchen.

"You might steal my baby and run off? Ha! You done said that so many times! But I know you better than that. Mama Ruby, you ain't the kind of woman that would steal another woman's baby."

Ruby stared at her kitchen wall as if in a trance. She took her time speaking again. "Let's have a cookout in my backyard to celebrate this new baby. I got that record by that new singer we seen on *The Steve Allen Show* the other week. That Elvis Presley. Remember him?"

Othella nodded vigorously and squealed like a teenager. "Oh yeah! He plays a mean guitar, and he ain't a bad singer for a white boy. A cookout is a good plan. I should be up and about, day after tomorrow, if it comes tonight like I have a feelin' it will." Othella got quiet as she drew imaginary circles with her finger on the top of Ruby's kitchen table. "Would you do that to me?" Othella asked, snapping her fingers to get Ruby's attention.

"A cookout? I've done it with all them other babies you had. What makes you think I wouldn't do it for this new one that's fixin' to come in a few hours?" Ruby replied, turning slowly to face Othella.

"I didn't mean that. I meant, what you said about stealin' my baby."

"Oh. Would I steal your baby?" Ruby laughed. She didn't answer Othella's peculiar question because at this point, she didn't know if she was the kind of woman who'd steal another woman's baby. She stopped laughing and snapped her fingers because she suddenly remembered something. "Oh, before I forget . . ." She stopped talking, removed a folded envelope out of her bra and handed it to Othella. "The mailman put it in my box by mistake. It's from your mama."

"More upsettin' news, no doubt," Othella sighed, stuffing the envelope into her bra. "I wonder who died this week, or what new affliction my mama done contracted."

Othella's letters from home usually contained depressing news, especially the last few years. But not that long ago, Simone used to send letters that contained lots of uplifting information. She had reported that none of Othella's three younger sisters had resorted to prostitution or a reckless lifestyle on any level. All three had graduated from high school. The two older girls had married truck drivers, and the other girl was engaged to marry a politician's chauffeur. Othella's brothers had also done quite well, considering the fact that they'd been raised by a prostitute. Two of her three brothers had finished high school, and all three had served in the military. They had all eventually secured respectable jobs. Every single one of her siblings occasionally attended Ruby's father's church, something they had never done as children. And every single one of them had children of their own. Othella smiled just thinking about all the good things that had happened to her family. But she still was in no hurry to read her mother's letter.

"You ought to read Simone's letter now, in case there's somethin' important in it," Ruby suggested, popping the top off another bottle of beer with the teeth of a bent fork.

Othella shook her head. "I'll read it when I go home. No, I'll wait and read it after I have the baby. I know it's goin' to be somethin' gloomy, so I ain't in no rush."

"When you write your mama back, tell her I said hi, and tell her to tell my folks I'm doin' real good," Ruby said, taking a long drink.

It was the one letter that Othella should have opened right away. Had she done so, it would have made all of the difference in the world to her, and to Ruby.

Simone wrote:

Dear Daughter,
My health is still as bad as it was like I mentioned in my last letter. If I live to see Christmas this year, I will be surprised. In case I don't, I need to tell you something because it's too heavy a burden for me to carry with me to my grave.

For years, you been trying to get me to tell you where Ruby's baby was left off at. Now that the end is near for me, I realize that it was wrong for one mother to deny another woman her motherly rights. Last Friday, I managed to crawl out of my sick bed and drive to Bolton Road in Manchester. That's where St. Augustine, that asylum home for the displaced and mentally challenged individuals, is located. I did a lot of checking around and it took me all day to get the information I needed. The folks who was in charge when I dropped off Ruby's baby are no longer there. The folks who are in charge now didn't want to reveal much information to me about Ruby's baby. But I didn't let up. Finally, one of the nicer nuns told me if I went up to the folks in the new wing office they added not too long ago, somebody there might be able to help me. The nun in that office told me that a lot of the original records was destroyed in a tornado some years ago. She told me to talk to her young assistant and she might be able to help me sift through what was left of the records and whatnot. That girl was off somewhere on a mission helping some other nuns feed the poor so I had to go back the next day. I went straight to the office where they told me the girl who might

*be able to help me worked. When I walked into that office
and seen that girl's face I knew who she was. She was
Ruby's child, all grown up. Oh! She is a beautiful and
smart young woman!*

*But that's not all. Lord help me! She IS my boy Ike's
child, which makes her your niece. There is no doubt whatsoever about that now. She looks enough like him to be his
twin, all the way down to that same cat's paw footprint
mess of freckles on her face like Ike! It was her! I busted out
crying and by the time I got the whole story out to her, she
was crying, too. We hugged and hugged and hugged, me
and my granddaughter. To make a long story short, she
wants to meet her mama Ruby as soon as possible on account of she's about to get married soon and she wants to get
to know some of her blood kin. Now I didn't tell Ike nothing yet. Maxine, that heifer he married, and them nine
kids they got, is enough for him to deal with right now. I
will not make another move until I hear from Ruby. Show
her this letter and we'll go from there. Ruby's sweet daughter understands why I did what I did that night and why I
thought it was wise to keep this information from Ruby's
folks. But once Ruby gets involved, she can decide what she
wants to do about telling her daddy and mama they have
another grandchild. This just goes to show that God is good.*

*By the way, Ruby's girl was named after the nun whose
arms I placed her in the night I dropped her off. That nun's
name was Sister Maureen and Maureen is Ruby's daughter's name. See, God is good!*
Love,
Mother

"Mama Ruby, don't you think it's time you wrote a letter to
your folks? Or maybe even go visit with them? It's been so
many years, and I am sure they'd love to meet Virgil and see
you all growed up and settled," Othella said, patting her bosom

where she had stuck the envelope that contained her mother's letter. "I know even without readin' Mama's letter that she's goin' to tell me to tell you to write home."

"I will. Let me know when you answer your mama's letter and I'll slide a note into the same envelope with yours. Simone can give it to my daddy next time she see him."

Othella looked toward the window with a heavy sigh on her lips. "The welfare woman said that after I have this baby, they'll increase my check. But I'm goin' to go back to work in the fields, too, and get paid under the table. That way I can have a little more money each month."

"And you know you can always count on me when I get a few extra dollars, Othella. Which is more than I can say for that deadbeat ex of yours," Ruby snickered, glad that the conversation had taken a slight detour. "That extra money you make workin' in the fields will be a big help to you, praise the Lord."

"Sure enough. And I can finally buy me a set of them fake foam titties," Othella said.

Othella would never purchase a pair of those fake foam titties. There would be no letter from Ruby to her family. There would be no cookout and no listening to that new singer Elvis Presley's record to celebrate the birth of Othella's latest child. There would soon be no relationship between Ruby and Othella after today.

In less than forty-eight hours, Othella would give birth to her last child and Ruby would finally carry out her threat to kidnap it to make up for the baby she lost. Ironically, she would name that baby Maureen after the madam who had taken them in, the same name of her real daughter.

Discussion Questions

1. Do you think that if Ruby's overly religious parents hadn't been so strict, she would not have been so promiscuous and eager to be part of Othella's wild crowd?
2. By hiding her pregnancy for the entire nine months, Ruby jeopardized her own health as well as her baby's. Do you think she should have told at least one person she was pregnant in case she had some serious complications?
3. Do you think that Ruby should have defied Simone and Othella and kept the baby that she gave birth to at Othella's party? Do you think that it was wrong for Simone to turn the baby over to that asylum orphanage to keep her from being "shunned" by Ruby's family and friends for being a "rapist's" child?
4. If Ruby had kept her baby, do you think her parents would have accepted her story about an escaped convict raping her, and him being the baby's father?
5. There were several hints along the way that Ruby's Bible-thumping father, Reverend Upshaw, was a philanderer. Were you surprised when Ruby and Othella caught him in bed with Othella's mother?
6. Ruby used the knowledge of her father's affair as leverage against him, so he eagerly allowed her to quit school and move from Shreveport to New Orleans with Othella. Do you think that Reverend Upshaw should have confessed his indiscretion to his wife, and not let Ruby blackmail him into letting her leave home?
7. Once Ruby and Othella made it to New Orleans and couldn't find a motel room, they got so desperate they trusted a stranger and agreed to spend the night in his residence. But when Glenn Boates tried to force Othella and Ruby into a sexual situation with him, he made it clear that he

was not going to take no for an answer. Do you think Ruby's retaliation, castrating Glenn with her switchblade, was too severe. If so, what do you think she should have done to stop him from assaulting her and Othella?

8. After Ruby and Othella escaped from Glenn Boates, things went from bad to worse for them. Their only choices were to go back home, live on the streets of New Orleans, or work in Miss Maureen's brothel. Do you think that they should have returned to their parents' homes?

9. During the time period that this story is set in, it was unacceptable for a black person to "sass" a white person, let alone assault one. Were you glad that Ruby didn't let that stop her from standing up for herself when she had to deal with hostile whites? Do you think she went too far when she beat up the man who had attacked her and Miss Maureen?

10. Once Othella and Ruby were kicked out of the brothel, they joined a carnival and moved to Florida, and eventually found husbands. Their plan was to forget about their sordid pasts as prostitutes and live wholesome lives. Othella's husband, Eugene, did not treat her well. But Ruby's husband, Roy, treated her like a queen, until she caught him with another woman. Instead of trying to reason with Ruby when she confronted him, Roy viciously attacked her with his fists—even though she was eight months pregnant. Did Ruby overreact by shooting him with the same gun that he made her carry for protection?

11. During her pregnancy, Ruby had convinced herself that her baby was going to be a girl. She gave birth shortly after she killed her husband. Even though it turned out to be a boy, that didn't stop her from treating her son, Virgil, like a girl. She dressed him in girl clothes, and styled his long hair in girly ponytails and braids. But the boy was too strong-willed to let his mother's bizarre behavior affect him. He eventually turned into a very "masculine" little

boy anyway. Do you think that if Virgil had continued to allow himself to be raised as a girl, Ruby would not have kidnapped Othella's last baby?

12. On the day that Othella went into labor at Ruby's house, Ruby gave Othella a letter from her mother that had been put in Ruby's mailbox by mistake. This letter contained some crucial information that would have made a huge difference in Ruby's and Othella's lives. Unfortunately, Othella delayed reading that letter, and she would regret it for the rest of her life. Did the information in the letter surprise you?

13. In her letter, Simone explained that she had contacted Ruby's now grown daughter and told her everything regarding her birth, and the girl was anxious to meet her biological mother. Had Othella read the letter in time, Ruby would have known everything she wanted to know about the baby girl that she'd let Simone turn over to the asylum. If Ruby had received that information in time, she could have reunited with her daughter. But because of Ruby's violent history, volatile personality, and peculiar habits, do you think that Ruby's daughter was better off *not* having Ruby in her life?

14. If you have already read *The Upper Room* (the sequel to this book) and know exactly what Ruby eventually did with Othella's last baby (and to Othella when she tracked Ruby down twenty-five years later and confronted her), does the *reason* for the obsession that Ruby had to have a daughter of her own make you feel some sympathy for her?

A Chat with Mary Monroe

Q. Mama Ruby and Othella are spirited, liberal women growing up during the Great Depression. Why did you decide to keep the hardships and racism of the times from affecting their optimism about life?

A. We hear and read so much about how hard it was for black women during the Great Depression. I didn't want to put too much emphasis on that because it would have changed the tone of the story. Despite the fact that Mama Ruby and Othella experience their share of racism and hardships, they are still young and "naive" enough to be somewhat fearless in a dangerous region during a dangerous time, and to believe in dreams. They are both unrealistic, but they have enough ambition and drive that eventually leads to some level of success.

Q. Mama Ruby was raised by strict religious parents, but she had no reservations about earning money as a prostitute and carrying a weapon. How did you come up with her unique, contradictory character?

A. There are a lot of religious people who know the Bible well enough to find a quote in it that justifies just about anything they want to do. Many people feel that when religion does not meet their needs it's okay to resort to desperate measures. Like countless others, Mama Ruby relies on religion only when it suits her.

Q. Why did you make finding a husband such an important goal for Mama Ruby and Othella?

A. Having a real career—other than domestic or farm work—was out of reach for a lot of black women back then. Therefore, to lovesick and disillusioned women like

Mama Ruby and Othella, landing a husband was a measure of success and the pinnacle of prestige, so naturally it was their ultimate goal.

Q. Mama Ruby *is the prequel to* The Upper Room, *which was your first book. How has your perception of these characters changed over the years?*

A. My perception of Mama Ruby and Othella has not changed over the years. However, it's because of my fans' reactions and eager acceptance of Mama Ruby and Othella that my perception of my current and future female characters has changed over the years. I gradually began to write about women doing things that the average woman would do only in her dreams. Mama Ruby and Othella were the original Thelma and Louise, and whenever I hear Cyndi Lauper's hit song, "Girls Just Wanna Have Fun," I think about Mama Ruby and Othella. I know that a lot of women—of all races—would love to have the kind of "take no prisoners" attitude that they had. When I first created these two women, they were strong-willed, frivolous, and independent, and all they wanted in life was to be happy—even if it meant using violence and deception. Unfortunately, it was because they lived by the sword that they "died" by the sword, so to speak.

Q. *Mama Ruby and Othella are single and living hand-to-mouth at the end of the story, but they seem content. Did you set out to address the struggles that single women face?*

A. I don't think that you can write a story about single mothers without addressing the struggles they face. That's another thing that I didn't want to put too much emphasis on because that was not the story that I wanted to tell. In spite of the many obstacles that Mama Ruby and Othella face, they *do* get almost everything they ever wanted. They get the excitement, the husbands, and the children.

But in the end, they are their own worst enemies. Deception, betrayal, and revenge consume them. They eventually lose the most important thing that they had going: their friendship.

Q. *Mama Ruby's background included other family members who were prone to violence. Was violence in Mama Ruby's blood, or was she just a woman who decided to get what she wanted using whatever means necessary?*

A. Negative personality traits, or "bad seeds" do seem to flourish in some families. But in the cases that I am familiar with, there are just as many positive characteristics in those same families. I think it's more about choices and what's going on in a person's life at the time that determines what he or she chooses to do.

Q. *Mama Ruby and Othella always seem to get involved with men who were also involved with other women at the same time— but they put up with it. Are they so afraid of being alone that they accept whatever they can get?*

A. As long as the husband is discreet, a lot of wives ignore the obvious and look the other way. Married women during that time had other priorities that didn't always include their husbands' fidelity. Because of the weak economy back then, security was more important to some women. If a women got that from her husband, in addition to some affection and children, she had it made. In Mama Ruby's case, she got it all. However, because of Mama Ruby's husband's public betrayal and his violent reaction when she confronted him, she was compelled to react accordingly.

Best friends Annette and Rhoda return
in the newest book in the acclaimed God series . . .

God Don't Make No Mistakes

Coming in June 2012

Turn the page for an excerpt from
God Don't Make No Mistakes. . . .

CHAPTER 1

MY MOTHER HAD TOLD ME YEARS AGO THAT IF I EVER got married, I'd better keep a parachute nearby because I was probably going to have to jump out of the relationship sooner or later. A parachute wouldn't have done me much good. A trampoline was what I needed. I did a lot of bouncing back and forth with Pee Wee, my estranged husband. Despite our bitter breakup several months ago, he still spent a lot of time in bed with me.

"I guess I still got it, huh?" Pee Wee asked with an anxious look on his dark, still handsome face. Except for his receding hairline and that spare tire around his waist, he was still attractive for a man of forty-eight.

"Still got what?" I asked, with my eyes on the five crisp one hundred dollar bills that he had dropped onto the nightstand next to my bed, just before he dropped his pants. Even though I had a high-paying job and we didn't have a financial arrangement, he gave me a couple of thousand dollars a month for me to spend on myself and our daughter Charlotte.

Pee Wee's eyes got wide. "Don't mess with me, woman. You know what I'm talkin' about. Judging from the way you was whoopin' and hollerin' in that damn bed a few minutes ago, I *know* I'm still handlin' my manly job well for a man my age," he teased.

I rolled my eyes and gave him an exasperated look. "So it's a job to you now," I pouted. The last thing I wanted to hear was the implication that sex with me was a "job." Because that's exactly what it had been to me at one time. I had made my money working as a prostitute during my teens. When my husband pulled out the five hundred dollars a few minutes ago, it brought back some painful memories. "You make me feel like a prostitute. . . ."

Pee Wee shook his head, rolled his eyes, and glanced at his watch. "Look, I got to get to my shop and open up. I got a lot of hair to cut today. So if you are tryin' to tell me somethin', hurry up and tell me."

"I did tell you something."

"So what if I do make you feel like a prostitute? Whores need love, too."

I threw up my hands. "If I were you, I'd stop while I was ahead," I warned. I rubbed the back of my neck and sucked in some air. We had had conversations similar to this one so many times that I felt like I was rehearsing for a play. "Look, I think we can still work things out and not do . . . *this*," I told him, patting the bed and hoping that he wouldn't agree with my last statement. "Every time you come over here now, we end up in bed. You don't have to sleep with me, and you don't have to pay me to do it. That's why I suggested we still date other people, until we can decide if we want to reconcile or not."

Pee Wee gave me a confused look. "Don't you enjoy these little get-togethers as much as I do?"

"I do, but I don't want you to think that we have to do it."

He gave me another confused look, this time blinking so hard and fast I thought something had got caught in his eye. "Why? Do you not want to make love with me? You don't find me attractive anymore?" he asked.

"Don't be so sensitive," I scolded. "You know I enjoy making love with you. I always have."

"Then why we talkin' all this crap, baby? You know that the money I give to you is for my daughter. I ain't payin' you to make love with me. I ain't never paid for no pussy before in my life, and I never will. Not even with you."

I didn't see any reason to remind Pee Wee about the times he'd told me that when he was in the army, he and every other member of his platoon had paid Vietnamese prostitutes for sex.

"You don't need to make our situation no messier than it already is," he reminded me.

"I know, I know. It's just that every time you come over here, we . . . uh . . . we end up in bed and you hand me some money. Just like I was still a . . ." Pee Wee knew that I had once worked as a prostitute. Even though that dark episode had occurred more than thirty years ago, I knew that he probably still thought about it as much as I did.

"Let's not bring up the past. We already have enough to deal with in the present. My mechanic is comin' by the house next week to take a look under the hood of your car to see why you keep hearin' that buzzin' noise. Do you need any yard work or anything else done around the house, baby?"

"No, I don't need anything like that," I told him.

"Well," he yawned as he rubbed his chest and licked his lips. "I'm feelin' real good. Even better than the last time I was here. Thank you very much!" he exclaimed with a wink "Is there anything else we need to discuss before I leave?"

"Since you asked, there is just this one other thing." I locked eyes with Pee Wee. Then the words rolled out of my mouth like marbles. "Will you tell your whore to stop calling my house?"

His jaw dropped so fast I was surprised it didn't lock in place.

"What? I—I ain't got no whore! You know you are the only woman that I'm involved with these days!" he yelled.

I gasped. "Is that right?" I asked, patting the side of my head. I usually wore my medium-length hair in braids, but lately I'd been getting by with a mild perm and a French twist. It had come undone during my ten-minute romp with Pee Wee. I could feel clumps of my hair standing up on my head, pointing in all directions. I must have looked like Don King.

"But . . . but . . . I . . . I," Pee Wee stuttered.

"Well, the woman I'm talking about is a straight-up whore! *Your* whore!"

I could see that my outburst had surprised Pee Wee. It had been a while since I had mentioned the woman that he left me for last March. He folded his arms, and a frightened look appeared on his face. He knew that he had to be careful about what he said to me, unless he wanted to deal with my wrath. The day that he had brought his mistress to my house to tell me that he was leaving me and moving in with her, I'd knocked out one of his teeth. And I had given his mistress a thorough, well-deserved ass whupping with my rolling pin.

"Are you talkin' about Lizzie Stovall?" he asked dumbly, shifting his weight from one foot to the other.

"Who else would I be talking about?" I hollered, giving him an incredulous look. "Lizzie is the only one that I am aware of! Was there another one?"

"No! No, there was no other woman other than Lizzie. You know better. You know I don't lie to you."

My eyes got as big as saucers, and I gasped. "You're lying *now*."

"Aw, Annette, you know what I mean."

"Do I?" I barked, giving him a critical look. "Whether I do or not, it doesn't matter. The thing is, that woman called here last week—several times—and she called again yesterday."

"She did? Uh, what did she want?"

"She was trying to catch up with you, fool! She claims she's been trying to reach you for days."

"Oh. Well, it's over between me and her, and has been since

she left me and moved in with Peabo Boykin. If she calls here again, just hang up on her. That ought to stop her."

"Don't you think I've already tried that?" I snapped. "But until you talk to her, she's going to keep calling here."

"I . . . I . . . I'll look into it," Pee Wee stammered, waving his hands in the air. I could see that he was nervous and anxious to get away from me now. His hands were shaking so hard that when he squatted down to put his shoes back on, he put them on the wrong foot.

CHAPTER 2

P EE WEE GAVE ME A DRY LOOK AND SHOOK HIS HEAD. Then, with a jerk, he turned and scurried across the floor like a frightened rat. He tripped on the area rug on the floor at the foot of my bed. He didn't like it when I brought up Lizzie's name.

"You don't have anything else to say to me?" I wanted to know, looking at him from the corner of my eye as he was about to flee.

Pee Wee's hand was on the doorknob, clutching it like it was trying to escape. He didn't even bother to turn around and look at me. He shook his head again. "I'll call you," he yelled over his shoulder, literally running out of my upstairs bedroom. He clip-clopped down the hardwood stairs so fast and hard, you would have thought that the cops were chasing him. This was the first time he had left without kissing me good-bye.

As soon as I heard Pee Wee shut my front door, I got up and went to the window with the sheet wrapped around me. I raked my fingers through my hair, holding several strands away from my eyes so I could see him better. I watched him scramble into his red Firebird.

It was only seven thirty. It had rained a few hours earlier, so it was a chilly day for July. Because of the low, dark gray clouds hovering in the sky, it felt and looked like it was much later.

I released a loud breath and eased back down on the bed. I didn't need to be at work until nine, but I usually went in earlier so I could be prepared for any unexpected issues. You could expect just about anything to happen at Mizelle's Collection Agency. A couple of weeks ago, I got caught up in a ruckus between two of the women who reported to me as bill collectors. The night before, Rita Lockett had discovered that Beverly Hawkins was dating her fiancé. Rita had come to work early to confront Beverly. It didn't take long for things to escalate into a violent physical altercation between the two angry women. They had hurled staplers, paper weights, and other desktop items at one another. I got scared when Beverly picked up a letter opener, but I quickly wrestled it from her hand. Had I not been present at the time, there was no telling how much damage they might have done. I had no choice but to fire both employees. I had been going in an hour early all this week, but two days ago the temp agency that we worked with sent me a young Asian man. Not only was he extremely personable, he was so efficient that he got us all caught up before noon on his first day. It was because of Daniel Hong that I didn't think it would be a problem if I took my time going in today.

I was even thinking about taking the day off. I needed to get my nails done, I needed a facial, and I wanted to run a few errands that I had been putting off. I also wanted to treat myself to a nice lunch and a movie. Afterward, I could come back home, put my robe on, and kick back on my couch with a large margarita. I couldn't get that comfortable at home on the weekend or in the evening because that was when most people dropped in on me unannounced. Another inducement for me to take the day off was that I would not have to rush home to cook dinner today like I usually did. I still had some of the barbeque in the freezer left over from the Fourth of July cook-out that I had hosted a couple of weeks ago.

I already regretted the harsh way that I had jumped on Pee Wee about Lizzie calling my house. It wasn't his fault that she was such a bold-ass bitch. As a matter of fact, I was even thinking about calling him up and offering to take him out to dinner as my way of apologizing. In spite of our separation, we still had one of the strongest relationships in town. I knew people who had never been separated who didn't have a relationship as strong and hopeful as ours. I couldn't deny the fact that Pee Wee was the best thing that had ever happened to me, as far as men were concerned. One reason I thought it was in my best interest to get back with him was because in spite of his cheating, he was still a good man. He was dependable, successful, generous, hard-working, smart, and family-oriented. I was all of those same things myself, so I felt that I was just as good of a catch as he was.

I decided that it would be smart for me to wait a couple of hours before I called him. I didn't want to seem too eager. And, I wanted him to cool off a little so that when he heard my voice, he wouldn't get defensive. In the meantime, I planned to relax in my bed for a few more minutes.

Before I could get comfortable and finish reading the latest edition of *Jet* magazine, the telephone on the nightstand rang. I looked at the clock next to the telephone. "Now who in the world is calling my house this time of morning?" I asked myself out loud. Other than my relatives and my closest friends, the only time my phone rang this early was when somebody dialed my number by mistake.

The telephone in my bedroom didn't have caller ID, so I had no idea who was calling me at this ungodly hour. It was none of the above. To my everlasting horror, it was Lizzie Stovall again, the woman who had broken up my home.

I was so taken aback, there was only one thing I could think to say: "Well, speak of the Devil!" I shrieked.

"Whatever!" Lizzie hissed. She sucked on her teeth before continuing. I didn't know if that was because she was tuning up her mouth to say something I didn't want to hear, which would be anything that slid out of her mouth, or if she was nervous. "Annette, I advise you not to hang up on me like you did the last time I called." This woman had no shame whatsoever!

"What the hell—" I almost choked on my words just as she cut me off.

"Let me speak to Pee Wee. And don't fix your lips to lie to me like you usually do, and tell me he's not there. I just passed your house a little while ago and I saw his car parked out front," Lizzie snarled, her words striking my ears like rocks. "Like I told you the last time I called, I've been trying to get a hold of him for several days! I am not going to stop until I reach him. You can tell him that. The sooner he talks to me, the sooner I can stop bothering you."

"Bothering me? Woman, as long as you live in this town you will be bothering me. You didn't care about bothering me when you were fucking my husband! Well, I've got news for you. Just hearing your name bothers me these days!"

Something that I didn't know, and didn't want to know, was the details of Lizzie's affair with my husband. Like exactly when it started, or which one of them initiated the affair. But the one thing that I really didn't want to know was *where* they'd made love the first time. The thought of her sleazy ass stretched out in my bed was unbearable. If I ever found out that they had been tacky enough to make love in *my* bed, I would not be responsible for my actions. There was just no telling what I would do to Lizzie—and Pee Wee—even though their relationship was over.

Or was it?

"Are you still fucking my husband?" Even if she was, I didn't expect her to admit it. But I had to ask anyway.

"Annette, you've got some nerve asking me that. How dare you!" Lizzie erupted.

I could not believe how calm I managed to sound. "Well, are you?"

"No, I am not still fucking your husband! I wouldn't let that man touch me again even if he had healing hands!"

My pulse was racing and my eyes were burning. I had balled my free hand into a fist. "Why did you call my house again? Why do you keep calling here? Don't you have anything better to do with your time these days? Can't you find another innocent woman to torture?" I jeered.

"You innocent? That's a joke! You've got a lot of nerve to even think of yourself as innocent—"

"Get your ass off this phone, bitch!" I hollered. "You're about to make my bowels move!"

"I will hang up when I am good and ready. Look, I know you're still jealous of me, but I can't help that. It is what it is. I gave your man something that you weren't giving him, and probably never did. That was some good loving. The very first time he was with me, he realized what he'd been missing. . . ."

These were the last words that a scorned woman—especially a scorned black woman—wanted to hear. If Lizzie had been standing in my room saying that shit to my face, she would be stretched out on the floor by now with my fist mauling the side of her head. I couldn't imagine what Pee Wee had said to her for her to think that I didn't give him what he needed in the bedroom before she slid into our lives. I didn't believe what she had just said for one minute—at least not her version

"Hmmm. Then tell me, why is he not still with you? Why is he coming over here to be with me whenever I let him? And I can assure you that we do a lot more than just talk when he's here. Does that sound like I don't know how to give him what he needs?" I taunted.

"What*ever*, Annette. I just need to talk to Pee Wee."

"Pee Wee is not here, goddammit!" I roared. "And let me tell you again—"

"You're a damn liar! He is there! Now you look, girl! I am not in the mood for any of your shit this early in the morning!"

I hated profanity. It was crude. I didn't like it when people cussed in my presence, and I didn't like to cuss myself. But under the present circumstances, there was no reason for me to act like a "lady" with Lizzie. "Now you look, bitch! If you don't want to deal with my shit this early in the morning, don't call my fucking house this early in the morning!"

There was a long moment of silence. I wasn't even sure that Lizzie was still on the line. I was just about to hang up when I heard her spit out a few sobs. Then she started to wheeze and cough like she was choking on some air. I had heard enough. I slammed the telephone back in its cradle. I felt like I was on fire now, so I needed to get out of the house as soon as possible. I no longer considered playing hooky from work. I couldn't wait to get to my office.

Just as I was about to go to my closet and pick out what I was going to wear to work, Lizzie called back. "You can't get rid of me that easily, Annette."

"Look, bitch, I'm going to hang up again. This time I'm going to leave the phone off the hook, so don't waste any more of your time calling here again," I told her.

"Don't you hang up on me! I advise you to put Pee Wee on this telephone, Annette," she ordered in a voice that was dripping with a combination of anger and desperation.

"I advise you to go straight to hell."

"Let me ask you again. May I speak to Pee Wee? I don't want to keep calling your house any more than you want me to, but I don't have any other choices." She had toned down her voice, but that made no difference to me. "This is really important. If it wasn't, I wouldn't be trying to get in touch with Pee Wee this hard."

"Why don't you tell me exactly what it is you need to talk to my husband about? I can tell him, and if he wants to talk to you about it, he'll call you."

"You'll find out soon enough," Lizzie mumbled in an ominous tone. It sounded like she had a mouth full of food, or that her hand was covering part of her mouth. "And believe me, *you won't like it.*"